AMBRYN

& The Cheaters of Death

A Reemergence Novel

Chris Philbrook

Edited by Linda Tooch of Insight Copy Editing

Designed and illustrated by Alan MacRaffen

Ambryn & the Cheaters of Death; A Reemergence Novel

Published in the United States of America

First Publishing Date 2015

Edited by Linda Tooch of Insight Copy Editing

Cover design and interior layout by Alan MacRaffen

This book is dedicated to all the people in the world who are wrestling with the daemons of their own mistakes right beside me.

Also by Chris Philbrook:

Elmoryn - The Kinless Trilogy
Book One: Wrath of the Orphans
Book Two: The Motive for Massacre

Coming Soon:
Book Three

Adrian's Undead Diary
Book One: Dark Recollections
Book Two: Alone No More
Book Three: Midnight
Book Four: The Failed Coward
Book Five: Wrath
Book Six: In the Arms of Family
Book Seven: The Trinity
Book Eight: Cassie

The Reemergence Series
Tesser: A Dragon Among Us
Ambryn: & the Cheaters of Death

Don't miss Chris Philbrook's ***free*** *e-Book:*
At Least He's Not On Fire:
A Tour of the Things That Escape My Head

TABLE OF CONTENTS:

Prologue

Vegas. The city where the desperate seek out fresh starts, gambling their past gains against their future. Every trip to Vegas has its winners and losers, and the bus filled with California retirees headed home at midnight from Sin City was no different.

Lucille, an eighty year old grandmother of three originally from Santa Barbara, had hit it big on the penny slots earlier that night. She'd gone to Vegas on the senior's bus trip with forty dollars saved from her Social Security check, and she was coming back with sixty-three dollars and fourteen cents and a belly filled with complimentary gin and tonic. She slept with a snoring rumble at the front of the bus, her breath reeking of alcohol, the pine of gin, and generic cigarettes. This was her heaven.

Gerald, a half Japanese spindly seventy-five year old Korean War veteran with a limp, sat two rows back from Lucille and had also hit it big on the penny slots. Five seats over from where she'd sat too. He'd taken down fifty plus dollars in winnings while putting back a steady stream of his drink of choice, vodka and cranberry. When they got back to Los Angeles, Gerald was going to spend the money on two new pairs of pants. Something that fit.

Peter had the saddest story of all of the elderly folks

who'd traveled to The Strip that day. Being that it was the fifth of the month, and that they were all flush with their monthly pension checks, he'd allowed himself to go a little overboard. But that was Peter's way. He'd gambled with his three wives and their emotions, he'd gambled with spending too much time away from being a good father to his three kids, and he'd gambled away every chip of goodwill he'd had with all of them. For him to lose nearly all his money at the low stakes Blackjack tables wasn't new, but this would be a painful month. He would have to pick up a few extra shifts at the parking garage booth he worked at, getting paid under the table. Hopefully the gang bangers dealt their meth on a different street corner this month, and he would be at ease.

Rory was the unofficial leader of the journey of sin. He was the driver of the bus with fifty passengers on it. He worked for the tour company as a driver, and he'd done the Vegas runs with the old folks for going on ten years, and it was easy money, especially if they won. On their way off the bus in Los Angeles, coming off of the rush of winning and still struggling to stand from all the free drinks at the Casino, he'd pocket a hundred bucks in tips. Pretty good considering they were old folks with little to spare most other days. It had been even better since the dragons had come back, and all the weird mystical stuff had started up all over the world. When that little baby was born a couple months ago in June, the flow of money from the geezers gushed like a prune juice induced dump. He'd slap that mothball-smelling cash right into his money rotation for burgers and fries, his meal of choice at least twice a day, unless the taco stand was nearby. Rory had the jowls to show his dedication to the restaurants he loved, and a belly big enough to have put ten kids through college on the price of double cheeseburgers with bacon (no lettuce, and put down that tomato Goddammit) alone. Rory was already hoping

Lucille would spot him a five on her way off the bus. She was good for a fiver, she also had that look to her tonight; he didn't have much cash, and he knew he'd want a burger on the way home after dropping the bus off at the company depot. The hope for the money distracted him from the rumble in his belly.

Ahead on the highway were a detour sign and parked beside it was a patrol car with its blue lights flashing. A uniformed cop stood in the road with orange sticks that glowed in the dark. The cop waved them in circles, telling him to take it easy. Rory got the bus slowed down on the desert highway and gently turned off the impromptu exit to the surface street on the western fringe of the city. The cop waved at him.

Rumbling over some flat ground covered in stones, Rory got the bus moving on a frontage road and kept it heading towards the Pacific. If this wasn't too bad, they'd still make it to Los Angeles in time for him to hit a 24 hour burger joint. Ahead he saw more flashing lights. Another police car rerouting traffic off the frontage road and into an urban area filled with businesses. This area of the city looked decrepit and abandoned. The economic recession hit Vegas hard a few years ago, and the city still suffered. Rory got the chills thinking about how many vast, empty buildings were in the city, and how the meth-addicted locals with their dry mouths, scaly skin, and cracked teeth were creeping around everywhere, just out of sight, thinking about *his* five dollar bill. Rory followed the cop's instructions and turned down another street.

Another block ahead Rory saw a group of patrols cars with lights flashing parked on both sides of the two lane street. It seemed to be definitely a side street, as most streets in Las Vegas were four lanes at a minimum. In between the thick flaps of skin and fat on his belly, Rory felt a sudden slickness of extra sweat. It made him nervous to be in the neighborhood; having the bus in such a narrow space made it more than worse. He couldn't turn the bus around even if he wanted to. He was behind enemy lines.

Another cop wearing an orange traffic vest stood in the center of the road where the yellow line should have been—or might've been years ago. He held up two orange batons crossed, giving Rory the X symbol letting him know he should bring the big bus to a stop. Rory obliged the officer and slowed the bus to a gentle halt. He put it in park and sat there, sweating. A quick glance over his shoulder told him the old people who were his charges were all still asleep. It was well past their bedtimes, even on a Vegas night. He was thankful they hadn't woken. They always bitched when there was a delay. Rory guessed disruptions were a bigger deal the shorter your fuse got.

A metallic rap on the bus door snapped him back to the front. He hit the switch and the bus' side door opened revealing two sandy uniformed LVMPD cops, and a tall man wearing a nice suit with skin that looked like day old, cold coffee with too much cream in it. He half expected to see a cigarette butt suddenly float to the surface of his cheek. Rory hid a rude laugh.

"Something funny bus-boy?" the tall man said after lifting his arm and taking a drag on a cigarette. He exhaled a thick plume of blue-white smoke, while Rory hunted for an answer.

"No, just uh, something caught in my throat," Rory said, rubbing his neck for emphasis. "Is there something wrong?"

"You got a burger caught in there? You smell like Sonic. Or Whataburger," the tall suited man said as he stepped up onto the bus, approaching Rory with a grace that seemed feline.

Rory's sweat stopped abruptly. He felt cold. Clammy. "I had a … uh … I had a burger earlier," he blurted, confirming the man's statement. He had no idea what else to say to the man.

"Yeah, I already told you that you smelled like it. Are you slow kid?" He had a faint accent.

Rory could see him better now in the bus' illumination. He was Latin. Mexican. Or a beaner if you asked Rory's Dad. But something about him wasn't right. For some reason Rory kept seeing the man as if he were bald, even though he had a head of black wiry hair that was perfectly coifed. Then it hit him: he looked cancerous. Pale and translucent like water logged skin. The revelation did no favors for Rory's whimpering heartbeat.

"What's going on here? Are you a detective?" Rory put his hands on the armrest of his driver's seat and started to stand, but the Mexican looked at him with eyes that were a pale shade of brown, like sun-bleached leather. Rory's nerve to challenge the strange stranger disappeared, and his girth settled back into the seat like a sweaty water balloon, spreading out to fill all the space it could.

"That's right. Sit the fuck down," the Mexican said as he patted Rory on the top of his balding head. "What's your name Sonic?"

"Rory," he gagged out, his mouth as dry as a blast furnace.

"Rory. Good enough, Rory. My name is Jimmy Romita, bud. I work for a man called Uncle Cosmo. You heard of Uncle Cosmo?"

"Is he like Uncle Sam?"

Jimmy laughed at Rory's question. "That's good. I guess in a way you could say he's like Uncle Sam. Uncle Cosmo has *needs* Rory. Uncle Cosmo *wants you,*" Jimmy said with a pointed finger and intense eyes. He turned and looked down the aisle of the bus and took in the fifty-odd elderly passengers of the bus. He looked faintly disappointed.

"Needs? What does Uncle Cosmo need with this bus? And why are the police here?" Rory realized the cops were listening to this entire exchange passively just a few feet away, like this wasn't the first time they'd seen the act go down. He leaned over and looked around Jimmy to see them. They were smiling strangely. Rory thought of wolves. Or vultures. It was surreal.

Jimmy put a hand back on the top of Rory's head and steered him upright. The fingers felt cold as ice on his scalp. At first Rory fought against the tall man's pressure, but his strength was incredible. Rory felt something pop painfully in his neck, and he acquiesced. He felt his whole head and neck twinge with pain over something now off in his spine. His fingers tingled.

"Pay attention, Rory. And don't worry, that's just a sprain. Jimmy didn't break your neck, *though I* kinda want to. Nothing to worry about. Little bit of pressure on a nerve or two. So listen here Sonic; Uncle Cosmo needs some friends, and you know what they say about the elderly…"

Under the icy-vise of Jimmy's hand, Rory shook his head and shrugged. It hurt his neck.

"They don't fight back all that well." Jimmy flashed a grin like a shark, revealing a mouth filled with pointed teeth. Before Rory could flinch, or fight, or escape, Jimmy's mouth was latched onto Rory's neck, and the neck pain he had been so concerned about a few seconds ago was a pin prick compared to the sensation of having his life ripped out of his carotid by the human lamprey draining him to death. He couldn't even scream to the old people for help. Jimmy's hand had clamped over his windpipe like a vice. Rory died in less than sixty seconds. There would be no late night burgers for him tonight. Ever again, in fact.

None of the lucky old folks woke up while the police officers boarded, and smiled their own hungry, shark-tooth grins.

In the end, Jimmy was right. The old people didn't fight back all that well.

Chapter One
Tesser

"You realize that Tapper has a plane set aside specifically for flying people like us all over the world right?" Matty asked Tesser, looking out the oval shaped window she leaned against. "I mean, specifically us."

They sat beside one another on a massive intercontinental airplane in first class, speeding towards dawn over the Atlantic at several hundred miles an hour towards Matty's parents and Norway. Baby Astrid rested on her mother's bosom, sleeping soundly, her little purple eyes shut behind flickering lids. The crown of violet hair atop her head had grown, as had she. Christmas approached a few weeks away, and Astrid had reached six months of age. It had been a good year for the world.

Tesser chuckled softly and looked over the aisle at his sleeping brother, Ambryn. The dragon of death had assumed human form frequently of late, and had insisted on staying at Astrid's side. The black haired man with pale skin who looked to be in his mid-twenties snored, and the older man next to him looked unhappy about it. *I wonder if that old man knows that drooling slob next to him is an ancient dragon? The truth that awaits just below the lies of reality.*

Tesser answered his love, "Babe, I think it's important that we retain normalcy when possible. I thought flying first class was a bit much, never mind getting our own plane. This makes us seem more common. Identifiable. This is plenty nice."

"Tesser, we had to check luggage. You're a dragon, and I apparently am the first mother of a dragon. I think that entitles us to our own plane every once in a while," Matty said snarkily, but with a grin.

Tesser looked at her and felt contentment. *The mother of my baby. So pretty. Prettier than ever before.* "Okay, how's this? Next time we fly, after we hang out in Norway with your family, and we meet the Troll envoys and tour their city under the mountains, I'll have Spoon get the Tapper jet for us. Will that do ya?"

"It'll be safer for the baby," she said to seal the deal.

"Our baby is a dragon. She is for all intents and purposes immortal. Even if we were completely incompetent, she'd survive just about everything someone threw at her. I'm not worried too much about her safety," Tesser said, leaning over to kiss her on the top of her soft baby head. *She smells nice. Partly like her mother, partly like baby powder and soap, and all like magic.*

Matty needled him. "Can she feel pain? Huh, babe? Do you want your daughter to feel pain? Because that's how you wind up single."

They shared a laugh. "She can feel pain. And I don't want her to feel pain, Matty, obviously, but pain in life is inevitable. We can't protect her forever, and flying first class on a plane with two other dragons and a distantly part-troll mother is about as protected as she can get."

"Speaking of which, you gave Spoon the trip off for vacation, and he's our direct line to Tapper. Another asset for our daughter's safety. *Not cool* hubby of mine; sort of hubby, at least. We can protect her for now. She can have all the pain she wants later when she's a big-bad winged mamma-jamma. But right now she's Astrid, my little baby, and there will be no pain for my little baby. Capiche?" Matty said with a smile that told Tesser the conversation was done.

"Did I hear she's in pain?" Ambryn—now awake—asked them with sleep in his voice from across the aisle.

"The overprotective uncle rears his groggy head," Tesser said. "At least the snoring has stopped. She's fine, brother. Matty is scolding me for not flying on the Tapper plane and bringing Spoon with us. She thinks this is a silly risk, and we're entitled to the comfort of a private plane. I think this," Tesser gestured to the thrumming quiet of the first class cabin, "is more than enough luxury and safety for us."

Ambryn nodded, his dark eyes bobbing up and down in agreement. "You're wrong. Matty's right. We should've taken the private plane. It would've been faster and safer."

Tesser looked at his brother incredulously. "You're taking her side?"

"This doesn't really have sides Tesser. She is the woman. She is the mother. She is right. End of discussion."

Tesser stared at his brother with wide, incredulous eyes as he leaned back in his seat again, crossing his feet, and closing his eyes. Hands on his chest, fingers interlaced, he was swept away by slumber immediately. Tesser looked back at the love of his life, and all she had for him was an ear to ear grin that couldn't be challenged.

Women. Can't beat them. Can't make a dragon without them. Tesser slunk down defeated in his chair and put his head on Matty's shoulder. It was the most comfortable place in the world, ever. It made being defeated easy.

*****

The pilot stuck the landing perfectly. The plane seemed to glide down through the clouds as if they were made of delicious, comfy marshmallows, and when the wheels hit the tarmac it was no more jarring to the passengers than a sip of a hot cocoa that came with the fluffy white treat in the sky. After getting their overhead luggage down, Matty led the way with Astrid in her arms, the two dragons in human form trailing with the bags. As they made their way to the plane's exit, the flight crew stood at the door, clearly at attention. Obviously the crew waited to say something to them.

"Excuse me, I'm Captain Danvers. Are you all who we think you are?" the Captain asked Tesser. He looked military and professional in ironed black slacks and a starched white shirt. His shoulder insignia made him and his copilot look very official. He seemed nervous to address the mother and two men.

Tesser answered him. "If you think I am Tesser, then yes, we are who you think we are. Danvers, eh? Isn't that a city near Boston?"

The whole flight crew plus the stewards and stewardesses started to shuffle their feet in excitement. To have two dragons on board! Father and daughter! It must've been a thrill for the ages. Something they'd tell their grandchildren about.

"Yeah, actually it is. More of what you'd call a large town I guess. I visited there once when I had a layover in Beantown. Just to say I'd been there. I have a picture of me standing next to the sign at the town line. You guys live near there right? Where it all started?"

Perspective my friend. Re-started. "Yeah. I like the city. Call me old-fashioned. Excellent landing Captain. I couldn't have done better myself. Thank you to you and your crew for an enjoyable flight."

The Captain blushed and became an embarrassed schoolboy in the span of a blinked eye. "Aww, shucks Sir. You've been flying a lot longer than I have. I'm just an amateur compared against you."

"Ah yes, but I don't know how to fly a plane, Captain Danvers. I have a strong hunch had I attempted to put this bird on the ground a minute ago like you did, the only people walking away from the crash would've been me, my daughter, and my brother." Tesser looked at Matty and had a sad thought. *She's so fragile compared to us. Mortal. That scares the shit out of me.*

Their fellow passengers backing up behind them in the aisle were starting to get frustrated with the delay in exiting the plane. Tesser could hear the angry whispers in a dozen languages before anyone else could, except for maybe Ambryn, who stood there dutifully carrying luggage. One of the stewardesses made the universal symbol for 'flapping dragon wings' and pointed at Tesser. After a few seconds of wide eyes and trying to point at him politely, the crowd turned from frustrated to excited. They now realized they were in the presence of fame, and more so— power.

One of the stewardess' put two and two together, and stared with shock at Ambryn. He winked at her. "Are you? Are you a dragon too?"

He bowed, smacking a suitcase into a wall. "Ambryn, the dragon of death, decay, and babysitting, at your service."

Three of the crew took a step back from the black dragon. The stories had already made their rounds on the media that Ambryn had been the one to kill Kaula in the subbasement from Hell below Fitzgerald Industries. Everyone knew now that he was the only thing on Earth that could kill a dragon. The ultimate trump card. To say he was feared by the world over was an understatement.

Tesser diffused the abrupt awkwardness. "He's harmless, I assure you. Feed him some crickets and a mouse from time to time, and he'll let you scratch his tummy."

Everyone laughed but Ambryn. He gave his brother a

dirty look as he shook his head. After a few seconds, the black dragon laughed too. *There you go brother. They'll love you when you're vulnerable.*

"You're just as funny in person as you are in your television interviews," the copilot said.

"Well, I grew up recently watching Jay and Silent Bob, and it's scarred me in a good way. I'm glad I didn't disappoint. We have a car to catch, it's been a pleasure. Thank you."

Matty, still clutching baby Astrid to her chest thanked them as well, and the trio departed the plane after some excited handshakes. As they headed up the ramp to the gate, Ambryn asked his brother a serious question.

"Are you going to make fun of me every time we're in public? Because eventually it'll get old, you know. You'll bore of it, then turn to making silly creatures like marsupials again."

Matty and Tesser both laughed at him. "Ambryn," Tesser said, "I will never tire of heckling you. We have an awful lot of history between us, and I plan on making you pay dearly for it. It is, after all, what it appears brothers do to one another nowadays." Tesser looked at the brother he'd been at odds with for so long and clapped him on the back. *It feels good to be this way with him. Not an adversary, but a partner. I hope this feeling lasts.*

Unless Tesser was mistaken, Ambryn looked loved, and all was well with the world. They headed to the baggage claim area, and the throngs of people who likely awaited them with cameras and microphones. Norway had gone to great lengths to advertise the great reunion of *The Dragon of Life* and the troll nation, and Tesser expected another media frenzy.

*****

Having made their way past the crowd of human flashbulbs, and all the posters of Tesser that a hundred teens and adults alike wanted him to sign (which he did, each and every one, each and every time) they were whisked into a large black limousine being driven by a European Tapper agent. Tesser and Matty sat in the forward facing rear couch, and Ambryn sat opposite them, facing backwards.

Oh my baby. Tesser held his daughter on his chest, giving Matty a break. *She is a machine. Lactating, carrying this bundle of poop everywhere we go. I offer to carry Astrid but nooooo.... Mommy has it. Not like I'll drop her and she'll* – the limo stopped suddenly, and Tesser nearly lost the baby to the floor. When he had her gathered back in his arms, Matty simply extended her own arms, hands opening and closing impatiently in request, and Tesser gave his daughter back to her mother, a sheepish look on his face. The daddy-holding-the-baby experiment had ended again.

In a stroke of what felt like divine luck to him, his Tapper issued mobile phone rang in his jacket pocket, alleviating his shame. Tesser only wore the jacket because he liked the way it looked. He wasn't cold. Style appealed to him. He pulled the phone out and looked at the screen. *Ah, my friend Spoon. Trouble already?* Tesser answered the call.

"Agent Spooner. What's shaking?"

"Tesser, buddy," Spoon said. "Sorry to interrupt your trip. So we got like a... potentially big problem happening back here in the States. Any chance you can get back on that plane and lend us a hand?"

Tesser laughed. "Spoon, I've been gone less than twelve hours and you're telling me something is already so fucked up that you need me to leave my wife on an international trip, a diplomatic trip, a family trip? Unless the Statue of Liberty is being torn down by dinosaurs with lasers for eyes, you're gonna have to bark up a different tree. Speaking of trees, just have Ellen deal with it. She's slow, but resourceful."

Spoon was humorless. "So there have been some buses that have gone missing in the southwest. Over a hundred people are missing, sort of."

Tesser put the phone on speaker and dropped it in his lap. "You're on speaker. Missing buses in the southwest, continue."

"Who's there? Who can hear this?" Spoon asked.

"Hey Spoon, it's Matty. Astrid says hello," Matty said. Astrid burped quietly as her form of oblivious greeting.

"Hello Agent Spooner, Ambryn."

"Ooh. I just had an idea. Okay anyway. Buses. One at first in August. FBI and ATF got involved, but nothing. An entire bus filled with senior citizens on their way back from losing their monthly checks just up and went buh-bye in the middle of the night. Few days ago."

"Continue," Tesser said, looking out the window as the limo sped out of the airport's perimeter. It was midmorning. Snow covered the Norwegian landscape. They had taken the red-eye, and the nation had roused, and began the drive to work.

"So another bus went missing in the middle of September. A high school football team plus cheerleaders, coaches, and a few teachers."

I remember seeing that on the news. "Didn't they find the bus crashed a few weeks ago though? Far off the beaten path, crashed in a washed out ravine like they were heading to a bonfire or something?" Tesser asked.

Tesser could practically hear Spoon gulping down coffee through the connection. "Yeah. A week ago. But get this: toxicology reports and autopsies are done, and the Feds reached out to Tapper. In fact, they tossed the whole case to us. There are some fucked up anomalies."

Ambryn leaned forward, suddenly far more interested. Strange deaths were his bread and butter. He looked territorial. "Such as what?"

"First off, not one of the dead bodies in that bus lined up with any of the missing folks. Not one student in there, or teacher, or coach. No dental records lined up. But wait, there's more. A few of the records did jive with a bunch of missing people reports from Vegas and all over. People who have been missing for months guys. And all of a sudden a few dozen dead bodies that all had a reason to be in Las Vegas turn up, but inside a bus that's been set on fire. That smell fishy to you?"

Sure as shit does. "Yeah. Anything else?"

"The hits keep coming here brother. As best as they can tell, all of the bodies were exsanguinated," Spoon said, almost daring them to believe him.

"What does that mean?" Tesser asked Matty. He hadn't heard the word before.

"Drained of blood, babe," Matty said soft enough for the speaker phone to not hear.

Tesser looked from her to Ambryn. Ambryn's recent face of serene duty and patience had twisted ever so slightly. He had a calmness to him still, but his lip twitched with a frustration Tesser hadn't seen in millennia. *That can't be good.* "Something you want to say?" he asked his brother.

"Any bite marks, Spoon?" Ambryn asked the phone as his eyes darted around, searching for an answer, or something to blame for whatever was running around in his head.

Spoon could be heart shuffling papers. "Couldn't find any. The bodies were burnt up real bad. You know what this looks like to the uneducated right?"

Ambryn answered him. "Vampires."

"I imagine it would have to be plural, yes. Too many bodies for a lone bloodsucker right?"

Ambryn sighed angrily. "It would really depend on the age of the vampire. The older ones are… shall we say absurdly thirsty, and rather crafty. Though I thought the eldest were all gone. It is possible my hunts have been insufficient."

"You seem to know shit about vampires, Ambryn.

Can you advise us on this? Come back? Lend us a hand? Hundred people might be dead. Oh, and shit. I forgot to mention. Another bus went missing last night. Get this: Marines out of Twenty Nine Palms on leave. Thirty jarheads just gone like a fart in the wind. As you can imagine, the Department of Defense has shown a sudden interest in us getting on this."

Ambryn looked at Tesser with conflicted eyes. Tesser knew why Ambryn was invested in the blood drinkers. *He wants to go.* "Leave," Tesser encouraged him. "Get on the next plane out."

Ambryn's eyes went to the baby in Matty's arms. "I don't want to leave you. I can't afford to leave the baby unprotected. The trolls might be playing a clever ruse to get at Astrid or Matty. I should stay."

Tesser dismissed the notion. "Nonsense. Times have changed. The trolls have changed too. They are now kin with our kind. Have some faith. I'm more than enough to protect Astrid, and we have Tapper agents, and there will be trolls that are distant family soon enough. Let's not even talk about anything being able to get past Matty and her parents."

I can feel her scowling at me.

"Are you sure?" Ambryn asked, seeking release from the self-imposed duty he'd assumed. *His guilt for killing Kaula.*

"Go," Tesser said, tilting his head to the window.

"So you're coming?" Spoon asked from the phone. I had forgotten about him.

"Yes. I'll head back now. To Boston?"

"Sure, that works; just let me know what flight you're on. I'm in New Hampshire right now at the main facility. I can get down to Logan and meet you there, and we can fly to Vegas together. I'll get some calls made. Mr. Doyle is already headed out that way to manage the ground operations, and I'm working on getting a critical response team sent too. Having you there will be a huge asset. I can't thank you enough," the ex-paratrooper said. "Do you have a Tapper phone?"

Ambryn patted his jeans pockets until he confirmed the little lump was the electronic device spoken of. "Yes. I do."

"Make sure it's charged. Talk to you soon." He hung up.

Ambryn rapped on the window between their cabin and the driver. The window rolled down with a powered hum. "Yes?" the driver asked as he navigated the traffic. He had a French accent.

"Pull the limo over," Ambryn said politely.

The driver was confused. "But the traffic— " he started.

Ambryn pointed to the car's occupants. "I'm a dragon. He's a dragon. Even the little one is a dragon. Pull over, please."

"Yes sir," the driver said, and immediately obliged him. Once stopped, Ambryn stepped out of the limo into the cold, carrying only his own small suitcase.

Tesser stepped out to see him off. "Do you think it's an old one?" Tesser asked.

Ambryn shrugged helplessly. "Hard to say. Could be a small nest of them, or maybe an older one. I thought the eldest had died out after Kaula disappeared. I haven't had to hunt one down in a couple of years. Uppity dhampyrs, sure. But no full bloods."

"Those are the half breeds, right? They have a name?" Tesser asked.

Ambryn nodded as the traffic whipped by them on the cold Norwegian December day. A spray of mist hit them both. "There was a real infestation in eastern Europe for a century or so. They sort of got out of control; things were handled eventually, but at great cost to your humans. They picked up the name there. Thank Kaula for silver and the sun."

This is what happens when you meddle in creating things

brother. Tesser didn't say that though. It wouldn't achieve anything positive. Kaula and Ambryn did the best they could to manage life in his absence, and he felt his own guilt flare. "Go, tie up your loose end. The humans will appreciate the effort, as will I."

"Take care of your daughter," Ambryn said fearfully.

He is petrified harm will come to her. So charming. "She is my daughter, the purple dragon of all things magic, and my greatest accomplishment. I will protect her like nothing else."

Ambryn shook his brother's hand and started running down the breakdown lane against traffic, suitcase in hand, heading back towards the airport. Once clear of the trunk of the limo, he shifted into dragon form. His clothes ripped away, revealing a massive black-scaled reptilian body, winged and fearsome, with a wickedly barbed tail, and full of a predator's grace. The rags fell to the wet pavement like dandelion fluff. His wings flapped in the newly falling northern Atlantic mist, and as the cars speeding below him slammed on their brakes to take in the spectacle of a dragon taking flight, he elevated higher and higher, disappearing like a serpent slipping below water into the heavy clouds forming above. He still held his tiny suitcase in a massive clawed hand.

May your scales turn away your children's fangs yet again my brother.

Tesser got back in the limo and snuggled up against his two loves, and they entered traffic shortly after.

Chapter Two
The Story of Something Gone Awry

During Tesser's lengthy forced absence from the world, the six conscious dragons needed to come up with a way to control the rampant explosion of his most successful creation: humanity. The balance had to be maintained no matter what. Without the gifts he had, they did the best they could.

Managing and creating life had always been the golden dragon's responsibility. Since creation had been forged, it was his duty to make life, to sculpt it and transform it as the needs and state of the world transformed over time. If Garamos built a range of mountains where the Sahara desert now is, then Tesser would alter the life around it in anticipation of the needs for survival there. The great balance was thus maintained.

Of course, when humanity as a species skyrocketed to

a global dominance, the initial kneejerk reaction by several of the six other dragons was to annihilate them. They nearly succeeded, and they don't like to talk about that, especially to the humans who they have hid that past from, and also to Tesser who felt the move idiotic. The dragons still argue about it to this day.

Humanity rebounded, as Tesser would've expected. He made them that way after all.

Chief amongst all the dragons in the charge of managing Tesser's creations was Ambryn. As Tesser was meant to create and evolve life, Ambryn existed to trim the fat from the world. He removed the unhealthy, unwanted, or the presence of the detrimental to the greater good of the planet. His initial attempts at creating plague and sickness to cull their herd were very successful for centuries, though a few of the illnesses he spat upon human society nearly repeated the pogrom from millennia before. In truth, the entire time of Tesser's absence Ambryn hated humanity and all that it represented. Their rampant tool use seemed like cheating in his eyes.

But Ambryn played the game, even though his opponent was missing.

After centuries of frustration, Ambryn reached out to Kaula long ago to move in a new direction. Instead of arbitrarily inflicting the species with illnesses and death, it started to make more sense to him that he needed to introduce a new predator to their kind. Something that would feed off of them, something that would keep their numbers in check and lower them on the food chain upon which Tesser had worked so hard to elevate them over time. The dragon of death wanted a wolf in sheep's clothing to do his bidding.

But the creation of life was Tesser's responsibility. It did not belong to Ambryn to make life, and even Kaula could not create something lasting without the assistance of their brother who lay still buried deep under the ground where Boston would be, comatose from daemonic treachery. They would have to do it without him if Ambryn wanted it done.

So instead of life, they created something between life and death.

They cheated.

Modern human society enjoys the use of the word 'undead' and it is as apt a description as any. The things born from Kaula's and Ambryn's ambition were not alive, nor were they fully dead. A dead body, reanimated and kept useful and sentient through magic, and a smidge of the very will and essence of the dragon of death, could be called undead. Why not? Nothing had ever existed like them before.

They experimented at length for over a rainy century, as Ambryn recalled. Each year or two they would finish a new form of undead and unleash it on the humans. They would move on to a new idea while the last experiment played itself out. Cruel? Possibly. But is a tornado cruel? Kiarohn would say that nature's fastest spinning winds were not.

Ghosts were entirely unsuccessful. The majority of deceased spirits were unable to affect any form of meaningful population control other than scaring a pair of humans into not having sex once in a while. Messing with the eternal spirit of a soul gave them both a bad taste as well, but once the precedent of their creation had been set, it could not be undone. Thankfully, over the years the number of ghosts and eidolons slowly dwindled. Now they are a rarity, and Ambryn is thankful for that.

Ghouls, wights, poltergeists, and more were set loose on the humans. Some did nothing, and some were wildly successful, like the ghouls. Ambryn and Kaula had to step in and trim their numbers manually down to nothing before they destroyed swaths of humanity en masse they were so good at killing.

But finally after a fashion, they invented the idea of a creature that would be as intelligent and cunning as a human. Not a wild monster that would abandon sense and self-preservation, but instead a predator that slinked in among their numbers, slowly trimming away, catching the tail of the herd, and keeping the human population in check. But what would that predator feed on if it wanted to still stay out of the suspicion of its prey?

Following Tesser's examples of mosquitoes, leeches, and a slew of liquivores, they decided on blood. The creature could bite quickly, drain a human to death, and be gone, leaving no evidence beyond the bite behind. They would even have teeth that disappeared when they weren't being used. And of course Kaula, in her joyous excitement, wanted them to have supernatural, magical powers as an edge. After all, they would be in the minority in the extreme, as Tesser had taught them with the predators of Earth.

Very quickly, of course, the vampire experiment failed. Wise and powerful were the dragons, but in this vein, these two were amateurs.

It took them a few months of watching a tide of the vampires spread amongst several European, Asian, and African civilizations before Ambryn stepped in and began to destroy them. The geographic spread of civilization made the work arduous. It didn't take him long after starting to discover why things had gone so badly.

They had used humans as the base for their experiment.

Life, in all its forms, seeks to create more of itself. Nearly every task undertaken by a living creature serves a very small list of desired effects. Generally, they are eating, or they are trying to make more of their kind. Most often, they are eating so they can have more energy to try and make more of their kind. It's a trait Tesser installed in life in a most infuriatingly successful fashion.

Vampires, being based on living organisms, and being based on the most intelligent living organism currently on the planet (no discredit to the dolphins, clearly) wanted to make more of their kind faster than the human population could sustain. The cart got in front of the donkey, so to speak. Predators cannot create more predators normally without adequate food sources to sustain pregnancy, or birth. Clever vampires, those who were drunk on the power and the blood, realized that if they were to take the numbers away from the humans, they could breed them like cattle, and rule the world.

A vampire needs only a human to make another vampire. Well, that and about a twenty day incubation period during which the magic and nature of what they are changes their new progeny. Drain them dry, fill them with vampiric blood, and allow it to transmute them over a moon's course, and the vampire has copied its condition to a new host. Every victim to an industrious vampire can be a new vampire, if that is what's desired.

Ambryn couldn't kill them fast enough, so with Kaula's aid, they cursed them at high noon. A potent dragon spell harnessing the power of the sun itself shunned the creatures to the ebony shadows of night alone, and if they should see the light of day, their flesh and bone would be struck down to nothing in seconds, purified and reduced to burnt cinders, leaving little behind of the mistake they were. Thinking their problem solved, the dragon of death and the dragon of magic sat back and allowed the sun to do their work.

A few years told them the curse merely slowed them down. No different than the sand falling through an hourglass. It may have been falling slower now, but eventually all the grains would be moved, fallen, and humanity would be taken outright. More drastic measures were taken by the two dragons.

An even greater spell came to Kaula, this time with the aid of the most disagreeable Garamos, dragon of the earth. They wanted a weapon to hand to the humans. A great equalizer. Something every human could use, and something that Garamos could help make common. On a lark, they chose silver.

Kaula imbued the grand element of silver with the essence of the sun, a kiss of her own magics of undoing, and a tear drop from Ambryn's eye, bringing the spell together and making silver the bane of all vampires. Garamos saw to it veins of the metal were pushed to the surface near human civilizations across the globe where the undead menace seemed at its worst, and only then did humanity take back the night. Eventually scientists and alchemists would theorize that Kaula's spell had the unintended effect of making silver scientifically more usable, and certainly making the metal more sought after, but that revelation had yet to come. Over the centuries since the harnessing of silver as a weapon, others have discovered that the metal also harms other magically imbued creatures like the shape shifters, also known as the two-skins of the world. An unintended effect, but one the dragons were not unhappy with.

Vampires finally retreated and took on something close to the role originally hoped for them. They became the skulkers and the bottom feeders, trimmers of the human fat. The Cheaters of Death. It became better still when Kaula disappeared. Her presence, her magical force of will, gave them their power, and when she disappeared the vampires faded away until none could be found unless every stone was turned over. You see, without her presence, their blood's power waned.

Given time Ambryn considered them his greatest failure. He has spent the time since hunting them out when he catches their scent.

Of course, what he and Kaula didn't understand when they played with fire was that they had created something that could evolve, change, and grow more powerful over time. Life, and even the unlife they had created, had that trait. The rarest of the vampires, the eldest, those first made and smart enough to survive the sun, silver, and the dragon of death themselves, were now fearsome monsters in their own right. Powerful with magics never intended for their use, ripe with cunning, and wealthy beyond measure. The eldest were centuries and centuries old now, but they were thinned. Unique creatures.

Now magic has returned. Astrid. Beautiful little Astrid, gatekeeper to the energy that binds the universe together.

And because of her gift to the world, the eldest of the Cheaters of Death has stirred once more.

Chapter Three
Mr. Doyle

The benefits of an endless budget.

Mr. Doyle rode in the air conditioned tactical motor home that The International Agency for Paranormal Response sent to Las Vegas for him. Tapper was multinational as well as regional, and this agency's black, converted RV belonged to the west coast Tapper group. Colloquially, the agency and the public called them 'Tanks.' Mr. Doyle had spoken to Agent Spooner days ago when he agreed to come out to Las Vegas to help with this incident and insisted one of the vehicles be assigned to him. The black bus stood as a library, an armored vehicle, and a mage's sanctum all in one—and all on wheels. It had a comfy bedroom, small kitchenette, and resources on board beyond mundane means. There were six of these vehicles in North America alone, and each of those and more across the world had been purchased using the exorbitant funds Tesser had allocated to Tapper in the wake of Fitzgerald Industries' downsizing. The generous dragon could afford to give away a fleet of them, and he did. When the private agency plane landed and taxied into the private hangar, the tank waited inside for Mr. Doyle. He hadn't even stepped out into the Las

Vegas heat, and he'd been in Nevada for two hours already.

I consider this a victory against Mother Nature's kiss of death; excessive dry heat, and the burning sun above.

The massive obsidian vehicle glided through the outskirts of the city heading west towards the spot where the burnt out bus had been found. The state authorities who had begun the investigation already had concluded the explosion and subsequent fire was suspicious. Mr. Doyle had come because all the bodies had even more questions to them that no ordinary means could answer. Magical questions.

"Sir?" the female driver of the massive bus asked as they turned off the highway and headed into the flat ground of the desert. Mr. Doyle had thought it strange he would have a woman as a bus driver, but the world had changed in more ways than one the past fifty years.

Wonderful. A conversation. He humored the agent. "How can I help you?" Mr. Doyle sat in the middle living area of the vehicle at a table that would double as his desk during the trip. He had folders and dossiers on everything the government knew about the crashed bus and its passengers arrayed in front of him.

"Sir, I'm Agent Alanna MacTavish. You can call me Anna, or Alanna if you like. I just wanted to say it's a pleasure to be assigned to you on this, sir," she said eagerly as she drove.

"Thank you, Agent MacTavish. Please focus on the road. It wouldn't do us any good if we were to crash only a couple miles from the reason for my visit," Mr. Doyle returned to his papers, hoping the blonde woman with her hair pulled back a bit tight was appeased.

"Everything that happened in Boston, incredible. And please, call me Anna sir," the fresh faced driver said, looking back into the bus using the rear-view mirror.

"I prefer to keep professional relationships as such Agent. We are not friends. I do not mean to be coarse with you, but you are an *agent* attached to the *agency* that I am employed by. For the time that I am here, you will be my driver, my source of local knowledge, and you will, if necessary, assist in my defense and the prosecution of this investigation to the best of your ability. You may refer to me as Mr. Doyle, or Sir. To be very clear; we are not friends. I am not your mate, or a father-figure you will look up to. My friends often die, and the longer you stay without that title or that idea in your head, the likelihood of your survival through my visit is far greater. If you wish to be my friend, we should turn around and stop at the nearest Old Navy right now, and bloody purchase you a *red shirt.*"

Agent Alanna MacTavish's jaw tried to work a response that didn't sound hurt, or impolite, but nothing came out. The woman clearly did not expect that in response to her reaching out. She returned her full attention back to the road.

"Nothing personal Agent. Boundaries are important," Mr. Doyle said. *Wouldn't want you broken like poor Abraham.*

Since the arrival of little Astrid, Mr. Doyle's life had changed along with the world. His enchanted wine goblet's magic had begun to flow once more, and his body had reinvigorated itself, returning him to a state of a fifty-five year old man who took good care of his mind and body. He still aged, but the rate was geological compared to normal. He now owned the underwhelming title 'Head of Arcane Studies' at Tapper. His connections across the world were indispensable in magical study and communication, as well as his extensive library, and perhaps most important of all, his knowledge of, and collection of, arcane artifacts. He had been the best qualified candidate, and the only candidate Tesser allowed to be interviewed. Predictably, the old mage got the job.

Some of his rare and powerful toys made the trip to

Las Vegas. He had them stored in the hard plastic cases in the back bedroom of the tank, most of which the old mage hoped to leave in the cases. Some of the things he'd collected should never see the light of day again.

"May I ask you a question, sir? It's relevant to the case."

Mr. Doyle pulled his glasses down the bridge of his nose and looked at the driver. "Of course."

"How did you know we were a few miles away from the crash scene? A spell or something?"

The uneducated are always looking for the mysterious answer. "No, Agent MacTavish. I looked at the maps while I was on the plane, and I've been looking out the window. Simple deduction told me we were in the area." The tank shook from the rough dirt terrain they had just turned onto. They were passing major crime trucks parked all about now, as well as a handful of Nevada Highway Patrol cars, Sheriff's cruisers, and unmarked police vehicles of unknown allegiance. The officers and detectives standing around moved out of the way of the massive black beast, looking at it like an unwelcome invader. *A bear in their pantry. This should be pleasant. Jurisdictional arrogance awaits.*

Agent MacTavish parked the tank in an open and flat spot, aiming the front of the vehicle towards the depression in the open flatlands that was the washout where the missing bus had 'crashed and burned.' Mr. Doyle got to his feet, and headed to the side door. As he put his fingers on the handle, he steeled himself against the expected heat. "I hate the desert, Agent MacTavish. Sweat, insects. All of it. I hate the heat."

Agent MacTavish got up from her driver's seat after swiveling to face Mr. Doyle. *She has a scar on her face. A bad one. Eye socket to jaw. How unfortunate.*

"It's sixty degrees today," she said with a smile.

"Hot as Hades!" Mr. Doyle exclaimed. "Have we enough fluids? How does anyone survive here on the surface of the sun?"

"Fahrenheit. Sixty degrees Fahrenheit," MacTavish said, obviously relishing her chance to make the old mage feel a little stupid. "I would've thought that with all your years here in the States you'd be more of a Fahrenheit guy now."

Well. "I now feel embarrassed, Agent MacTavish. Well served on your part and I am unable to volley. We shall call that an Ace." He cleared his throat. "Onward to the comfortable temperatures outside then." Mr. Doyle twisted the handle of the tank's side door, and stepped out into the harsh glare of the Nevada desert sun.

"You must be the Brit," a gruff man's voice greeted him before he'd put his second foot down in the hard sand.

Mr. Doyle gathered his wits immediately and assessed his greeter. The first thought that came to mind was one of Frankenstein's Monster. The man was goliath. As wide as a rhinoceros and well over six feet tall, the man wore a Las Vegas Police Department uniform that practically strained in the audible spectrum to contain a barrel chest. His black hair was razor short on the sides, but longer on the top and slicked down. He wore mirrored sunglasses and chewed old, previously minty gum. Mr. Doyle wanted to board the tank and call to have someone else be there awaiting him instead of this person.

"Greetings to you, Officer. You must be the man standing in my way," Mr. Doyle said, allowing his irritation to shine as his eyes adjusted to the sun.

The big man stepped back, giving Mr. Doyle room to put both feet on the ground. "Yep, you're the Brit. Welcome to Clark County. Your name is Doyle, right? I'm Lieutenant Rosen. I'm here to officially hand the scene off to you."

We are not in Las Vegas. "You're awfully far from home aren't you, Lieutenant?" It came out like left-tenant. "I was under the impression the Highway Patrol would be in charge of the scene after the FBI left."

"Yeah well, shit happens. Ever since the state labs came back with all the weird results no one wants to be anywhere near this place. A few of the local cops are calling it the Clark County Triangle."

Curious. "In reference to the Bermuda Triangle? Is there a triangular reference here? Mountains, hills, rivers, roads even?" *Geometric oddities can have peculiar effects on the world, more now than ever perhaps. Leylines and such. If there is such an anomaly here…*

Lieutenant Rosen crossed arms that resembled a nest of wrestling anaconda bodies. They rippled with the fruits of many hours spent lifting heavy things. "Yeah, they're referencing the triangle, but there ain't anything out here like that I'm aware of. Other than the Native American mysticism and Area 51, we don't have much in the way of real magic in Vegas. Hell, tons of fuckers on The Strip pretending like they're Harry Potter, or Gandalf, but the really real… I'd wager you're the first true person with half a clue to step foot here in a long time. Shamans being the exception possibly. People are afraid of what happened here. The missing buses have spooked people."

"They should be afraid, Left-tenant Rosen. The events of the past year-plus have altered our present world in ways we have not yet discovered."

"People ever tell you that you have a knack for making them feel negative?" Rosen asked Mr. Doyle as he turned and surveyed the crime scene just out of sight in the ditch.

"Such things are only said behind my back when they think I can't hear them being said. I think they are afraid of being turned into frogs," Mr. Doyle said with a wink.

Rosen didn't know what to make of that statement, so he turned and took a few steps towards the crime scene. "Want me to show you around?"

Mr. Doyle took a step away from the tank, and stopped suddenly. *I'm hungry.* "Yes, thank you Left-tenant Rosen. Please let your officers know that I will require them to be leaving the area. Their presence will affect my ability to do my job. Agent MacTavish," he said as he turned. The agent was right in the door, only a foot or two behind him and about to exit. "Is there a place that offers food to go around here that provides decent, say, lamb?"

Her eyes warbled around as she tried to think of an answer. They settled, and she nodded. "Yeah. Lamb stew; that kind of thing you mean?"

"That or an ale pie. Something with a flaky, buttery crust. I'm famished, and it's near midday. Run and fetch us our lunch while Left-tenant Rosen here shows me around the staged crash of our missing bus. Fetch my briefcase and the duffel bag next to the table before you go, like a good lady."

MacTavish didn't seem too pleased with the assignment, but she got back in the tank, handed Mr. Doyle the bags, and a moment after the door shut the heavy diesel engine turned over, and she started to pull away.

"Follow me," Rosen said.

Not for long, Lieutenant Rosen. I prefer my solitude when thinking.

With arms stronger than they looked the old man carried his bags and walked after the hulking brute of a peace officer towards the ravine that hopefully held clues.

Chapter Four

Wayne Simmons

"Wayne you need to come home. Your son misses you. Do you have any idea how what you're doing is affecting him?"

Wayne stood on the side of the road next to his Sonata, looking out into the southeastern Nevada desert through binoculars he'd only purchased a week prior. He'd needed them to see the bus crash site better after the feds pushed him further back. The air of the day had been cool. Pants and sweater weather for locals.

Do you know how losing your wife and daughter affects a man Marsha? He looked down at his dark brown left hand and the perfectly polished golden band that rode on the ring finger. The simple ring that bound him forever to a woman most likely dead. He felt an ache in the middle of his stomach again. He hadn't eaten a proper meal in days and had little interest in rectifying that problem. When Wayne ate he felt like he was feeding that twist inside him. Better to starve it out than feed it.

"Marsha, look. I can't just give up on this. If I came home now, with Shauna and Melanie gone… I mean shit, gimme a fucking dead body. Something to bury. Something to bring home to Shauna's mother and father in Tennessee at least. Those weird people in that Tapper agency just arrived now. Big black motor home thing came and went after dropping some old fool off with some bags. If anything's going to happen, it'll be now. I gotta stay a few more days. You can take care of Trevor right? Just give me a week more."

"I don't have the money to feed a ten year old boy, Wayne. I got two of my own, and Chris is already working two jobs to feed the four of us and pay rent. Send me some damn money, and I'd be glad to take care of my nephew on top of all the other shit I gotta do," Marsha said.

Thanks for the unconditional support, bitch. So much for family. "I'll do a transfer tonight from my hotel. Will a hundred work a week?"

"Mmhm," she said, but Wayne could hear she wasn't pleased. He didn't take the bait.

"Is he being good for you?" Wayne asked. He had raised a good boy. He and Shauna worked hard to be good parents.

"Yeah, he's good. Active 'lil fool. Looks just like Shauna too, thank *God* for that."

Wayne felt relief. His stomach's churn paused. "Thank you, Marsha. Tell your husband I said thank you as well. I won't ever forget this. I'll be home soon. Tell Trevor his daddy loves him, and he's looking for his mom, and his big sister, okay? Tell your kids I said hi too," Wayne said, peering through the binoculars again. *Lots of movement up there.*

"I will brother. Don't do nothing crazy. You got out the Marines in one piece to have two children, don't do nothing dumb that'll leave your son without his father," his sister advised him. It felt more like being scolded.

I'll do whatever it takes. "I won't. Talk to you soon. Keep an eye out for the money later. Bye."

They ended the call, and Wayne watched as the cruisers and trucks peeled away from the scene of the bus incident one by one. *Why the hell are they all leaving?*

Across the road from where his Sonata was and where he now stood was a Highway Patrol cruiser. The cop had taken up a position here days ago for the sole purpose of keeping Wayne away from the scene. The big black former active duty Marine had been threatened with arrest seven times now for interfering with the crime scene, though all he'd done was try and ask questions and get close to where he thought his wife and daughter might be. The cop, this cop, had let him off because he too had been a Marine. Was still in the reserves.

Wayne crossed the road and approached him congenially. He'd gotten the cop coffee the last three mornings, and they were becoming near to friends. "Hey Marty. What's happening? Case called off?"

Marty was a small guy. If he weighed a hundred fifty with his gun belt on Wayne would eat shit and smile about it. Marty hiked up that gun belt and gave Wayne a strange look. "Wayne, the weirdoes are here. The Paranormal Agency people. Tappers. FBI punted to them, and we're just holding the scene. I guess their guy wants us all gone. Their problem now." Marty looked suddenly sad. "Hell Wayne, I am sorry. I don't know what this means for you."

"Good news, I 'spect," Wayne said. "This is some supernatural shit. I can feel the work of the Devil in my bones."

"Well, let's see if the Tapper dude feels it in his bones too." Marty stuck out his small hand at Wayne's big black fist. They shook, Wayne's mitt draping around Marty's like a black hand towel. "Don't let this shit eat you up, devil dog. Things happen for a reason. Remember your wife and daughter, take care of that kid you still got, and let the professionals whup some ass for you."

Wayne's voice was as cold as the desert breeze. "I ain't never let no one whup ass for me when I could whup it myself."

"Yeah, I thought as much. Be careful at least. Don't get any bracelets put on you," the cop said, clicking his wrists together. "Thanks for the coffees." Marty got into his cruiser and pulled away when a spot in the exiting order of cars made itself apparent. A couple minutes later the only vehicle on the lonely stretch of road was Wayne's burgundy Sonata.

I hope I can watch this guy work from here.

*****

The giant black RV came back about an hour and change later. Wayne watched as a shades-wearing blonde woman wearing a shirt and tie under a black suit jacket cut the wheel and lumbered the giant monster vehicle onto the packed earth towards the accident scene.

This bus crash was no accident. I gotta call it something different. Crime scene maybe.

The female agent driving the big RV gave Wayne a long look as she drove, and were it not for the sunglasses both wore, they would've stared straight in each other's eyes. The woman held his obscured eye contact confidently, and he instantly had more respect for her. Wayne wasn't intimidated by her, or her badge and gun, just curious as to who they were. *What kind of people work for the magical FBI?*

Wayne made it another hour before his patience failed him. Despite the intention to eat nothing all day again, his belly was so tied up he succumbed to the hunger and ate a handful of gas station trail mix. It wasn't enough, but it muted the crying from his guts. Not long after that he moved up and down the road, trying to get an angle on the destroyed bus around the new big black one the Tapper brought. *Fuck it.*

Wayne got in his car and started it. Tossing it in gear, he drove it across the road slowly, and rolled up on the black bus. He parked a car length from it and got out slowly. *I don't see anyone, but I also don't wanna get shot by an invisible secret agent.* He made it to the corner of the bus before the woman who he'd seen driving it stopped him. She had been waiting on the other side.

"This is crime scene, and you're about to enter it. May I help you sir?" the woman who had driven the bus earlier asked. Wayne could see under her black suit coat that she indeed had a pistol on her hip. The comfortable angle of the hang of her gun hand told him she'd draw it on him fast if she needed to.

Shit, she's got a huge scar. Fucking must've hurt. "Hey sorry. I was, uh ... I'm a father of one of the victims, my daughter, and husband of another. I been here for days trying to find out what happened to my babies. I saw the new rig here you got," he tipped his head at the tank, "and with the cops gone, I thought I'd come over and see if I could be of any assistance."

The agent looked at him skeptically but didn't harden and tell him to leave immediately. "What are your daughter and wife's name?"

"My wife's name is Shauna. Our fifteen year old girl is Melanie," Wayne said sadly. "Thank you for asking."

The agent nodded, trying to show she felt Wayne's pain, even though she couldn't. "Do you have information that could be useful to Tapper? Something we haven't already been told by the local authorities? Anything at all?"

Wayne shrugged and peered over the agent's shoulder. He could see the burnt out hulk of the bus. He knew it was the same school bus his family had ridden on the night they disappeared. "I don't know anything for sure. Well, I don't know nothing. I'm a Marine, retired. I just wanted to say I could help, and was wondering if there was anything you all could tell me. I'm hurting real bad you understand?" Wayne felt the knot in his belly tighten, and his lips and chin quiver. *I hate when I cry.*

"Agent? Is there a problem?" a foreign old man's voice asked from beyond. The voice began to calm Wayne's tremulous emotions. *He sounds Irish.*

The agent turned to talk to the man, but not so much that she turned away from Wayne or exposed her sidearm. "Grieving spouse, Sir. I was just talking to him."

Wayne took a step sideways after willing his chin and lips to cut the shit. His eyes calmed down and he averted a stream of tears. The old man wasn't as old as he'd looked at a distance. Wayne thought he was mid-seventies through the binoculars, but up close he was no more than a long decade older than he was. He had short gray hair, wire framed glasses, and a vaguely turtle-ish look to him. He steamed up the slant away from the bus towards them, intent on finding out what was going on. *But there is something odd about him. The way he walks, talks. He seems old, real damn old, but he isn't. Must be the accent.*

Wayne seized the initiative. "My name is Wayne Simmons, Sir. I believe my daughter and wife were on board that bus when they disappeared. It's my belief they are dead. I'm looking for answers and I hope to be proved wrong. Seeing if I can be of any help."

The old man reached the side of the agent and stopped, taking Wayne in. They were just about the same height. He felt scrutinized, assessed. The old man's face softened like melting butter and he hummed sadly. "I'm very sorry for your loss, Mr. Simmons. I apologize also for the fact that we do not have answers for you at this time. Your daughter's name is Melanie, yes?"

What the hell? Is he psychic? "Yeah, how did you know that?"

"I overheard you tell Agent MacTavish as I came up the hill, and I also recognize your name from the files of the missing. Three busloads of people, only two claim the surname Simmons. No sorcery, just deduction. I am sorry for your tragic loss. To lose a wife and your daughter so suddenly is a cruel joke played by the fates. My heart goes out to you."

Damn chin. Sit still. "Yeah, thank you sir. You're a Tapper?"

"One of the original, yes. You said you wanted to help?" the old man asked him softly.

"Yes. I'll do anything. I'd sell my soul to the Devil if it meant bringing my girls back," Wayne said without thinking.

The old man's face stiffened with disappointment. "The words of a desperate man are often said without proper thought to their weight. I'll forgive you for what you said because I know your intentions are pure, but I assure you Mr. Simmons, you must be quite careful when you talk of souls and selling. Nowadays there are notably more interested parties that might hear you and attempt to solidify such a statement."

Great. Now I feel stupid. "Yeah, I know. I'm a good Christian, I'm just lost."

"I understand. Perhaps as a good Christian you should stop by a local church later today and try to find some solace. You need inner peace, Mr. Simmons. Your anger will cause you to do and say things that won't be helpful, which is regrettable, because your intent is to help."

"Yeah. Damn man, are you Sigmund Freud or something? All wordy and whatnot."

The old man smiled. "I am, Mr. Doyle. I am a sorcerer, or mage, or wizard, or warlock, or whatever word that approximates users of magic for you. I am no psychologist, or psychiatrist. I am an old man that has seen much, and I like to tell people what they are doing wrong as if it were a hobby."

The lady agent snorted a laugh.

"I get that. My grandpa was like that," Wayne said. *In truth, he does remind me of Grandpa Simmons. Except he's white and from Europe.*

"We tend to lose some of our uniqueness as we age. Less motion in the atoms I suspect. Tell me this Wayne: do you have a piece of your daughter or wife handy?"

What? The hell kind of question is that? "A piece? Like Dahmer? You need a blood sacrifice or sumthin?"

The man named Mr. Doyle chuckled. "No, no sacrifices are needed. If you were to have a small token of them. A piece of hair, a shoe, a toothbrush. Something with their essence. Something important to them. Something personal to them alone. Their DNA will work if you have it. I could perhaps use it to garner a lead."

Wayne's mind took flight. "I live a few hours away from here. I could head home and get my wife's hairbrush and toothbrush. Same for Melanie."

Mr. Doyle seemed pleased. "Then we are agreed. Tomorrow morning we will be back here, continuing our search for clues. Bring what you can here, and I'll do my best."

"Jesus, thank you, Mr. Doyle," Wayne said, sticking his big black mitt out again.

The small British man took his hand and gave it a firm shake. "Rejoice, Mr. Simmons. The truth shall be found soon."

Wayne shook the hand of the aged agent and made his way back to the Sonata. He got it going and pulled out onto the road. The fuel gauge was a fingernail above the E line, and his stomach had lost some of its anger towards him, leaving only a hunger pain that scratched at his insides.

Gas up, and I get another bag of that trail mix. Home, here I come. I hope you're telling me the truth, Mr. Doyle. I don't like to play games.

Wayne brought the car up to sixty on the side road, and headed towards fuel and the trail mix.

Chapter Five

Jimmy Romita

Jimmy Romita's phone rang. *I fucking hate it when people call me before I wake up. More now than ever.* He opened his eyes and looked up at the ceiling of his penthouse style apartment. Each wall consisted of a bank of very expensive high definition television screens that ran constant images of the Vegas Strip. There were no windows in the room, but you wouldn't know it at first glance. Jimmy reached over out of his plush King sized bed with its silk sheets and picked up his iPhone. It was the cop. His cop.

"Yeah?" Jimmy grumbled. "The fuck you calling me for at two in the afternoon? You know I am a fucking vampire, right? Sunlight and the day aren't my shit anymore, yo."

"I know, sorry. It's just... the Tapper people are here. They took the scene over and asked us all to go. I wanted to let you know."

That's probably not good. Uncle Cosmo will want to hear about this. As soon as he wakes up on his own. "Okay, alright. Sorry for being a bitch."

"Understandable. What do you want me to do?"

Jimmy tried to think smart. Smarter than usual. It was

a challenge for him. He normally served as more of the enforcer in these matters. *I wanna tell him to shoot the Tapper people in the face, but that won't do.* "How many of them are there?"

"From the looks of it, just two right now. A female agent named MacTavish, and an old British guy who goes by Mr. Doyle. Weird old dude. He was involved with the shit back in Boston and the dragon. He's legit man. These are the major leaguers when it comes to the supernatural."

Fuck. Uncle Cosmo is not going to be pleased. "Can you keep an eye on them? Tail 'em while they're here? Let me know if they get more people, or are sniffing around any of our assets."

"Not a problem at all. I'll get a few of our off-duty guys to do it in their private vehicles in plain clothes. Totally off the record. It shouldn't be that hard. They're riding around in that big shiny black fucking motor home. Hard to miss. Very high profile."

"Good. Great. Anything else changes, get back to me," Jimmy said as he fished a cigarette out of the pack on the bed stand. He lit it and took a drag. It did nothing for him. He was dead. Despite being deceased in the larger sense, it appeared old habits died even harder than he did.

"I'll be in touch," the cop said, and then he hung up the call.

Jimmy lay back on the bed, resting his cold head against the leg of a sleeping girl he'd picked up at the club the night before. He had ridden her hard, like he always did with disposable women. She'd been wearing a short dress that could've passed for a large belt, and a translucent blouse that told everyone looking at her she had pierced nipples and hated her daddy. It took Jimmy two drinks, one flash of his roll of hundreds, and a few sweet words before she came back to the casino where he lived with him. She did think it was weird that he had a basement apartment instead of a penthouse suite, but once she got a few lines of coke in he and he turned on the sound system, nothing really mattered to girls like her.

I love sex. Jimmy took a drag on his cancer stick and exhaled into the air. Jimmy wanted kids of his own, but he was dead now. Taken to the other side and made into something no longer quite human, having a normal baby wasn't an option any more. Uncle Cosmo had told him about making half vampire babies though. He just needed to focus hard while fucking, and when he blew his nut, the magic inside him that kept him alive even though he was dead would slide over into the girl enough to get her pregnant. The baby would be like him a bit, but still alive.

I don't know if this bitch is pregnant yet, but whatever. We'll find out in a few weeks. Until then... Jimmy rolled over and pulled the silk sheet off of her long, exquisite body. She still slept. She'd seen the touch of surgeon to look this good, but Jimmy didn't give a shit. *Who cares what's in the hot dog as long as it tastes good right?* Jimmy traced a finger from the small patch of pubic hair over her bump, and across her pierced navel. He circled her breasts, gently tweaking each pierced nipple, and then up her neck, slowly rotating her head to the side so the artery was aimed at his face.

With no more effort than it took to chew gum, Jimmy sprouted a single tiny fang, and sunk it slowly into her neck, letting a solitary gush of rich arterial redness squirt into his mouth. None of it got on the silk. His skills at feeding improved night by night.

Oh, that's the shit. I can taste the coke in her still.

"What the fuck Jimmy? Ow!" She tried to sit up, but Jimmy's mouth was pinning her neck and head down into the pillow. One slow, flat hand pressed on her chest, and she might has well of been the witch under that house in Oz. *Bitch ain't going nowhere.*

Jimmy let his fang retract and he nibbled the tiny wound shut. For some reason, that clotted most of his bites. Some vampires could lick them shut, like Uncle Cosmo, and some couldn't shut a bite at all, but this worked for Jimmy. Once the hole stopped bleeding, Jimmy licked his lips to clean up, and she stopped struggling.

"Just a nibble baby," Jimmy said. He let her up like it wasn't anything. She got to her feet and started to look for her underwear and dress on the floor of the darkened room. The only light came from the screens faking as windows. She seemed borderline frantic after the surprise he'd just given her. She didn't even know what happened other than he'd bit her. *Shit bitch. Normal people bite each other all the time.* "Where you going? You gotta work? Cuz you don't gotta work no more. You're a Romita girl now. Kick back and relax. I'll get you some new clothes, get you did up. Whatever you want."

She stopped and looked at him as if he were insane. "I'm no one's girl, Jimmy. We've known each other like, eight hours max. Last night was fun, but I gotta get going. My roommates will start wondering where I've been. Plus I gotta call my Mom."

Jimmy got to his feet, fully naked, dick slowly rising. He gave the cigarette a tug and took it down to the filter as he rounded the bed towards her. She looked at his cock and the borderline panic started to bubble over into something more intense. Something worse.

"Yeah, about that baby. I'm gonna need you to stay with me here at the Casino for a few weeks. You see, I think you got my baby inside you now, and you can't leave with it. You see, I wanna be a daddy, and Uncle Cosmo has plans for this city. Gonna have to lay off the coke for a bit."

She backed up, her underwear hanging off her wrist like some absurd silk bracelet. "Who the fuck is Uncle Cosmo? Your dealer? Are you kidnapping me for white slavery? What year is this? Let me the fuck out!"

That's rich shit. You know she's pretty when she's angry. "Not exactly. But I do need you to get pregnant with my baby. And if that doesn't happen, well shit. I'll just make you my girlfriend forever. You'll have to share me with the three other girls I've turned over, but hell, you'll get over it. You'll have forever to work on that and your daddy issues. And if you don't, then you get the closet," Jimmy said as he tilted his head to a smooth, otherwise nondescript portion of the wall in his room.

She was hyperventilating as she retreated and tripped on one of her own shoes, falling back into a plush red chair in Jimmy's suite. "The hell you mean forever?"

Jimmy gave his teeth a little flex, and he sprouted two fangs for her. "Forever baby. Like in the horror movies. Like in Twilight." *Bitches love Twilight.*

She screamed bloody murder, but in the comfy confines of Jimmy Romita's basement suite in the Casino with its television-windows, far from the real sun above and any kind of help, no one who cared heard her cries.

Chapter Six
Ambryn

Ambryn stepped off the Tapper Lear jet in a distant open space of the airport runway with Agent Henry Spooner just behind him. Their Boston flight had come to a long end. After the few steps to the tarmac, Ambryn sat his bag down and waited for Spoon to finish talking to a ground crew member and surveyed the urban sprawl around the airport. It was late afternoon, and the sun looked about to set.

Las Vegas. There's a first time for everything. I see the infamous Strip over there. I thought it would be bigger. But then again, we are a ways away from it still. It is cooler than I expected, but then again it's December. I'm sure it gets much hotter. Heat's good. Kills the old and the sick efficiently. Gives venomous insects a better home too. Less effort required on my part.

"You ready?" Spoon asked the dragon, interrupting his musings.

"I don't like the way it smells here," Ambryn said back to him, answering a question that hadn't been asked.

Spoon looked around and sniffed the air, trying to find the scent the dragon didn't like. "Smells like jet fuel, maybe a little bit of burnt rubber. Smells like an airport from my porch."

No, that's not it. "It smells strange here. Not like any of your silly engineered chemicals. It smells like an emotion. It has the scent of lust. With a little," Ambryn inhaled until his chest was puffed wide, "with a *lot* of despair."

"You can smell despair?" Spoon asked, pointing the dragon towards a fairly mundane looking Sport Utility Vehicle.

The dragon followed him. "You can tell when someone is afraid of you, right? Or when a dog doesn't care for someone? Or when a storm is brewing in the night?"

"Yeah, sure," Spoon said as he loaded a gym bag and a long hard plastic case into the back of the SUV. Once Ambryn's things were in the vehicle, he shut the back door, and they got in the front seats. "But that's different."

"It's no different really. It's a sense. Something you absorb through more than just a scent, or words said, or body language. I am the dragon of death, yes? I see, and smell, and taste a considerable amount of despair as matter of course. I can tell here. Too many come here and watch their dreams die. Despair and a host of other emotions have taken root right in the sand. And in so few years. Sad really."

Spoon drove them off the tarmac towards an exit a TSA car was leading them towards. "I guess Vegas is pretty new in the big scheme of things. Not like London."

"Or like Babylon. Or Heteroxi."

"What's Heteroxi?" Spoon asked.

"It's a dragon thing, forget about it," Ambryn said, scratching his head and turning to look out the window. *The cities they don't know they had...* "What's our first stop?

Spoon reached into his suit coat pocket and dug out a smart phone that looked just like the one in his jeans pocket. "I'll get in touch with Mr. Doyle. See where he and his handler are. We'll meet up with them and then figure out what they've put together. Where we need to go."

Perfect. Only a few hours of daylight remaining. Maybe we'll get lucky and find a few of the Cheaters of Death wandering about after sunset. Easy pickings.

Ambryn yawned. Flying in a human airplane for so many hours was surprisingly tiring.

*****

Spoon ended the call as they got onto the highway. "Doyle says he's still with the bodies."

Good. I wonder if the bodies still have the stink of the Cheaters on them. "How far away is that?"

"I dunno. Not far. Let me get the GPS up and running." Henry was already flipping through screens on his phone setting up the destination.

"Is that safe?" Ambryn asked him, pointing at the phone use. "We are doing sixty miles an hour on the road, and there is a good amount of traffic."

"Not safe at all," Spoon said, ignoring the dragon's implied request.

Humans are so self-destructive. I suppose I should be more appreciative. "If we crash, I will walk away, and you will probably be dead, or worse—paralyzed and shitting into a bag the rest of your life."

Spoon chuckled. "I count the dragons of Earth as close friends. If you think driving and operating my GPS at the same time is an excessive danger to my well-being, step back brother and look at my big picture."

"Tesser really has changed the world, hasn't he?" Ambryn posed as Henry sat the phone down, his programming of the GPS complete.

"Yeah."

"We, the dragons, we've always avoided humanity, Tesser's incessant meddling aside. Dealt with them from as far away as possible. And now, Tesser's dragged us out into the world and put us on display. Integrated without our permission. Did you see the damned advertisements in the airport? What lows we have allowed our kind to reach."

"Zeud's ads? Shit, Ambryn, she looks good. So what if she's selling makeup on the side to make some cash?" Henry said.

I hear the sound of admiration and attraction in his voice. "Dragons don't need cash, Henry. We are eternal. Above petty wants. We exist to manage the world. Not to put on Revlon, or Maybelline, or pitch the newest kind of jeans to the teenage human audience. It debases us. Makes us less than we are."

"Ambryn, buddy," Spoon started, "You gotta understand that this world is not managed by just dragons anymore. Humans and all we've done have taken over more than I think you've ever admitted to yourself. There are billions of us, and I know with a wave of your giant fucking dragon wing you can end us, but we are entrenched in the workings of shit now. Zeud, Tesser, shit even Kiarohn, have figured out ways to integrate with our society to find ways to better do their jobs. Don't hate the player bud. Hate the game."

Ambryn sighed. *He raises a point. Humans have taken over far more than I would like, and there's no way to cull Tesser's favorite and remove their influence.* "You say it's better to work with you than against you?"

Henry nodded, and turned the vehicle towards an exit. "There's a system in place you can't just destroy. Might as well use the system instead of fight it. Think hard on that."

A novel idea.

*****

The state and city had set up a special portion of the county coroner's office for the sole purpose of storing and examining the dead bodies recovered on the wrecked bus. The coroner's office would be large by any standard; many people died in Las Vegas, and the examiner's office was suitably sized to deal with the load. This incident, however, stood out as a bit of an anomaly even by their standards. The regular flow of the city's deceased had been routed to a nearby coroner's office while Tapper took over.

The single story affair was covered in a brick red stucco finish. It struck the eye warm, and had a pleasing appearance, blending in with the desert. Spoon and Ambryn parked and headed inside. It took only a few flashes of Henry's face and badge for them to get laminated visitor cards on lanyards and access to the rear locked areas where the bodies and autopsies occurred.

They came into the sterile, cold lab only after the stressed and rude staff insisted they put surgical masks on. As soon as the heavy steel door shut behind them, Ambryn took his blue paper protection off and dropped it in a steel waste bin. Henry kept his. Across the room Mr. Doyle had three bodies arrayed parallel to one another on a series of steel tables. The bodies were all burnt fiercely, and bore the traditional Y shaped incision indicating they had been opened up and their insides explored. Off to the side stood a suit-wearing professional, her face covered with a paper mask as well. She had her arms crossed, and her body posture screamed boredom through her suit.

Mr. Doyle stood wearing a white lab coat and bright blue gloves. He had a clear plastic shield covering his face to prevent spatter, and he looked entirely out of place. He looked over at them as they approached, and he raised his slightly bloody hands as if he'd been caught stealing.

"Mr. Doyle," Spoon said happily, his voice slightly muffled by his mask.

"Henry!" Mr. Doyle responded. "I've no idea what I

am doing here. I am not a doctor or a forensic pathologist."

Comforting that the old man is doing something he has no idea how to do. "Mr. Doyle, it's a pleasure to meet you again," Ambryn said with forced charm.

The old man came down the length of the table towards the new arrivals and nodded. If he knew the dragon was faking the pleasantries, he hid it well. "Ambryn. It's been too long. How are Tesser and Matilde? Little Astrid?"

"They are well. I wish I was with them to be truthful. They're in a foreign land with inadequate protections," Ambryn said. *I should be with them.*

Mr. Doyle pulled off his gloves and put them in a specially marked waste bin. He lifted his plastic hood. "Perhaps that is so, but I am glad you are here Dragon. I feel this is a fair bit above my head. All our heads."

Let us hope that's not true.

The aged sorcerer hiding in a younger man's body pointed to the masked fellow to the side. "This is Agent Alanna MacTavish. She is my local liaison. Henry, she has done very well by me the last two days. Ensure that she is recognized accordingly please."

"Hey, Mac. Good to see you again," Henry said to her with familiarity.

"Hey, Spoon," MacTavish said back. "And you're the dragon, Ambryn?" she asked Ambryn.

"I am."

"No shit. In the county coroner's office I finally meet a dragon. Talk about it not going like I envisioned," MacTavish joked.

"You two are familiar?" Mr. Doyle asked Spoon, charmed by the exchange.

Henry nodded. "Yeah, we served in the 101st together. She's a fellow Rakkasan, same as me. I needed someone to watch your back I could trust without doubt. Made a few calls and had Alanna reassigned."

"Ah," Mr. Doyle said, approving of the news. He turned to MacTavish. "A paratrooper. That increases your stock with me Agent. But remember, we are still not friends."

MacTavish sighed, defeated. "As you please, Sir."

"Are you being an asshole again?" Henry asked his British friend.

"I have but one setting," Mr. Doyle said by way of an apology to the world.

I have always almost liked this man. "Mr. Doyle, what can you tell us about what you've discovered so far?"

The old man's face came back to business. "Yes, of course. The crash site told us next to nothing we couldn't have surmised with creative thought and deduction. The fires were started by hand with accelerants and not the result of a crash. The vehicle was brought out to the location at a reasonable speed and then sped up and crashed into the ravine in a spot that is curiously hard to see from the ground. A setup of a frankly amateur nature."

Hm. Curious. "And the bodies are drained of blood?" Ambryn asked.

"According to the reports, yes. I am not a doctor and have little experience in identifying when a burnt body is empty of blood, but they assure me these bodies are drained." Mr. Doyle pointed to a pile of papers on a steel desk near Agent MacTavish.

"These then were not vampires when they died," Ambryn said.

"Vampires would have blood in them then?" Spoon asked.

"Yes," Ambryn replied. "They drain and retain blood similar to a vehicle needing and storing fuel in a tank to operate. The blood they drink is expended over time by the magic that keeps them in their semi-living state."

Spoon put his hands on his hips. "Ha. I imagine the dragon of death would know a lot about vampires and the undead huh?"

"I find them an aberration of the cycle of life and death. One of the world's greatest mistakes. They have been of interest to me since their first appearance."

"A mistake? I bet that's a helluva story," MacTavish said.

Ambryn gritted his teeth and shook his head. "Not really." The room fell silent as Ambryn walked around the bodies, touching them, feeling them, and moving limbs here and there. He opened the mouths of each slowly, examining the teeth, and in a final, strange moment, he lowered his nose a fraction of an inch from the flesh and sniffed their corpses intently. Everyone cringed.

"Can you smell despair on them?" Spoon asked, baiting him with a bad joke.

So funny. "A bit, yes." Spoon looked guilty. *Or does he feel stupid?* "These were just vessels. Drank to death, and then left as husks. No different or more important than a discarded cola can. Not meant to be turned. I've seen this before. Definitely the work of vampires."

"Well, shit. Any guess as to how many could've done this?" Spoon asked as he stood beside Mr. Doyle. "This is a giant pile of bodies, and there's still a shitload more missing. I get the feeling we're going to have another crashed bus on our hands soon."

Ambryn made a noise that sounded like frustration. "No. Could be several undead, just one, or a hundred. It's impossible to know."

"A hundred? How is that possible? How fast can they reproduce?" Spoon asked.

"A day for the hunt, the bite, and the full transfer of blood let's say, then it takes approximately three weeks for the magic to set in. Give or take. It's a loud, painful process for the new vampire. It would require seclusion. Many old vampire traditions require the burial of the new vampire. The rumors alluded to the soils being important, but in truth, no one could hear the new vampire screaming as their insides died and rotted away."

"Do you think it's more likely that this was done by a single vampire then? If it's so hard for them to reproduce?" MacTavish asked the dragon.

"It is very possible. An elder, one with great hunger could feed on this many in a month and then turn them. It is feasible. Though this appears shoddy. Half-witted to send so many bodies to the trash all at once. Vampires, especially the old ones, are wiser. They adapt, learn from experience, and then use it. No vampire old enough to feed like this would dispose of bodies in such a way."

"So we can't yet decipher how many have done this, but can reasonably assume that it was done someplace outside of Las Vegas then?" Mr. Doyle offered.

"Possibly, yes. There are three buses missing? How many total missing passengers?"

"One hundred thirty eight," Mr. Doyle said without pause. "We now have thirty eight bodies recovered from this bus, but as I'm sure you know, these are not those missing passengers. These are vacationers gone missing, derelicts of society, homeless people and whatnot. No locals with families. The original passengers are gone, replaced with others taken theoretically from off the street."

"And no leads?" Ambryn asked the sorcerer.

"The police have nothing. Not a single videotape, audiotape or photograph to go off of for the missing people from the city. We had a chance encounter with a father who was wishing to help. A pleasant fellow, though he had the stink of alcohol and unchecked sorrow on him. I asked him to fetch a token of his wife and daughter who died in one of the crashes and have not been recovered yet. I have a pair of goggles; they are enchanted to discover the whereabouts of persons who are missing. Very old, very powerful. Using the hair he brought, I tried to search for them, but they failed to trigger the magic of the seeing tool. Henry, you must remember them from our jaunt below the ground in Massachusetts with Tesser."

"Sure do," he replied. "You looked like a mad scientist."

"They're dead," Ambryn said. The room went silent. All were taken aback or confused by the dragon's morbid statement.

Mr. Doyle offered hope. "The device has led me to bodies before. I suppose they could shield them from the scrying effect with a layer of lead, but that would require a fair amount of lead, and some knowledge of how to defeat the divinatory magic."

Always a blind spot. "I would suggest that the device failed to locate them because they are neither dead, nor alive, and naturally adept at avoiding detection by humans."

"Undead?" Mr. Doyle asked. "Isn't that just semantics?"

"Words matter, Mr. Doyle. Say them in the right order, with the right tone, inflection and thought in mind, and you know better than most they can change the world," Ambryn said as he lifted the police papers, and scanned what they said. *Legal nonsense. Human medical mumbo-jumbo. Scientific sorcery. Words.*

"I suppose you are right," Mr. Doyle said with a hint of sadness.

"So you think maybe magic is shielding them? Do you think a wizard or sorcerer is shacking up with a vampire to hit buses like a series of fucking food trucks?" Spoon asked.

"I sure as shit hope not," Ambryn said, sounding like Tesser for a moment. "It is more likely that they are just undead and are foiling Mr. Doyle's toy. The solution is most often the simplest."

"Ockham's razor. The bodies then are a dead end? We

can glean no more from them?" Mr. Doyle asked.

Ambryn cracked his knuckles and dismissed the bodies with an irritated wave. "No. We need to enter the city. Sniff around. Sense what is happening first hand. I can identify a vampire at a hundred of your paces by look or smell alone. I am your hound. Unleash me."

"As you wish," Mr. Doyle said. "There is someone I could call that might be of assistance to us as well. Tapper would have to sign off on his presence in America, of course."

"Who is he?" Spoon asked.

"I don't know if he's even available, or would be willing to travel here, but I can make a call," Mr. Doyle said.

"Who is he Doyle? Who is this character? I'm not sticking my neck out for someone I don't know unless you vouch for him as being necessary for the case."

"His assistance in this could be very helpful. We call him The Romanian."

Chapter Seven

Belyakov

The old places of Earth kept magic the longest after Kaula disappeared. Magic coalesced in the abandoned and lonely places like tidal pools after the tide goes out. The hedge mages, sorcerers, wizards, and warlocks felt the slow draw of the power fading, and when they found places that had more of the tingle than others—the pools of remaining magic—they ran to them. They scurried to the fonts of remaining energy like starving beggars to dropped food or as a drowning man fights to the water's surface.

In the great nation of Russia, the magic faded slowest in the snow and cold of Siberia. Far from the rusting hub of Moscow and the coastal gem of St. Petersburg, the white fluff of snow and the isolation from science and banality insulated the northern land, protecting it in some fashion from the curse of Kaula's absence.

Of course, moving to the ancient and uncivilized tundra of an already unstable nation meant leaving behind niceties and comforts. It meant no phone, no internet, no caviar, and certainly no pretty ladies.

Unless you were Mr. Doyle's good friend, Belyakov. He had whatever the hell he wanted, wherever the hell he wanted it.

Belyakov, like Mr. Doyle, had accumulated many years. Older than his sun darkened, wrinkled face led others to believe he was. Mr. Doyle could only venture a guess at Belyakov's age, but he knew from the way the wily old Russian spoke, he had to have seen the First World War with his own eyes, the same as he. Regardless of his age, Belyakov made his fortune at the height of the Soviet Union's power. In fact, he had been a highly prized asset of the secretive KGB. When the west heard about mind reading Soviets and psychic powers flourishing behind the Iron Curtain, they were hearing about Belyakov's parlor tricks.

In a decidedly noncommunist fashion, the communists paid him very well for said parlor tricks.

Belyakov took his money and invested in the west with it right after the Berlin wall fell. One of the many benefits of being someone who can work with magic, is luck tends to fall on your side an unnaturally large amount of times. If a spell caster who knows the right workings flips a coin a hundred times, they can tell you how many heads will come up with exact certainty. Not because they guessed correctly, but because they used a spell to guide them to the truth of what would happen before it became. Many magic users have been accused of counting cards on more than one occasion.

One of Belyakov's spells told him to invest in the American computer company called Dell. A fifty thousand dollar investment on his part through a few intermediaries in 1990 ballooned to a fifty million dollar payday a decade later and wise investments since then had seen that number grow.

You can bring a lot of nice to the tundra with fifty million American dollars in play money.

Belyakov answered an eighty year old phone that had been restored to its early glory. The handset came off the cradle and he lifted the base to his mouth. It looked like a

French horn. Both pieces had been enchanted long ago to prevent electronic eavesdropping, and he was as confident in the spell today as he was fifty years ago when he cast it. Confidence was paramount to a sorcerer.

"Da?" he said in his thick native tongue.

"My old friend, I'm sorry to bother you at this hour," a familiar voice said in English. *True English too, not American. It is my old friend, Doyle.*

"Do not worry my limey friend. It is always a good hour to hear from old friends. Are your adventures treating you well? Are you still in a single piece, or has someone cut you open again and spilled your gravy and magical wine?"

The British man laughed. "Still in one piece. Holding your vodka as always?"

"Da, comrade. Speaking of which, I have found a new vodka. Slovenian. Very good, I will send you a case," Belyakov said, remembering the bite of the smooth, clear candy. *I should have another glass before I retire.*

"I'd be honored. I wish this was more of a social call, Belyakov, but it is not. I have need of an urgent favor," the old sorcerer said.

He sounds troubled. More than when the dragons came. What could be the problem? "What can I do for you or your special agency?"

The mage coughed, clearing his throat. "I think we have an outbreak on our hands. Something like the Ukraine incident of '73. Do you recall?"

Vampires again? Not possible. Not since the purple dragon went to sleep. "How is this so? They have not been around since your Kaula went away. What proof have you that the blood drinkers are back?"

"Thirty eight dead bodies found drained of blood in a crashed bus in the outskirts of Las Vegas. Another one hundred and thirty eight missing."

Fuck. "That is worse than Ukraine. Are they returning? The elders? The ones who sleep? Can they make more again? We haven't seen a new vampire in a decade."

"It would appear so. Ambryn, the black dragon of death is here lending a wing and claw in the hunt. He seems to have a vested interest in the dead. Well, the undead specifically. I'm not sure how to question him on it as of yet, but I'll get to the bottom of that story. In the meantime, I feel that we have need for our special resource in these matters."

No. Not in a city. You keep monsters in the woods. "I cannot do this for you. He is not like his father, or his father's father. He is too dangerous. A wild animal. He calls only when death is about to happen, and it too often comes because of him. He has become careless."

"I'm surprised he hasn't called you already, in that case. No one alive is a better hunter of their kind Belyakov, and you know it. He has been civil before. A good hunter. An honor to his family name. I can keep him on a leash, so to speak."

"He is not a dog, Doyle. He may at times walk like one, but a dog he is not. He *will* bite the hand that feeds him just as soon as do what you ask," Belyakov warned.

"I'm aware. I have a dragon here. If anything can keep him in check it will be that."

It is hard to argue with such things. "How do you think he will act with the dragon there?"

"I think he will act like his kind tend to. He will obey a greater power so long as he fears it. Ambryn is an alpha in the strictest sense, Belyakov. Should The Romanian step out of line, he'll have teeth at his throat he'll find hard to shake."

I wish not to do this. "Against my good ideas, I will do this."

"You mean against my better judgment, Belyakov. I know you speak English better than that; don't play stupid with me, I've known you too long."

The trouble with having old friends that know you well.

Secrets are fleeting. "I will call him. That failing, I will head to Romania to his home and get him for you. But you, my friend, will owe me a great debt of gratitude for this deed. This is not a task I take lightly, or relish."

"The International Agency for Paranormal Response will pick up the tab for this one, and that might be better than a favor from the lowly likes of myself," the wizard said as humbly as he could.

"I say bullshit. Time will tell. Until that time has passed, be wise. Da Sveedaneeya."

"Indeed. Let me know when you have news. Da Sveedaneeya."

Belyakov sat the cylindrical ear piece of the phone in the horseshoe shaped cradle with the French horn mouthpiece and sat it down on the antique, matching French end table in one of his many living rooms. This room was decorated lavishly with artifacts dated from the French Revolution. Out the window the winter raged, trying to shake the heavy insulated glass he'd had made to never shake in such weather. Inside he shook like the windows fought not to.

The Romanian. I suppose a reliable man if all you need is the killing of the dead.

Belyakov got up from his couch and went in search of a bottle of the Slovenian vodka he told his friend about. Sending a case to Doyle would have to wait. He might need one to build up the nerve for a trip to Romania.

Get drunk first. Then call Romanian. Da. This is good plan.

Chapter Eight

Sandra "Sandy" Brown

Sandy Brown had always put effort into maintaining a reputation as a ball-busting bitch. Some upwardly mobile women who were assertive picked up that title unfairly in a very sexist fashion, but not Sandy Brown. She was born a bitch, grew up into a bigger bitch, and now she was a fully grown adult bitch practicing being a bitch, because she liked it. An upwardly mobile, ball-busting bitch, of course.

And if she was being honest with herself, she loved it.

Sandy came into the world the way every mother wants a daughter born, and the way every father dreads. Pretty straight out of the womb with a lock of honey colored hair, bright blue eyes, and a smile. As she grew, her good looks and sharp wit intimidated or angered other girls and eventually other women. Sandy became a cheerleader against her father's will and the captain of her volleyball and softball team in both high school and at Virginia Tech, where she graduated Cum Laude with a degree in business management. She was never invited to pledge to a sorority ... if that tells you anything about her.

Straight out of college in the early 90's, Sandy received an offer to work in management at a Casino near her hometown, and she took it. The idea of making her living off of gambling appealed to her. It challenged her to think of ways to manipulate the systems of chance to earn. It felt sneaky. High risk with high reward.

She took her professional yet short skirts and her demanding attitude to the Jersey Shore and did well there for nearly twenty years. She rose all the way up to assistant casino manager there, demanding hard work from those below her and above her and, eventually, another opportunity came calling. That happens to people who are competent, attractive, and accept nothing less than a job done exceedingly well.

A wealthy businessman wanted to open a new casino in Vegas, building it on the skeleton of a chain casino that had been abandoned mid construction just a few years before. Realtors made the land available for cents on the dollar, and finishing the building itself would've been a steal when compared to erecting a cathedral to sin of a similar size. Her new benefactor's name was Sheikh Alumaidi. The Sheikh had billions in oil money, and when he went out on a limb to build the casino on the cheap, he wasn't doing it to save a buck. He did it because he wanted a deal. Alumaidi made his living being a financial vulture, picking the carcasses clean of everything that had value wherever he roamed. The dead casino presented an opportunity, and he needed someone to run it. Someone who knew the industry and wouldn't take shit from the old guard of Las Vegas business. In short, he needed a ball-busting bitch.

Enter Sandy Brown. Highly recommended by the casino industry in New Jersey, Alumaidi handed her the wheel of the casino to-be and told to make it in the image she chose. She chose a theme that hadn't been done well in her opinion in Vegas: The Arabian Nights. It helped that the Sheikh found great amusement in her quasi-homage to his culture.

Built on the edge of the city, far from the vaunted Strip, they would have to stand out to draw the crowds needed to be viable, world famous, and more importantly, profitable. Enormous golden minarets were constructed at the pinnacle of the hotel and casino that reflected the desert sun for miles around. As tall as buildings on their own, the onion shaped architectural features quickly became the subject of media attention and started the talk for the new casino. They stood as beacons crying out: come here, and spend your money. Enormous columns of white marble were erected all along the outer wall, and giant sweeping windows with high arches opened the building up to the sun, giving it a spacious and airy feel. Even the glass elevators rode the outer walls of the casino hotel, giving anyone headed to the upper floors a sensational view of Las Vegas.

Of course, the gambling rooms were hidden from the light of the day. It didn't make good business sense to let your gambling customers know when sunrise came. That experience from the Vegas old guard stood the test of time.

The exterior of The Arabian Nights casino had a half dozen pools, a concert stage with space for nearly five thousand raging fans, tennis courts, basketball courts, ten full service bars, spas, and every luxury you could want in a five star resort hotel, let alone a casino.

To help The Nights compete with the carnival show that was the Vegas Strip, she went out on a limb and tried two dangerous ideas of her own. Sandy called for the construction of a rollercoaster that circled the building and spiraled through it, cutting into a passage that allowed the strapped in riders to fly through the lobby, thirty feet above the atrium floor and all the folks checking into the hotel. The coaster was built in such a way that it appeared that the riders were sitting atop an ornate Persian Carpet. She called it The Flying Carpet ride, and it proved to be a stroke of genius.

She also instituted the Genie. Every day at The Arabian Nights a single employee was chosen at random to be "The Genie." If a guest of the casino or hotel approached an employee and declared with certainty that someone was "The Genie," and they were correct, one person per day would win five thousand dollars in chips, and a five day stay. People got a single guess each day, and enough people guessed it correctly for it to be wildly popular. Websites sprang up keeping track of what employees had been asked each day, and it became a wild goose chase to track down the employee every day.

It didn't take long for The Arabian Nights to climb as a destination in Sin City, and Sandy Brown reaped a healthy reward from Sheikh Alumaidi for all her hard work and ingenuity. She'd taken that healthy reward and had a nice surgical upgrade performed on her chest, and she had a beautiful home built in the Summerlin area of the city. Then Uncle Cosmo came, and things got better. Sort of. There had been some change with the new 'owner', but Sandy knew what was good for her, and she went with it. Like many changes, they came with pain, but some pains were worth bearing. One of the smaller changes needed was that Sandy's office had been relocated to one of the casino hotel's massive subbasement floors where the sunlight couldn't affect her job or her new… condition. The fact that her skylights at home weren't being appreciated properly seemed to be the greatest drawback in her mind. Tonight, because of all the changes, she had a subordinate to educate.

"Jimmy, you do realize that this is a clusterfuck of Hindenburg proportions right?" Sandy said, stabbing a finger with a perfectly French manicured nail in the air at the idiot lackey she was forced to deal with on a nightly basis.

The Mexican bodyguard-turned-vampire enforcer looked down at the floor and shuffled his feet. *I love how I make this man nervous. He knows power when he sees it.* "I'm sorry, Miss Brown. I really thought with the crash and fire and all that we could get rid of the bus and the bodies at the same time. I was trying to be efficient."

He's so simple. He's going to get us and Uncle Cosmo killed long before the plan is completed. "Jimmy, this isn't 2010. The police have wizards, and dragons, and things that are just as scary as us now. Things that are scarier than Uncle Cosmo, Jimmy. Picture that for me okay? Wrap that up in a little mental burrito and digest that thought, honey."

Jimmy looked at her with pale brown eyes that looked washed out and meth ridden, but she knew better. He was dead, and meth wouldn't do shit to him or for him. He looked like hell because he'd lived a hard life, and the transition to undeath hadn't done his skin any favors. "I know Miss Brown. I fucked up, it won't happen again."

It better not. "I certainly wouldn't want Uncle Cosmo to find out exactly how badly the disposal has gone. There's too much on the line for us all, and with the Feds taking the case over, our men on the force are nearly useless to us. That's a protective layer that we can't use Jimmy. It's like paying for a winter parka and leaving it at home on New Year's Day."

"I got the cops on it, Miss Brown. They're tailing the big black bus and checking them out 24-7 so we know where they are going and what they are doing. They're still useful. Cops on the payroll always are," Jimmy pointed the fact out to her as if it were a secret only he had ever been privy to.

Thank God for that at least. "It's smart you had them do that. It might save your life, or what passes for your life now."

Jimmy flashed a tooth filled grin. Some of his fangs had popped out in a show. *Is he doing that on purpose? Disgusting savage. We are noble creatures of the night. Eternal and wise, and he shows his teeth to me like I'll be impressed.* She sighed. "How many bodies do we have downstairs that need disposal before they start to reek?"

Jimmy thought for a second. "I think we have thirty more already. Some of them already stink. I've been worried the smell will make it up to the main floor."

"We wouldn't want that. Jesus, the babies are thirsty. We can hardly pick them up food fast enough. We can't afford to nab another bus right now either. Ration them Jimmy. We need them hungry for the big night anyway."

Jimmy nodded emphatically. "Yeah, you got it. I do need to get rid of these bodies, though. Plus we got those buses still. No one can see 'em down in the back of the garage 'cept our people on the special payroll, but it still makes me nervous. I only trust those of us who have been turned, and Uncle Cosmo's people from where he came from. They speak shitty English, but they're like cousins."

That's... actually fairly accurate. "Jimmy sometimes you speak shitty English. The two remaining buses must stay right where they are. If they are seen outside of the casino now it could be catastrophic, and they're part of Uncle Cosmo's plan. We can't afford to draw the attention of the Tapper people to any of us, and certainly not to the Arabian Nights. They can make our lives very difficult Jimmy. The word of the day is *innocuous*."

"Is that like inoculated?" he asked.

Moron. "No. It means to be subtle. Unseen. Simple in execution. Elegant. Competent, and above all Jimmy, it means do this without being caught. Can you get rid of the thirty or so bodies in an *innocuous* way Jimmy? That'd make Uncle Cosmo pretty damn happy. Do you have an *innocuous* plan for this yet?"

He seemed undecided. "I know we need to dispose of

them in small chunks. Two or three a day somehow so it stays off the radar of the cops and the feds. I debated having our own cops take them out late at night in their cruiser trunks and dispose of them. It might take some time, but that could work."

It could, but it also puts evidence in the back of patrol cars. "I don't think that's a good idea Jimmy. I do like your mention of the word chunks though."

"Whatta you mean?" Jimmy asked her.

"Cut them up. Get them out of the casino in trash bags if you have to. Have a few bags go out in the trash too so it gets split up. Then burn them somewhere. Take them into the Red Rocks or something and have a good old fashioned bonfire."

Jimmy's eyes lit up. "What if I have a money truck do it? No one fucks with the money trucks."

Dear lord. A bright idea. "Now that is an idea Uncle Cosmo would like. Just make sure you have a good place for a fire that no one will happen upon, and I think you're on to something Jimmy. Well done."

"Innocuous."

"Yes. Now head out. Uncle Cosmo will be rousing shortly and I don't want him to see you until you've righted the foolishness with the bus. And make sure the cops are on the tails of the Tapper people, comprende? No more mistakes Jimmy. I can only protect you so much."

"Yeah, totally. I'm on it," he said as he fished a cigarette out of a pack from his inside suit jacket pocket.

"Not in here," Sandy scolded.

"Yeah, yeah. I won't. Have a goodnight, Miss Brown," he said as he stuck it in his lips.

Get out. "You as well, now go."

Jimmy left. Inside her Spartan concrete office Sandy leaned back in her plush leather chair. *The only luxury I afford myself here. A nice place for my ass.*

She stood and walked over with impatience in her

step to a steel door in the corner of the room that had been painted a warning yellow color. On the center of the door at head height was a sign that read in bold lettering; 'Danger: High Voltage.' The sign was a lie. Sandy grabbed her key ring off her belt and pulled it from the retracting, spring loaded affair that kept them attached to her. She found the right key and inserted it into the knob. A twist later, and she opened the door into a densely walled closet that had floor to ceiling padding.

Her eyes had been made more acute since she'd been taken by Uncle Cosmo. Not taken sexually of course, the old vampire had no interest in the pleasures of the flesh anymore in that sense she felt, but taken in the whole and literal sense. He'd drained her dry and filled her to the brim with the dark red life that ran in his own veins. She'd suffered through the change like she'd never imagined, but when she emerged from the other side of her vampiric chrysalis, she was a dark butterfly with blood red wings, pale white skin, and the remnants of a soul that was far less than human. Many would argue her soul was unchanged in the affair.

And with her better vision and enhanced sense of smell, she inhaled the frightened scent of the teenaged black girl sitting on a futon mattress in the closet, shaking, crying, and trembling. A bucket sat in the corner where the girl had been instructed to piss and shit, and like a good girl, she'd had impeccable aim. Sandy kneeled.

"Hello again, Melanie. I hope you haven’t been too distraught stuck in the dark all day again. I'm really sorry to keep you like this, but you're such a delicious treat for me."

Her eyes were beat red, and her face puffy. Her hands were wrapped up into tiny, angry fists. She was too weak to punch with them, but they trembled with the urge to strike at Sandy. *That's a girl. Let it hit ya. Be pissed at me. When you get turned, that anger will help you do what Uncle*

Cosmo needs you to do.

"Please let me go. Puh-please. Let me see my … muh … mommy. Tell me mommy is okay. Let me go. Let us go. My daddy will find you. He's a Marine. He'll shoot you in the fucking head," the girl named Melanie rambled and threatened with words strung together between sobs. The girl had no composure. Both physically and emotionally the girl had become a mess.

"Your mother is doing much better now. She saw my friend Jimmy a few days ago, and now all her pain is going away. Just a little more suffering, and then she'll have forever. Forever with your mom, Melanie. Won't that be swell? And you know, Melanie, threats aren't kind. I'm trying to be your friend, Melanie. I have such great gifts to give. You don't make friends and get precious gifts with threats."

"Fuck you," the little black girl shot back.

Ungrateful cunt. Sandy slapped the girl's face hard enough to send her whole body careening off the concrete wall of the closet that served as prison cell. Her brow hit the concrete hard, and split open down to the bone hidden underneath. The scent of rich blood hit Sandy like a tidal wave. *Such… Deliciousness.*

Sandy dropped to her other knee like a pouncing jaguar, her trademark brown skirt riding up, revealing her garter belt and panties. She lunged into the closet and grabbed the teenager by the head and dragged her forehead over to her mouth. Melanie's eyes were dazed and glassy, her brain shaken by the slap and the impact with the wall. Sandy sucked at the inch long gash hungrily, running her tongue back and forth inside the salty, sweet wound, letting the skull underneath serve as her dinner platter.

The little girl screamed, but again, no one in the casino who could hear her cared. She might as well have been at the bottom of the ocean for all it mattered.

So Sandy had herself a little black snack before

waking Uncle Cosmo. Like licorice, only it tasted good and would let her live forever.

Chapter Nine

Ambryn

The second week of December brought on what the locals described as an "arctic front," with the wind chill the temperatures in Las Vegas dropped all the way down to 30 degrees Fahrenheit during the day, and close to the bottom of the teens when the sun went down behind the distant mountains. When the desert wind picked up, it struck near zero more than once in the dead of the night. Everyone in the city wore as much clothing as they could muster, and they shuffled around like stiff, frightened penguins everywhere they went. News of the bus' reappearance had cast a long shadow over the city, sending many folks home to shiver not only from the cold, but from fear.

It was ten in the evening, and Ambryn and Spoon were driving around downtown Vegas in their rented SUV. The heat in the SUV churned out warm air, and they were on the hunt.

"These cold temperatures aren't good for the hunt," Ambryn said as he stared out the window of the truck. *Fucking cold.*

"Why's that?" Spoon asked.

"Vampires struggle to moderate their body heat."

"Are you saying they are cold blooded? Like turtles?"

In a way, yes. "They aren't alive. They're dead. They have no pumping heart and are sustained by magic, and that magic is fed by blood. They can turn up the temperature of their body for short periods of time by consuming the blood they've drank, but that means they must feed more. Temperatures this cold at night will keep them off the streets, or force them to bundle up heavily. They will literally freeze solid."

"Ha," Spoon laughed. "A vampire Popsicle. Count Chocula has some fucking competition now brother."

Spoon turned the vehicle onto a more primary street. Hundreds of people were stumbling down the street, huddled together for warmth, and half of them drunk. "Who is Count Chocula?"

Spoon laughed again. "He's a character on a box of cereal. A cartoon vampire that wants chocolate and not blood."

That's not funny at all. "Why would they put a vampire on a cereal box? That seems silly to me. But then again, I am not a human."

"And there you have it. If you were human you might get the joke. No offense, Ambryn," Spoon said.

"None taken."

The pair rode in silence for the better part of a half hour. They kept their eyes riveted on the streets, peering at every detail of every person, trying to pluck the predator out from the prey. Every so often the dragon would hit the down switch on the window to get a nose full of something, but every time he scowled and put the window back up. They were finding nothing again, and that made insufficient sense with so many missing and dead. By now, they should've accidentally found a vampire.

"I don't know what I'm looking for," Spoon said in a dejected way. "I can't smell despair or spot a vampire man. I'm sorry. Got any tips?"

"Your movies have it mostly right, though some of the little details are off. Pale skin is a good first indicator."

"You must hate the fucking Irish," Spoon said joking.

Ambryn laughed. "No more than the English. But beyond that, there isn't much to look for using human eyes. A lack of silver jewelry can be a good indicator—or it used to be. Nowadays there are many choices for people in terms of ornamentation."

"Silver is bad for them right? Mr. Doyle made sure I was issued a silver dagger and silver weapons. No pure silver bullets though."

"Silver is bad for them. A very long time ago Kaula enchanted all of the silver in the world to work as a bane against the vampires and to serve other purposes. Every speck of the metal carries some of her most powerful magic. To this day."

"No shit. Far out."

"Far out. They are cold as I said, unless they have prepared to be warm ahead of time. If you are unsure, or suspect a vampire, grab their wrist suddenly. If it is cold, you might be dealing with the undead."

Spoon looked at Ambryn like the dragon was insane. "You want me to play grab-ass with a vampire?"

"You said you have a silver knife. Tesser swears by your combat prowess. I'm sure you'll be fine against most of the vampires we're apt to encounter," Ambryn scratched his neck and continued his search. "As my golden brother would say, don't be a pussy."

"Most of the vampires. Right. Whatever man. Let's change the subject. I've been thinking about all the disappeared people."

Consider my curiosity gained. "What are your thoughts?"

"Huge groups of people nabbed off of buses, and the buses they were on taken as well, right?"

"Correct."

Spoon continued, "And now we have a crashed bus

with thirty eight dead bodies in it, and these bodies aren't the right bodies. Some are homeless, some are missing locals, and more than a few are still unidentified. Hopefully DNA turns up some links, but what I'm getting at is I think we need to investigate the dead we have, instead of wandering around every night until dawn looking for random vampires walking the streets. The city is too big. And shit man, we need to keep a low profile. If the world finds out there are vampires running rampant in Vegas, and Tapper felt it was bad enough that we needed to call on a dragon for help, the levels of panic could be catastrophic. We need to be low key, and this kind of roaming the city patrolling to contact is the kind of shit that leads to very high profile results."

Could be a good idea to investigate the missing people. I'm not too worried about keeping a low profile. I'm a dragon. "How do we investigate these missing people? No one cares about the homeless. They've already been discarded and forgotten."

"True, but I think we need to take over looking into the missing locals that aren't homeless. If there's a connection, we could narrow down our search considerably. And Ambryn, you gotta admit this is going nowhere fast."

It couldn't hurt, I suppose. "Alright. Let's look into it. Where will that information be?"

"Mr. Doyle should have it with him in the tank. I say we spend tonight out hunting, then tomorrow afternoon when we wake up we meet up with him and MacTavish and go knock on some doors. Ask some questions, and see what kind of answers we get."

"Deal. Spoon, do you know where a good strip club is?"

Henry was shocked. "Um?"

"Sex is a natural draw for the young 'immortal' vampire. Flush with new power and the ability to keep their dick up endlessly, I've found more than a fair share of males where sex was easily obtained. Females too actually. Tesser's gift of a powerful sex drive to all things living plays right into their hands. It might be worth it for us to pass through a few of the local establishments of ill repute. That is unless you know of a brothel. That might be more direct."

Spoon let out a deep belly laugh. "There are a good number of ballets around here if you know my meaning."

Huh? "Ballets?"

"Yeah, ballets. Same as a titty club if you break it down really, lots of people dancing, except the ballerinas wear more clothes and the strippers have the option of using a pole."

Clever play on words. "As you see fit, Mr. Spooner, take us to a local ballet. One with a pole or two."

"Low profile, Ambryn. Low profile." Henry already knew where a nice dancing establishment was.

Chapter Ten

Belyakov

The Romanian didn't answer his phone. Belyakov drank like a fish for hours to maintain the proper level of foolishness required to attempt to talk to the reclusive killer, and it had all been for naught. He would have to go to Romania for his British friend and find the person he dreaded spending any time near.

Fucking Romanian. Why can't he be like his father, and his father's father? Honorable and able to answer a phone call? Belyakov left his Siberian home and drove the eight hours south through rough back roads and village streets in his heavily upgraded Range Rover, to the Siberian city of Irkutsk, home to nearly half a million cold Russians and the Irkutsk International airport, where he kept his small private plane.

A luxury I can afford. Nyet. A tool I must have.

Even with his wealth, Belyakov was entirely unknown where he lived; that was by choice and attained through effort to remain off the local radar. He shopped online via intermediaries, and had his goods delivered anonymously to multiple addresses at random times of the day, week, and year. He often wore disguises or used whatever magical power was available to him to hide his appearance, and whenever he was asked who he was, he had a new story available every time. As a former KGB agent, he had plenty of experience in making up new stories. Belyakov was the Siberian Ghost, and that suited him just fine.

A retired Russian military pilot named Sergei operated his plane. Belyakov knew him from years of working together doing secretive things for the Soviet government and then the Russian government. Sergei enjoyed a fifty thousand dollar a year salary to live near Irkutsk and fly Belyakov around Russia and Europe as needed. Belyakov called on him typically no more than a dozen times a year, and Sergei enjoyed the ability to continue flying, as well as the relaxed and safer schedule. Belyakov enjoyed his silence, his complete lack of interest in asking questions, and his ability to fly a plane anywhere on a moment's notice. It was a friendly but polite relationship that had benefitted both men.

Belyakov had called ahead to Sergei, and when the old Russian met his younger counterpart at the airport, the plane was fueled, the flight plan ready, and the engines were running.

"Zdravsvtvuyte Sergei," Belyakov greeted his pilot, as he always did. There was no smile.

"Zdravsvtvuyte, Mr. Belyakov," the pilot said back, as he always did. "To Bucharest, da?"

"Da," Belyakov replied. "Ochen' bystro, pozhaluysta." *With haste my good pilot.*

Belyakov loaded three bags and a small hard-cased trunk into the passenger cabin of his jet. The case was very heavy, as if it was filled with nothing but stones, or a small brick collection. He never travelled without it. He had avoided the questions of the ground crew and security by flashing his newly issued FSB identification. The KGB dissolved when the USSR collapsed, but the Federal Security Service of the Russian Federation had stepped in without missing a beat. They were almost as feared as the old KGB. Soon they would be feared just as much as the KGB had been. *It is sometimes good that old habits die hard. Show FSB identification, and people are afraid to question it. And better still, as soon as you put it away they wish nothing more than to forget that you even showed it to them. It is most helpful. It also saves the effort of manipulating thoughts with spells.*

Belyakov settled into the plush red fabric of the second chair in his twenty seat plane and buckled in. As soon as they reached cruising altitude he'd crack open one of his bags and fetch another bottle of that Slovenian vodka. *I should get more on the way home. And have it billed to Mycroft. Won't that get him in a bind? A bill for vodka, not tea! I should like to see his wrinkled face when he gets his charge card bill.*

Belyakov chuckled as the plane taxied towards the runway for takeoff. He sobered up quickly when he remembered where he was going.

*****

Sergei's experience made him a talented pilot, but no amount of talent could avoid some wide spread turbulence from time to time. Belyakov heard him hail each flight control authority as they traveled, asking for a different altitude to avoid the storms and the choppy air, but each time his request to adjust the plane's flight path was insufficiently granted or flat out refused. The air was full of planes apparently.

Christmas travelers. Christians making the pilgrimage to their birthplaces and families to celebrate the birth of Christ, and the giving of consumer gifts. It is for days like these I wish the world was simpler.

They flew through the night for ten solid, sleepless hours, skirting the angry air. Belyakov fought against the shaking winds with more vodka when he was able to stand, but he didn't bring enough to drown out the world, to chase away his fleeting dreams. It wouldn't do to be exhausted when he tried to meet with The Romanian. He would need to be ready for anything. The Romanian was like that nowadays.

Sergei put the plane down with the crack of the dawn's light at the plane's tail in Bucharest, Romania. Belyakov had very mixed feelings about returning to the country.

The nation was beautiful. God's country, truly. Rolling green hills, the Carpathian Mountains, deep river gorges, old cities and castles, and beautiful dark haired women who loved as powerfully as they could hate. Romania had become a growing nation, expanding and safe, and many called it a place to enjoy a full life. It also housed some of the oldest memories of mankind, and not all of those memories were happy. Belyakov had to weigh the good against the bad. The scales tipped to and fro in his mind and may never settle on a side.

At least the city is beautiful. And it was. Despite the two plus million souls calling it home, it felt small for some indefinable reason, and it exuded a feeling of history. More of the memories of old, perhaps.

"Sergei, find hotel. Relax. Enjoy Bucharest. I will contact you when I am finished," Belyakov said as the two men loaded his bags into the trunk of a rented Volkswagen Touareg SUV. It wasn't his Range Rover with the brush guard, armored windows, ballistic panels, or protective enchantments, but it would suffice. *Once I hit the country, I will enchant the vehicle. There are a few quick abjurations that will help should violence happen.*

"Da, Sir. I will wait for your call. Do you expect nasiliye? Should I be ready for goryachiy take-off?"

Belyakov shook his head, indicating it should be a safe, normal take off. "Nyet. If anything bad happens, I will die. I won't return with anyone wanting to kill me. Ya nadeyus'."

Sergei seemed pleased by the good news, and after

saying goodbye he returned to the plane and its needs. Belyakov got into the white SUV, started it, and shifted the manual into first. He nearly

popped the clutch (it had been years since he'd driven a stick shift after all) but saved face, and he pulled away, leaving the hangar and his pilot behind.

To Pitesti.

*****

Halfway to the small industrial city of Pitesti Belyakov got off the A1 at Corbi Mari, a quaint collection of small villages. He had traveled far enough from the city for his spells to work on the Volkswagen. He found a dirt road a few miles off the highway that had a picnic spot that wasn't being used. The day was but a few hours before the high sun. *A good time for good spells.*

Belyakov got his small hard-cased trunk out and rested it on the hood of his Volkswagon. A combination tumbler kept the case locked shut. A few deft flicks of his thumb later, the Russian opened the case, revealing contents that might've confounded someone who didn't know him intimately.

Mr. Doyle called Belyakov a 'Stone-worker,' or more accurately, a 'Geomancer.'

The Russian was able to harness the inherent power hidden within stones. He could squeeze them with his effort and mind to wield magic, bringing something out of nothing, and leaving the stones unharmed in the process. So long as Belyakov had earthen elements at hand, he had magic. Now, with Astrid returned, the stones he had been forced to work for hours to illicit the smallest of responses now sprang forth with a replenished reservoir of arcane energy.

My box of rocks.

Belyakov quickly found four small pieces of lodestone after removing a pair of nested trays in the case. He had hundreds of pieces of crystal, stone, and gem inside it and knew exactly where each stone lay, and what each stone did independently and when combined with the presence of another. On the inside of the top of the case lay a belt with a series of tiny pouches that would contain his 'battle kit' of stones. He'd put that on later. Before shutting the case, he grabbed a stick of red wax, and a Zippo lighter.

Now, to find the proper locations. Belyakov circled the vehicle and opened all the doors. He walked around the car with intent eyes, searching for the points where the four lodestones would be most effective. One spot jumped to him immediately, right in the back near the handle that lifted the floor cover.

With reverence, Belyakov sat the four lodestones down in an accidental diamond pattern, and took the stick of wax and lighter out from his pocket. He struck the lighter and held it to the wax until a fat red dollop fell off onto a piece of hard black plastic. He sat the tools down and selected the stone at the bottom of the diamond.

"Bud'te kak obolochki cherepakhi," he whispered to the tiny piece of gray before lovingly placing it in the cooling wax. He blew on it once it was sat down and watched with a childish smile as the stone settled into its temporary home. His anchor stone placed, he walked around the vehicle until he found a good spot under the hood for a second stone and two more spots under the front seats as well. Each time he told the stone the same thing; "Be like a turtle's shell."

In all, the whole process of the spell took an hour. He got his belt of stone pouches from the case and after tying it around his waist, he got back into the car.

Now for food. Tochitura and plum brandy, with strong coffee. Then, to Pitesti and to find The Romanian.

Belyakov's stomach shuddered, and he wasn't sure hunger caused it. He turned the vehicle around and started the hunt for a good place for fried pork.

*****

Pitesti was ancient. The city nestled against the southwest foothills of the Carpathians had been inhabited in one form or another since the Paleolithic era. The locals no longer lived in caves and beat their dinners to death with clubs and rocks, thankfully, though they were still a hardy and occasionally violent lot. The Wallachian city of almost a quarter million people had transformed into a rail hub of Romania, had an oil refinery, and was a substantial center of the eastern European automotive industry. Rough and tumble hard workers and hard drinkers called Pitesti and its long history home.

It had been the base of operations to the men known as The Romanians for as long as Belyakov had been alive, and for as long as many hidden history books recorded the unseen events of the world. The family Belyakov searched for here had a reputation amongst the things that had fought to stay out of society's eyes. They were killers. Hunters of the hunters, slayers of the dead. The Romanians Belyakov searched for were a family of vampire hunters, and there were no others who could claim their skill or their successes. But now, after a decade of dying magic, the family had dwindled in size, and now only a few of the line remained. Belyakov knew ways to contact them via the telephone, but with no one answering he'd been forced to their doorstep to knock.

It just so happened that knocking on a killer's door was a sure way to wind up as one of their victims

The Romanian had a series of residences in the city that he rotated through to remain safe. Belyakov knew of three of the safe houses, but he suspected there were as many as ten. The Romanians were traditionally not known for cutting corners. This Romanian might be very different than his predecessors, but Belyakov knew some traditions lasted no matter who they were passed on to.

A poorly lit apartment building rose up from the streets of Pitesti, groaning against the power of gravity. The Russian made it the first place he visited. One in a line of dreary, identical post-Soviet tenements that had been constructed quickly and with little regard to long term safety, the building begged to be demolished. The blinking light in the rattling elevator didn't soothe Belyakov's nerves on the way to the seventh floor in the least, where he knew the special apartment was.

He stepped out into the yellowed, nicotine stained tiled hallway and took a right. Out of a pouch on his simple belt he fingered a small piece of bloodstone and a fleck of citrine. He made sure the band on his middle finger had the copper ring touching his flesh. The presence of the metal helped the energy of the stones meld.

I feel stronger already. I hope he does not try to hurt me. We have been very civil for years, and I was good friends with his father.

He stopped at apartment 708. *Always a seven followed by an eight. Never more than three numbers. Always.* He took a deep breath, drew on the tingle already emanating from his rocks, and rapped his knuckles on the door. Surprising the Russian, the door felt hard, and sturdy. *Must be an upgrade. Oh. I hear shuffling. Not an adult.*

He heard the sound of a heavy bolt unfastening, and the door cracked open. A buzz in the back of his head told him a powerful warding spell was just inside the door. If he were to enter unwanted, there would be dire consequences. A short girl no more than thirteen peered around the edge of the door. She had hair as black as ink and mismatched eyes; the left green, the right blue. She looked him up and down, and with wisdom beyond her years, she simply shook her head at him.

Belyakov pressed her politely. "Rumynskiy?" *The*

Romanian?

She shook her head again. "Kukol'nyy teatr." *He's at the puppet show. She speaks good Russian. Definitely a member of the family. She's clean though. No taint of the hereditary… gift.*

Belyakov dipped his head down to the young girl, and turned to leave. He'd heard what he needed to hear. He knew where the puppet show was. "Zhdat!" she said loudly. *Wait.*

The Russian stopped and turned to face her. He clenched the stones and prayed she wasn't about to attack him. He hated killing children. Even the evil ones. She had stepped into the hallway, past the protective wards of the apartment. *Something must be important for her to leave such safety.* "Da?"

"On vypil segodnya. Byt' ostorozhnym." *He has drank today. Be careful.*

Belyakov's guts twisted again, and he wished for more of his Slovenian vodka, and quick. "Spasibo."

She nodded with fear in her dark eyes before slipping back inside the protective cocoon of the warded flat. He heard the locks turn again, sealing off the dangers of the outside world and the man in her family who she clearly feared more than Belyakov.

"Fuck."

Chapter Eleven
Jimmy Romita

I miss the sun, Jimmy thought as he looked up at the moon. *It looks like a Cadbury Mini-egg tonight. Not thin enough to be a crescent, and not fat enough to look full. Fucker is a fence sitter.*

"Jimmy, the fire won't start," a voice called out to him. He'd come to the middle of nowhere with just one other man for assistance. They'd come to set fire to some body parts.

The vampire looked down from the cloudless Nevada sky and looked at the baby vampire that told him the shitty news. The guy was a security guard for the casino but had been turned into a vampire by Jimmy on Uncle Cosmo's orders. Cosmo wanted more muscle—vampire muscle—and this guy was a willing convert. He was short, but thick necked with close cropped hair. The blonde fuzz was illuminated by the moon's glow, like he wore a thin netting of light over his skull.

Lots of people want to live forever. "Why the fuck not? You brought starter fluid. How complicated could this be?"

"They're meat, man. Meat doesn't burn. Have you ever seen a steak burn on the grill like it was a piece of coal? We need wood or something to put underneath them. Something that'll burn for a while."

"You want to get wood in Las Vegas at three in the morning? This isn't fucking Wisconsin," Jimmy said to him as he fired up another cigarette.

"I'm out of ideas. We already poured a half gallon of gas on the body parts and that helped, but it petered out after just a little fire," the guard said. Jimmy could tell he was scared to keep saying this shit to him. No one disappointed Jimmy. Not without consequences.

"Fuck. Fine. Where do we get lumber at this time of night? Craigslist that shit?"

The guard laughed. "I can head back to the casino with the truck and hit the maintenance storage area in the garage. I know they have some lumber sitting around. I can be back in an hour."

Fuck, yeah, whatever.

The guard stood there, waiting for an answer.

"The fuck you waiting for?" Jimmy said after spitting on the ground. The act had no meat to it. His mouth no longer created saliva unless he willed it to.

"Alright, I'll be right back," he said before jogging away.

*****

True to his word, the guard returned an hour later. He'd gotten one of the casino maintenance dump trucks and filled the bed of it with at least forty lengths of 2x4s. He grinned, happy as a pig in shit.

"About fucking time," Jimmy said in feigned anger. Always make 'em think you're unhappy. *Always make 'em think they gotta work harder.*

"Yeah, sorry Jimmy. Had to switch to the truck quietly. Wanted to make sure I was bringing enough wood. I think this is enough," the guard said, carrying a giant stack of the lumber past his vampire boss and into the secluded dead-end canyon where they were trying to burn the numerous bags of body parts.

"It better be. You get more gas too?" Jimmy said as he took off his expensive suit coat. *No need to get this new Armani dirty. I shoulda worn fucking overalls. Or Dickies.* He grabbed a massive armload of lumber out of the truck bed and carried it over to the pile of body arts as if it weighed no more than a rolled up blanket. He had to have been carrying two hundred pounds of wood. Jimmy dropped it all and started to arrange it with the other guy in a pile to put the bodies in.

"Yeah, I got a big can from the facilities garage," he said.

Kid's not half bad. Maybe he's got potential. "Not bad kid. Half a brain to ya. Serve me well, and I'll put in a good word with Uncle Cosmo for ya."

The guard stopped suddenly and looked over at Jimmy as he approached. "No shit? You'd do that for me?"

Hooked 'em. "Yeah, I might. You gotta put some more time in, you know, pay your dues and all, but you know, I think you got potential. Just keep doing everything I say, and uh, Uncle Jimmy will take good care of you."

"Great, thanks." They worked silently for minutes, neither of them breathing, or sweating. Being dead had some advantages. Finally the guard asked a question. "Hey, Jimmy, this might be too much to ask but do you know where Uncle Cosmo is from?"

Europe motherfucker, duh. "Yeah. He's from Europe."

"But where? Is he from Transylvania like Dracula? Some of us new guys just got that feeling." They were almost done with the wood, and the guard was grabbing burnt body parts off the desert ground to put on the stacks of lumber.

Jimmy laughed. "I don't think so. He won't tell anyone anyway. Neither will the handful of guys that came with him. The dhampyrs he calls them. None of 'em will say shit, not even to Miss Brown or me. I think he's from Russia. Maybe Greece. Can't tell though. I don't think I would tell you if I knew. Gotta be loyal—" *shit what's his name? Andrew.* "Andy. Gotta stay true to who takes care of you in this new world. Vampire or not, we need folks to have our backs."

"Yeah, totally Jimmy, I get it. Hey, even we burn in the day, right?" he said with some cheer.

That's fucking creepy. "That's right."

"Do you at least know how old he is?" he asked hopefully.

This'll fuck with his head. "I don't know exactly. But Uncle Cosmo told me once that 'the only good music is classical music' and then he told me that 'I would understand if I had seen Bach live, like he had.' Shit Andy. I wonder if that means he's German. You think Bach is German? I think so."

The guard named Andy thought about it as he poured out a huge gush of gasoline on the body parts and the wood. A good soaking ensured a solid fire. "Yeah, I think so. Man, that means Uncle Cosmo is at least what? Four hundred years old? Holy fuck Jimmy, if that's true… He must be powerful as all get-out."

You have no idea. "Andy, Uncle Cosmo is a force of nature. I'd bet you that shirt you're wearing he could rip the teeth right out of that fucking dragon's mouth. The one on television? He ain't scared of shit."

A tossed match caused a powerful fireball that nearly set the two vampires on fire, but they'd backed away just enough. The voluminous roar of the flames very quickly told them both that the fire would be hot enough to do the job if they fed it enough wood. The two blood drinkers stood twenty feet away, basking in the warmth that kept their dead bodies from cooling and hardening. The chill December night air of the desert felt like rigor mortis setting in if a vampire wasn't careful. The cold could be a hard teacher for the undead.

"You said you'd put in a good word for me?"

"Keep doing what I say, Andy. Uncle Jimmy will take care of you."

"You got it, boss," Andy said back without hesitation.

Good little boy. Jimmy lit another cigarette, and the two men watched the fire consume the grisly evidence of mass murder.

Chapter Twelve

Mycroft Rupert Doyle

Waiting for Henry and Ambryn to awaken after their nights of roaming the streets is wearing my patience. Mr. Doyle looked over Agent MacTavish inside the tank and saw a similar look of impatience and disdain on her pretty but scarred face. *The two boys play all night long while she and I pore through paperwork, sifting for the detail that could rip this case wide open.*

A knock came on the tank's side door. Mr. Doyle had a minor spell running on the hull of the vehicle that whispered to him that outdoors awaited Ambryn and Henry at last. Behind the closed eyelids of a blink he could see a ghostly outline of them. "Ah, at the crack of 1300 hours the rest of our team arrives. Do come in."

The door opened, and the former Boston detective and the dragon masquerading as a human climbed up the steps and inside the cabin of the modified RV. *They look ashamed. And Henry appears not a little hungover.*

"Sorry we're late; we tried a new idea last night," Spoon said after taking a sip from a Starbucks coffee. He made a dissatisfied face.

A Dunkin's man. "Oh? A new tactic? Do tell." The wizard found it hard to hide his frustration as the dragon slid into the bench seat across from him.

"We went to a strip club."

Lord grant me the patience... "A strip club? Strictly for business of course?"

Spooner and Ambryn exchanged a guilty glance. "Yes," Ambryn said devoid of any shame or guilt."

"Are you serious?" Mr. Doyle asked them. "Why would going to a strip club be a good idea when we need to stay out of the limelight? We can hardly afford for anyone to recognize any of us right now. The media has already had a grand old time reporting on my presence. Imagine what they'd do if the 'hero cop of Boston' was here? Or, heavens forbid, they were to find out that Ambryn was here. Rubbish. Pure rubbish."

"Calm yourself, mage," Ambryn said, the taste of hostility in his voice. "Vampires have a powerful sex drive, especially newly created ones. A strip club was a likely place to find a fledgling looking for an easy meal. It was worth the effort. Your scolding of us trying something new is not necessary. We are aware of the risks in exposure."

If he weren't a dragon I would slap him across the face. "You're playing with fire, both of you. One of our greatest assets is that no one knows you are here, Ambryn. If you are discovered by whoever is behind the missing people and the buses, they will disappear, and we may never find them again."

"I'm aware," the dragon replied.

Infuriating. I could choke someone right now.

Spoon's phone went off. The sound playing was the eighties hit Eye of the Tiger. MacTavish laughed. "That's Tesser. I wonder what he's up to." Spoon thumbed the call to accept it, and immediately put it on speakerphone and sat it down on the table.

Look at Ambryn. Excited and nervous. He's so invested in his brother and his new little niece. Or is it sister? Incestuous ways.

"Tesser, buddy. How's Norway?" Spoon asked his friend.

"Shhh. Geez man, Astrid and Matty just fell asleep," Tesser said, whispering. "Norway's great. Cold as you might imagine but still beautiful. We just got done with a huge tour of the deeper parts of the subterranean troll city. Quite the place, man. Bigger than I thought. And far more beautiful. The way the light plays off the ice they've carved. Just radiant. I've never been there as an acknowledged guest before, and I gotta say, they are good... people. They've changed a lot."

"They've got a vested interest in the world at large now, Tesser," Ambryn said to the phone. "They are now related to the dragon of magic. Matty's got troll blood in her, and that means Astrid does too. Instant credibility on the world scene."

"True," Tesser said. "How are things in Las Vegas? Any news on whether or not our missing and found buses are linked to a vampire or vampires?"

"It is a Cheater of Death, there's no doubt. I think there might be many," Ambryn said.

"Cheater of Death?" Spoon asked the dragon in the vehicle.

"Ask me later," Ambryn said, dismissing him. "Tesser, is the baby fine? How is Matilde?"

"They're good, thanks for asking. Tired. Matty doesn't get much sleep with Astrid wanting to be fed all the time. We're in a hotel for a couple of nights, then we are heading back to the city for a few troll familial rituals. Some kind of acceptance thing. I've seen it done before; family is big for them. They want to officially welcome Matty and her parents, as well as Astrid into the troll nation as citizens and more. Should spark some interesting conversations about nationality and ethnicity in human culture."

"Nothing is simple," Mr. Doyle said.

"You got that right. How are you, Mr. Doyle?"

Ah. My soapbox has arrived. "Tesser, I'm quite frustrated with the activities of your brother and Agent Spooner. They've seen fit to go out to a strip club, and I'm concerned that they'll be spotted in public, revealing our full hand before we've caught the tail of the monster we're after. Never mind the public relations issues of having a Tapper agent at a business where women undress for money."

"They'll do a lot more than undress," Spoon muttered under his breath. MacTavish laughed again.

"A strip club? Really guys?" Tesser asked.

"They're highly sexual, Tesser. A club was a good enough place to find them as any. It was a calculated risk. Tell me, is Astrid getting enough rest?" Ambryn said.

"Don't change the subject on me, you know she's fine. You guys gotta be careful. This sounds bad Ambryn, and knowing you, it can only get worse. Have you any leads?" Tesser asked.

"I resent that accusation Tesser," Ambryn said with a defeated voice.

"Nothing solid as of yet," Mr. Doyle replied, ignoring the hurt feelings of the black dragon.

Spoon added, "Ambryn and I were sitting down today to pore through the missing people with Doyle and Agent MacTavish. Specifically, the dead bodies we've identified from the crashed bus. I think tracking down how they went missing, or any connections they have to the living or the dead might lead us somewhere. We need to find out who put them on that bus."

"I've also reached out to get assistance from someone intimately familiar with hunting vampires. I am hoping to hear news soon," Mr. Doyle said.

"Who is this?" Tesser asked.

"You wouldn't know him, but he is known in the

circles of magic as The Romanian. He is the most recent of a long line of vampire hunters. He also happens to be a two-skin," Mr. Doyle said.

"A werewolf?" Spoon asked. From down the length of the bus Agent MacTavish became suddenly interested. She closed the distance to the conversation. Up until that moment, she'd been a distant spectator, laughing only at Spoon's jokes.

"Yes. His family has been hunting undead in Europe and western Asia for generations. They have been very successful and have ways that I do not fully understand, despite my efforts. If The Romanian agrees to help, he will be an asset of tremendous use to us," the old man said, sipping a cup of now cool tea.

"Is he a liability?" Tesser asked his friend.

Absolutely. "No. He has had a few incidents in recent years where he might have been considered overzealous in his hunt, but I am told he has calmed down notably in the past few months. He is worth the risk if what we believe to be true here, is true." *Lying is such a delicate thing.*

No one said anything. The whole situation felt frustrating, and the sense of desperation for some help—any help—was palpable.

"Whatever it takes, right? We can't afford mass murder or the spread of vampires. I gotta go guys. I think I hear Astrid, and I don't want her to wake Matty. I can bottle feed her. Be safe guys. Nobody get bitten," Tesser said.

Everyone said goodbye, and the call ended.

"Here to research the missing people, eh? Agent MacTavish and I have been diligently working on that since yesterday," Mr. Doyle offered, looking to his lady cohort.

Spoon defended his statement. "There's got to be some link. Something. More eyes on the data might reveal a morsel we can use. I know you're angry Mr.

Doyle, but we're grasping at straws here. I'm not a wizard, I'm a cop in a world that's a lot different than it was a year ago. I'm used to hunting down car thieves, and drug dealers, and frat guys who chased too much fucking vodka with too much fucking Viagra. No academy in the world teaches vampire hunting."

"Not yet, Henry. But I assure you when we are finished here, someone somewhere will be teaching it," Mr. Doyle said.

"Good," Spoon said back.

"Each identified person of the thirty eight has a folder stacked there," he pointed to a thin wall-mounted table, "and each of the Jane and John Does are over here." It was a larger stack by far.

"Forensics is running DNA on the bodies, right?" Henry asked.

"Yes. I am told the county office should have results to us in a day or two. They've fast tracked it as best as possible, but twenty five DNA tests is a large amount for any facility to process on short order. I've requested that labs in the southwest with capacity be tapped to help. We've also asked multiple forensic dentists to assist as well. I think they might offer us more than the DNA, and faster as well, but we won't know for a bit regardless."

"Alright. Sounds like the gears are turning for us. Let's dig in to what we got already," Henry said as he sat down next to Ambryn.

"Agent MacTavish, would you be so kind as to fetch us a few menus? It's lunch, and I'm famished yet again. Good on you."

The agent sighed at the undignified task and went to get the take-out menus. The look on Henry's face told Doyle that he, too, didn't approve of how he was utilizing the young woman.

Chapter Thirteen
Belyakov

In the city of Pitesti there is a theater. It's an establishment of the fine arts, named after the noted Romanian diplomat and public administrator Alexandru Davila. He's quite a big deal for the locals.

The actual building housing Davila's theater was bulky, uninspired, and lacked any architectural grace or flair. It reached perhaps six stories in height and stood apart from the other buildings in the middle of Pitesti. It had too many lines, too many right angles, and had been built out of too much concrete and gray, and too little glass or color. The most beautiful aspect of the entire place had to be a few well-trimmed green hedges in the courtyard, and a worn bronze statue of a bearded man wearing a cape. The place lacked all of the culture and creativity of the plays that occurred inside it. It made anyone near it feel tired, like they were walking into work on a dreary Monday morning.

Reminds me yet again of the brutal, ignorant grace of the Soviet Republic. So ironic that so little beauty surrounds a place such as this.

Teatrul Davila had a special show for children every so often. A puppet show, and a well-known event across a good portion of Romania. The girl at the apartment had said The Romanian would be at the puppet show, and that's why Belyakov was buying a ticket. *Hopefully the Romanian is sitting watching, and I can speak to him in a public place where we will both feel safer. I hope to speak like two gospoda. Gentlemen.*

He fingered the stones resting in his palm that he'd made ready. *It is wiser to prepare for what you expect and not for what you hope. I don't wish to kill him if he attacks me. But I fear I may need to use great force should he shift to his monstrous forms. Varcolac can be... unpredictable when shifted. Especially this one.*

The Russian made his way through the lobby, whose glossy tile floor saved the entire building from a complete loss in terms of beauty. It had an old geometric flair to it with strong, black shades of golds and reds, and he found his eyes dancing across the repeating radial patterns. Parents and their children meandered about in the theater lobby as he walked. The mothers and fathers holding hands, leading their little boys and girls to the bathrooms, or to a series of benches where they could organize a small snack before heading in to watch the masterful puppeteers work their magic. Belyakov smiled at every child who looked up at him with wide, innocent eyes. *There is real magic in the eyes of a child. I wonder what my child would've grown up to look like. Ugly, like my life? Or handsome, like my hopes? Bah. Such thoughts cloud the mind and vision. I must focus. An error now would cost me more than just my indulgence in old memories.*

With his empty hand he pulled the theater door open. A blast of laughter hit him from deep within, and it was infectious. He smiled and walked around the wall just inside the door that blocked the light. He stopped at the top of the bowl shaped theater with its hundreds of red velvet seats, and he searched for the man he didn't want to speak to. First, he had to look away from the shrunken stage where the puppets were reenacting some tragic

Greek play done with a childish glee. Puppet soldiers dressed like warriors tabbed innocents with spears the size of drawing rulers. It had an odd morbidity to it that was not lost on the Russian. *Is that meant to be Achilles? With the blood-soaked spear?* Belyakov shrugged and looked away, disturbed by the play. He started searching into the spaces of the darkened theater for the specialized killer for hire he sought for his friend.

No. No. Too short. Not him. That's just a tall woman. Oh. There. Alone. As I remember him, though he slouches. That must be the drinking the girl spoke of. He does not sit proudly as he should. And he laughs too loud. He will embarrass himself if he continues. Look at the parents around him. Moving slowly, escaping. They can sense the monster inside him. Just beneath stretched skin. I must go to him. End this and speak to him.

The Romanians, each and every one of the bloodline who took on the family's title were tall. Like something else more sinister, the lean bodies ran in their blood. Belyakov had met three of the hunters in his lifetime, and each had been no less than a foot taller than he. The current Romanian was even taller. He stood well past six feet, just over halfway to seven feet. And like his father and his father's father, this man had long black hair, silky and smooth, tied back into a tail that hung high on the back of his skull. When the Romanian went to battle the hair would be braided tight or discarded entirely when he left his human form. This Romanian wore baggy sweatpants and a loose zippered sweatshirt that hung open, showing a stained undershirt beneath. He looked more like a drunk hoodlum than the most recent in a long line of heroes.

I am sad.

Belyakov circled the theater around the back of the seats so as not to block the view of the paying patrons. He came down the five rows, walking silently until he stood just a dozen feet from the man he came to speak with. His heart throbbed. This would be a very dangerous moment.

Here we go.

Belyakov shuffled sideways like a crab until he was two seats away from the killer of vampires wearing the tracksuit. *He reeks of plum brandy. I don't remember him being a drinker like this.* Belyakov sat down a long arm's length away with the Romanian still oblivious to his presence. He laughed loudly at the dancing puppets as they sparred with spears the size of chopsticks. *How does he not know that I am here? He should've caught my scent by now.*

The play continued far below on stage, causing the happy children gathered at it to shriek with joy. It was loud enough in the theater to have a quiet and polite conversation without anyone caring, and Belyakov took the initiative. *Better now than later.*

"Artur Cojocaru," Belyakov said just above a whisper to man sitting near him.

The Romanian continued to laugh, transfixed on the puppets acting foolish on the stage. The children laughed as he did, though not with him. He appeared to be ignorant of the Russian's presence just a few feet away, as well as the mention of his name.

"Artur Cojocaru, varcolac of the Carpathians, and the most recent of your line," Belyaov said, but again the Romanian either didn't hear him or ignored him. *I don't dare reach out to touch him.* "Artur Cojocaru. Do you remember me? I am Belyakov. I have come to speak to you about important business. Family business. People have died, *many* people have died, and even more need your help."

One of the puppets fell from tripping on a dropped soldier's shield, and the children and the werewolf wearing a tracksuit laughed hysterically, all clutching at their bellies.

"Artur," Belyakov pleaded with urgency.

The Romanian exploded out of his seat, hands stretched open like monstrous bear paws, his long fingers tipped in ebony talons that hadn't been there a millisecond before. His teeth had sprouted massive canines that forced his mouth open, and something else had changed about him. The stretched skin that had hidden his nature from the world had torn away, and the true beast inside clawed to get out. "I FUCKING HEARD YOU THE FIRST TIME, OLD MAN!" The scream was in English.

Belyakov recoiled, nearly calling forth the magic out of the stones clutched in his hand. The show stopped. All the children were shrieking, though now out of some primal, base fear of a predator in their midst. A monster had stepped into their presence, and they knew it. The parents scooped up their precious offspring and retreated to the side of the theater like rabbits fleeing the fox. They took their children opposite the two men in the theater, and they hid low behind seats. It was all they could do after the bellow. A puppeteer dressed in all black stood up slowly from behind the boxed stage and looked on with wide, frightened eyes. The illusions of the world were peeling away.

"Artur. Calm yourself. Do you remember me? I am your friend," Belyakov said in a voice a soft as silk. He'd dealt with drunks before, and he hoped this would be at least somewhat the same. *May God help us if I am wrong.*

Belyakov could barely hear him over the cacophony in the theater. "Shut your mouth, Russian! I know you. I know what you are," Artur hissed. "You're a charlatan with your magic. Impure. So unfair. You can't *learn* to be one of us. Born with all you need. You just steal your power from the world. Making magic. So impure," he slurred as his teeth grew longer on both sides of his tongue, and the hair at his jaw line grew thicker. Instead of the smooth black hair on top his head, his new growth was snow white, thick and coarse.

He will expose his kind here. I can already see phones coming out to record this. I must move this outside, or his hand will be played forever, and The Romanians will never be the same.

Belyakov slid to his feet, backing away towards the side exit door he knew was just feet away. The Romanian had selected his seat wisely, despite being inebriated. Belyakov would use his escape route to draw him away from the screaming children. "Vspyshka!" he shouted in Russian as he drew on the power of the citrine stone. It flared warmth in his palm, and in the space between he and Artur, the air erupted into a flare of light accompanied by a loud, piercing bang.

The magic explosion temporarily blinded and deafened the werewolf. The insanely tall man staggered back, his jaw working reflexively as Belyakov turned and dashed as fast as his legs would allow out the fire door. It led to a narrow alley sandwiched between another wing of the blocky gray building. *Not much room here, and I'll never outrun him. I must make my stand now.* The Russian ran another ten paces and slipped his stones back into their proper locations at his belt. He found another rock that would have to do, unless he had to visit great violence on the Werewolf. He turned, and planted his feet, waiting for the Romanian.

The fire door blew open like a truck hit it from the inside. It slammed off the wall beside it and the drunk werewolf exited, larger still than when Belyakov had last seen him. His arms had lengthened, as had his legs, though his gait had become different, like his knees were stiff, or broken. They bent in a decisively inhuman way. He lowered his head like the wolf he was and growled as the door shut behind him. *The children are safe. If only for a minute. He nears the shift. The full change. I have little time. He must be made pure in blood.*

The werewolf changed faster than a shirt could be shed in a lover's presence.

The Cojocaru name came from a strange trait the family owned. As strange a trait as their ability to shift into wolf form. In Romanian, Cojocaru means 'winter coat,' and like the white hairs that had grown from his jaw, when Artur shifted into one of the full inhuman forms of the two-skin he was, his black hair was shed, leaving only a thick pelt of white covering him from wolf head to wolf toe. The beast was massive, the size of a compact car, and just as wide and fast. The monster's black eyes were disconnected, lost in the haze in the middle of a lake of brandy and an ocean of mindless hate. It charged him, trailing ropy strands of saliva and tearing at the pavement below.

Belyakov had a fraction of a second to get his spell off before the wolf-Artur hit him full force, and gutted him with teeth the size of steak knives. He held aloft a piece of carved blue calcite the size of a table cracker. It had been delicately carved into the shape of a tiny funnel.

"Chistka!" he screamed with direct intent at the chest of the wolf. A beam of blue light the width of a man's arm erupted from the stone in his outstretched hand and pierced the wolf, passing through the length of its body and exiting a different color. The bright and translucent oceanic blue laced with white exited Artur's body as a navy blue with swirls of violet and jade. The beam hit the far wall of the alley with a sticky wet slap, leaving a descending stain of the brandy that had driven Artur to madness. Belyakov's spell had blown the alcohol straight from the blood of the hunter and rendered the beast unconscious in the same instant.

The spell did not stop its forward momentum, nor make the old Russian any more agile or durable.

The white body of the beast smashed into him with the force of a dump truck. The Russian felt crushed in slow motion. He heard and felt muffled snaps inside his body. *I've broken ribs.* He flew backwards through the air, its weight and girth pushing him like he was a tiny nail and it was a giant hammer. When they landed, the hundreds of pounds of wolfen weight crushed him against the hard pavement below, flattening him out and careening his skull off the hard stone. Belyakov felt something crack behind his ears, and the light coming into his eyes diffused and became dark as the werewolf's body settled on his chest, crushing him. He fought to get air into his lungs, and mercifully Artur's body atop him began to revert to human form, giving him some ability to breathe. *My air feels wet. I want to cough but can't. I might be drowning.*

Belyakov's mind struggled to stay focused. He was hurt. Badly. *Ribs... Broken... Can't feel my feet... Where have my toes gone? And I'm wet. Blood. So much blood... I can feel it around me like a halo. I'm going to die. Damn you Doyle. I will find a way to haunt you. Break your wine glass.* Belyakov laughed, imagining the look on his friend's face as a ghost pushed the wine glass off his desk. The act of laughing nearly blacked him out. *Very hard to breathe.*

Something gray and large moved in front of his eyes, obstructing the cloudy sky high above the narrow alley. *What is that?* He blinked repeatedly, and even that hurt.

"Erou prost, bătrân," a familiar female voice said in Romanian.

Old man? I know that voice. The girl. Belyakov looked up and saw the black haired girl from apartment 708. She was opposite him, upside down in his eyes, and looked somewhere between frustrated, and outright furious. He saw her mismatched eyes; the left green, the right blue. *But wait... she is upside down. They should be the other...*

Belyakov died before he could finish the thought.

Chapter Fourteen

Ambryn

I am a killer. Henry and Mr. Doyle, and even Agent MacTavish would like to think that I'm different, more than that, but I am the dragon of death. I cut the circle of life where it has spun for too long, or where it has grown fat, and should be trimmed. I exist to kill. I exist to restore balance in life, by bringing death. I cannot change my nature any easier than a leopard could lose its spots or the sun could stop shining.

I am content to help my human friends in their search for clues during the day. Henry has a knack for investigation. It's as clear to me as the hair on his head that he sees things, facts, motives, details, and plots where others do not. I'm confident that sooner or later we will find something in the science that we are poring through. At a bare minimum, I am learning more about how humans conduct investigations. In the future, these new skills might help me find other vampires or things much worse.

I cannot afford to wait for later. I must act on my own despite what they wish. I am a dragon after all, and I answer to no human.

Tesser confounds me. His blind loyalty to this species he loves goes against so much of why we exist. We dragons are above it all, behind the scenes. We are directors, not actors.

And yet he chooses to remain down in the dirt with the life he creates, giving them influence and power over the world that is our dominion.

Is it love? What sense is there in loving something other than duty? Has he lost his sense because of his love for Matilde?

An alien thought if there ever was one for a dragon. The only thing our kind should love is the world and all that we are here to protect. But Tesser … he has fallen in love. Matilde, she is … his first and greatest possible weakness. Her death would bring madness upon him.

And she will die. None of us has the power to stop it.

Why would anyone put themselves in such a place? Intentionally assuming risk for no good reason?

Although he would argue that how he feels is reason enough, and I've no idea how to counter that logic. I am a killer, not a lover or a maker of life. I am so very different than him, and yet we work in harmony to ensure the balance. I suppose the eighth true wonder of the world is all the proof Tesser needs for love.

Astrid.

Ambryn sat in the back of a very large adult club just off the Vegas Strip. The music chattered loudly, reverberating inside his chest, and shaking the crystalline chandeliers, preventing anyone from striking up meaningful conversation with him. Ambryn appreciated that, regardless of whether or not it was thumping electronic music, or the grinding rock or pop from an older decade. It was all the same in the end.

No one from Tapper knew of his forbidden presence at the club. Henry, Mr. Doyle, and MacTavish all believed he was curled up in miniature dragon form on the King sized bed in his hotel room back at the Wynn. He had been very adamant about his need for sleep and how he hated to be disturbed.

Ambryn was hunting.

It doesn't suit me to sit still and pore through paperwork. I wasn't made for that. I must act.

Like every other time Ambryn took human form, he became a modest looking, faintly handsome man of average height. He was slim, and his hair short and parted neatly to the side in a haircut that seemed stylish, yet from a different decade. His skin was fair, like a redhead's, and his expression detached and ethereal. He always looked like his gaze passed through you. Like every other dragon who had taken human form, the members of the opposite sex were drawn to him when it suited his purpose. Death can be seductive.

Not quite like how they are drawn to Tesser, but then again, we serve different purposes, and so does our seduction.

Women liked Ambryn because of his inner nature. Just as how Tesser radiated sexuality, Ambryn exuded a sense of pending mortality. To stand near him was to be unconsciously on the edge of death. To skirt the void of the great beyond and yet not fall and perish. He was the ultimate thrill. The adrenaline rush only those who have nearly died experience. He was death incarnate, and many men and women wanted to chase the feeling he gave them, though they never knew why. Ambryn wanted nothing to do with them. Sex wasn't his thing.

It certainly wasn't his goal for tonight.

The working women at the club— the dancers—came to him steadily, leaning over seductively and offering the presence of their long and exquisitely sculpted bodies for cash. Ambryn made an effort to be pleasant to them. Thanking them kindly for the offer, but declining. He then explained that he was there to enjoy a few drinks, that he needed a distraction, and that he wanted to think about 'things.' He said his phrase with a forced and false sound of melancholy, telling the women of his suffering, that his heart had been broken recently, and that he needed to be surrounded by something that would distract him from the state of affairs his life had fallen into.

Saying no got him three free lap dances and two phone numbers written discreetly on condom wrappers in permanent marker. Ambryn put the signs of sympathy away with a grateful smile after thanking them for their compassion. He had nothing against the women. But it was difficult for him to watch for a cheater of death when he had a pair of silicone-enhanced breasts pressed into his face.

Patience.

Periodically Ambryn would inhale deeply, forcing the thick club air up his nostrils and through his beyond human nasal passages. He'd keep his mouth just slightly ajar as he did so, allowing all of his sense of smell and taste to mingle, giving him a supernaturally powerful sense of the environment.

I smell cancers. There are at least ten people sick with it in this building. One is near death. Two I doubt even know they have a ticking time bomb inside them. I wonder if they'll see a doctor in time, or if my little check and balance will do its dirty work in time…

I smell body odor. Perfumes in laughable excess. Cologne applied as if the man had marinated in a tank of it instead of spraying it on. Don't they know they're masking their own natural sex-smells? Tesser gave you pheromones for a reason. Silly humans.

I smell alcohol. I smell cocaine and methamphetamines. I smell gun oil and the steel of hidden knives. I smell a man with fresh stitches. He should sit, wherever he is in here; he is bleeding a bit. Wouldn't want you get an infection now.

I smell sex. Yeah. Most of all I can smell the greasy, slick, primal smell of arousal. The girls, the men. It's as thick as an English fog in here, and just as hard to make a good decision on what to do in the middle of. The crushing, twisting, gyrating need for life to fuck itself into a new generation. And right beside that is little old me, keeping the numbers in check and giving them half the motivation to do just what they came here to do. More of us died, we should have more children, they think. Funny. That my role in the world inspires what I am trying to cull to breed faster. The balance is a strange thing.

I smell food. Fried food. It smells good. I also smell death. Death.

Ambryn sat up out of his plush lounge chair and sat his half drank mojito down on the cherry table beside it. He closed his eyes and focused on the unmistakable scent of the walking dead. Each of the great mistakes Ambryn and Kaula birthed onto the world and all the similar monstrosities that had come about before and since had different, distinct odors. Call it an olfactory fingerprint. Zombies smelled like rot. Old decaying flesh and ruptured bowels left in the forest beside a mold crusted tree for the sun to cook. They were potent. Ghosts and the immaterial smelled like dampness mixed with old incense and the perfumes of lost loves. They were almost impossible to smell unless you were blessed with a nose far beyond the ken of a human. Humans wondered why dogs barked every once in a while for no reason. Ambryn knew many animals could smell the dead long before the humans could.

Vampires smelled imperceptibly of corruption and taint, of bad decisions, and greed. They stank of hidden secrets, and spilled blood. They were hard on the nose, like spilled gasoline being obscured by a drift of old burnt rubber. Harsh if your nose had been designed for great use. Perhaps worst of all, over the top of all that they truly were, the vampires smelled like the humans they hunted.

The scent that made the hairs on Ambryn's arm stand on edge came mixed in with an air conditioned gust that moved to him from the main entrance. He'd chosen his seat to have a view of the door. Ambryn squinted ever so slightly and assessed the group of fresh arrivals.

Which of you is it?

Standing happy and gregarious at the entrance of the club stood a veritable posse of mismatched goons. He counted seven new faces at the door. As he leaned forward to watch them, a song about cherry pie started to blare on the club speakers, and the girl appearing on the stage nearest to him began a mind-boggling series of twirls on her golden pole. Ambryn tried to tune her act out, but her talent made it somewhat of a struggle. *Even I have my weak moments.*

He narrowed his dark eyes and watched each man in turn. Most were tall and thickly muscular like athletes. The others were all walks of man. One was fat and short, nearly round, and with a hairline trying to escape off the back off the back of his head like a convict with a stolen purse. One was entirely forgettable. Neither short nor tall, thick nor slim. He had a haircut that said he could be professional, but he wasn't at work right now. They were all grinning, already deep into a night filled with alcohol and elated to be suddenly surrounded by a herd of beautiful women who wanted their attention.

The three tall ones are sweating from veins filled with drugs and liquor. They are alive. Though perhaps not for long if they don't get fluids. Good riddance.

The wide one… breathes heavily.

The plain one. He stands apart. But… they all look to him every few moments, seeking his approval. Seeking his permission. Ambryn studied his chest. *He does not breathe.*

Electricity coursed up and down the dragon's spine as he readied for the kill. He got to his feet and took several strong strides toward the entry of the club and started to envision just how he'd rip the vampire into pieces and how satisfying it would be to rid the world of another parasite.

From the shallow depths of the previous night's memory, Henry's voice spoke to him. "*True, but I think we need to take over looking into the missing locals that aren't homeless. If there's a connection, we could narrow down our search considerably. And Ambryn, you gotta admit this is going nowhere fast. We need facts. Clues. Leads. Killing a random bloodsucker is gonna leave us with a body, not answers."*

Ambryn stopped his predatory approach two steps in as the group of men drifted away with several dancer escorts, up a flight of wide, curving stairs to a VIP room on the second floor of the club. The dragon gritted his still-human teeth and cursed under his breath. *Fuck. Henry is right. I need to ask that damned thing questions or take it captive.*

"Honey, you look angry. Can Azure help you?" a female voice asked close to his ear.

She got very close to me. I'm tunnel visioned. I need to be aware. Wait. I have an idea. Ambryn shook his head clear, put on a smile, and turned to face the dancer. She was short, with chocolate colored skin and long, straight hair that reminded him of a waterfall at midnight. Her plump breasts were barely contained by a silver bikini top. She was exotic, and beautiful. "Your name is Azure? Blue?"

"Look at my eyes, baby," she said, pulling down a lower eyelid with a finger tipped in a two-inch long silver nail that matched her top. Her eyes were crystalline and bright blue. Real, with no outline from colored contacts. "True blue honey."

"Beautiful. Really beautiful. Maybe you can help me. I saw some guys go upstairs just a minute ago. What happens up there?"

"Oh that's the exclusive rooms. Very. Important. People. You get four girls, champagne, and the best night of your life," she said, her long finger trailing an erotic circle around his ear. "Of course, it ain't free." She circled the lobe, and caressed his jaw line. *Quite an expert at seduction.*

"I'm very important. Would you take me upstairs? I'd like to have some champagne," Ambryn said, staring at her with his black eyes. He pushed a tiny flair of his immense dragon will into the look, and ensured her compliance.

The tiny bit of Ambryn's relatively weak magic hit her like a sirocco smashing on the sand and she lit up, excited to fulfill his request. "Sure thing honey. Follow Azure. Tell me what kind of girls you want to watch." The ebony goddess took his hand in hers and led him toward the curved stairs.

Chapter Fifteen

Agent Alanna MacTavish

Alanna knocked on the hotel room door, later than she should've been. Urges were tough to fight when they'd been years in the making. *I hope he's not asleep already. It looks like the lights are on inside.*

She watched the peephole turn dark as whoever was inside the room looked out of the fish-eye lens. Out of instinct, her right hand dropped down to the handgun holstered at her hip. The door cracked open, stopped by the metal loop that had replaced the chain technology years ago.

"Mac? Everything okay?" Henry Spooner asked her through the crack in the door.

I am so nervous right now. "Yeah Hank, everything is fine. I was just awake and wanted to say hi. I brought a six pack if you want a beer? It's Sam Adams seasonal. Your favorite." She hefted up the six pack of beer in her left hand, and watched as Henry smiled. *He still has a nice smile.*

"I, um ... I was heading to bed, but yeah, a beer

sounds good. Hold on," he said before closing the door enough to slip the metal loop off the stud. He opened the door all the way and motioned for her to enter. He had a tank top on underneath his open blue button-up shirt. His belt hung off his waist, undone. In his left hand he held a heavy pistol. *I guess we have the same instincts. He still looks great.*

Alanna walked by him deeper into the hotel bedroom and handed him a cold beer from the six pack. "Thanks. I've been meaning to stop in and say hi. Thank you face to face for getting me into the agency. That and getting me this assignment."

Henry put his pistol on the television stand and used the corner of the same to pop the cap off the bottle. It spun on the top before shooting off onto the thick rug. "You're welcome. I knew you were looking for work on the west coast, and I knew you had experience. You're a good fit. I'm glad it worked out."

"It's been great," Alanna said as she sat at the foot of the still-made bed. It was springy, just like the one in her room several floors below. She used the bottle opener on her keychain to open her own beer. She tossed the cap into the tiny waste bin nearby. "I can't believe you pulled strings to get me on the transfer here. I get to be Mr. Doyle's attaché? His personal driver too? Such an honor."

Henry snorted, nearly coughing up a mouthful of Boston beer. "Yeah, well he's kind of an asshole, it isn't that much of an honor."

Is he serious? "Henry, we talk about him in the Oakland office like he's the second coming. All the after-action reports you wrote of him with that sword in the basement of Fitzgerald Industries? The spells and how he's teaching new recruits all kinds of magic tricks. He's our version of Gandalf, or Dumbledore. With a dash of Sean Connery and Stallone added in for flavor."

"I assure you he is like none of those people. He's more like Oscar the Grouch. With some of the Balrog for flavor maybe."

He's still funny. "Well, regardless of what you think of him, he's a celebrity around my parts. We talk about him like he's a super hero. And really, you too. You're like, upper echelon cool. You hang out with dragons, shoot guns, kill monsters, and get paid for it."

Henry downed the rest of his beer. "It's not all glitz and glamour. Most of it is trying to figure out what Doyle and Tesser are talking about as they talk to each other. I write so many reports on their conversations, it isn't even funny." He walked over to the bed and pulled a beer from the six pack beside Alanna. Without her brain being a part of it, her hand reached out and touched Henry's as it withdrew. *Shit. That's going to be awkward.* Henry smiled at her and returned to his spot next to the television stand. He popped the beer open once more using the edge of the furniture. He made it look easy. Paratroopers made a lot of things look easy.

"Well, we aren't east coasters. We're late to the game," she said with a shrug.

"We're all late to the game," Henry said, taking another swig. "What actually brings you here?"

I'm gonna need another beer to answer that question. She finished her first off, and slid the empty into the box as she fetched her second. When she had the bottle open, she started talking again. "What happened to you and me?"

Henry leaned against the stand and held his beer in both hands. He looked at his feet. "Deployment ended Alanna. We went home. I guess things changed."

Something in her chest fluttered, less like a butterfly, and more like an angry wasp. "But what changed? I mean really. I thought things were good between us."

Henry kept looking at his feet. *He won't even look at me.* "Yeah, I guess they were good. Alanna, I know this is bullshit, but this was never about you. This is on me."

"It's not you, it's me. Yeah I've heard it before."

Alanna's hand ran up to the scar on her jaw. The ugly grand canyon carved in her flesh. "Tell me it wasn't about this. Tell me I was pretty enough. Tell me I was an asshole. I can live with being an asshole."

Henry's eyes finally lifted up to her, and he looked almost angry. "Fuck no. Shit Mac, you're beautiful. That mortar—look, fuck that thing. You have a scar, so what? When we got back to Kentucky I wanted nothing to do with you because I'm a shitty boyfriend Alanna. I can't handle the real world and a real person in my life at the same time. I'll forget about you. I'll work too much. I'll fuck some young girl at a club just because I can. I can't love like you wanted me to. Not yet at least."

That makes me feel somewhat better. Not all better. "Have you been seeing anyone? Since you got out?"

Henry snickered. "Dates here and there. Some sex. Nothing that lasted more than a month. I'm not made for marriage, Alanna. I'm not that guy. I'm sorry to say that to you now. And I know I messed up when we got back from deployment. I need to see someone that I can't be in love with or possibly marry. I need to date a small horse or something. But whatever. The sins of our past are on me. Not you. Speaking of you, what about you? You seeing anyone?"

Alanna's hand unconsciously rose up to the scar again. "No. I focus on work. Try not to think about it."

"Think about the scar? Or think about finding a man?" Henry teased.

She grinned. Alanna took a swig from her bottle. "Both I guess. Funny how things go, huh? Both of us are on the top of the world here, doing what we love, and we're both emotional derelicts over an affair we had in Afghanistan."

"To be fair, I was an emotional derelict long before we deployed."

"Ha, maybe me too. Henry, it's good to see you. Really good. You look great."

He looked at her for a long minute, warmth in his face, and in his eyes. *Maybe it's the beer, but I think he's still attracted to me.* He walked over and sat down on the bed next to her and leaned his head over until it rested on her shoulder. His head felt warm.

"If you can handle it, and realize that I am going back to New England after we wrap this up, I have a King size bed," he said softly with a tiny slur from hitting the beers fast on what she guessed was an empty stomach.

This time, her chest had butterflies. "If only for a night?"

"Like good old times."

She leaned away, and he lifted his head up. They were inches apart and his scent had snuck in her nose. Musky. Like fresh deodorant and the tiniest amount of sweat. *Haven't smelled that in a long time.* She leaned in for the kiss she'd thought about for years, and his phone rang.

He sighed hard as he pulled away. "Fuck. I gotta get that." He answered it on the third ring after looking at the screen. "Spooner. This Ambryn? Dude what's up? I thought you were sleeping."

Chapter Sixteen

Ambryn, The Dragon of Death

The black woman with the bright blue eyes led Ambryn around the club, picking up three other gorgeous models as if she were a wholly new breed of pied piper. Ambryn couldn't help but appreciate how easily she got the attention of the women through the noise and chaos of the club, and how fast they agreed to come upstairs to perform for him and him alone.

I am wondering how much cash this will cost me. I only brought a thousand dollars of the money Henry gave me. I hope that's enough. I would feel bad if they missed out on money because of my ruse. This is how they make their living after all. I suppose I should also be concerned with their health should a fight break out. And I do certainly intend on visiting great violence on that vampire as soon as I have the answers I seek.

The crescent shaped staircase in the club lobby was wide enough for all five of them to walk with their arms interlocked, the women's hips swaying softly, full of erotic potential against his. *It is difficult to fight the urge to want to have sex. I must admit. I feel guilty. But then again, I am about to hunt a vampire down and rip him apart. I have things to think about.*

"What do you do for work baby?" Azure asked him.

"I work in healthcare management," Ambryn said with a wry grin. "It's a killer job." *Jokes.*

The stairs spilled out into a rug so white it looked like fresh fallen snow. *How is it that they keep the floor so clean? Surely the shoes of the patrons track in dirt all night long? Have they recruited fairies to sweep through every five minutes and pick up each grain of sand as it is left behind?*

Ambryn turned his gaze away from the milky carpet and looked to the side of the wide hall with its sand colored walls. Spacious, open entryways revealed opulent rooms to each side where the champagne was doled out in mass quantities alongside smooth thighs and curvaceous chests. Sweeping couches reminiscent of the stairs gave the girls plenty of room to maneuver on the laps of their clients and still be able to glide around the room on heels that were precariously tall. Ambryn glanced into each open doorway as they walked to their own room, past security guards standing at attention waiting for an unwelcome hand to stray.

"We're in here, sugar. Have a seat, and one of us will pour you a flute of bubbly," Azure said, gesturing at a room nearly identical to the others they'd walked past.

I haven't seen the vampire or his group yet. There was one doorway beyond they hadn't walked by. A bathroom was just past it at the end of the hall. "Go ahead and pour for me. Here's six hundred bucks. I'm going to use the bathroom." Ambryn handed Azure a wad of bills from his pocket and broke free of the ladies. They groaned in feigned displeasure as he walked away. He smiled, aware of their little ruse.

The doorway sat ten paces from where he left the girls, and as he reached it, he dropped to a knee casually and retied his shoelaces. He spied into the dark depths of the room and assessed the men again.

The five athletic men were all sitting. Each had a buxom performer riding up on them in one fashion or another to a rapid fire beat thumping in the club's speakers. *Reminds me of a rap video.* The large man sat off to the side with a bottle of champagne, swigging directly. The vampire had moved to the rear of the room, sitting in a large, semicircular lounge chair as if he were the king of a pornographic court. He had two women all to his own, and he looked at them with an expression that could only be compared to that of a very hungry animal. *He looks downright peckish.*

Ambryn memorized the layout of the room, and went into the bathroom after getting to his feet. It was empty save for the echoes of the music and the wet sounds of a dancer on her bare knees in the corner stall, pleasuring a generous client with her tongue and presumably the depths of her mouth. *You go girl.* Ambryn dried his hands using the air blower and prepared to act inebriated. He pulled the bathroom door open just as the man in the toilet grunted in rapture, signaling his sexual finish. Ambryn began to stumble, his mouth contorted into a slack-jawed, mouth-breathing grin. In two loping, tipsy strides, he walked straight into the vampire's room.

Two of the athletic men got to their feet with alarming speed, picking up and setting their girls off to the side like they were lap trays instead of people. They moved to block his further penetration into the room. Conspicuously, they aligned their bodies between Ambryn and the unseemly man with two girls in the back. *They're here to protect him. I don't think they are dhampyrs. They don't smell like the half-dead.*

"Whoa buddy, wrong room," the biggest of the duo said, putting out his hands, stopping Ambryn's forward progress like a football linemen. "Let's turn you around."

"What?" Ambryn asked, intentionally looking past the big man with glossy eyes at the ceiling beyond.

"Shit, he's drunk. Let's get him in the hallway. Maybe

the security guys can steer him back into whatever room he's supposed to be in. Fucking tourists, man," the other goon said, moving to flank Ambryn. The dragon leaned heavily into the hands on his chest, letting the big guy hold him up.

"Wait," the undead man in the back of the room said. His single word froze all the other men in the room. It reminded Ambryn of a dog trainer calling his pets to heel. He excused his body from the two girls and came around the S shaped couch until he stood behind the muscle holding Ambryn up. "Where are you from, stranger?"

Shit. What places have I been to? "Cleveland, or Akron if you don't like Cleveland," Ambryn said, slurring his words slightly. *The smell of this dead cunt makes me want to tear him apart right here. I'll paint this white carpet red. See if the fairies can get that out of it. Grant me patience. Grant me resolve.*

"Nothing wrong with Cleveland in this room," the young man said with a sudden look of pleasure. "You here with anyone else tonight?"

Ambryn shook his head as if it were barely attached.

"Great. How about you join us in here? We're always looking for fun new people. Do you have girls in another room?"

"Yup."

He smiled. It reminded Ambryn of a cobra spitting venom. "Great. What room? I'll have Todd here go get 'em and bring 'em over for us. The more the merrier, right?"

"Yeah, totally. Right across the hall," Ambryn said, pointing erratically in the approximate direction of the room where the party he had paid for and his women were located.

"Todd, why don't you go get them. What's your poison? You know, I didn't catch your name either Cleveland," the sinister vampire said disarmingly.

Ambryn perked up like he'd been shocked with a cattle prod. "I am Paul. My mom called me Paully."

"Paully, do you like Jagerbombs?"

"I like alcohol," Ambryn said back to him.

"We're going to get along just fine. Come on in. Tell me about your stay in Vegas, Paully; what hotel are you in? How long are you in town?"

Ambryn allowed the dead body to put an arm around him and guide him to the couch. *Now, I learn as much as I can about these people. Then I kill him.*

*****

The liquor came out at a torrential pace. *I think they have skipped directly over 'get me drunk' and moved all the way to 'drown.'* The men had the dancers drinking too, and a half hour into the attempted conversation most of them were unable to stand in their platform shoes let alone dance. They were kicked to the side, and the girls continued their gyrations, though the sexiness generated had diminished relative to the level of alcohol they'd consumed.

Ambryn had determined that the large, jacked up men were not athletes. At least not professionally or actively. They wouldn't comment directly when Ambryn asked them repeatedly what they did no matter how much humor he injected into his inquiries, but he did overhear a single exchange that he thought might be helpful.

"Hey, you working the floor or the money room this week?" the one named Todd asked his friend. *So at least these two work together. Likely the others as well.*

The man shrugged excessively, letting the liquor guide his body. "I haven't checked the schedule yet. I worked floor two weeks running over at the cash elevator so I'm hoping I get money room or the ops center. I haven't fucking dispatched in forever."

"Oh man, ops would be tight as hell!"

And that ended the useful part of the exchange. *I think they work in security. Armed security as well, judging by the way they carry themselves. They have a slight swagger to their movements. They sit with their backs to the wall, or at the very least facing the entrance at all times. All of them have a bulge at their waist under the shirts that are perhaps one size too large. They aren't new. And as for where… they work at a casino. That doesn't narrow it down much in Sin City, but it's a start.*

Ambryn moved over to the lonely overweight man.

"Hey man. Hey. Hey, what's your name?" Ambryn asked him as he collapsed into the couch beside him.

"Brandon," the balding man said.

"Nice. Brandon. You look like a Brandon. Hey, can I ask you a question man? Like, man to man, man?" *I hope I'm not overdoing the drunk act. I've never actually been drunk. I don't even know if we dragons can get drunk.*

"You ask a lot of questions, Cleveland," the man with the shiny head said with narrowed eyes.

He's less drunk than the others. I need to be careful. "I am a lawyer. I ask lots of questions. Witnesses, judges, experts, and shit. You should see me. I'm like Boston Legal."

The expression on Brandon's face told Ambryn the explanation eased him slightly. That or the attention from someone made him feel good. "What's your question, lawyer?"

"This party costs mad money, don't it? Like, a clean grand for the girls, the booze, and the room right?"

"At least. Simon likes his girls. We got what? Six chicks in here, plus your four. Plus the good champagne and open bar. Easily two grand. Probably three before we're done here."

"Where you get all the money? I mean, I get that the big guys are hired muscle. They're the goon squad to protect you and Simon or whatever his name is, but what do you guys do to make that kind of cash? Does Simon work for Microsoft?" Ambryn tried to seem interested and confused at the same time. So much so that it he wanted the balding man to think the lack of knowledge created actual pain for him to not know the truth.

Brandon looked around for Simon, wary of saying anything that the smaller man might hear. The vampire had a girl in his lap and seemed entirely consumed by her presence. Brandon leaned in. "We've got some serious casino connections." He winked.

"What casino? All of them? Shit."

Brandon opened his mouth to answer Ambryn, but Simon appeared at his shoulder like a materialized wraith. He came out of nowhere, impossibly fast. The humans in the room couldn't have seen his movement as anything but a teleportation. Ambryn watched as the larger sitting man winced in pain as Simon's fingers dug into the flesh beside his neck, silencing him.

"Now Brandon, why don't you go fetch Paully here another Jagerbomb?" the vampire named Simon said just loud enough for the two men to hear over the dance music. His command sounded pleasant, jovial even, and was anything but.

"Sure. Sorry, I'll uh ... yeah." Brandon got up as Simon's claw unclenched from his meat. He scampered away to the back of the bar as quickly as he could, clutching at the flesh that would surely be black and blue in an hour.

Simon took Brandon's spot sitting next to Paully. He had arrogance coming off him in waves, right behind the attempt to intimidate his lesser. *The baby vampire, flush with immortality and brand spanking-new power.* "Who are you, Paully? You stumbled in here, acting the fool, and all you've done is ask us fucking questions. Are you some kind of narc? Some kind of fucking cop?"

Shit. How do I play this? "I'm not a cop dude, relax. You have drugs in here? I could care less."

Simon eyed him with suspicion on his face. "Bullshit. I'm starting to think you have a plan. You came in here on purpose." He leaned in towards Ambryn in a move designed to intimidate the unknown man. The dragon watched as the vampire's brown eyes suddenly seemed lit from within by a muted red glow. The big men in the room caught on to the unfolding drama, and Ambryn felt and heard them getting ready for some kind of confrontation.

The best part about being me is the lack of fear I have about being hurt. "You're planning on doing something with me. When the big one behind me said I was a tourist, you lit up. I suddenly became a victim." Ambryn spoke with no hint of the effects of any alcohol.

If Simon noticed the abrupt sobriety, he hid it. "You're wrong."

"No, I'm not. When Brandon started to tell me more details about where you all work and where your money came from, you bolted over here and stopped him. Odd that you could hear a whisper through all this loud music and commotion, eh? You're afraid I'll find something out."

Simon's pale white hand clenched into a fist. "Your attitude sucks, mister. I think it's time for us to go for a walk."

"Are you going to take me back to where the locals have gone missing?"

Simon's expression froze.

Got ya. "To where the new vampires are fed? Was I to be baby food?" If it were possible for a being with no physiological activity to have the color drain from their face, Simon's would have gone even whiter.

"Kill him," Simon said.

Ambryn smiled in relief. The act was over. *And now, to do what I was meant to do.*

Simon blinked his body off the couch and towards the doorway, covering the ten paces in the span of a single breath. Once their leader had gotten clear of the line of fire, his steroid infused cartel opened fire on the dragon in human form. The sound of the pistol fire inside the club was strangely muted against the music. Their ears were already being assaulted with heavy bass and rattling treble, so when the snaps of mid-caliber bullets being fired started, no one initially reacted. Not even Ambryn as the slugs pounded into the back of his head and shoulders harmlessly. The rounds might as well have been made of Styrofoam and shot at him with rubber bands for all the damage they did.

Drunk or not, they're good shots. Ambryn rose from the curved couch as the dancers caught on to the sudden eruption of gunfire. *Shocking how long it took them to realize the men they were just dancing for are shooting guns. Must be the drinking. Oh good. Brandon has fallen to the floor covering his head. He won't be a threat.*

The other five men continued to shoot at the dragon as he took the few steps towards them, his clothing perforated by the onslaught. The one named Todd died first. Ambryn was a few inches shorter than the armed and firing goliath, but that didn't stop him from pistoning out a hand and grabbing his face like it were no more than a melon on a fruit stand. The dragon lifted him off the floor as Todd's pistol emptied into his midsection impotently. With a chuckle no one heard, Ambryn savagely twisted his body and slammed Todd's head into the snow white carpet, breaking it apart like an egg and putting a dent in the floor below. Brains, blood, and more ruined the uniform purity of the rug. The gunfire halted as the guards stood with their mouths ajar, their violence halted by the horror they had just witnessed. *Sorry about the rug.*

"Now come on, boys," Ambryn said as he stood up straight. "You can't tell me after working for the bloodsucker that just ran away that seeing a little bit of brain spilled on the floor puts the fear of God into you?"

"Jesus Christ! We ain't afraid of you, freak!" one of them had the balls to scream as he slapped a new magazine into his handgun.

Ambryn turned to face him, the dragon's face stark and devoid of emotion or sympathy. "Christ won't save you from me. Nothing will." Ambryn was on the man before the slide of his gun snapped forward and chambered a round. A single upward punch to the midsection hit the man with the equivalent force of an artillery shell. His ribcage liquefied, and his internal organs ruptured under the incredible impact pressure. He fell to the ground, no more than a pile of jelly beside two of the dancers who were screaming bloody murder for help.

The three remaining men had seen enough. Two ran for their lives out the doorway and into the hall from where they had all originally arrived as two of the club's security guards rushed in. They stopped at the threshold of the room, appalled by the gory scene the dragon was making. The third bodyguard tried to run as well, but when he leapt over the edge of the couch his trailing foot caught on the cherry colored fabric and he went down hard, face-first onto a knee high table. The way his body slumped to the floor Ambryn knew he was knocked out at the very least. The way his head came to a rest suggested his neck might have broken in the fall. A quick glance over his shoulder at the big bald man curled up in the fetal position told him Brandon was still harmless. *I'll chase down the guards, then the cheater.*

The dragon walked towards the club guards, covered in blood. They parted for him without hesitation, backing far away to avoid his wrath. Once in the hallway, he picked up his pace to a run, sprinting down to the end of the hall where the wide stairs descended. He reached the retaining wall and looked over at the crowd of patrons and dancers alike that were leaving the violence as fast as they could. *I seem to have sparked a stampede. It's like someone rang the dinner bell for a MDMA giveaway down there.*

He narrowed his eyes and searched for the two men who were trying to elude him. A muzzle flash and impact on his forehead told him where one of the men was. The crowd dove away, some running out of the club, and some back into it to get away from the fresh bloodshed. The man below steadied his pistol and snapped off a trio of rounds at Ambryn, all sailing high and hitting the ceiling.

Well, fuck you too. Ambryn grabbed the top of the waist high beige wall and jumped over it, falling through the air and landing just a few feet away from the man who'd just shot him again. The shooter stood paralyzed in fear, shocked that the man chasing him had just fallen nearly two stories and landed as if it were no different than the last step on a stairway.

Ambryn backhanded him so hard his cheek and jaw broke like fine china. He fell to the ground on his back, blubbering, spitting up teeth and blood. He gathered his faculties for a moment and aimed the gun again. The dragon kicked him in the crotch, sending him into a catatonic state and a wild spin on the hard tiled floor beside the patrons trying to lay low. He was done.

"Where did the other armed man go?" Ambryn yelled to the crowd. "He just came down the stairs!"

"Outside!" one of the dancers—a tiny redhead—said, pointing at the door with a finger tipped with a javelin shaped sparkly fingernail.

"Thank you. Thank you very much," Ambryn said appreciatively and with an honest smile. She looked at him quite aghast. *Must be the blood.* The dragon bolted out the door to search for the guard.

*****

He caught up with the last guard three blocks away. The big, strong man was huffing and puffing from sprinting for his life, and he was doubled over, hands on his thighs, utterly oblivious to Ambryn's approach until the dragon had his hands nearly on him. *Nothing escapes death without my permission, silly. Now you die tired and sweaty.*

"Let's talk," Ambryn said conversationally. The man responded by spinning and squeezing a pair of rounds from his gun into the dragon's chest. His shirt was history. Ambryn gripped the man's wrist and squeezed, snapping the small bones at the base of the hand with a sound like popcorn popping inside a wet paper bag. The man screamed and dropped the pistol to the ground. Ambryn twisted the man's limb and his eyes rolled in pain. He collapsed to his knee, no longer able to stand. His agony must've been epic.

"Stop, please! I'll tell you anything. Please, just fucking stop!" he man pleaded.

"That's the attitude. I'd hate to have to kill you too. I guess hate is a strong word. I just need a few questions answered. That's all. No need to make this difficult."

"Fine! Please, shit, just stop. Let go of my hand. I'm begging you." His words were laced with delirium. Ambryn let go, and he fell to his ass, clutching his shattered hand.

"Where are the baby vampires? Where are the missing buses?" Ambryn asked him.

The man looked from his swollen and quickly turning purple hand to the crouching stranger who'd just killed his friends. "Look, they'll kill me."

"You think I won't? If anything I would imagine watching me destroy your coworkers just a minute ago upstairs would convince you that I am indeed the thing you need to be most afraid of in your life. I can protect you or I can kill you. It's not too late to make a good decision and save people's lives. Vampires are evil. A terrible mistake that should be wiped from the world. Now tell me."

The man opened his mouth to tell Ambryn what he wanted to hear but instead of words coming out, his teeth and tongue exploded into the dragon's face. Ambryn felt another bullet hit him in the bridge of the nose after destroying the guard's head. *I have brain in my mouth.* Ambryn looked up.

Down the street leaning around the corner of a brick building stood Simon, the vampire. He held a handgun of his own, and had a bead drawn on the exact spot where the guard's head had just been.

You're mine.

Ambryn rocketed up from his crouch and closed the gap to the alley where the vampire stood before the undead monster could escape. Ambryn knew the vampire moved fast—far faster than a human—but he couldn't escape the embrace of death this time.

The dragon felt another shot careen off his cheek right before he slammed his shoulder into the small frame of Simon, propelling him into the far brick and mortar wall of the alley. The vampire's body smashed into the hard surface with enough concussive force to crumple the mortar and bricks alike. It spoke to the power of Kaula's ancient magic that his body didn't do the same. Simon slumped a bit, almost falling to the ground, but he caught himself, bared his fangs, and hissed.

Ambryn obliged him with a roar that told the vampire he had been outclassed by far in the dark streets that night. Simon tried to run, but Ambryn had pressed into him, smashing him again into the wall with a driven shoulder. The vampire's neck and head snapped out, biting the dragon on the side of the head just above the ear. Unlike the harmless bullets, the enchanted fangs of the vampire broke the dragon's human skin and drew blood. Ambryn felt pain for the first time in decades.

Like a bull rhino, Ambryn lowered his head and

rammed the vampire despite the fangs still sunk in his flesh. The angle and force of his motion snapped Simon's canines off, still lodged in his arm, and nearly broke the neck of the monster in the process. Simon screamed a shrill, inhuman wail as his life-stealing weapons were ripped free from his mouth. Ambryn pulled his now-free head away and grasped the vampire's neck, pinning him to the wall, his feet dangling.

"Who made you?!" Ambryn spat.

"Fuck yourself, monster!" Simon said back equally vile.

Ambryn squeezed his hand until he felt vertebrae strain to their limit. "Monster?! You know nothing, Simon! You are the monster. Begat as a bastard of death and sorcery, an abomination I *shall* abort! Now tell me, who made you!?" Ambryn leaned into close, his hot breath spilling out on the face of the undead he had pinned.

The vampire went limp, no longer fighting. He sensed the opportunity for survival. "You will free me? If I tell you who made me?"

An opportunist. Anything to survive. "Of course," Ambryn said. *I will not. You will die where I hold you right now.*

"You promise?" Simon asked him, scrambling for life.

"Of course, now tell me. Who gave you their blood, and made you into a vampire?"

Simon licked his bloodless lips, his tongue lingering in the gaps in his smile where his missing fangs just were. "Uncle Cosmo."

Uncle Cosmo? Who the fuck is Uncle Cosmo? "Where is he? Tell me. Where can I find him?"

"I don't know where he is, but we all work out of…" the vampire suddenly stiffened, obviously in pain.

"Speak," Ambryn said. But a gush of dark red blood erupted downward out of Simon's nose, and he started to flail wildly as if electricity coursed through his body.

What the fuck? Ambryn dropped the vampire as his skin started to slough away, rotting a century in a moment. Before the vampire's body could even touch the ground below, he had nearly liquefied, broken down into the cursed base parts of which his once human body had originally been made. In mere moments, all that remained of the monster was a pile of thick sludge and clothing amongst the garbage on the ground.

The dragon of death stood looking at the pile, confused at what had just happened. *That's a first.* After a few seconds of debate on what to do next, Ambryn reached down and pulled his Tapper issued phone out of his jeans. *Well then. It didn't get shot or broken. Miracles do happen.* The dragon went to his contacts and dialed Agent Henry Spooner. As the phone started to ring, Ambryn pulled the two broken fangs out of his arm. He put them in his pants pocket absently.

He answered on the third ring, even though it was near two in the morning. He sounded groggy. "Spooner. This Ambryn? Dude, what's up? I thought you were sleeping."

"Henry, I have made a bit of a mess. You're going to be rather cross with me."

Chapter Seventeen
Brandon

When the violence ended and the club cleared out, the music blared on without the DJ at the turntable. Brandon had always suspected the DJ's at these nightclubs were a bunch of fakes, and this confirmed his suspicion. *I knew it. Playlist running on iTunes from a damn memory stick. And some of these assholes make a hundred grand a year spinning tracks. Bullshit.*

Brandon had avoided a lightning fast and likely painful end at the hand of the strange man Simon called Paully by playing petrified at the private room bar. Brandon had faked freezing up from fear on the floor, covering his head and sobbing like a child in the fetal position. He had mimicked the dancers. Cowards can, in fact, get ahead.

When the room emptied—other than the screaming women on the floor—Brandon got to his feet and walked over to Todd's body. *His head is fucking mashed like an Idaho potato. What the hell can do that a man? Another vampire? Even Simon or Jimmy ain't that strong. Gotta be Uncle Cosmo level. Shit. What the hell was up with that guy?* On the floor beside his body lay Todd's pistol. He bent over and picked it up. A quick check on the magazine told him it had one bullet left. He fished Todd's last magazine out of the holster under his shirt and slid it into the gun.

"Dude, who the fuck are you?" one of the club bouncers asked from the entrance of the room.

"Fuck off," Brandon said in a tired voice. From his hip he shot the bouncer in the gut, and he fell to the floor moaning in pain. Brandon thought he'd live. Maybe.

Edgar had fallen face first on the floor, his legs and torso still on the couch. His head lay at an unnatural angle that told Brandon he'd eat applesauce through a straw for the rest of his life. He put a .40 caliber slug into the back of his head and made sure Eddie wouldn't need a wheelchair. Better to be dead than crippled. Once he was sure both men were dead, he fished their wallets out of their pockets and made sure they had no identification left. He left the room, leaving nothing but corpses behind.

The guard wheezed as he crawled away on his back towards the relative safety of the bathroom in the hall. Brandon watched as the escaping guard rolled onto his stomach and started to crawl away faster. *Fucking witnesses.* Brandon put two more rounds into the man's back, and he stopped trying to escape.

He made his way to the stairs and wandered down to the first floor, watching for cops or armed patrons; anyone who looked threatening, really. The lobby seemed abandoned save for one of the other Casino security guys that had come in with Brandon. He lay curled up on the brown tile floor in the center of the open two story foyer, clutching at his groin. A pool of thick blood dotted with yellow teeth spread from where his mouth was. He groaned softly.

"Shit, Craig, you alright?" Brandon asked the man.

Craig was crying. *Jesus he has blood coming out of his pants at his dick. What the fuck happened to his dick? That asshole bite him in the junk?*

"Mmmm. Glaurg. Hulp," Craig said with a broken mouth. Only then could Brandon see the extensive damage that the man had suffered to his face. The shape of it had been changed through incredible strength and damage. He had been deformed like a plastic toy left on the dash of a car on a hot day. He'd never look the same again.

Brandon sighed and shot him in the temple before he could move any more. In Brandon's mind no one deserved to live a life with a messed up face and a busted, dead dick. He took Craig's wallet before leaving.

The heavyset balding man walked out of the club and into the cold December Nevada night. It was only then, as the music faded inside, that he could hear the LVMPD sirens heading closer. He tucked the pistol into his waistband and started to jog. *I dunno where Simon or that other fuck is, but they can take care of their own shit. Gotta get to the car and back to the Arabian. Sandy and Jimmy gotta hear about this.*

Uncle Cosmo won't be happy.

Chapter Eighteen

Artur "The Romanian" Cojocaru

I have made a terrible mistake. Many mistakes. I am a failure in every possible way today. Rahat.

Artur's two daughters flanked him in a small apartment in Pitesti. The apartment served as one of their rotating residences in the hard working, dingy Romanian city. They fretted over the body of the Russian sorcerer Artur knew only as Belyakov. The Russian man's body lay on its back on the coffee table his family took tea at when football played on the television. *My daughters. They are not failures. No. Perhaps they are the only good thing I've ever really done.*

"Papa, he's not all-dead," Georgeta said to him with a hint of hope. His daughters sat flanking Belyakov's body, seated so that their blue eyes were closest to their father, and their green eyes further away. They always seemed to move in unison when together.

Sometimes they move like a mirror, my twins.

"Can you bring him back to life?" Artur asked. Rom magic had never been his strength. His girls however, were born rich with it, and with the magic of the world flowing once more, they were powerful in their own right. *Perhaps more powerful than I am.*

His other daughter Rodica answered him. "We can bring him back, but neither of us knows a way to knit him to be the same again. You broke him. Too much brandy, Papa. When will it stop?" she asked, scolding him and sending a dirty look his way.

I feel sick. "I am done with brandy. And vodka. Never more. Rahat, all of it. I hurt a friend of the family and I will never live it down," Artur said, near tears in shame. *My father would disown me. Leave me in the woods to be a wolf without a pack.*

"You killed a friend of the family today," Rodica said angrily, challenging her father. She'd had enough of his failures and misery.

"Help me my daughters. Bring him back to us," Artur pleaded, gesturing at the body of the old Russian man. "I must speak to him. Hear why he came so far."

The girls looked at each other over the body and got to work after a silent agreement to end the conversation. Artur stood and took a step back, afraid that his presence would alter the spell somehow; perhaps ruin the flow of the magic in the room. His presence had caused nothing but trouble already that day, and there was no reason to taint the moment.

Rodica had followed Artur to the puppet show to ensure something like this wouldn't happen. She had been unable to stop him from getting drunk in the morning, but when Artur charged Belyakov in the alley, raging and unable to control his irrational fury at the stranger, she had been there at the end after the sorcerer's spell stupefied her father. A dumped cola on his head got a newly sober Artur back awake, and the two of them got

Belyakov into the street where the family car had been parked. A short drive and a ride up in the lift later, and they were home in the forgettable apartment. Artur's skin still felt sticky from the soda. His conscience might never feel the same again.

The girls were chanting in Romanian softly, holding hands over the chest of the broken man below. Pungent incense burned alongside candles that were a hundred years old and nowhere near their end. Ornaments, relics, talismans of a wide variety were placed on Belyakov's body at crucial points, his internal leylines, channeling the remaining life force in his body and serving as a mystical beacon for his nearby soul to return. They were speaking louder now, calling out to his spirit; slowly pulling on the tether than kept it close to his mortal form.

It is lucky that he is not all-dead. Even the most powerful spells have their limits.

Belyakov's body hitched and gasped as the girl's voices built up and reached a crescendo. When they stopped and silence dominated the room, all the electric lights in the flat snapped out as if the fuses had blown.

By the light of the candles alone, Artur could see Belyakov's chest rising and falling minimally and with considerable with effort. "Belyakov, can you hear me?" Artur asked the Russian as his two daughters slipped away, their work done, and their bodies drained for the moment.

"Of course, I can hear you. Why am I alive? You killed me. I remember dying," the old man said in a gruff voice. He sounded weak and in pain still. "I hurt."

"I am so sorry. I have not been myself for many years, but this you know," Artur said, resting an apologetic hand on the leg of his victim.

Belyakov lifted his head with more than a wince and gave the werewolf a nasty look. "Goddamn you, Artur Cojocaru. Your insanity cost me my life. What have you done now to bring me back? Is my soul promised to the daemons? Or something worse, knowing the circles your family has entered over the centuries? You should've left me dead in that alley."

He shook his head. "No promises were made with your soul. Georgeta and Rodica worked their spells and brought you back. They tell me they cannot fix your body though." As he finished, Georgeta reappeared in the room. She had a glass of water in one hand, and some pills in the other.

"Bea pentru. Drink please," she said softly, indicating for Belyakov to tilt his head for the water and the medicine.

The Russian tried to sit up, but his body didn't do what he wanted it to do. The look of alarm on his face was sobering. "I… I can't feel my legs."

I will never be able to make this right. "I am afraid I may have broken your back and paralyzed you. I am very sorry. We will take you to hospital." The look the Russian gave Artur could've curdled milk. It lasted long enough to make the Romanian look to the floor. Only then did Belyakov wiggle to get his head tilted and take the medicine. After he swallowed the pills and Georgeta had left, Artur continued. "I will do everything in my power to call favors in. I know healers in Greece that can mend things. I trust them with the health of my daughters. I know they can do right by you."

The Russian looked pissed, but the frustration faded, and his head slumped onto the paisley patterned throw pillow on the coffee table he lay on. "Why?"

"Why what?" Artur asked back.

"Why have you become a savage? Why do you drink like you did earlier? Yours is a noble family, Artur. The way people speak of your grandfather, and your father, let alone all the others before … the pride you would have. But why? Fruit should not fall so far from the tree. There must be a reason for this … this madness."

My stomach twists. Shame. "My family ends with me,"

Artur said.

"Nonsense. You've two girls, yes? Your family will live on."

Artur shook his head. *You don't understand.* "No. Not the same thing, friend. When the magic faded… my kind were unable to make copii. Babies, Belyakov. Varcolac children did not come to us no matter how many babies we made. Sure, we had twins more often like always, but none were born with the blood to change shape. My people have been denied a future. My girls, they can work Roma magic, but they cannot become wolves. They are not varcolac."

"And with no werewolf child…"

"I am the last hunter in my family. The final Cojocaru varcolac," Artur said, his eyes swelling with emotion. His chin shook. "Our gift dies with me. I have let down my family. I should have spent more time with my wife before she was killed. I should have focused. I should have had more sons and daughters. And I *knew* Belyakov. *I knew.* Ten years I knew. I could've killed fewer vampires and had more children. What helps Romania more? What helps the world more, eh?" Artur's daughters watched and listened from the kitchen as their father wiped tears from his cheeks. They hadn't seen their father cry like this in years. Not since their mother was taken in the night.

"So you turned to the brandy?" Belyakov asked, his head pointed straight at the ceiling.

"I turned to whatever I could find to forget."

The hurt old man shook his head in disapproval. "You've killed so many innocents on your hunts these past few years. You used to be reliable. Discreet. It makes some sense now," the Russian said.

"A drunk werewolf trying to fix the world by killing will make many mistakes. Far too much blood is on my hands and stains my teeth," Artur said as he looked at his hands. Killing hands. *Too much blood. I can still taste it.*

"Do you know why I came here Artur? What was so

vazhnyy for me to get in my airplane and fly to Bucharest? To then drive here to Pitesti to find you?"

Artur shook his head.

"Vampires in America."

"Fuck America. What do I care about them? I need to make babies, not rescue Ronald McDonald." Artur could see Belyakov smiling. *It is good to see him smile.* "What is funny?"

"They're now able to make more of their kind, so it would seem. Do you remember Doyle, Artur?"

Yes, yes I do. "He was kind to me once."

"Consider yourself lucky, he is kind to few. He works for the agency now, you've heard of them, yes? The one that protects us from other things like us."

He had. "Tapper?"

"That's the one. He is investigating missing buses in Las Vegas. They are fairly certain that three entire busloads of people have been taken by vampires. Forty are dead already. If the buses have been taken by their kind, and they are making more… then soon there will be hundreds of them. In a city. It could be like Ukraine in '73. When your father came to help us. Only worse. Doyle has asked for you by name."

Artur felt a twinge of pride. *This was how my father and his father felt. Proud to do what we do best.* "I… I could go, yes. I've never been to America. My father had been twice before he died I think. I suppose it is time for me to cross the ocean too."

"Three times actually. And you do not 'suppose' you will go. You broke my back. You owe me this much, and you owe Doyle near the same for the kindness you spoke of. I remember that day myself. You will pack your things. Prepare for the greatest hunt of your life."

Artur was thrilled, his tears halted. *A chance at redemption.* "I will get my things ready now. My girls will help you get well, arrange for anything you need. They are good. Trust them." He stood.

"Wait. There are a few other things to contemplate before you rush off to the airport and America."

He sat down on the wooden chair again.

"There's something I want you to think about. Kaula, the purple dragon was the font of all magic, and when she disappeared, everything special began to fade, da?"

I've watched the news Belyakov. "Yes."

"Now, she has died, and a new dragon has been born. Astrid. Born to Tesser, the golden dragon, and a human woman," Belyakov said, still staring up at the dingy ceiling in the seldom used apartment.

"I have watched the stories, yes."

"Her birth has brought back magic. I can do things I haven't been able to do in a very long time, and I'm sure your daughters are thrilled to be able to do what their aunts and uncles told them they once did."

"Yes, Rodica and Georgeta have taken to new spells and are very happy. What are you getting at?"

"I am getting at the fact that new magic is here. If the vampires are now able to make more of their ilk, then perhaps your kind can as well. Babies conceived in the wake of Astrid's birth might be born with the two-skins gift again."

Good Lord above. "Do you think?"

Belyakov shrugged. It looked funny because his body lay still on his back. "I do not know Artur, but I know if you were not able to have varcolac babies before Astrid, you should try making more now. Find yourself a pretty woman. Or that failing, one with wide hips, lots of patience and low standards. Less anger in your life and more love."

Artur's heart swelled. "Yes. It is worth it to try. I will clean myself up. Dress better. Try and meet women. Give my daughters brothers. Give my family a future."

"Las Vegas first. If they are spreading like Doyle fears, your varcolac children won't survive to follow in your footsteps."

"Yes. I do this for you. And Doyle. I am sorry Belyakov. So very sorry. I am ashamed for what I have done to you," Artur said, his words genuine and pained.

"There's one more thing. In Las Vegas, you will work with Doyle, and at least one other. You may... have conflicted feelings about the other."

Artur looked at the old man strangely. "Who is it?"

"Ambryn, the black dragon. Brother to Tesser. He is there helping."

"I will fight alongside the dragon of death?" Artur thought about it for a bit. "I like this idea. It will be a great honor for my family to have hunted beside such a creature. This convinces me." He stood again, energized by the thought of killing vampires alongside a winged dragon, ancient and powerful beyond measure.

"Artur."

"Yes?"

"If you have any... slip-ups. Mistakes. If you are messy. If you find the vodka and rum and whiskey that flows so freely in the City of Sin... You will answer to American law, but more importantly, you will answer to Ambryn. I suspect the dragon of death, killer of Kaula, will be far less forgiving of your transgressions."

Artur's energy left him as if he were a drained battery. He looked to his daughters with their two blue eyes, and their two green eyes. He made his decision after seeing the hope there.

"I have made my last mistake Belyakov. No more."

Chapter Nineteen

Cosmin "Uncle Cosmo" Dorinescu

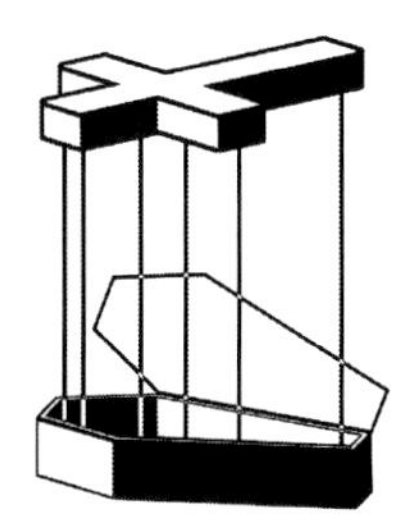

Time had weight, and no one felt the pressure of the centuries on their shoulders and souls more keenly than an ancient vampire. Assuming, of course, the magic that made the undead what they were allowed for the soul to survive. Amongst vampires, Cosmin Dorinescu felt the weight of the years on his deceivingly youthful shoulders more than any other. Any other vampire he knew, at least.

Cosmin opened his yellowed, bloodshot eyes and allowed them to focus in the dark of the room he'd chosen as his own. Deep underneath his acquired casino the room by design had been locked in the center of a subbasement, far from the burning caress of the daytime sun. Someone would have to level the entire structure above with an atom bomb to get sunlight to his bed, and that pleased him a great deal.

The piles of money the business above raked in twenty four hours a day helped with any fears he might've had as well.

Time made the magic inside his body potent, refining him in the same way a fine wine changes over the years, but arising from rest became more and more difficult every evening for the vampire. He looked no older than forty, but inside, his blood and bones rivaled the centuries that the castles of Europe weathered. As the days grew into years his mind struggled to rouse itself from slumber, and it took him far too long to regain all his faculties with each passing year. *I used to be able to sit up immediately, and stand. Go about my business with no lethargy weighing me down. Now… now I must lay and think first, opening and closing my hands, wiggling my toes, moving the blood I've drank about my body for minutes before I feel invigorated enough to sit up. I fear for the hunter that comes at dusk as much as how the living fear for me at midnight. There are nights I consider staying up to watch the sunrise now. Unthinkable for so long.*

Cosmin had reinvented himself in Vegas. He'd heard on the news of the new casino being opened by Sheikh Alumaidi on the television back in Europe, and knew that very soon it would be ripe for the plucking. A plane ticket to Dubai, a few kind words, and two fangs sunk into an Arabic artery later, and the Sheikh became his pawn. And now that the organization and its riches were in his back pocket… Cosmin would move on to the whole city. Perhaps even the world.

Soon.

The name Cosmin Dorinescu was old. It hailed from Romania and wasn't the name he had been born with. His true name was much older, but if all had gone according to Cosmin's ancient plan, everyone who knew that name looked up from six feet under, had been burnt to ash, or fared even worse. Cosmin decided he needed a new name for his umpteenth reiteration in Vegas. He settled on the nickname "Uncle Cosmo." It struck him as very Mafioso, very 1950's America, and it made him smile from time to time, a luxury that he often only afforded when fresh hot blood ran down his throat. *Besides, everyone in America wants a cool uncle.*

Uncle Cosmo got out of his bed with its expensive sateen, Egyptian cotton sheets. He had slept alone that day, and the bed had stayed as cold as his flesh. For a century in the 1800's Cosmo had slept with dogs to help the blood in his body stay warm, but too often his vampiric nature would spook the beasts midday, and he'd get bitten. No dog was forgiven for the slight. It didn't matter if it had been in the creature's nature to bite something frightening or not. Now, he slept alone or with a meal after sex when that urge struck him.

Vampires of my age have painfully few urges. Urges lead to poor decisions, and if you strive to live forever, one must be very deliberate. Very urge-free.

Vegas is an over-the-top place, and despite centuries of hiding under the stage of life, allowing others to assume the lead roles, Cosmo had taken to the culture of Vegas quickly. The city of Las Vegas had been made for the nightlife, made for the traveler, made for someone to be anonymous in, and so far as Cosmo believed... made for the undead.

He headed to the shower.

*****

Cosmo left his sanctum with a brisk energy in his step. Tonight he had planned a meeting with his upper echelon vampires to gauge their progress on his various schemes. He was expecting good news. He would demand it.

A board room had been constructed in the basement at his request. It had a long steel table that admirably fought the frequent bloodstains it suffered and fancy metal backed chairs that did the same. It had enough space to seat a dozen, though typically it held no more than half that. Crowded rooms led to crowded thoughts. As his steps took him closer to the meeting room, the old vampire could hear Sandy speaking on the other side of the door. She had the tiniest trace of fear in her voice and anger enough to match.

"Bran, shut up. You're going to tell him, to his face, like a big boy, tonight. He'll appreciate your honesty and courage. Uncle Cosmo is not a savage. Stop worrying."

Another voice came back immediately. Cosmo paused to listen. "Malarkey, lady. You want me to tell him so if he snaps he kills me, not you. I ain't falling for it. My momma didn't raise no fool. I already told you both the whole story. Let me walk. I don't wanna take the fall for something that wasn't my fault. Hell, I cleaned the mess up. I left no witnesses. I did what I was supposed to do and then some."

"You're going to sit right there. And when Uncle Cosmo gets here, you're going to tell him what you told us." *That's Jimmy. Good little dog. Bark away. I think I'll enter now.*

Cosmo adjusted the part of his still-damp chocolate brown hair and pulled the double doors open. He strode in as if he were gliding on the air. Undeath—or in his opinion, the vampiric state at the least—conferred a grace and agility that exceeded the superhuman. Sometimes, it felt good to just *move*.

He swept into the room like the angel of death, his arms spread wide like wings, and a smile on his face that had been practiced for hundreds of years. He wore a midnight black suit over his athletic and lean body. He had crafted an image of success with a smile that could sell sand to a Saudi prince. He had in fact. Six feet of it and recently to boot. Jimmy and Sandy looked upon him with unbridled admiration and love. The bonds of blood. A chubby balding man looked at him with thinly disguised horror. *That is a man that expects to die right here, and right now.* "Good evening my friends. Thank you for coming."

"Happy to be here, Uncle Cosmo," Jimmy said jovially.

Sandy simply nodded her head. Brandon waved, but his hand shook. A male fledgling vampire wearing a suit shut the doors as Cosmo took a seat at the head of the table. He lounged comfortably, ensuring the large man a better chance at relaxing in his presence.

"I couldn't help but overhear from the hall that Brandon has some bad news for me. Brandon, rest assured I am not the 'kill the messenger' kind of vampire. I am a level-headed and even-keeled ancient. You have little to fear if what you have to tell me is truly not your fault. I encourage you. Be at rest. Speak truthfully," Uncle Cosmo encouraged. He tried his very best to be persuasive and legitimate. *I do want the truth, unfiltered by middle men.*

Brandon's jaw worked, but no sound came out.

Clearly the man is still fearful. "Please Brandon. I won't kill you for telling me the truth, but I'll put you down like a dog for being a coward about telling me bad news."

Brandon nodded, his small jowls shaking. "A few of us went to a titty bar last night. I mean a strip club, sorry."

Cosmo waved the uncouth words off, and Brandon continued.

"Simon was with us. We got a VIP room upstairs, everything was going great, and then some drunk guy stumbled into our room. Said he was a tourist. Simon wanted to bag him to bring back here for food, like we've been doing." Brandon paused, searching for words.

"Continue. Something went awry I take it?"

He nodded again as sweat began to trickle down his forehead. Cosmo watched it slide down the smooth skin in fascination as the man spoke again. The memory of sweating was distant for the blood drinker. "Strange drunk guy is, like, asking lots of silly questions. At first we didn't think nothing of it, but Simon got the heebie-jeebies, and he sweeps in, and confronts the guy. He asks him 'what's with all the questions?' All serious like."

"Go on."

"I went over to the bar, and I didn't hear what the guy said, but immediately dude's stone cold sober. Like the booze he'd drank all night was gone from his system. Guys says some shit quietly to Simon, and Simon pops out of the way, and tells the crew to light the dude up, so they did."

"Right in the VIP room?" Uncle Cosmo asked.

Brandon continued to nod. "Yeah. All five guys opened up point-blank on him. And Sir, the guns did jack shit. Bullets bounced off him like he's Clark Kent or something. He didn't even flinch. Not once. They would've done more damage with harsh language."

Well, that's profoundly bad news. If he's a vampire, he must be close to my age or older. "Call me Uncle Cosmo, Brandon. Simon instructed them to shoot right in the club?"

"Yes."

"He must've gotten a very bad feeling to risk that much exposure. That or he overreacted in the moment. It would seem his reaction was justified in the wake of this person shrugging off being shot. Tell me, what happened then Brandon?"

"Dude got up," Brandon said, his eyes glazing over, and staring at the wall beyond.

Clearly something impressive happened then for him to not answer me with more detail. "Please. Spare no details. Use many adjectives. It could be very important."

The witness to the event snapped to, and everything came out in a torrent. "He stood up. Quick. Walked over to Todd, I don't know if you know Todd, but he grabbed Todd by the head like he was a fucking little kid and smashed him into the carpet so hard his head came apart. Brains fucking everywhere. Simon left. Ghosted us. The other guards went down one right after another. I hit the floor and played scared as shit. I figured if I didn't seem like a threat, he'd leave me be. Ask me questions later maybe. He chased the crew down after they ran and hurt them all, or killed them."

Sandy added more information. She sounded frustrated. "This happened late last night. We found out about all this just a few minutes ago through our Vegas police connections and from Brandon here. They said they found a pile of... liquefied human in the street. I think that might've been Simon. They found all the other bodies."

He tried to betray me. The geas in the blood held firm. My investment returns as wise once more. "Simon... got what was coming to him. He violated the blood. My blood. Let his death be a lesson to you all. Betray me, and you too will end up no more than dog food."

The vampires in the room looked at each other, frightened more than a little. They had no idea what he spoke of.

"But Sir, the good news is I took care of everything as best I could," Brandon said, a hint of pride showing.

"Do tell," Cosmo said, intrigued.

"When the dude left, I got one of our guy's pistols, and capped the hurt guards. I had to shoot a bouncer who came into the room too. I knew the guy would come back and start asking questions, so I left no one to answer any. Then I got out before the cops came."

"Smart," Uncle Cosmo said.

Brandon shrugged. "I did what I thought you'd want."

He has potential, despite his girth. An overweight vampire has its uses though. We can't all be pretty. It would be suspicious. "Brandon, tell me, do you have family?"

"Single child, both parents dead. Why?"

"Girlfriend? Wife?"

"I have never been good with women, Uncle Cosmo," Brandon said, almost apologizing.

"Excellent. I'm sure that nightclub had security cameras, and I'm sure the police will be looking for you. It would be smart of you to lay low for a month while our connections in the police department work out a suitable solution. I am promoting you. The portion of the month it takes you to turn will be more than enough time for everything to work out, I suspect. Granted, you'll miss Christmas due to the agony of the change, but it's a sad excuse for a holiday anyway."

"Are you shitting me?" Brandon said, all his fear evaporated away.

"No, it really is a sad excuse for a holiday. Now, come to me and present me your throat," Cosmo said as if it were a chore. As Brandon approached timidly, Cosmin spoke to Jimmy and Sandy. "Speak to the police. Find out what they knew. Find footage of this bullet-proof character. I need to know who is on to our presence here, and I need to know it immediately. We must handle this carefully. We need to speed up our acquisitions of new citizens as well. Seek out something other than a bus. I'd like to add another hundred to our numbers by the end of the week. And don't protest how hard it will be. We have absurd amounts of money, use it."

Both vampires nodded. They already knew the deal.

Brandon dropped to his knees beside the vampire and lifted his chin, baring the throat Cosmo asked for. He swallowed hard as more sweat ran down his forehead.

"Wrong side. That's the vein side. I prefer my meals a bit more oxygenated."

"Sorry. I didn't know," he said as he waddled in a half-circle on his knees, giving the vampire the other side of his neck. His legs shook, and Cosmo saw more of the sweat trickling down his forehead.

"You'd best not taste fatty Brandon. I despise a greasy

feast," Uncle Cosmo said with a grin. Brandon thought he was being serious, but saw the look on Cosmo's face. He laughed, and Cosmo chose that moment to strike. His fangs were long and snakelike, well over the length of a pinky finger when completely extended. They sank into the neck deep enough to pierce the carotid, tearing it open and releasing a powerful explosion of blood into his mouth. He formed a seal with his lips, and pulsed the muscle of his tongue, creating suction.

Yes. This will do. A nice treat, and a crafty new vampire in my herd as well. Cosmo sucked hard at the holes in the neck as Brandon's body sagged, his life being pulled from him one gulp at a time. *And soon, this whole city will be what I want.*

A metropolis for the half-dead.

Chapter Twenty
Sandy Brown

"I'm not sure that idiot deserved to be turned," Sandy said to Jimmy. They'd just sat down in her drab office after leaving the board room with its stainless steel furniture and fresh blood spatters. Both were somewhere between frightened and pissed off. "Brandon made a couple good calls last night, but I don't think he has the resume overall."

"Uncle Cosmo makes those calls Miss Brown. Then we roll with it," Jimmy said with a shrug of his shoulders, somewhat deflated.

"I'm aware," Sandy said, checking her computer for emails. Her fingers danced across the keyboard, her nails clicking away like muted gunfire in the distance, sending back a curt administrative message. *So many people who can't make a decision on their own. Morons.* "I still wonder if he was lying to Uncle Cosmo just to cover his ass."

"If we can get the tapes from the club, we'll know right off," Jimmy said, picking at his teeth.

At least he has the good grace to leave his fangs sheathed. "Speaking of which, can you take care of that? Call the Captain and ask about getting copies made for us? I'd like to see them. We already know Uncle Cosmo wants eyes-on."

"Yeah. I can call him right now," Jimmy said, reaching into his suit to fish out his cell phone.

"While you're talking to him, make sure you ask him if he has any ideas about where we can add another hundred undead in a hurry for the boss. If the cop has an idea, I'd like to hear it. Tell him Uncle Cosmo will fast track his application for vampire status and line his wallet in the process. And while you're at it, we're going to need a rather large portion of storage space to house another hundred baby vampires. Building an army requires barracks. As it is, all the spaces here and at the warehouse near the airport are full. Get us a good deal, but get us something fast. We can always strong-arm them later to cut costs."

"Done and done," Jimmy said as he pored through his contacts.

"And make sure it's safe, or out of the way. No accidental open doors like the first time. I don't want to lose another twenty soldiers. There's no way we're going to follow through on Uncle Cosmo's plan if we don't do this right." *This is coming to a head very fast and all of a sudden. I didn't like the look on Uncle Cosmo's face when that ass told him the guy shook off being shot. I'm scared of Uncle Cosmo. I'm petrified of whatever makes him afraid.* Sandy indicated Jimmy should make his call elsewhere, and as he left her office she returned to the overflowing inbox she had to sort through. She tried to keep the thoughts of the dark man that eviscerated her guards in the club out of her head.

"And what the hell did he mean about betraying the blood?"

Chapter Twenty-One

Mr. Doyle

Mycroft Rupert Doyle had a disdain for hotels. In his mind they were nothing more than vermin infested lairs that gave his potential enemies an address where to find him. He'd been attacked enough times at hotels and motels to know that staying on the move when in unfamiliar territory would always be a good idea. The shiny, sleek Tapper tank he had been assigned served like a gift from God in that regard.

Covered in armor plating, heated comfortably in the desert winter, it also gave him substantial storage and workspace, accepted several forms of protective enchantment, and could be relocated anywhere each and every night by his liaison-driver or by himself if need be. Right now he had it parked alone in the subterranean parking garage of one of the more massive casinos in the city.

Granted, someone could follow the vehicle to any location they moved to and merely attack him there, but by being in a different place every night they had no ability to prepare for the environment they would have to fight in. Unpredictability always favored the defender. Advantage: Mr. Doyle.

He had just eaten a small dinner while watching the security camera footage on a laptop from the club incident the night prior. The sun had only dipped below the horizon for perhaps an hour, and his blood pumped sluggishly in the too-cool massive bus. Doyle let his thoughts wander. *I fear the vampires will retaliate against someone for this incident at the club. I hope their discretion is better than Ambryn's. We should be so lucky to have impatient, vengeful, and thirsty enemies. Perhaps the loss of a few lives in a meaningless act of revenge will push them to play their hand and reveal their location or identity to us.*

His phone rang from the hard, synthetic table surface. He scooped it up with fingers that should've been stiff and arthritic but were supple and steady instead. *Ah, Belyakov.* He answered it on the third ring.

"My friend, how are you?" he asked.

The Russian answered him slowly, as if he had a mouthful of food he had to deal with first. "I have been better."

Worrisome. "Are you okay? Is there something I can do for you?"

The old Russian had no food in his mouth, but he sounded as if he hesitated to answer regardless. To Mr. Doyle, it sounded like he struggled to find the right words to say. "I am in Romania. I have found The Romanian."

Something happened inside Mr. Doyle's chest that seemed indescribable. It landed somewhere between a flitter of nervous palpitations, an electric shock and instant petrification. "Were you able to persuade him to come to Las Vegas and help? How did it go?"

More hesitation on Belyakov's part. "After this settles down comrade, you will owe me dearly, and let me leave it at that."

Oh dear. The last time he said I owed him, he lost an eye. It took almost a year to grow it back. "Are both your eyes are intact? Your balls? Tell me your baby makers are alright."

The Russian couldn't hold back a tiny laugh. "My family jewels as you say are fine, and I see straight. I am not entirely well and will bear scars from this. I hope my sacrifices will prove worth it. I know my KGB bosses of old would laugh at me for doing such things to save American lives, but times are different, da?"

"Yes, they are my friend." Mr. Doyle had a strange regret welling in the pit of his belly. *I hope he will be well.*

"He is on a plane. I was able to pull an old string or two and get him a very temporary visa, but he will need proper documentation very quickly. I trust your Tapper connections can achieve this, yes? I will text you the flight number and the information needed on your end. He should be arriving with the sun at his back tomorrow morning," Belyakov said, his voice loaded with a warning.

"Should I be worried? He hurt you, didn't he?"

"He had been drinking, but da, he hurt me. Things are mending Doyle. Forget about what he has done to me, and give him this chance to redeem his failings. I will heal with time. He is a Cojocaru. His blood is old, and strong. It will prove its worth soon enough."

Mr. Doyle chewed on his friend's statement. "We should keep him away from booze then?"

"Lyuboy tsenoy, Doyle. If he tips a glass you slap it from his hand. The monster in him could come out without restraint. He will be the indiscriminate ubiytsa that so many fear now. Keep him clean. Put the dragon with him. He respects the dragon. He fears it. He will serve you and the black lizard to regain his honor and his family's honor."

I guess we are pot-committed now then. Suitable seeing as how we are in the gambling capital of the world... "Very well then. I will make this up to you, Belyakov. Know this. I hope whatever it is you've had to deal with hasn't been too terrible. And you know that if there is anything I can do to make things right, I'm a phone call or a spell away."

"I know my friend. Da sveedaneeya, comrade. Good luck," the Russian said.

"Goodbye," Mr. Doyle said softly, and the two men hung up. After setting his phone down ruefully, the Brit waited, his mind wandering to and fro, perseverating about his friend's possibly injuries, and how difficult it might be to manage the Romanian when he arrived. He distracted his thoughts by sifting through some police reports about missing people and sipping on a freshly poured cup of Nescafe. It wasn't Kenyan AA, but it served its purpose well enough. In half an hour his patience was rewarded with a ding from his phone. A check of it told him that he had received the flight and immigration information for The Romanian from his Russian ally. He jotted the information down on a notepad and called another number.

"Spoon here," Henry said in a friendly tone.

"Henry, I have some good news," Mr. Doyle said. He could hear a television murmuring in the background.

"Been a few days since I heard any of that. Fucking Ambryn and his night club shenanigans. Judas motherfucker. Covering this up has been a spear-sized thorn in my side. Let's hear it if you got it," Spoon said.

"The Romanian is on his way here to lend us some assistance."

"The special vampire hunter you mentioned?"

"In the flesh. He's on a plane headed to the States as we speak. He requires some documentation to remain in-country, though," Mr. Doyle said. "I hoped you could assist with that."

"Email it to me? I'll get our travel department on the horn, and they can talk to the State department. Figure it out before he lands here. Does he need a translator?"

"Excellent, thank you. I don't think his English is perfect, but he should be able to make-do without a translator. Less ears and eyes involved is a good thing, I imagine. I'll email everything you need shortly. Before I let you go, there is... one little thing I should mention about Artur."

"Is that his name? Artur?"

"Yes. Artur Cojocaru. He is a bit of a... I guess you could say he's a special kind of werewolf." Henry didn't respond. *I look forward to the day where I can say such things, and people don't react with shock, or awe.* "Are you still there?"

"Uh, yeah. I 'guess' he's a werewolf huh? How does that work exactly?"

"Not just a werewolf as I said before. He is a varcolac, specifically. He has a few more tricks up his sleeve than a regular run of the mill werewolf, hence his value to us and the case. You have little to worry about. Artur is a masterful hunter of the vampire race, and is no more savage than you or me."

"Was that meant to make me feel better? I've done some horrible shit man," Henry said with a laugh.

Mr. Doyle smiled on the other side of the phone. "He won't eat any children, if you're worried about that." *I hope.*

"Is he monstrous? Do we need to hide his presence or can he blend in? We're having a hard enough time keeping that security tape out of the media's hands from Ambryn's thing last night. Alanna's been running interference nonstop."

"No, he'll blend in quite fine. Just get his feet on the ground here in Las Vegas, and allow Ambryn and me to manage him and all will work out. Having this man here will help us. He can do things we can't."

"I sure hope so. We're banging our heads against the wall here trying to find leads. All we're getting is dead ends, bruises, and a pile of bodies with toe tags on them."

"Have we found any connection between the bodies from the nightclub yet?" Doyle asked.

Spoon sighed, frustrated. "Nothing yet. As you know, none of our bodies from the club had ID on them. We've got a rush on their prints and dental, but it doesn't work like Law & Order or CSI. It takes a day or more to get a single set of prints run. DNA has a much longer turnaround. I've made a few calls to put some pressure on, but it takes a long time to get several sets of prints checked. If you want it done right, you can't speed the process up too much. You want to make a quick buck Doyle? Cook up a spell that speeds up the DNA identification process."

That's not a bad thought at all. "Well, let us hope our friends at the crime labs are quick and competent. I fear the longer they take, the more toe tags we'll need."

Chapter Twenty-Two

Tapper Special Agent Henry "Spoon" Spooner

After getting past the airport security people and a handful of confused sheriff's deputies, Spoon drove the obsidian SUV straight onto the massive tarmac of the Las Vegas airport to nearly the same spot he and Ambryn had arrived at not so long ago. The black dragon—sedate and silent—rode in the car beside him. Since the dragon's debacle at the titty bar two evenings prior, the ancient being had been near to silent. Ambryn had achieved the death of a vampire without injury, but no leads had come of it, and his presence had been nearly revealed, tipping off their enemy that something or someone very powerful in the city was out stalking their kind. It had been a disaster, and it seemingly had humbled Ambryn.

Now they were headed to retrieve someone who supposedly could crack their nightmare scenario open, and show them the way to the enemy. His name was

Artur Cojocaru, also known as The Romanian.

I can't get over how many infamous murderers and heroes there have been in the world that my government has no idea existed. There are thousands and thousands of years of shadowed history hidden so well from the public. According to Doyle, Artur and his family alone have put down almost a full hundred vampires in the past century. I can't fathom how many people those vampires have killed on top of that. I wonder what mysteries can be solved by laying them at the feet of the supernatural. Jimmy Hoffa got eaten by a goblin in New Jersey? Was JFK taken out by a gun-toting sprite on the grassy knoll?

"You seem nervous," Ambryn said out of the blue. His first words in hours.

"Yeah?"

Ambryn nodded, watching the airport buildings slide by. "Your breathing is more rapid than it was earlier. You are sweating. I can smell it."

Spoon mentally checked down and realized the dragon was right. "I suppose having never met a werewolf before, I am feeling a bit uneasy about it."

"Seems natural," Ambryn said. "You've nothing to worry about. I don't think this Artur character poses you any danger. I can protect you as well."

Gee, thanks. "Have you met him before?" Spoon asked.

"No. Why would you think I have?"

"It's obvious you hate vampires Am-bro. Based on your hatred of vampires, I sort of thought that if this guy was the werewolf equivalent of Wesley Snipes or Van Helsing you might've crossed paths at one point or another."

Ambryn thought about it. "No, not to my recollection. I have some admiration for what Artur has accomplished now that I am aware of who he is. The man and his family have somehow managed to track down vampires that I've hunted fruitlessly for years. Werewolves have no skills beyond an excellent sense of smell to assist them in hunting anything to my knowledge, leaving me to wonder why this man and this man's family have such an impressive track record. There's a story to be revealed here Spoon, and I'm excited to see what it is."

The truck rounded the corner of the hangar building just as the Tapper private jet stopped inside it. Ground crewman chocked the wheels to keep the plane still. "Well buddy, we'll be able to ask him in person in a few minutes. Chew some gum, your breath stinks."

*****

Spoon and the dragon leaned against the side of their car watching the ground crew roll a mobile staircase over to the opening door of the small plane. Spoon had a cigarette lit and was taking a few puffs before he had to put it out and act professional. The door opened up and down like the maw of a strange robot, revealing a lean and imposing man standing within. He radiated both impatience and excitement. He wore a black leather jacket that reached just below his belt, and jeans that had seen profuse wear. They were frayed at the knees, and had barely visible stains that had waged war against hundreds of washes. His long hair, fine and thin like ink stained corn silk, was tied back into a ponytail. His skin had the tone of a Mediterranean's, though there were many fine scars from what looked to be an active childhood. He looked as if he had just stepped out of a music video from the 1980's that had been shot to appear as if it were about the 1200's. With jeans. And cowboys.

"He's a long one," Spoon muttered as he exhaled rich blue smoke. *And not that hairy. I imagined Teen Wolf.*

"Indeed," Ambryn replied, judging the werewolf.

Artur's dark eyes searched the interior of the hangar with a practiced experience. He looked for exits and threats initially, and only then did he settle his gaze on the two waiting men. At first the expression on his long face seemed newly somber and guarded, but then it softened, and a wide smile appeared. With lanky legs he clambered down the steps to the hard concrete.

"Stop! Sir! Your bags!" one of the Tapper flight crewmembers said from the open plane door. Artur stopped cold, looking embarrassed, and turned around. He returned to the doorway and accepted the two leather bags from the crewman. The crewman struggled to lift them, but in the pass Artur took them as if they were no heavier than pillows. He dropped them to his side and left the plane behind, fearlessly walking straight towards Spooner and Ambryn. All negative expression had slid off his face, leaving nothing but positivity.

His nostrils are flaring. He's sniffing us. Spoon stood up straight and adjusted his suit coat after flicking away the filter of his cigarette. He could hear an airport worker nearby sigh angrily as the little white piece of litter flew away. "Artur Cojocaru?" he asked the man.

The Romanian's face lit up even more at the sound of Spoon's voice. "You are Yankee? A Yankee, from the north? New York City? Joe DiMaggio? Brooklyn? Statue of Liberty?"

Fuck the Yankees. "Boston. Red Sox. Big Papi. Bunker Hill Monument. Dorchester. Tea Party, ... but yeah, I'm from the north," Spoon said, trying to hide his irritation at being mistaken for a New Yorker. "I'm Tapper Special Agent Henry Spooner. You can call me Spoon if you prefer. Or Henry I guess. You're Artur Cojocaru?"

If the foreign man had any idea his question had irritated Spoon, he didn't let on. Nor did he pay attention to Spoon's introduction or question. He turned his attention wholly to Ambryn. "And you are... the dragon?"

Ambryn was still leaning on the car, indifferent to the arrival of the werewolf. "In the flesh. And to clarify, I am *a* dragon. Not *the* dragon."

Artur dropped his bags to the concrete, a knee

touching down a scant half second behind. He dipped his head down in reverence, showing tremendous respect to Ambryn.

Jesus. Strong reaction much?

"Please. Stand. I am not a God to be worshipped, just a dragon," Ambryn said, reaching out and lifting the kneeling werewolf up to his two feet.

Spoon watched as Artur's eyes gave away his disappointment. The vaunted hunter was offended by the dragon's lack of appreciation for the act of appreciation. "But you are the dragon of death," Artur said. "If you are not a God, what is?"

Ambryn stumbled on a reply. "Your kind—humans, that is—have worshipped us in the past. Temples were built and sacrifices made in our honor. I have a strong feeling many of you will do the same again. It didn't work out the way your people wanted. We were not meant to be worshipped. We have no interest in being fawned over. We have duties. If you think we are worthy of following as we go about our lives, then so be it. But Artur, you do not need to bend a knee to me. If you want to show me I matter, then help us find the vampires that have chosen to infest this city."

Artur slowly nodded, his eyes transfixed on the dragon's face. He hung on every word and digested them, absorbed them. "Yes. I see. I will fight alongside you. Forgive my English. I don't speak it enough."

"Your English is better than fine," Ambryn said.

I can't wait to tell Alanna this story. This is some weird shit. "Artur, you are welcome here indefinitely in America so long as you are working with Tapper. If and when we close this case and find the vampires, I can get you an extension for a month or two to see the sights, but our primary focus is to hunt and kill whoever or whatever took those people and those buses," Spoon said. "I've secured you a standard contractor's wage, and your reasonable expenses will be covered by the Agency."

Artur pried his eyes off the dragon and pointed them at Spoon. "Yes, I was told all this on the plane. I had to sign forms."

"Good. We have a room for you at the hotel where we are staying. Do you require any special equipment that we need to get? Firearms, arcane substances, body armor, anything?"

Artur thought for a moment. "No, I think I am all set. Can we meet women? I have a need for finding a woman soon. I need more sons or daughters. I care not which. I think a half-American child would be good for the babies. Good citizenship."

Are you shitting me? This guy wants an anchor baby? Is that a serious question or is this guy a comedian? "I think we need to focus on the vampires first, Artur."

Spoon watched as the werewolf's mind came to agreement. "Yes, of course. Maybe after."

"Maybe after," Spoon said, reinforcing the idea. "We have a car here. If you're ready, we can head out and link up with Mr. Doyle and Agent MacTavish and get started."

Artur looked pleasantly surprised again. "Ah, the British man. He has been good to me. I am happy to see him again. But first, may I step outside to get more fresh air?" He indicated his head towards the wide open hangar door and the cool desert city outside.

"Sure," Spoon said. "Just don't walk out too far. The media likely has cameras all over the place and we'd like to keep our faces off the evening news. People are riled up enough right now."

"Riled up?"

"Worried. Scared. Agitated. We don't need to give them any more of a reason to lose sleep or panic," Spooner said as they walked to the invisible line marking the inside of the hangar from the outside. As they walked, the agent watched as Artur's nose wrinkled and he inhaled big lungs of the Nevada air. Right when they stopped, the Romanian's face soured, like he'd gotten a taste of garbage. *That can't be good.* "Catch a whiff of something?"

Artur turned back to Ambryn, who was still back at the SUV waiting patiently for the agent and the werewolf to return. "Can you not smell that?" Artur asked the dragon.

Ambryn walked over to the two men, lifting his own nose high, sampling the air. "This city smells of many things, not all of them pleasant. What are you smelling?"

Artur turned back to the opening of the hangar and the city of Las Vegas, a solid scowl now infecting his face. "This city stinks of the dead."

Chapter Twenty-Three
Uncle Cosmo

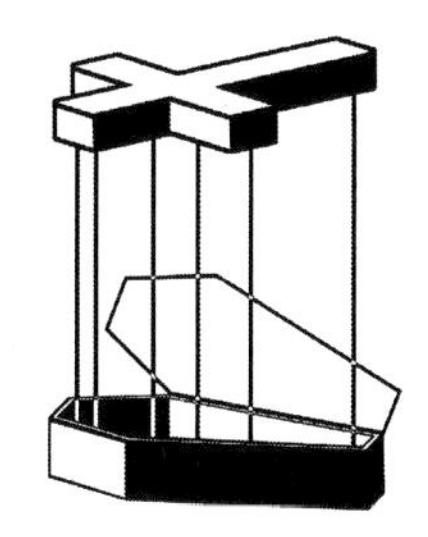

Uncle Cosmo had awoken once more. An evening first meal of fresh hot blood had already crossed his tongue and slid down his throat, and he felt the warm tingle of someone else's life deep in his belly. It was rejuvenating. Empowering. Intoxicating.

He sat at the same steel boardroom table in the basement of the Arabian Nights, and he sifted through paperwork his chief aide Sandra Brown had given to him minutes before. She sat two seats away. The papers concerned mostly business matters and were of peripheral importance to the ancient. *Money doesn't matter right now. I don't need to afford what I want when I can take it anytime I want it.*

"And you can see here once more the wheels were our gain leader on the floor. We don't land whales on them of course, but on every dollar they take in, we keep almost all of it. I'm thinking I talk to the marketing people and see if we can come up with a more Arabic or middle eastern theme to the spin so it's more flavorful. Get some new wheels made," the woman said as she pored through a copy of the same report in her hands. Jimmy Romita was the only other occupant of the room, and he sat silently, staring at the wall, fidgeting with a soda straw. It danced across his knuckles with surprising dexterity and wound up in his mouth where he chewed on it.

He wants a cigarette. I wonder how long it'll take him to realize that his lungs aren't absorbing any of the nicotine from his habit-sticks. "Jimmy, do you want to get some fresh air? Perhaps put a lighter to one of the Marlboros in your pocket?" Uncle Cosmo asked congenially.

Sandy hushed and Jimmy lit up. "Uncle Cosmo I'd love that. I've never been one for board meetings."

I'm well aware. You are a simple tool used for hitting things I need hit. A thug. Though inside you, I sense great potential. Your loyalty to family is of great use to me, and one day soon, I think I'll give you the opportunity of a hundred lifetimes. "Go right ahead friend. If we need you, Sandra will have you paged. Take your time." Jimmy got up and excused himself from the meeting. Once the double doors shut behind him, Cosmo nodded his head to Sandra. She continued her briefing on the casino's finances. *Competence is hard to come by these days.*

A knock came at the door, and her frustration at being interrupted strained the skin on her face into angry wrinkles.

"Open," Cosmo said to the visitor.

One of the two doors swung in, and a young vampire entered. He had only been fully awake and undead for a few days, but according to Sandra, he had already been useful as a reliable errand boy inside the casino. He had mouse-brown hair and thin glasses that were a size too large for his face. The whole look made him seem more youthful than he likely was. Another asset in his favor. In his hands he held a padded manila envelope. He froze solid when his eyes passed over Cosmo.

Seeing your new father for the first time will do that to you. "Yes, son?"

He straightened up and gathered his wits quickly. "This just came in via a police officer. He was very discreet and said it was for Miss Brown."

She turned, no longer frustrated by his intrusion. "Let me have that, Casey. Thank you, you may go."

The baby vampire—Casey—according to Sandra, handed the envelope to her and turned to leave his superiors. Cosmo stopped him at the door with a comment. "Good job, Casey. Thank you."

Casey looked star struck by the tiny accolade. "Thank you, Sir."

"Call me Uncle Cosmo. We're all family here now," he said back to the boy.

"Thank you, Uncle Cosmo," he said back, thrilled. Casey left, and the door shut behind him with a metallic click.

"The big Lieutenant came through. This is the tape from the other night," Sandy said, getting up and walking over to the DVD player in the corner of the room. The playback device was linked to a large flat panel television on the wall. She tore open the package and pulled out a shiny disc with a canary yellow note stuck to it. She read it. "Note from Rosen. He says his Captain couldn't get the recording easily, so he did it on his own. There are some photos in here too. He says the footage is pretty impressive."

The Captain fails us. It would seem that we need to remind him that things must be done whether they are easy or not. That bodes well for the Lieutenant. And as far as what's impressive, I'll be the judge of that. "Play it."

Grainy and soundless, the video had low quality. The image had been recorded in such a manner that it split into four equal rectangles, one camera angle for each quarter of the screen. As the video played, the images flicked, showing even more angles, and soon, the story of that night played out. Other than Sandra's intermittent gasps of shock and surprise, the first play through of the hour long video they watched together in silence.

"Again," Cosmo said, leaning in, looking at new

panels of the video for information he might've missed.

The black haired man that destroyed his employees and frightened off the vampire named Simon started the video sitting downstairs, avoiding the advances of the female dancers. When Simon and his entourage appeared at the front door, the black haired man sat up like a lion that had caught scent of wounded prey. *So he can sense our presence. From smell? Or something arcane?*

The group went up the wide staircase, and after picking up an attractive black skinned dancer, the man followed. More women joined in as they walked. *Like white hair to black pants, and just as difficult to get off of you.* When the group arrived upstairs to their separate VIP room, the man went to the bathroom, and faked tying a shoelace. From a crouch he watched Cosmo's people for a time, went into the bathroom, and on exit, put on an act of slobbering drunkenness. He made his move, and stumbled into the lounge.

They almost kicked him out, but Simon stopped them, sensing an easy mark. *Greed is strong in the blood of the vampire, isn't it my dead child? Your greed that night even cost you your life.* The man played drunk for a time, and Simon's guards fed him alcohol at a torrid pace, ensuring that the act would become reality. But it didn't. The stranger sat down next to Brandon and leaned in close, obviously engaging the plump man in conversation. *Perhaps he thought he was the lowest hanging fruit? The other easy mark in the room.*

Within seconds Simon came over to the curving couch visibly bothered by the interaction. The vampire ushered Brandon away from the stranger. The body language wasn't hard to read between the undead and the mysterious dealer of death as they spoke. There was a stiffening, a realization leading to a sobering moment for the vampire as he sat on the couch and engaged the man. Some form of verbal confrontation happened, and Simon issued an immediate command. A raised finger led to drawn guns, and soon after the video was drowned out by the muzzle flashes of innumerable shots, all hitting the trespasser without exception. *At least the men were accurate.*

After that, the violence became as one-sided as it could've been. The guards might as well have been babies thrown into a pit with a hungry tiger for all the good their guns and training did them. He moved fast, faster than Simon did, and his strength exceeded that of a human being's by far, and perhaps most importantly, nothing they could do would harm him.

After killing or maiming Simon's entire security crew, the powerful stranger left Brandon cowering at the mini-bar in the room and followed after Simon as he fled the club. From what Brandon had told Cosmo already, the stranger caught up to Simon not long after. In the wake of the murderer's exit, Brandon got to his feet, and true to his story, dealt with the remaining witnesses. He showed a level of cunning that Cosmo appreciated. *But he could not silence Simon before his escape. And then, of course, the bastard tried to betray me. Heh. The blood spell holds true when the will cannot. Brandon has earned his turning. I'll see to it he is rewarded handsomely when he awakens.*

Sandra stopped the video after the second play through and looked to Cosmo. He waved an indifferent hand, and she left the footage video stopped. "So what now?" she asked her vampiric father.

Uncle Cosmo forced an unneeded sigh out of his useless lungs. "You said there were photos in the envelope? Are they isolated pictures from the video or something else?"

Sandra picked up the padded pouch and pulled out the sheaf of photographs. They were rough images printed on regular copier paper, not glossy photographic prints. There were many. "These aren't from the club. Another note from Rosen though. He says these were taken this morning at the airport by one of his off-duty officers tailing the Feds. Well, look at that," she said with an un-surprised smile. She slid one of the images across the table to Cosmo. Cosmin picked it up with long gray fingers.

The image had been taken from a great distance with a high-powered lens. It showed a plane half shadowed inside a hangar and a pair of men leaning against the fender of a large federal black SUV watching it. A suit wearing man in his late twenties or early thirties with a short military haircut puffed on a cigarette, and the man at his side could only be the mysterious wrecking ball from the club. *They are familiar to one another. Comfortable. Well then. It would appear the Agency has added an enforcer to their payroll. But who? Who is this dark man, but perhaps more importantly, what is he? He isn't human.*

"Looks like they picked someone up off that plane," Sandra said, sliding another print across the meeting table at Cosmo.

The paper spun around in wild circles at it approached him until it stopped just shy of his fingertip. The image settled right-side-up, and he could see the two men from the first picture standing just outside the hangar with a newly arrived third. The face of the third man had familiarity to Cosmin. It jarred memories. Unpleasant memories. Cosmo couldn't stop his lip from curling up in displeasure.

"You know him?"

Uncle Cosmo's eyes darted up from the picture to Sandra's face. With bright blue eyes she gauged his reaction to the picture, and she didn't look pleased with whatever expression he'd let slip. "Yes. This man I know."

"Who is he? Should we be worried?"

"He is The Romanian. The most recent of a long line of prolific European vampire slayers. He roams not far from where I spent many years. I have crossed paths with them before. In Czechoslovakia they once almost caught me. That he is here means one thing."

"They know vampires are in Las Vegas?" Sandra posed.

Uncle Cosmo nodded somberly, his undead fingers clenching into fists of frustration. "They are as they say, 'on to us' my dear."

"That sounds to me like we should be worried."

"I was worried when the mysterious man made mincemeat of one of our security teams and strong armed a vampire into nearly confessing my secrets. Beyond worry, we now have cause to be frightened. This escalates matters profusely."

Sandra shifted in her seat. "What do we do? Call it all off? Go to ground?"

"No. We are far enough along that even with his presence and the strange monster of a man at his side, we can proceed. Too much is in motion for us to abandon ship. It's all about leverage my dear, and they do not know yet what leverage we have over them and the city. Not to mention I have other irons in the fire. I suppose it's high time we inform them just what's at stake should they take action against us."

"What can I do to help?"

The ancient vampire stood up, reaching his full height. Cosmin had never been a tall man, but somehow he knew how to loom over anyone near him. He slicked back his full head of dark brown hair and adjusted the way his white dress shirt sat on his body. He shook off the temporary demeanor of concern, and replaced it with one of confidence. Yes, it might be identified as false bravado, but Sandra would never know the difference if he played the part correctly. "Contact the Lieutenant. Inform him we need The Romanian followed at all times. If he does anything, we need to be made aware of it immediately. His location must be known to someone every moment of the day and night."

"I can do that. Anything else?" she asked as she rose to her feet as he had.

"Yes. I'll need to contact some people you're unaware of as of yet. Please block off an entire floor of the casino. I'll be needing space for around fifty more people."

"Fifty? Are you kidding? Are they vampires? Do I need to have maintenance block out the windows?"

"No, they are dhampyr. My living flesh and blood. Shooters from the old country that have been living near to here, waiting for something like this to happen."

"Like the handful of guys you brought with you?"

"Yes, like them but with bigger guns. Go now. Free up a floor for them. A lower floor so they can take the stairs if need be. The first will be arriving within a few hours. Some of them have a drive to get here, and I don't want my family kept waiting."

"Very well," she said. Sandra turned and walked towards the door after gathering up the papers she'd spent so much time preparing that were now discarded in the wake of the bad news from the photographs and video.

"Oh, and Sandra," Cosmin said, the gears in his mind churning.

"Yes?"

"I'll need something that can take high quality video. Plus a camera operator. And someone to edit it as well."

"We have people for that on the payroll here," she said with confidence. "Might need to put them on the special payroll after."

"Good. And stop feeding the new children. I want them hungry. Very hungry."

<u>Chapter Twenty-Four</u>

Lieutenant Aaron Rosen

The twelve year veteran of the Las Vegas Metro Police Department closed the hinged burner cell phone and discreetly slid it into the pocket on his tight uniform shirt opposite his badge. Aaron couldn't feel the warmth of the battery through his Kevlar and wished he could. His office felt cold in the December evening.

Want me to watch this motherfucker, eh? I'll do you one better. Rosen grabbed his phone off the base from his desk and dialed an extension inside his command building. *If I can manage this fast, the rest of my life with be golden. Fuck the Captain. Pussy.*

The line picked up. "Danny."

If you sent a refrigerator to a police academy, you'd get Danny's younger, less hairy, smaller brother. Danny worked in the gang unit, had a reputation in the department for being harder than the rock the mountains were made out of, and had a special place inside Rosen (and thus Uncle Cosmo's) inner circle of loyal and well compensated police officers. A thick tuft of hair perennially poked out over his shirt and body armor, his thinning hair was trimmed into a perfect flattop, and beads of sweat ran down in all directions from his crown.

"Danny, it's Aaron," Rosen said. He kept his voice hushed, despite his closed office door.

"What can I help you with Lieutenant?" Danny asked back. Rosen couldn't help but think Danny's voice would've seen him into a successful career as a backup singer somehow. Despite his girth and occupation he had a lyrical quality about how he formed words. Had you never met him in person, after a phone conversation you'd think he looked like a teen pop star and not a linebacker with a square jaw.

"So there's a hotel case I'd like to talk to you about in person if you have a minute," Rosen said.

"Time sensitive?" Danny asked, his singing voice dropping an octave. A hotel case was their secret code for anything that involved Uncle Cosmo. In a city with a hundred hotels, if anyone had the chance to be listening to them the expression was as innocuous a sentence as could be.

"Yeah. Right now works best. My office?"

"Gimme ten minutes."

Rosen hung up the phone and let his mind wander to the dark places where murder plots were born.

*****

Danny shut the sheer glass door behind him and twisted the Venetian curtain rod, forcing the slats to rotate. The room darkened as the sunlight winked out.

Something I'm going to need to learn to live without. The sun.

Danny squeezed his keg shaped body into the wood and vinyl office chair that looked like it had survived the set of The Brady Bunch. The tuft of chest hair had already made its escape. The two huge men seemed to fill the room with muscle. "What's the Uncle want?"

Rosen reached into a file drawer in the bottom of his desk and produced a manila folder filled with printouts. It looked tiny in his massive hands. He slid it across the desk wordlessly and watched as Danny's small, alert eyes devoured the images inside it one by one. He analyzed each photograph, each face on each page, and assembled everything he could see into a puzzle that he could solve. "The Tapper people, eh?"

Rosen lifted a finger to his lips. "Outside influences, yeah. I just got off the phone with the Ice Queen, and she said our mysterious benefactor requires us to keep eyes on the dude with the long black hair. Apparently he's an old school vampire hunter from Europe and he being here ruffles feathers."

Danny sat the folder down on the desk and leaned back as much as he could in the too-small chair. "I can't believe this shit is for real. Vampire hunter? That's already a profession? What the hell is the world coming to?" He laughed. "Alright. We're spread pretty thin right now though, Aaron. We've got some normal shit cropping up, the incident at the night club now, and you've already got off the clock guys watching the old dude in the big black bus. Half of my gang team has already been re-tasked. I don't have a lot of resources—trustable resources—to help. I mean, I wanna help, you know I wanna help you, but I don't know how to squeeze blood from a rock without drawing attention from the cops in this police force that aren't on the special payroll." He sang it all prettily.

Rosen's eyebrows flared, and he flashed a wicked grin. "I'm with ya. We don't have the manpower to watch this guy twenty four-seven, but we could spare a small crew of guys for an hour or two to set up a hit."

Danny's flesh darkened to the ruddy color of bricks. "Wait. What are you thinking? You want to kill him?"

"I think we can do it. You have a bunch of Zebras on

the payroll right? A few of the older guys?"

Danny nodded. A zebra was the internal nickname LVMPD SWAT officers got. "Yeah, five guys. Solid dudes."

"Pull a few of 'em in. We've already got surveillance up on these feds as you said, and we put the SWAT guys to task. Make it look like an accident. Carjacking. Gang related shootout. Act of terrorism. Plot of Lethal Weapon. Who knows?"

Danny shook his head, unhappy about the idea. "Aaron, this sounds like bad juju to me. Taking out piece of shit assholes here in the city is one thing, but going after a dude working with the feds is another. What if we hit one of the agents, man? You realize the kind of heat that's gonna come down on us? Having the Tapper people here is scaring the guys already."

"Jesus Christ, Danny; I thought you had a pair of balls. Sack up. You want to live forever right? That's what we're talking about. *That's what this is all about.* What we're putting our neck on the line for. Eternal life, no bullshit, no movie special effects. This is a bold move we can pull that swings us straight into the good graces of Uncle Cosmo. I ain't claiming it isn't risky. I'm not saying it isn't dangerous. But if we pull it off, we jump right up to the top of the totem pole because we *got shit done.* Go big or go home right?"

Danny leaned forward, still red and now angry. His voice had lost its melody and had dropped into a gruff baritone. "I got plenty of balls you Jew prick. And you know what? Where the fuck is the Captain in all this? Why isn't this coming from him? What's your angle? This a power play of another kind too?"

"Fuck you, Danny. Angry 'cuz my dick is trimmed. No need to bring religion into this. And look, Sandy called *me,* not the Captain. She made it sound like she was pissed at him for dragging ass on getting the club video to them. I made it happen, and they're impressed.

Bold moves Danny. If you wanna get noticed you gotta do something worthwhile. I'm not excited about waiting ten years to get turned into a fucking vampire. I want to be young forever, not wrinkled and fucking disgusting."

Danny chewed on Aaron's words for a moment, and the tension in the room faded the tiniest bit. "What's our window?"

Rosen shrugged. "As soon as we can. A day or two would make us both look really good over there."

Danny's color settled out, and he remained forward, elbows on knees. *He looks like a bowling ball with a sidearm.* "I'll see what I can do. Maybe we can do it clean. High powered rifle from a rooftop or something."

"Not too clean. We don't want to arouse suspicion that a sniper took a shot to do this. Too premeditated. Too professional. That's how a cop thinks. Besides, there are still far too many people on the force who aren't with us on this just yet."

"But quite a few who are. More every day from what I hear. There's gonna come a time when everyone's gonna have to take a side, you know that right? Blue on blue for real," Danny said. "I'm probably going to be forced to shoot friends when this gets real. Dark days no matter how you look at it."

"Judgment day comes for everyone. No one escapes the Grim Reaper, right? Except those that don't really die. And may I remind you, that is our chief motivation in this."

"Yeah, you're right. Okay. Okay." Danny stood, the seat sticking to his wide hips for a moment. "Sorry I called you a Jew prick."

Rosen dismissed it with a wave of his hand and a toothy smile. "I *am* a Jew prick. But I'm also a smart and ambitious prick, and so are you. I've known you long enough to know when it matters most, I can lean on you and whatever needs to get done, gets done. We pull this off? We take down this fucking vampire hunter dude from Europe, and our shit won't stink for the rest of time. Endgame brother."

Danny grinned and nodded. "Endgame. Gimme some time to get the guys together and see what we can work up."

The two men shook hands and parted as conspirators in murder. Rosen leaned his thick body back in his swivel chair and let his mind wander to the dark places where eternal life at any cost lingered.

Chapter Twenty-Five

Artur

Georgeta and Rodica were on the phone. The night had slipped away in Pitesti, and Artur called his daughters to make sure they were alright before they went to bed. He hadn't ever left them behind alone for a hunt. Cojocaru family had always taken care of them when he'd left on a hunt or when he had drank too much to be around them. To be able to have an entire conversation in Romanian quieted the unrest he felt at being so far from home and so far from his babies.

"Georgeta, you are well?" Artur asked his eldest twin daughter.

"Yes Papa, things are good," she said back. "Are you drinking?"

"No little one. No more drink for me. Rodica you too are good?"

Rodica sounded happier. "Yes Papa. We finally have the flat to ourselves again. Fresh air has come back with the old man gone."

"Belyakov? He has gone back to Russia?" *How did he leave? He was paralyzed because of me. His back shattered. His ribs busted. He couldn't have magic that powerful.*

"He had a driver. A pilot. He drove up from Bucharest

and helped the old man into a car. He was angry with everything, but he is Russian. They are always angry at something. We gave him some of your vodka, and that helped," Rodica said.

"Oh, good. Get rid of it. Get it all out. From all of our homes in Pitesti. Brandy too. Pour it down the drain," Artur insisted to his two daughters.

"We already did," Georgeta said.

A twinge of something uncomfortable hit Artur in his belly. Jealousy? *I'm so thirsty all of a sudden.* "Good. Thank you. You do your father great service."

"We know," the twins said in harmony.

My girls. So beautiful and smart. I should be more proud of them than I am. I disgust myself with the hunt for what I don't have, when I already have so much.

"Is it hot there? It's desert, yes? They have cactus there?" Georgeta asked, the edge in her voice seemingly faded for the moment.

"Yes, they have cactus. It is flat here. Some mountains far away. Pretty in a plain way. It is cold now. Winter. Sweaters or jackets everywhere. Many flashing lights. Your cousin Dmitri would like the lights. The city is smaller than I thought it would be. It reminds me of mold on bread. Just a spot on something flat that shouldn't be there." The girls laughed. "But there is evil here, no mistaking it. It is in the air like oil on water and I think it spreads just as fast."

"Can you hunt them soon?" Rodica asked, now solemn.

"I hope. The Americans haven't told me everything yet. I don't know what I can eat here that will lead me to them, but I will fight alongside the dragon when it happens. Be proud of your Papa girls. Finally."

Rodica whispered in excitement, fearful of someone hearing her enthusiasm, "What is the dragon like? Is he powerful? Have you seen him fly?"

I don't know. He isn't what I expected. "He seems strong.

He appears as a man so far. They do not want anyone to know that he is here. Handsome. He is in the other room right now. We are at a casino hotel. I haven't spoken to him much yet. Mostly a special agent called Spoon."

"Spoon? Like a fork?" Georgeta asked.

"Yes. A nickname. He is an army man I think. Or used to be. His hair is cut short and he smokes and uses curses a lot. You know the type. I think I will fight alongside him as well. I recognize him from the television when the first dragon appeared. He is important somehow. I think he knows the other dragons."

The girls babbled with muted excitement. *They are happy for me. Finally. I am doing something worth being proud of. This is a feeling I could get used to.*

Artur heard a knock on his room's door, and he got off his King bed and walked over. He inhaled deeply as he approached and caught the acidic and woody scent of Spoon's recent tobacco use. He opened the door, phone still held to his ear.

"We're getting together downstairs in a conference room for a briefing in ten minutes," the man named Spoon said a little too loud, and a little slow.

He means to speak slow for me to understand. "I understand English, Spoon. I am not a retard. Speak at your normal pace, please. I'll be down," Artur said with a smile.

Spoon flushed the smallest bit and laughed at himself. "Sorry man, didn't mean to offend. I've watched Borat too many times, I guess."

Artur nodded like he understood what Spoon was talking about, though he didn't. "Where are we going?"

"I'll wait for you in the hall. Get dressed. Mr. Doyle will be there, plus a few other local officials. He can be an ornery prick when he's kept waiting. We're trying to find a way to coordinate with the Vegas authorities to canvas a larger area. Trying to find all these missing locals and tourists is proving to be a real bitch," the agent said, running a hand through his cropped military style brown hair. Artur saw the bulge of a handgun at his hip just above the bottom of his suit jacket.

Guns everywhere here. One for every truck. "Give me five minutes to say goodbye to my daughters. Thank you." Artur shut the door and returned to the phone call with his beautiful and smart girls, with their blue eyes, and their green eyes.

*****

The small conference room Tapper rented in the hotel had a single overly large oval table at the center of it. Gathered around it was a hive of uniform and suit wearing activity. The lone exception to the unannounced dress code was Artur, who wore his worn Levi jeans and a paisley patterned button down shirt, and the man Artur knew to be Mr. Doyle. He wore a simple pair of dark wool slacks, and a dress shirt that was the color of clover honey. Somehow he seemed more important than all the people gathered wearing more expensive clothing than he.

Across the room their eyes met, and Artur had a shudder run up and down his spine. The old man smiled in a friendly way, but somehow the gesture rang as sinister to him. *The sorcerer looks no more than a year older than when I last saw him. That was twelve years ago. I don't understand wizards or shamans. Give me what my blood offers and no more. I cannot trust what I cannot taste and feel.*

Spoon pointed to a seat at the table, and Artur took it. The agent sat down beside him. Mr. Doyle moved across the room, about to sit at the middle of it all, clearly directing the gathering.

"Ladies, gentlemen, please have a seat. There is a lot to discuss today, and time is slipping from us," the spell caster said. The accent Artur remembered had faded some. *Too long away from the island he was born on.* "Thank you. You'll notice there is a rather large sheaf of papers arranged in front of each of you. Contained therein you'll find a brief case summary you already have likely seen, as it is identical to the one prepared prior to Tapper's arrival here in Las Vegas. Beyond that, you'll find a second summary of my arcane findings of the bus crash site, followed by a police report regarding the club incident from the other night, and an internal Tapper report for the same. Peruse said papers, and I'll continue once everyone is finished." Mr. Doyle let the room start reading. He sipped out of a paper cup that had a faint trail of steam rising out of it. Artur let the papers rest where they sat, flat in front of him. The papers wouldn't tell him any more than what he could find out on his own soon enough.

"So there's a substantial amount of censorship in your report, sir," one of the suit wearing men said. *Must be a politician.* "We were hoping to confirm the identity of the man who did all the damage inside the club." The man looked over to a silent Ambryn, who tipped his head and winked back at the speaker in return. The man in the slate suit licked his lips nervously and looked to Mr. Doyle.

"His identity is still unimportant, hence the redactions in the report. It is sufficient enough for you to know that he is a 'good guy' and that he is very much on our side in this," Mr. Doyle said, ending the curiosity of anyone else in the room.

Why such a secret? Soon enough someone will recognize him from the few times he has been on the television? Such an elaborate ruse to protect something they should be shoving down the throats of the vampires that are laying in wait here. You must frighten them. Scare them back under their rocks for another decade. Show them the atomic bomb you have, and end the war before it starts. You are Americans, you like dropping bombs on your enemies.

The British man continued, "You will also find a

summary page of lead assignments. Many of you will be tasked with door knocking on the few leads we have that we believe are worth checking into. Please do not be offended if you feel this is below your station. I assure you, time is of the essence, manpower is critically short, and your experience in all things will be an asset no matter what we ask you to do. I thank you, and your government thanks you."

A murmur ran through the gathering of officials. *I can see that many are insulted. They feel above base tasks. Silly Americans. All about titles and perceived importance. Swagger means little when lives are on the line.* Artur's patience steadily moved downward as his frustration rose.

"Okay, so you won't tell us about that guy," an aging uniformed cop said, pointing to Ambryn, "but will you tell us about the hippy?" He moved his finger in the direction of Artur. "He some new age shaman that's going to do a spirit reading and tell us who our totem animals are?"

Cunt. Artur was about to lash out at the disrespectful man, but Mr. Doyle beat him to the punch. "Captain Reilly, your attitude smacks of ignorance and a lack of respect for your equals. Not only are you doing yourself a disservice by insulting a complete stranger, but your words harm the reputation of the Las Vegas police."

The old officer, the Captain, made fists, crumpling the papers he had just read. The man's voice slipped an octave down into a restrained growl. "I'm sick of your shit, Doyle, and I know I'm not alone here in the room in that thought. Since you assholes rolled into town with that big black bus you've bossed us around and kept everyone in the dark with your mystic mumbo-jumbo." He flipped the misshapen papers, scouring for something. When he found it, he started reading. "And I quote: all attempts to use scrying devices, and clairvoyant spells or effects have failed to determine the whereabouts of any survivors. What the fuck does scrying mean? Clairvoyant spells? I would've thought that speaking plain English would be easier for an Englishman. Need a goddamn interpreter to read this garbage." He tossed the papers into the center of the table, almost as a challenge to the older man.

This time it was Artur's chance to cut off Mr. Doyle. "Mr. Doyle, if I may?" Artur asked. Artur tried to be deliberate and intense in how he formed his words for the mage. He wanted to sound angry, but intelligent at the same time.

Something in Mr. Doyle's eye told Artur the sorcerer trusted him. "By all means, good sir."

Artur leaned forward, his long black ponytail swishing around his head and landing on his shoulder. It had the effect of making him appear ancient and formidable, like the wise barbarian king of a savage tribal nation. "Captain Reilly, is it?"

The cop with the bushy gray eyebrows gave him a nasty look back. "Yeah. Surprise, another foreigner. Country as big as ours, you'd think we'd be able to solve our problems with people inside our own damn border."

Artur let it slide. *Nationality means nothing to me.* "I am sorry to disappoint you in that I am not from New Jersey, or Florida, or Texas. But I have come a very long way to help with this, and I am happy to. I am not a hippie as you say. I am a varcolac. A varcolac hunter of vampires, the last in a long line of glorious men and women who have given all for centuries from the shadows to hold back the rising black tide of the undead that has appeared again here and now. I offer you my assistance and my respect. But know this; I do not suffer fools. Mind your tongue around my friends, and you'll be happier for it."

Reilly fought to hide a sneer and lost. "A varcolac? You're a varcolac? Is that like a gypsy? Some mystical title or something? Or more like a goblin? We should ship you to South America where the rest of the goblins live in their holes."

Artur felt his temper flare, but he squelched it. The reputation of his family was more important than tearing this insolent cop's throat out and tossing it into the center of the table like a discarded pork chop. "If you think there are no goblins here, you are wrong. A varcolac is a kind of two-skin. Or, as your movies might say, a shape shifter."

The room hushed, and then like the winds stirring before the storm the whispers started. Even Captain Reilly had to take a second to gather his thoughts before sending back another salvo of acidity. "You're a werewolf?"

"I am a type of werewolf. A rare kind with... how do we say... mixed breeding."

Reilly looked confused. "Like, you're half-wolf, half-bulldog?"

Artur laughed, he was genuinely amused at the quip. "No, not like that. I am all werewolf. A varcolac is a special kind of werewolf, one whose blood has been mixed with a dhampyr's."

Ambryn turned and looked at Artur with an expression of betrayal. "I did not know that about you," he said with coldness in his voice.

"I am sorry," Artur said humbly. "Many generations ago, one of my kin took to bed with the living offspring from a vampire, and the stars aligned. The resulting offspring shared some traits of both creatures, creating a formidable being. My ancestors. It was then my family decided to hunt the undead. A dangerous but noble profession."

"Do you drink blood? Do you kill as they do?" Ambryn asked him, eyes narrowed, and his knuckles white on the arms of his chair.

He means to kill me if he does not like my answer. "I kill only those who deserve it, or at least that is my intention. I have been... I have lacked caution at times, and innocents have been hurt or killed, but that time has passed. I do not drink blood to survive, though flesh... Flesh speaks to me. It is the thread that a varcolac unravels that gives us our ability to hunt so well."

"Explain," Ambryn said. By then Reilly had been silenced by the palpable, hostile presence of the dragon among them. No one knew who or what Ambryn was truly, but at that moment every soul understood that they all answered to him. Depending on how this conversation went, they might see a replay of the carnage that happened at the club.

"Wait. What's a damper again?" Reilly asked, interrupting the dragon and the werewolf.

Artur said it slowly, "A dahm-peer. Dhampyrs are the living offspring of a male vampire, and a human female. Born with some traits of the undead, but nearly none of the negative side effects. For example, sun does nothing to a dhampyr, nor does silver. We also do not need to drink blood. Have you heard of the sin eaters?" Artur asked the dragon beside him.

"I have. You claim to eat the sin of the dead then?"

"No, but a varcolac can, with a bite of flesh, divine information about the person or thing we have bitten. Our innards are special, they see pieces of the life of what we eat, and with years of practice, we can funnel the insanity of what we see into an experience that shows us useful things. Things that lead us to vampires, for example."

"So if you were to eat a bite of a dead vampire, you might be able to see a memory that vampire had of the original vampire who bit and turned him?" Ambryn asked.

"I might see that, yes," Artur said confidently. "Fresh meat is always better, but it could work. There is only one way to find out."

Ambryn looked to Spoon and Mr. Doyle, and without a word, they all knew exactly what was to happen next.

Mr. Doyle stood. "Meeting adjourned. Study what is needed of you, and begin your tasks immediately."

Chapter Twenty-Six

Tapper Special Agent Alanna MacTavish

Alanna got to her feet at the same time her charge, Mr. Doyle, did and just before the rest of the room. *Secure the exit. Check the hall.* She went to the wide double doors of the conference room and pushed them open into the corridor, wary of threats. Daytime or not, there could still be danger. Something tiny clinked against the bottom of the door, but pushed out of the way easily. She pressed the doors open until they locked, her eyes bouncing up and down from the base of the door where she'd heard the noise, and the two ends of the hallway. *Something must've been placed there while the door was closed. A cup maybe?*

Alanna peered around the edge of the door and saw what the door had hit. It was a small black piece of plastic the size of a pinky finger. *A USB drive?* The agent pulled a rubber glove out of her suit interior pocket and after crouching, picked the drive up using the glove like a napkin. The drive had no markings on it and other than its location, had nothing special about it. It was ordinary. Alanna knew better than to dismiss it. As she slipped the tiny piece of what could be evidence into her pocket, the room emptied. She stood out of the way and watched as the locals all dispersed down the hall and into the lobby like a bucket of minnows dumped into the sea.

"Something wrong?" someone with an accent asked her.

Alanna turned. She already knew it was Mr. Doyle. "I found something behind the door just now. A memory stick." She produced the small item from her pocket using the loose glove.

Mr. Doyle's eyes furrowed at the device. "Interesting, and quite suspicious. Ask the hotel staff who came down this hallway after our meeting started. Good eye, Agent. I suppose we should plug it into a computer and see what's on it, eh?"

"There's a suitable laptop computer in the tank. It's set up to protect itself from malicious code and has nothing on it that's worth stealing," Alanna said.

"Brilliant. Artur, Ambryn, and Agent Spooner are going to head to the Coroner's office. Let's view the contents of the disk first and head over."

"It's not a disk," Alanna said as the two men began walking in step.

"I am not technologically savvy Agent. That's your role in this. Have I told you about my apprentice, Abraham? A charming young man, if you could ignore his foul mouth and loud music. Now *there* was a student I could be proud of. Very technologically savvy."

*****

Alanna had the heavy cased laptop out and open on the small kitchen table in the tank. She had the tank parked in the hotel parking lot, and Mr. Doyle stood at her side, watching intently over her shoulder as the younger Tapper agent inserted the drive into the appropriate slot. With a few clicks of the laptop's pad, Alanna had the drive's contents open.

It had a single mp4 file. It was titled; View me immediately. *Ominous.*

"Shit," Mr. Doyle said as Alanna double clicked the video icon. It prompted for a password. Above the field was the lone hint: Name the vampire killed unjustly the other night. "What did Ambryn say the man's name was?"

Alanna was already typing it. "Simon."

*****

The first few frames of the recording were stomach churning, particularly for Alanna, whose years in Afghanistan were littered with fears of her or her friends being captured and beheaded in a video that looked very much like this one. She shuddered as she watched a sitting teenage boy struggle against bonds of duct tape and rope. He had a strip of the silver material across his mouth, and his stifled moans were jarring. His eyes were wide, and danced around like a pair of whirling dervishes shot up with opium. Sweat ran in heavy streaks down his dirty face, and his lopsided haircut hung limp and desperate off to the side of his head. The sad and terrifying spectacle took place in front of a coffee colored sheet draped just-so to obscure the background of the room.

The light had an eerie, looming quality to it, casting harsh shadows with edges that looked too much like sharpened daggers. Mr. Doyle and Alanna watched the boy's eyes widen and focus as an adult man walked into the frame. *This is not going to end well for that kid.*

Like the light, the man loomed over the sitting boy,

and judging by the sudden intensity of the kid's squirming and his attempts to escape the very approach of the man, he was likely as dangerous as the imagined daggers the shadows pretended to be.

He wasn't tall, or short. He had a robust physical character underneath a pair of slacks and a white dress shirt, but he wasn't bulky or muscular. He seemed healthy, average even. His hair had a chocolate color to it, and its length was short like a businessman's should be. Against the stark white light his skin looked like milk. *He is creepy.*

When his eyes caught the light coming from the camera they reflected in a pair of disc-shaped flashes like a cat's might. He circled around the boy like a plotting vulture in the sky, like hunger given wings.

"If you have worked out the password, I trust this message is being watched by those I have intended it to reach. I am Uncle Cosmo. I am the man—the vampire—whom you seek most ardently."

"Cheeky fucker. Are you recording this?" Mr. Doyle said, staring at the screen.

"No," Alanna said breathlessly as she watched the Uncle Cosmo character run long, gray fingers around the circumference of the boy's neck. Alanna's fingers hovered over the keys of the laptop, frozen straight, her simply painted pink nails hanging in the air.

The vampire looked down at the child lovingly, and somehow that made it all so much worse. "I come here with an explanation, and an offer of peace." As the vampire moved in and out of the voids in the light, his skin seemed to change colors. At times it was white, pure as bleached bone, and then it would turn gray, like a storm cloud at dusk. All the while, he looked down on the struggling, impotent boy as if he were his own child cooing softly in a rocked cradle below. "For far, far too long, for as long as I can remember, my kind have been hunted. Persecuted for what we are. Unjustly persecuted for a curse laid at our feet whether we wanted it or not. And many of my brethren were not given the choice," he caressed the teen's cheek with the back of his hand, "and yet they too were hunted like animals."

"When was this video taken?" Mr. Doyle asked Alanna.

"I don't know. There's no timestamp. Might be able to check the file properties."

"And when we as a kind were nearly hunted to oblivion during the drought of Kaula's imprisonment, I laid low. But now, in the glory of the return of all things magical and arcane, my powers have flourished, and once more my kind may be born. And as the spring storms bring the autumn harvest, I have brought greatness to this world once more."

"What the fuck does he mean?" Alanna asked Mr. Doyle. The old soul didn't respond to her.

"But where does a father take his children when they are born into a world that will hate them so? A world where every human will want to kill him or her at the drop of a hat, simply for being what they were born to be? Where?" Cosmo ran his fingers through the hair of the boy, teasing it affectionately, tucking it behind his ear. "I need a home. A safe place to raise my children, my wonderful children of the night, my children of forever. A city that will understand them, embrace them, and offer them succor and sanctuary for all time."

"Oh no," Mr. Doyle whispered.

"New York City, that place they claim never sleeps, was far too much work to change. Too much industry and commerce. Too many global connections I didn't care for. Too many hands in the cookie jar. The same turned out to be true of London, and Brussels, and Cairo and a half dozen cities more. Although I must confess I lingered for an extra night in Bruges. Stunning city. I'll regret not choosing that for a century, I'm sure of it. But nevertheless, I searched and searched, and my trusted children advised me, and in time we chose a city large enough, sinful enough, and profitable enough in the deep desert of the great American state of Nevada. I am proud now to claim Las Vegas as my family's home."

"Ambryn is going to shit a brick," Mr. Doyle said, using a curse word for the first time in Alanna's presence.

"Ambryn is going to shit a brick *building*," Alanna said back.

"As you can imagine, populating a city with a family such as mine takes some work and tremendous sacrifices. Hundreds of good natured locals willingly joined my family at the first offer after I arrived. You've no idea how tantalizing the offer of eternal life is in a world that has been turned upside down as ours has so recently by the dragons and all the things such as myself ... and of course even then we needed more sons and daughters, more nephews, and nieces, and niblings ... so we took some. Call it a land grab, if you will. Conscription perhaps. In days of old nations would simply move their borders at the command of a King, and the locals would be forced to adopt their new nation's customs and laws and religions, and let's be honest—this is no different." Cosmo kneeled beside the boy as if he were about to have a heart-to-heart discussion with him. Blood ran cold as he put his hand on the kid's trembling knee. "Right down to the bleeding, it's really all the same."

Cosmo moved so fast the camera registered nothing but a blur. *Oh Lord, no. No no.* The boy didn't have the time to flinch or struggle. The vampire had lunged and grabbed the folding metal chair by the seat, and he had lifted the boy into the air as if he weighed no more than a terror-stricken rabbit. His mouth was latched firmly onto the teen's throat, and the two men could hear a wet, slapping, and sucking noise as the vampire forcefully drained the poor boy's blood. Five seconds into the murder, Cosmo reared back, and an arterial spray from the boy's neck hit the coffee colored sheet, leaving a graffiti-like spray. He laughed a satisfied laugh, and put his mouth back onto the limp boy's neck and finished what he started. It didn't take long.

"I don't use words like this much Agent MacTavish, and I beg your forgiveness as a lady, but that *thing* is a *cunt,*" Mr. Doyle said as the murder took place.

"Couldn't agree with you more," she said softly, watching the teenager's eyes loll about in his skull, glazing over. She'd seen it before. The moment life left the body for good. But perhaps in this case…

Cosmo sat the chair holding the boy down and turned to face the camera. His face and white shirt was slick with sticky, red blood. He licked his lips like a grinning father who'd gotten strawberry ice cream on his face from licking a cone after a hot summer day. It disgusted Alanna. "Now, that's a roundabout explanation for why I am here in Las Vegas, and why a few 'errant' buses were 'lost' recently. I assure you that you know little of what has actually transpired, and that the buses you search for and the people who were aboard them are the mere tip of the iceberg. And my offer is this: I can help you steer your investigation—let's call it your *Titanic* to maintain the imagery—and help you save more lives than you can imagine."

"This should be good," Alanna said.

"It's apt to be horrible," Mr. Doyle quipped back. "Villains rarely have a grasp on the real meaning of how to save lives."

"I have annexed Las Vegas. It is now a reservation similar to the ones your Native Americans are forced to live on. We will enjoy a similar status of fealty and protection by your government, and in return, we will turn no more living humans into vampires against their will. Willing applicants must fill out the proper paperwork and submit themselves to our admissions process. Furthermore, we will police and regulate the consumption of human blood in our 'nation' and ensure that only willing donors are fed from. In addition, we will police our own kind, and protect humans from those of us who disobey our laws and customs. I offer you, summed up, the ability to control the spread of vampirism in America, and quite possibly the world. And all for the low, low cost of the city of Las Vegas. Of course, there are other details, legalities and whatnot, and those have been over-nighted to the Tapper offices in New Hampshire, as well as to all of the Nevada Senators and members of Congress. I trust this matter will be a priority for everyone."

"What the hell is he thinking? No one will go for that," Alanna said, alarmed.

"I wouldn't say that just yet. As he said, this world has been turned upside down of late," Mr. Doyle said ruefully.

"I will give you a full day to consider my *reasonable* and *generous* offer. And I remind you that the spread of vampirism and all the diseases that come from drinking blood in our manner will happen one way or the other, and I think the American public will appreciate the efforts put forth by their government to protect their health." He looked back at the dead boy, his expression now more filled with love than before. "I must attend to the birth of my new son. But please, use the local media to broadcast a response to me by the dawn of the following day. If I don't get your response by then, I will continue with my plan, and whether or not you are able to stop us, there will… there will be a river of blood running down the Las Vegas Strip and all across the heartland of this nation. And those lives, and all that precious blood, will be on your hands."

Chapter Twenty-Seven

Ambryn

The dragon, the werewolf, and the ex-policeman reached the coroner's office long before Agent MacTavish and Mr. Doyle did. Ambryn's impatience and nagging had urged Spoon's driving to a speed that bordered on reckless, especially considering their rental SUV didn't have police lights or a siren. The two had an argument about Spoon's driving choices on the way, and Ambryn had been forced to swallow his words and let the human do what he felt best.

They walked past the front desk with Spoon flashing his Tapper credentials at a startled police officer serving as the security guard. The thick necked man wearing a too-tight uniform had tried to stop their entrance by standing, and barking out 'halt' in a low voice, but a solitary stare from Spoon sat the man back down. *The alpha wolf raises its hackles, bares his teeth, and the rest of the pack sits down. It is as it should be. And he's not even the wolf among us…*

Now, only a minute and no more than fifty yards from the very same front desk, they were pulling a black, zipped up body bag out of a refrigerated locker that held what passed for the remains of the vampire named

Simon. The shape filling out the bag had no discernible human qualities remaining. No face where a head should've been, or legs splitting to feet with the toes pointed to the ceiling. The bag could have been filled with amorphous, congealing oatmeal made with blood instead of a human body.

"So explain again, please. You eat something, and you get visions of their life?" Ambryn posed. *I don't understand all the strangeness of these living creatures. Such complexity woven into their existences by Tesser and Kaula. Give me the simple, stark reality of death. It is luxurious in its elegance.*

"Yes," Artur said. "Memories. It takes much practice for a varcolac to see the visions, and even more practice to make sense of them. They can be maddening."

"Do you need to swallow? Or can you just... chew?" Spoon asked with a disgusted look on his face.

"I must consume the flesh to absorb the images."

"What if it's something fucking gross? Like, could you do it to a daemon? Or some fucked up hairy ass mountain gnome?" Spoon asked.

"My enemy is my enemy, Spoon. I am a werewolf. Like a wolf in the wild, if I must kill, I will bite my prey. In battle I cannot stop the flesh and blood of my foes from trickling down my throat, so there is little sense in worrying about what a mouthful will do. I trust my constitution. The risk is worth it when I know what I can learn if I take just one bite," Artur laughed. "No one can keep a secret from a varcolac if we can get our teeth into them."

"He's right. It's no different for me. If I were to be in a fight, I would bite my opponent in half and think nothing of how clean they were," the dragon said idly, looking down at the bag. *I wonder what secrets you will taste like?*

"I guess the logic of it all doesn't really apply to humans. We don't naturally bite things as a method of aggression," Spoon said, flipping the bottom of his coat open to show the grip of his handgun.

"How did you discover your people had this ability?" Ambryn asked the werewolf.

Artur's posture changed. His chest puffed, and his voice took on a proud lilt. "Members of my family discovered our gift many generations ago. When our werewolf bloodlines crossed with the dhampyr, the ability became ours. We do not know why. We have discovered over the years that if we do not regularly imbibe some blood of the vampire through killing them, then the gift fades. We must keep our blood mixed with theirs for the vision to work. It also means that my family hunts vampires. We hunt them for honor, for profit, and for a taste of their blood to retain our gift. That is our way."

"Very interesting," Ambryn said, mulling the explanation. The dragon took the zipper and slid it down the length of the remains, opening the bag. A strange, toxic odor sifted up into the air. It was foul and wet, like sewage mixed with ash. It stuck to the inside of the nose like greasy clay, and it stung. *Foul thing, this dead vampire. What could've done this to his body? Sorcery?* "Are certain body parts better than others? If you can identify anything in the bag, I suppose."

Artur reached over with hands that showed no signs of trepidation. He pulled the bag wide open, revealing the gelatinous, unidentifiable gore within. Spoon bent over from a loud retch and walked to the other side of the room, unable to watch.

After perusing the contents as if he were an interested culinary consumer at a bizarre butcher's counter, he shrugged. "I would prefer the heart. It seems to give the clearest and most potent visions, but I see no heart. After that, the liver is best. I see no liver. After that… anything but bone seems to work equally, unless I can boil the bones for a day to make a broth. Then, sometimes I have worthwhile visions."

From the other side of the room, "Boil the bones?" Spoon shouted through a gag. "Are you fucking kidding me? You wanna make dude soup?"

"No," Artur said back seriously.

What a world, eh Henry? "Take a bite please, Artur. Tell me if you see anything."

"Wait, whoa, are we really doing this?" Spoon said, his stomach suddenly under control. He had his hands raised in the universal 'whoa' position as he approached the lunacy at the steel table. *He really doesn't want us to do this.* "Are you suggesting that he takes a bite out of a dead body? There are laws against this kind of thing Ambryn. Quite a few of them, I might add. You can't just disrespect the body of a person like that. It ain't legal, and it sure as shit ain't right."

"Perhaps not," Ambryn said to the flustered agent. "But we are running out of time, and if Artur believes he can give us a clue or a path to follow, then we must try. My attempts to hunt down the undead were as you may recall, largely disastrous in relation to lying low and led us to here. And further, Agent Spooner, this is the tainted, evil corpse of a vampire. A murderer at the very least, and a creature of pure evil. A monster. An aberration of the cycle of life and death. This is a sin we can afford to suffer."

"Fucking dragons." Spoon threw his hands up, and left the room. The thick metal door slammed shut behind him, sending an echo through the room.

Artur reached into the miasma of foulness that was Simon with his bare hand, and found something meaty after poking around in the goop. He pulled it out of the sludgy remains and snapped his wrist twice, flinging off some of the wretchedness clinging to it. He whispered some words in what Ambryn guessed was Romanian, and held the meat high to the dragon, as if it were a toast. He popped the morsel into his mouth, and started to chew with his eyes closed, breathing heavily through his nose.

Ritualistic. I wonder how long this will take.

Artur's body tensed. His eyes opened and looked directly at Ambryn, but the dragon knew the man wasn't seeing him or seeing this world at all. The werewolf grunted something approaching the sound of pain as bright red spidery veins of blood coursed through the white of his eyes. The werewolf coughed out the piece of meat, nearly hitting Ambryn with it, and went down hard onto the smooth floor of the county morgue. Ambryn rushed over to his twitching body.

Shit.

Chapter Twenty-Eight
Artur

After saying a few prayers and invoking the favor of a few old spirits back home, Artur popped the piece of what he thought might have once been a kidney into his mouth. The piece of meat had a chewy consistency, almost rubbery and unlike anything he'd ever eaten. Normally meat was meat, regardless of what animal or person it came from. Only rare and strange creatures had flesh that defied the norm. Artur had once taken a bite from the arm of a mermaid in a very strange altercation that took place on the shore of The Black Sea, and her flesh had tasted watery and loose, like a congealed mouthful of old pudding and blood mixed with salty sea water. He had visions of the vortices and denizens of the deep oceans that night, and his dreams haunted him with memories of it occasionally to this day.

But this flesh, it was not fishy, nor was it comparable to oats or gelatin. It was old meat, cured by the process that made it undead, and something else unknown. He discovered it hard to chew like dried jerky but moist and somewhat pliable to his teeth. It yielded under the strength of his jaws and came apart, giving off a liver-like and coppery flavor that he found vaguely pleasant, but not entirely enjoyable. It tasted off.

Trickles of blood and flecks of the flesh escaped down the back of his mouth and into his throat, and he swallowed it down easily as a predator would. Artur opened his eyes to see what the dragon did as he ate and experienced the flesh. Ambryn watched him across the cold steel table with eyes like a viper. *Right now, he looks a dragon. His eyes cold and black with no bottom, his body taut. He looks coiled. Tense. Ageless. He looks …*

Artur's eyes speckled over with flecks of white light, as if a field of stars had emerged from the depths of the blackest night. They interrupted his thoughts and captivated him. The intermittent dots flashed a billion times, exchanging color and location in his field of view, quickly drowning out the real world. *Ah, faster than usual, but the memories are coming strong.*

The white in the world soured to gray, and then rapidly to black, starving him of reality. Panic hit him like a sledgehammer. *No, something is wrong. Something is quite wrong. Poison. Something I couldn't taste. Something I couldn't smell. Something inside –*

When the world turned red, Artur's bleeding eyes rolled up into his skull, and his consciousness departed.

*****

When a varcolac of the Cojocaru bloodline stole memories from the flesh, the pain inside the remembrance-visions never came along for the varcolac to experience firsthand. It remained a morbid cinema of the mind. Fiction nearly. Observation only. Sight and sound without pain and suffering.

This time, much pain came for Artur. Ungodly, unholy, unbearable suffering that ripped at Artur's innards like a murder of rabid crows trapped in his belly. The flaring, roaring agony tore up his spine and through his chest as it ran through his pelvis, down the length of his cock, through his balls and straight to the soles of his feet, sizzling every nerve as it moved. Every single atom of his supernatural body shuddered in frenzy, tearing about and trying to come apart at seams that didn't exist. It felt like forever in every breath he took.

From the floor, his vision flooded with the hot, acidic blood that streamed out of his eyes, he wished for death, but that was the domain of Ambryn, and the dragon was either unaware of his suffering, or unwilling to do him the kindness of giving him the release from it.

Please, why? What have I done? Why now? I have come back to the fold. I have turned from arrogance and pity.

An image flashed. Whole and intact in front of his eyes like an old, cracked photograph cast in shades of sepia.

Or is that shades of red blood?

Artur focused on the image. It gave him miniscule relief from the boiling ruin that worked to undo him inch by inch.

A boy wearing a prep school uniform loomed over Artur (Simon). He wore a white button-down shirt that was starched to an unnecessary degree, and his dark blue slacks, just like the slacks Artur (Simon) wore, and just the same as the pants the other boys standing around wore, were clean pressed. The angry faced boy had a fist entrenched at Artur's (Simon's) collar, and another reared back, ready to punch. Artur (Simon) lay on his back, outside somewhere. A gray sky filled with clouds loomed above.

Artur's (Simon's) hand reached up and touched below his nose, and the fingers came away bloody. He watched as a tiny cord fell in front of his eyes, an ear bud dangling at the end of it against his (Simon's) chest. The thin white wire had a smear of blood on it. People were laughing like hyenas. Laughing at Artur's (Simon's) misfortune and humiliation. It scalded, scarred. It felt far worse than the busted nose and loose tooth. The boy laughed again, and the cocked back fist slingshot into Artur's (Simon's) cheek, and as his head jolted back, stars swam in the cloudy sky, and consciousness slipped away. As the memory of the flesh went, Simon's thoughts repeated inside Artur's mind over and over…

"*Never again. Never Again. Never again. Never again.*"

And as a different blackness took Artur out from the depths of the stolen memory, he knew beyond any doubt that Simon would've given his soul for the power to fight back against others like that angry boy with the perfectly white shirt, and the perfectly blue pants that day.

Giving his life to a vampire for that power must've been easy then.

*****

Artur awoke in a hospital bed. Everything hurt, right down to his finger and toenails. *I am not dead then. In a hospital. An American hospital. I wonder how much they want to charge me for being disintegrated by vampire taint.* Artur laughed and immediately regretted it. Something moved in the corner of his eye, and he flinched. *That was a terrible mistake.*

"You're awake," the voice of Ambryn said.

Artur tried to speak, but his throat felt torn and dry. Instead of words, he made rasping sounds and quickly fell into a fit of coughing that nearly snuffed out the consciousness he'd just regained. When his vision came back a moment later and the world leveled out, Ambryn's hand supported the back of his head, and he held a cup with a bent straw poking out of the lid in the other. The dragon lifted it to his mouth and let the plastic tube poke between his lips. Artur took a tiny draw from the straw, and a trickle of ice cold water covered his tongue.

Blessed relief. A swallow followed by another tug led Artur to the promised land of normal breathing, and understandable words. "Thank you."

Ambryn backed away a few inches, but held the cup

close. "You're welcome. We nearly lost you."

Artur nodded. *Another mistake.* "I felt very lost. There was more than a moment where I wished you would grant me a swift death, dragon."

Ambryn put on a smile that seemed proud. "Would that everyone and everything that was as close to death as you just were greeted me with such open arms, Artur. I am glad you did not die. I would've felt guilty."

What? "The dragon of death would have regret over my dying? So peculiar, that thing, that I am more important alive to you. I am honored."

Ambryn's expression seemed conflicted. "Don't let it go to your head. Part of my role in this world is not only seeing to it that people and things die as needed, but also that they remain alive as needed. Things die so that others may live. I am not merely a dealer of death, I am its master. You are a powerful asset in my fight against the undead and I wish you to remain alive. If we can get you back to health, I foresee you and me working together for quite some time."

Artur's heart soared, and that didn't hurt him at all. "That would please me. That would make my family very proud."

"Good. Do you have any idea why that happened to you? Was his flesh poisoned?"

"It has never happened to me before. To no other I know of. Something about his blood. Something about what made him a vampire maybe. When he tried to tell you secrets, he exploded, yes? And when his flesh tried the same, it too revolted. But this time, it happened inside me. Something wicked. Something special about his nature. It may be more difficult to gain truths about what we are hunting than I had hoped." Artur looked out the hospital room window. Daylight dominated the sky, though the sun seemed near to setting. "How long have I been here?"

"About eight hours. A few minutes after you went

down, Doyle and the other agent arrived. He did something to you with a wine glass that somehow slowed whatever was happening to your body. He poured some kind of enchanted wine in your mouth," Ambryn tossed his shoulders up in a shrug, "and it worked."

"Maybe that is why I feel hung over," Artur said as he scratched his head. IV tubes dangled loose from his wrist. "Was it that bad?"

"You were bleeding from everywhere."

"*Every*-where?"

Ambryn wagged a finger indicating Artur's entire body. "Everywhere."

Artur sighed, embarrassed. "It would figure that I meet a dragon and the first thing I do is bleed from my sezut. I hope I did not make a mess."

"I didn't have to clean it up. Matters not to me. Tell me Artur, was this all for naught? Did you have a vision of anything useful?"

He won't approve. "I saw a moment from his past. Something from his grade school years. Maybe I think they call it high school in America? He got beaten up. It was an old memory. That means it was very important to him. Formative. Like a foundation for the house of his mind. He was beaten up and humiliated, and he swore never again."

"So what does that tell us?" Ambryn asked the werewolf.

"Much, though it may not prove to be useful in the hunt. In the vision he wore clothing from the past twenty years I would say. Of course, I could be wrong. I do not dress fashionably and never have. He had the same hearing thing that my daughters use for their iPod." Artur waved a sore hand at his ears, unsure of the word he needed.

"Ear buds? The little speakers that fit inside your ear canal?"

"Yes. This tells us he was a young boy, alive in the daylight within the past two decades. And yet he appeared what? Thirty years old as a vampire to you in the club?"

"Yes, about that," Ambryn said.

"Vampires do not age after they are turned. Then he could not have been turned long ago. No more than a few years. He is a copil. Well, he was. A baby."

Artur watched as Ambryn's eyes flashed, searching the room, like the light on a computer that blinked when it worked hard. "And yet he was in charge of several men. And was intending to bring me back somewhere. For his own meal, or something else."

"Fishy, yes?"

"Indeed," Ambryn said as the door to the room opened.

Mr. Doyle and the pretty younger agent with the old, ragged scar on her face named MacTavish entered, both with unpleasant demeanors about them. The British man saw Artur, alive and responsive, and brightened. "You're looking decidedly improved since I last saw you my Romanian friend."

"Less bleeding, I am led to believe," Artur said back with a smile that made his neck hurt.

"Yes. You bled enough to make the Thames run red for a day and a night. Are you feeling better?"

"Much, thanks to you and your wine. No more wine for me please. No alcohol in my life any longer."

"I regretted giving it to you, and I assure you I felt it necessary."

"I am still not all well, but thank you. I am sure it has helped me. Where is the Spooner?"

"Agent Spooner is downstairs, coordinating some affairs that require opinions from men and women who believe they are far more important than we are."

Politicians. The dragon sighed, validating Artur's thought. Artur looked to the gathering of allies around his bed, and knew something was off. *They are not telling me something.* "What? Did something happen while I was gone?"

"Does the name Uncle Cosmo mean anything to you?"

Artur suddenly had a frog in his throat. The name meant much. "Yes. Cosmin Dorinescu. Some of my informants in the old country heard that he had fled. Gone deep into hiding or fled far away to escape our hunt for him. Years ago he did this. Do you think he is here? Do you think he is the one behind your buses? He is a very bad person."

Mr. Doyle huffed, a frustrated sound. "I think our buses might be the least of our pending problems. Artur, there's a short video I think you should watch. And when you're done, we need to hear everything you know about Cosmin Dorinescu."

Agent MacTavish produced a laptop from a leather bag, and opened it. "This is going to be hard to watch," she said.

Chapter Twenty-Nine
Ambryn

Uncle Cosmo's videotaped act of murder and subsequent offer of secession via annexation had changed everything. A few hundred missing people had created a tragedy of considerable proportions, but an ugly war between the undead and the living on the streets of Las Vegas was another thing entirely. The potential for loss of life and property damage in the event of a vampiric uprising would be astronomical, and when humans were put in a situation where they could be parted with their money, the amount of attention directed to a problem increased exponentially. *Greed trumps tragedy. If Tesser and Matilde bring an eighth dragon into this world, it will be the dragon of Wall Street.*

The small team Tapper had assembled to investigate the buses and their missing occupants were once again gathered with the same local officials from earlier that morning in the very same hotel conference room. They were even sitting in the same seats around the massive oval table, with the same cheap paper coffee cups in front of them, and everyone seemed just as frustrated as they were that morning. Likely more so, and now with a far stronger sense of impending doom. The sense that everything could spiral out of control within hours seemed to wear on the darkened faces of all those gathered.

A video conference system that had been spun up by one of the local FBI techies sat on the wall of the room. The image on the big screen television looked like the introduction to the Brady Bunch, broken up into multiple equal panels, each with a different face at its center. Center among them all sat a very worried American president. The meeting had reached its third hour, and despite intense discussion from a multitude of angles, no decision had been made. *So worried about a few deaths. Many human cultures put an abnormally high value on every individual life. When will they understand that some lives are more precious than others? That some should survive when other should not? That some must survive when others must not? And that engineering a good life for your people at the cost of a few lives here and there is a noble sacrifice? A lesson I have failed to teach them over time, it would appear.*

The president listened intently to a talking head on the television that had a law degree. "Understanding fully that we as a nation do not have a lengthy history of negotiating with terrorists, we are in very new territory when it comes to paranormal species, and conditions of life, and their individual rights. Should we fail to acquiesce to this Cosmo character's wishes, we stand to alienate untold amounts of newly discovered races. Races that may or may not promote the growth of the nation. One of the great questions, I believe, is whether or not we set a precedent now, moving our national culture and economy forward, or maintain the status quo?"

Another lawyer on the television picked up the ball and ran in the other direction with it. *I don't like his beady eyes.* "We also can't afford to lend legitimacy to any… race of things that decides to take a few hostages and declare Cleveland or Tampa, or Denver as 'their country.' Taking hostages and forcibly converting them to your way of life is not a legal or ethical way to go about fighting for your rights. It certainly isn't the way to get your backyard declared a new sovereign nation."

"I think there might be a few Native Americans that could talk at length about the right and wrong ways to fight for your intrinsic national rights," the president said.

Murmurs in the meeting indicated that there were mixed opinions on the matter.

A third advisor spoke up. "At a bare minimum we need to fully examine the idea of the rights of a dead body. Vampires are deceased by definition and then reanimated somehow. They are at least entitled to the same rights as a corpse, and perhaps no more. We need to start looking at redefining what passes as eligible life for citizenship. I suspect when family members suspected missing or dead start turning up as zombies or ghosts, or in this case vampires, we are going to experience some serious legal issues. Inheritance, property ownership, copyrights, you name it. Imagine if Walt Disney turns up as a vampire. Or Hemingway, or Tesla, or Amelia Earhart. What happens to patents when someone decides to bring back Henry Ford or Thomas Edison from the dead? What do we do when some asshole resurrects Stalin? It's all going to come up, and it's going to be ugly, and it damn sure well will be costly."

"Ambryn," the president called out on the television. He leaned in closer to the camera filming him and the screen that displayed the conference room on his end. He squinted to look for where the dragon sat.

"Yes?" Ambryn replied to the talking head of the American leader, holding up a hand for identify where he sat.

"You're a dragon. Like your brother. I've taken his advice a few times recently and the results have been primarily good. I've heard from people with law degrees about legality, and I've heard from military and police people about my tactical options, and I have heard from the religious authorities about their beliefs, and medical people about the health concerns, but I have yet to hear from someone with some meat on their bones regarding the... magical side of things. I know Mycroft Doyle is there as well, and I'd like to hear from both of you now if I could."

Ambryn looked to Mr. Doyle and he nodded, letting the human go first. "Doyle here Mr. President. I will attempt to be delicate, even when we are in a position that offers us little time to be so. There has never been a time for human society quite like now. Magical energies and inventions, supernatural creatures and beings, whatever you wish to call them or us, have erupted onto the world consciousness like never before. We all know they are not going away any time soon. It's brilliant really. As your highly educated legal team has said at a nauseating length, there are layers and layers of legality to consider. Rights of the citizens of Las Vegas, rights of the kidnapped, rights of the state of Nevada, rights of the United States government, and then the ethical balance between protecting all of those rights, and the rights of the undead population, and then of course the astronomical financial impact to the city, state, country and world from a large-scale incident should one happen here as early as tomorrow morning."

The room listened. Mr. Doyle continued. "I cannot speak to the vampire race as a whole. In fact, we have no actual data on how many vampires there are in America or the world. Are they an ethnic group? A race? Or are they a subset of people more akin to a group that has been infected by a virus? If that's the case, then I would wonder aloud whether or not giving them their own nation is, in effect, making a modern day leper colony?" The Brit let that idea sit in before continuing. "Do we want all sufferers of cancer to declare a community in their name at the center of say, Manhattan? We are at a crossroads, and I am certain that no matter how we navigate our choices here this night, we will have more of these meetings than we all care for. It is my opinion that we find this Cosmin Dorinescu and annihilate him. If we choose to at a later date, perhaps immediately afterward, we can negotiate these same ideas in a less distasteful fashion, with an elected leader of their people instead of the person we've been forced to deal with."

After a pause, the Commander-in-Chief thanked him. He looked to the dragon. "Ambryn, if I may hear your opinion on the matter."

To be elegant, or blunt? "All of you will eventually die," Ambryn stated, choosing the blunt option. The room's collected shocked response made him chuckle. "And here you sit, debating the lives and rights of a few thousand people, and possibly as few as a hundred monsters, as if the entire world's existence depended on it. Allow me to illuminate a fact for you—it doesn't. The world has survived far worse than a greedy vampire who is smart enough to leverage a few craftily written human laws against its government. What I ask you all is how much of your governmental responsibility actually stems from fear for your career? Or guilt over letting things progress to where they are?"

The president interjected, supporting his peers. "Now listen here Ambryn, not a one of us here is thinking about our career tonight. All we want … "

"Stop it," Ambryn said. "I've met with greater people than you. Certainly better liars. Your arrogance is insulting. Your pride. You think you need the moral high ground. You believe that you need to be seen as right at all times, and that your nation must always be portrayed in the best light possible to the world. Foolish. What is right, and what must be done is far separate than what is best for a nation, or for a people, and especially for you. Tell me, how many people at this table and on the television are up for reelection soon?" The room was awkward and hushed as Ambryn looked face to face. "I thought as much. Now, for my pure opinion in the matter. Vampires are an aberration. A grand mistake in the grand scheme of things. By your standards I have dedicated an enormous period of time to their eradication. More time than this country has existed. It is my advice then that we focus all our efforts on locating Cosmin Dorinescu and all his progeny—with haste—and encourage them at gunpoint to go for a brisk mid-day walk."

That got a round of nervous laughter and a few claps. The president still seemed offended by the dragon's comments though, and his words illustrated as much. "Well, Ambryn, we will make the best decision for the nation, and I thank you for your *candid* words."

So sarcastic. "Mr. President, I believe my brother Tesser once had a conversation with one of your representatives about the domain we dragons have claim over?"

He seemed confused. "Yes, I believe there was some conversation in the matter. What of it?"

"Then you should be aware that regardless of what you and your advisors decide, my actions will be focused on the annihilation of Cosmin and all vampires wherever they may be, Las Vegas or otherwise. If you give them sanctuary, all you will achieve is making my task that much easier."

"That could be ... an unwise decision Ambryn. Think of the public outcry. I wouldn't want our relationship harmed by a rash quest for revenge," the president warned.

Ha. "The public outcry means so very little. Nothing about what I've said is rash. And as far as what's unwise, your nation of three hundred years, give or take, has a pittance in the way of comparable experience to my brethren. My family—my kind—watched the Earth birth from the clouds of stardust in space. We watched the first raindrops fall. We presided over the rise and fall of a million species before yours, and I personally will preside over the fall of yours. It is inevitable. Despite what you're thinking right now, my actions here today are intended to lengthen the stay of humanity on Earth, not shorten it, and you would do well to heed my wishes. It would be an unwise decision to do different."

Now the leader of the free world had open contempt for his challenger. "Listen here. Your brother Tesser is going to hear about this, and he's not going to approve of your statements today. Open threats even. And then the two of you can mince words over who has the last say about what happens here."

"Sir?" Artur said meekly, cutting the argument in half.

"Who are you?" the president barked.

"Artur Cojocaru. I am a varcolac from Romania. I am known to many as The Romanian."

Engaging his mind seemed to calm the president somewhat. It distracted him for a moment at the least. "Yes. I remember your name. Another person we don't know enough about. Someone remind me to look into funding more intelligence gathering activities about the paranormal. You're a werewolf right?"

"Yes. Correct."

"Not a Nazi experiment gone wrong?" the president joked.

Artur didn't laugh. "No. Though my grandparents told me many stories about the Nazis and how my family went against the Romanian government and fought against the Germans during the war. They were smart enough then to take advantage of the magic the world had, and it nearly won the Third Reich that world. Not everything is an evil, Mr. President, but some people, they are very evil."

The president got serious. "This Dorinescu, are you alluding to him? Is there history you can share about him that might sway our decision either way? Some facts would be great if you have them."

Compelling. I wonder what the werewolf knows.

"My grandparents told me many stories as I was growing up. Some were about Cosmin. I can tell you of my own hunt for him in the old country, but I think a story about why my family has sought him out for fifty years might sway you. Something my grandpapa told me. In all this, we mustn't forget *who* we are dealing with, because that is more important than *what* we are dealing with."

"Then by all means, tell us a story."

So the werewolf did.

Chapter Thirty
Artur

Artur made no attempt to hide his accent. "It was before the time of Ceaușescu in Romania. A few years. Early 1960s I believe. Right when the Berlin Wall was going up, my bunic told me. Before I was born. The Soviet Union was pushing our country into industrial work, and we toiled under the communist regime. You could not speak out against the government. I'm sure you have heard all the stories of our labor camps and prisons. I do not tell you that tale. I hail from a small city called Pitesti in the heart of Romania, but my family has roamed the region for more than a century. We spent much time in other countries, moving to where we were told the undead were. Hunters, we are. Paid assassins of the living and the dead where our services were needed and could be afforded."

"Your family served as mercenaries?" the president asked him. "Did you kill more than just vampires?"

"In a manner, yes. I prefer to think of us as exterminators of a very clever kind of vermin. We find evil, and we snuff it out. Sometimes that evil comes in the form of a vampire, and sometimes not."

"Well said," Ambryn muttered.

"Continue, please," the president said softly.

Artur picked up again. "My grandfather was The Romanian at the time; the known hunter of my family, and the man who spoke as our voice, as I do now. He was in the employ of a small village in, I believe it was Czechoslovakia, or maybe Germany. He had been brought in on the train to find out why so many people were sickened or missing. You see, there were many Roma there, many gypsies, people like my own family, and they had magic enough to sort out that there was evil in their town. Gypsies are unwanted, untrusted. We are the … hated people. The minority. We are treated like the bogeyman, and rightfully so I fear. When the local Roma begged for police help they were beaten, laughed at, and left to rot and die in ditches on the side of the road. There was no justice for my people back then."

Artur sipped at a paper cup filled with lukewarm coffee from a hotel cistern. Across the room MacTavish got up and fetched another cup, this one hot, for the speaker. "My grandfather would not suffer our people being abandoned. If we would not be given justice, we would take it ourselves. He went north from Romania and worked for them in exchange for favors to be repaid later. Favors they are still working off to this day; but if it were not for him, they would not be alive to owe favors. A small price they say." Artur took the hot cup of coffee from MacTavish and thanked her.

"Rosice was the town. It was small town," Artur trailed off, reminiscing about something, like a lover remembering a first kiss, but he quickly came back. "My bunic arrived at day, as we wish to do as much as we can. We always want hours in their town while they rest. It gives us time to track down their dhampyr, and taste them to learn."

"I'm sorry Artur, but what's a dhampyr?" the president asked.

"When a male vampire has sex with a human female,

it is possible for her to become pregnant. It is uncommon but not rare. The offspring are called dhampyr. They are stronger and faster than most humans, and are not affected by silver or sunlight. Daylight guardians of their vampire sires."

"I thought vampires were undead? How can a dead thing get a woman pregnant?" one of the talking heads on the television screen asked. Artur knew the man worked in medicine, based on the questions he fielded earlier.

Ambryn answered before Artur could. "How is it that vampires are coherent and able to grow fangs? How is it I am a dragon, yet I sit here as a man? Science cannot explain everything that this wondrous world has to offer. Magic fills in many of the gaps for which science still has no explanation . The binding wonder of the ethereal energy behind all things."

"Voodoo," the doctor said.

"It could very well be in many cases, though vampires do not originate from voodoo practices," Ambryn said back with a knowing smile.

Artur continued. "My bunic, my grandpapa spent two days in Rosice talking to the gypsies and the police he could trust, avoiding the Soviets and seeking out the weakest links in their chains. He slept in the woods at night in the form of a wolf and came back to town during the day as a man," Artur laughed, "it is hard to find a man who doesn't always need to *be* a man. When he finally caught the scent of a dhampyr in the village market at dinnertime, he went in for the kill," Artur's eyes flared in excitement. "He transformed to the dire wolf in the daytime, with the Roma all about, and dragged the dhampyr into the forest with his teeth to seek out his answers."

"How do these incidents not get reported?" one of the other analysts in the room asked aloud. "We have spies everywhere. Wiretaps, paid informants, double agents, you name it. But when we dig back through, there's almost nothing reputable about anything paranormal, and what little we do have is half wrong."

Artur had the answer in his mouth as if it were the only sensible response, "People keep secrets. They are suspicious of authority. They revel in their rituals and their superstitions. It should be no surprise to you how little you know. The wonder of the world must be protected. And the common man and the common women are its guardians."

"There should be a religion built around what he just said," Ambryn said, deadly serious.

"I think the world has an abundance of half-baked faiths, Ambryn," the president joked. The dragon didn't laugh.

"My grandfather said the boy dhampyr tasted rotten, like an old fruit. But the child gave up the face of his father and even remembered where he lived in the village. My bunic ran, and when the Roma who knew of what he hunted saw him running, they ran too. They ran at his heels with knife and pitchfork, with Kalashnikov and Makarov, with fire and steel. They wished their village free of the damned, and they knew that where my grandfather went, their salvation was at hand. Damn the Soviets."

"So to be clear, your grandfather ate a kid, and he had a vision that told him where Cosmin Dorinescu was hiding out?" the same skeptical analyst asked, an incredulous look on his face.

"Yes."

The analyst laughed. "You eat people and learn their secrets? If that's the case, we have a menu of grade-A assholes for you to take a bite out of."

Artur laughed as well, dismissing the idea. "Yes. To a degree, yes I can. But it works best when what we consume is vampiric. The blood is powerful," Artur explained, "It can bring a body back to life, and that's the simplest things it does. There is a… there was an estate in the middle of the village. Big and square, made of white stones, with a bright orange roof of tile with many chimneys to keep it warm, and with tall walls all around topped with iron spikes tipped in the blood of dead thieves. Cosmin hid there, right under the noses of the Soviets and the police. Doing the unspeakable." Artur stopped talking.

"Finish Artur. Please," Ambryn asked the hunter.

Artur coughed, hiding the catch in the throat. "My grandfather leapt the wall, and inside there were more dhampyr. He killed them, but he was shot many times. But it was okay. In the half-wolf war-form we heal fast, unless silver is used, or fire. He said they came at him like wasps, buzzing and stinging his body until he smashed them, bit out their throats, and tossed them away. The villagers, the Roma, smashed at the metal gate as he fought his way inside the home. I remember his face now. Wrinkled, scarred from battle like mine, and trembling with sadness. I can still see his eyes, hazel and whitening with the cataracts of old age, getting wet and looking away as he told me what I am about to tell you," Artur said, his own eyes searching out each person in the room to ensure that they were listening. *Memories like these must be shared. Never forgotten. Never allowed to happen again.*

"Varcolac, like all werewolves and all the wolves of the wild, smell the world before we see it. You see browns and greens, but we catch the scents of sweat and earth. The richest aromas of lust and love, and the heady, gagging reek of fear. My bunic said the smell of death and suffering in the home nearly turned him away. Imagine that? A werewolf stopped at the moment of triumph because of how rotten something smelled. He compared it to the Nazi graves filled with Jews and the enemies of Hitler's ideas. He said it smelled of rotting blood, piss and shit, and cooking meat. And he kept talking of the smell of fear. The scent of desperation. The odor of the captive."

"He had prisoners?" the president asked.

"My grandfather followed the scent. That's what we do, you know? He went to the kitchen, and after tearing the bowels of a dhampyr that had tried to hit him with an axe out and throwing them in the fire, he found a heavy barred door. Locked with padlocks. Big locks on the outside. Locks meant to keep things behind that door. He ripped and tore at the locks, and if it were not for his great strength, they would've held. No human could get past that door with ease. But he did. He tore the door open, and stairs descended into fire-lit darkness. The smell was so bad, he claimed, that he had to shift to human form, to a more ignorant nose—to hide from what he knew would be down there." Artur sipped at his new cup of hot coffee. The only noise in the room came out of the heating vents. A faint whooshing of warm, dry air.

"The basement had been modified to be a dungeon. Wooden tables stained with blood and human filth—dozens my grandfather said—were arranged in crowded filthy rows like at a hospital. Each bed had a woman or a child in it. Each woman was with a baby. Pregnant, I mean. To a one they cried when he entered the room. And each child ... each baby, was being bled. Bled for food for Cosmin. This was how he stayed hidden you see? Stealing women when he could, making them with his babies, and then growing them up to serve him. And when he had enough loyal servants, he fed on his own children as they were born. Safe way to feed. Imagine the mother's horror. To suffer nine months bringing a monster's baby into the world, only then to watch that very monster eat your child? This is a plan twenty, thirty years in the making. Can you not see his madness? Even then he tried to remake the world to better serve him. You say his kind needs rights, and maybe you speak wisdom. Maybe one day they do deserve rights. But I say he is a monster. Any vampiric nation he is the leader of will surely pursue madness and violence as their way."

The absence of blood from the faces of those gathered struck Artur as remarkable.

A young woman moved to tears blew her nose and got Artur's attention. "What happened to the children? The women?"

Artur's voice was distant. Cold. "The women who were redeemable were set free and supported. Brought back to the families and safety again. Some went mad, some killed themselves. Others disappeared. Some did fine. The children were feral ... or simple. They were born into a cold stone basement to be someone's meal. They were never given love. They never experienced the embrace of a mother the way it should be. They were not redeemable."

"They...?"

"The estate was burnt to the ground that night when people saw the basement. Priests and police stood watch until nothing but ash was left."

"Where was Cosmin in all this?" the president asked.

Artur looked helpless. "Fled. Probably gone the first night my grandfather arrived. He left it all to survive. The will to survive is strong in the vampire. They have forever to lose you see. Not just a few decades as we do. And that is why we must find him now. If he says he wishes to make his stand here and make a vampire nation, then perhaps he has decided to make his fight. Perhaps this is our chance to kill him and not be left with a room full of bleeding babies. But again, perhaps he's chosen not to fight until now was because he has never before been prepared to take on the world."

The leader of the free world pinched the bridge of his nose. The worry came off him in waves.

Mr. Doyle cleared his throat, and pitched an idea. "Mr. President, we have until dawn to reply to him as Cosmin's offer indicates before he does whatever it is that he's planning on doing. If I might suggest, you allow our team on the ground here to press. Mobilize whatever military and police support you can to come right now. We search for him at a roughneck pace while you and your advisors find wording on a speech that is sensitive to the needs and rights of the non-humans of the world. If we find him, we'll handle him. If we do not find him in time, your speech puts him on his heels should he follow through on his violent intentions. The United States appears thoughtful, we hopefully kill a heinous villain, or at least delay him until we can find terms that are stomach-able, and should he act, he appears to be an impatient villain to the public."

The president nodded, digesting the idea. "Doyle, I like it. Boys and girls, get on that speech. We have less than twelve hours until dawn, and I want to be on the air with the networks before then." A chorus of replies in the affirmative rang out. "And to all you people on the ground in Vegas," the president said, some steel creeping into his voice, "find that motherfucker."

"Bravo. Finally, a sensible statement," Ambryn said as he got to his feet. "Tell whoever comes to help us to bring silver and fire."

Chapter Thirty-One
Sergeant Danny Ronan

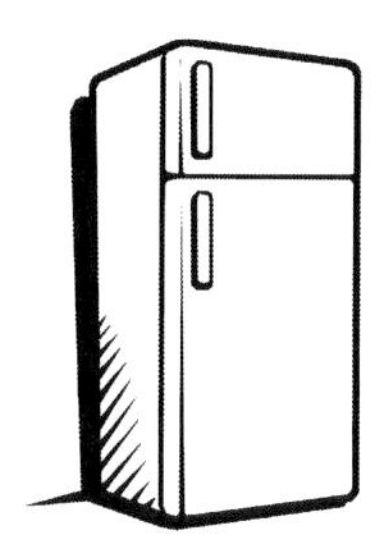

The sun had set on Las Vegas, but the city wasn't any darker because of it. The lights of the casinos cast out in every color of the rainbow lit up the night, bouncing off the clouds and glass sides of the buildings, giving the illusion of safety to those who didn't understand the city, didn't know who hid under the surface, and didn't know who ran the colorful show for real. At a distance, the smooth surface of the ocean of Las Vegas only hid the sharks swimming below it.

Danny had his boys gathered, his sharks, and they were getting ready to hit the long haired freak. When SWAT spun up for a normal job, they geared up at one of the district commands. Body armor, holsters, weapons loaded and rounds chambered, helmets, facemasks and all, were normally adorned and prepared behind a wall, out of the public's eye.

Taking out someone who worked for a federal agency off the clock and entirely against the law meant doing everything a little bit different. For this, they had assembled in the far back end of a dive bar parking lot. The trash that frequented the place would either be drunk off their asses, or such shitty people they wouldn't dare interrupt four big me with guns and a plan.

Danny had put the call out on the 'down-low,' and his four men who served on the Las Vegas metro SWAT team had come running. As they prepared, he gave them a pep talk. "Boys, we got a good shot at impressing Uncle Cosmo right here, right now. I know we're walking a thin line between being in the clear and slipping a noose over our necks, but if we can pull off a single hit on someone tonight our yellow brick road will be laid out for us."

Their yellow brick road didn't lead to the Emerald City. It led to an eternal life, free of sickness and fear. The plan they forged needed to be simple and it had to be based on the need for secrecy. When the night ended, the four men had to be able to return to their normal lives. To that end, a car large enough to hold all the men was stolen from a long term airport parking lot that the police knew had shit security and no cameras. No one would report the car missing for days, and if they got out clean, they could drive the car back and leave it where they found it. *You get what you pay for.*

The cops used their personal weapons. They couldn't use department issued gear. That would be too traceable. Fortunately, men who worked on the SWAT team were firearms enthusiasts by nature, and a substantial selection of choice military grade firepower was at hand straight from their gun safes. Each man brought a selection of pistols, rifles, and shotguns to the back parking lot of that dive bar on the outskirts of the city near the hotel where they knew their target was located.

Danny slid a magazine into his just-bought Ruger SR45 pistol. He'd chosen it not because it was the weapon he was most familiar with, but because no one else knew he owned it, and the heavy .45 hollow points it spit were a pretty versatile answer to aggressive problems. The pistol was a gift he bought for himself less than a month ago. He drew the smooth slide back and chambered a round. He then put the firearm into his waist holster he'd gotten for the gun. *Neat. The loaded chamber indicator works and doesn't snag either. Slick.* He turned to face the gathered men. They all looked far different than they would have during a normal shift or on a regular door-knock. He watched them as they too loaded their weapons.

To mimic a criminal and allow for the blame to land easily at the feet of a group that might be involved in a random shooting, they needed disguises. Only one of the guys was Hispanic, so pretending to be members of MS13 wouldn't fly. None of the men were black either, so posing as either the Bloods or the Crips was a stretch, but they could easily pass for members of one of the biker gangs that rolled through the southwest pushing meth. A few bandanas over the mouths of the men, and some dark sunglasses when the deal went down, and they would easily be fingered as Hell's Angels, Outlaws, or maybe even the Mongols if the light hit them just right. *Doesn't matter who they think we are, so long as they don't think we're the cops.*

"When they get out of the hotel nearby, we'll be in the parking lot. They roll out, we drop in behind them, and as soon as the local cops in the meeting are out of the way, we do it. We have to make sure we don't hit any friendlies. Captain Reilly is in there, and as you all know, he's on Uncle Cosmo's payroll. We need to hit it as clean as possible, make it look like a random shooting, and get the fuck out," Danny said as the men loaded the magazines into their weapons and chambered rounds. The most common rifles amongst them were AK-47s and tricked out AR-15s.

One of the men added after putting his weapon on safe, "And no matter what, hit the tires. We don't need them following us. We don't know what these guys are capable of."

"What if the guy with the long hair gets into the big fucking motor home? What then? My buddy at the ATF heard that it's armored to fuck. With what we have on us right now, there's no way we can knock that thing out. We might as well try and hit an Abrams tank."

Danny racked a shell into his 12 gauge shotgun and set the safety. "If he gets into the tank, then we follow and wait until they get out. We can take a shot at long range if we need to. We're all in the same vehicle, so no one shoots unless it's a go from me, okay? I'll use the scattergun to hit the front tire, and then we're game on. Light the vehicle up," Danny told the men, and they all nodded. One of the men tied a red bandana loosely around his neck. "Everyone ready?" They indicated they were. "Everyone remember why we're doing this, right? Live forever. Young forever. One night of risk for a million nights of happiness, right boys?"

The chorus of approvals was enthusiastic, like a fraternity party with too much beer. They high-fived and knuckle-bumped and started to get into the vehicle.

As the men loaded into the minivan they had stolen not long before, a suspicious and freshly drunk man watched them from the side of the bar not far away. His vision swam as it tried to counteract the jelly in his knees. He considered what he should do about the strange looking criminals that had just driven off, talking about shooting up a tank. On his life he couldn't think of a single good reason a tank would be in Las Vegas, but he was still swimming at the bottom of his deep bottle, dealing with his own demons.

He suddenly thought about a business card in his wallet with a number on it that he knew he could call. He tried to focus on whether that was a good idea or not as the van filled with gunmen pulled out of the bar parking lot and into the orange night of southeast Nevada.

Chapter Thirty-Two

Wayne Simmons

Wayne slid his back down the outside of the bar until his ass met the cool concrete. He slumped like a pile of old laundry. Smelled like it too. *It's cold. Real cold. What the hell, Lord? Why am I here at yet another crossroads?*

He looked down at his brown hands, the palms lighter than the backs. *I served my nation. I am a Marine. And yet you test me Jesus. So I can fail? You take away my daughter and wife, the two women I love more than life itself? What must I do to earn peace? What I am tested so?*

Wayne looked up from his hands just as the taillights of the minivan winked out of eyesight. *I don't know what those men are doing, but they aim to kill, and soon. But who are they on the hunt for? Are they going to kill the vampires? Should I get my pistol and help them?* Wayne tilted his body, lifting one cheek of his ass off the ground an inch and slid the wallet that matched his leathery skin from his pants pocket. With fumbling fingers he tugged out the card he'd remembered earlier, but dropped it between his legs. A gentle gust of cold desert night air blew it several feet away, and panic set in. He dropped his wallet to the ground and leaned forward, grunting to reach out to it.

A slender hand appeared from up high, seeming

angelic, and picked the card up. Wayne's eyes climbed the steep mountain of her thin body and saw the face of the bartender. Wayne remembered that she called herself Heather, but he thought that had been a fake name. She didn't look angelic in the face. She had teeth that had seen better days and skin to match. Her straggly blonde hair fought to escape the unruly ponytail that clung to the skin of her neck. Wayne had enough beers sitting at her bar recently to know her story, if not her real name. Recovering meth addict, and not a good one.

"Wayne, you can't sit in the parking lot like a fucking bum. Conduct yourself like a gentlemen and be a drunk inside with the rest of us. Let me help you," she said, reaching one of her stick-thin arms out to put under his armpit.

Wayne sat back on his haunches, and awkwardly slapped her hand away. The two hands meeting sounded like a wet towel being snapped lazily. "I don't need no help from you, Heather. I just sat down to… Sat down to think on something." He slumped back against the wall of the bar with her looking at him.

She wore a thin shirt that exposed her arms to the cold, and as she shook her head in disgust at him, she rubbed her arms to warm them. He could see the goose pimples on her pale skin. "Wayne, you're pathetic. What would your wife and daughter say to you right now if they were here? You think they'd be proud? Get your shit together man."

Wayne looked up at her, pissed. "Don't talk about my wife. Or my daughter. I know you live in a glass house Heather. You're not perfect. Shauna and Melanie are out there somewhere, and I gotta help them. Gimme that card." Wayne extended a hand up to her, fingers gesticulating for the card. His head pounded. Somehow the hangover had started before the buzz left.

Heather looked at the card and read it. "The International Agency for Paranormal Response. Special

Agent Alanna MacTavish." She looked down at Wayne. "What have you gotten yourself into, Wayne Simmons? You messing around with the boogey man? You going out hunting for the chupacabra?"

"Tapper took over the investigation of the missing buses. They think something evil is at hand, I believe. The Devil's work. I was helping them a little," Wayne said as if he was embarrassed by it.

"You were helping them? Tapper? The spooks? Suit wearing wizards?" Heather asked him in disbelief.

Wayne nodded at her, arm still extended. "I am a Marine, Heather. And yeah. They think something weird happened to the people. Something paranormal."

She crouched down and handed him the card with two extended fingers. "Do you think it was vampires? Or fairies? I do love that show True Blood."

Wayne took the card from her and looked at the writing. "Maybe vampires. Maybe werewolves. I don't know, Heather. What I do know is that with my very eyes now I saw a van filled with big men with guns leave this parking lot, and they was talking about taking down a tank. For some reason, I feel like I need to call this woman. And I know I should just call 911 instead. Can you tell me why I want to call her instead? I can't figure it out…" Wayne sounded despondent. Lost.

Heather produced a cigarette from her waist apron pocket and lit it up with a lighter as she thought on it. Her eyes popped open. "You trust her. That's easy. Wait. Those Tapper people have been in town right? Is that big black van I keep seeing theirs? The big bus? I saw it on my way in tonight at the hotel just down the way. Whole mess of cruisers and state cars there too."

Wayne's guts flushed with adrenaline, forcing a sobriety onto him he suddenly wished he didn't have. "They call those buses 'tanks' damn it all. Those thugs. That's why I want to call her. They goin' after the Tapper people." The connection made, Wayne reached into his other back pocket with far steadier hands. He produced his phone, and after coordinating his digits, he dialed the number on the card. *Lucky I didn't crack the phone when I sat down.*

"Do you think?" Heather said as he waited to talk, tugging on her cigarette with pursed, cold lips. "Is there going to be some kind of shootout? Lord, we should get inside. I don't wanna be turned into a pile of red Jell-O or shot with a beam of light."

As the line rang in his ears Wayne extended his arm to Heather, and she helped him to his feet. It took the wall's support as well, but he was upright when the line picked up.

"Agent MacTavish, how can I help you?" a woman's voice said into his ear.

She sounds pretty on the phone. Too bad about that scar. Hell, she's still good looking. Scar just show she's tough. A man needs a tough woman. Alright. Don't sound drunk. "Miss MacTavish? This is Wayne Simmons, you remember me?" *That sounded good.*

"Yes, I do sir, you have a daughter and wife involved in the case we're investigating. Thank you for your assistance the other day. Is there something I can help you with?"

"I think there might be something I can help you with Agent. I am over at the Bighorn Saloon, I think maybe not far from where you are, and I just watched a handful of white guys get into a minivan, loaded up for some shooting."

"Have you called 911 yet?" she asked him.

"No, I wanted to call you first. I overheard them say something right before they left, and I think you should know," Wayne said. *I hope she listens.*

"Yes? Is it relevant to the case?" MacTavish asked him. He could hear her moving. A door shutting in the background.

"Right as they left, one of them said something about

hitting a tank. Something armored. Can you think of any tanks in Las Vegas? The only tank I can think of is that big black bus you were driving the other day." *Listen to me. Listen to me woman. Something isn't right with this. You're the people to call when something isn't right, right?*

"What did the minivan look like, which direction did it head in, and when did this happen?"

Chapter Thirty-Three

Artur Cojocaru

After waiting for the slew of vehicles to depart ahead of them, heading to various parts of Las Vegas to intensify the search for Cosmin Dorinescu, the black rental SUV glided away from the hotel parking lot leisurely with Spoon behind the wheel. The night sky above was dyed a bluish orange, the color of a bruised peach from the sodium arc streetlamps covering the metro area.

"Alright so we've established that eating dead vampires is bad for you. What do you think would work?" Spoon asked Artur.

Ambryn sat beside him in the front passenger seat. "Would one of the guards I killed in the club fetch you a worthwhile vision?"

Artur was in the truck's middle seat row, sitting behind the shorter Spoon. "If they had seen something worth remembering before their deaths, then yes. Visions from the flesh take only minutes for me to experience. If you take me to their bodies, I can taste many quick. All if there are just a few."

"Might be five of them. I'll head back to the county coroner's office. We haven't released the bodies to the families yet. Hey Artur, how are you feeling? Can you even risk trying more of the... meat?" Spoon asked him morbidly as they took a turn into the traffic on a different surface street.

Artur looked out the tinted windows as the buildings flew by, a blur. "I feel much better. Two-skins heal faster than a full blooded man or woman. If I could get time in my wolf body, I would heal even faster. After say, a ten minute time as wolf, I would risk the flesh of the thugs. I think their bodies are safe."

"What can your body heal from?" Spoon asked innocently.

The hunter learning how to hunt a new prey. I know how to seek out weakness. "We are very strong and fast, but I am quite killable, if that's your concern Agent," Artur said, laughing. "If you wound me bad enough, I can bleed out and die, but that is hard. Strike my head from my shoulders, pierce my heart or liver, drown me, or set me aflame, and I will die. Never mind our allergy to silver."

"So that old wife's tale is true?" Spoon asked as Ambryn listened, looking out the window.

"Yes. Wisdom passed down through the years from the educated. Something I wish of course that had been forgotten," Artur said. "Something about silver makes the wounds we suffer from them refuse to heal. It is a bane to our very existence. Ambryn, dragon friend you said silver was special from the Kaula?"

Ambryn's head bobbed in acknowledgment. "We needed a weapon humans could use against the vampires. Against many things they—you—were ill-equipped to kill on their own. This is long before the age of science that propelled you all forward the past six or seven hundred years. Firearms and explosives, and all the things you've created have leveled the playing field far more than we could've anticipated. In all, I'm pleased. Your science mixed with silver, and now with magic flourishing more than ever before... it will lead to the extinction of the vampire. I'll see to it."

There is a story here. He chooses to share moments of it, but not the whole tale. "She, Kaula, cursed the metal?"

"Yes, I suppose that'd be one way to describe it. We needed Garamos as well. His manipulation of the earth below made silver more prevalent, and absorbent of the energy, thus more deadly for our purposes. I gave some of my personal essence to the metal, and Kaula bound it all, casting her spell out across the entire world."

Fascinating. "If what you three did so long ago was intended to kill the vampire, I forgive you for the suffering of my people. Two-skins of the world should know this. We would curse silver less. It is a badge of honor."

"Strange that you would celebrate a weakness," Ambryn said with a grin.

"Strange that you do not embrace your weaknesses dragon friend. There is power when you can take away your fears. To stand against your nemesis, and look it in the eye. Is good."

"I think that is a conversation to be had with someone other than a dragon Artur," Ambryn said.

Spoon's phone rang, and he answered it using the car's Bluetooth system. Apparently he and Ambryn had an argument prior about using the phone while driving. The dragon thought it was dangerous. So *responsible, the dragon of death.*

"Hello?" he said aloud.

"Henry we've got a big problem. I think," the lady agent's voice said. "I just got a call from a guy who helped Mr. Doyle and I when we hit the ground here, and he said as many as four to six heavily armed perps loaded into a minivan less than thirty minutes ago, not far from the hotel we met at. He said they were going to try and hit the tank. He had been drinking, but I think this is on the level. Spoon I think the vampires might be coming after us before we go after them."

"Fuuuuuuck," Spoon said softly as he squinted and looked more intently at the side and rear-view mirrors. Ambryn and Artur followed suit and did the same. *Some cars around us. But we are not the bus.* "What vehicle are they in?"

"Dark colored, late model minivan," she said through the car's speakers.

They all looked out the SUV's windows, searching for a threat in the flow of traffic. Artur saw two minivans that might've matched the description. "Two, behind us, several cars back."

Spoon was already zeroed in on them, and Ambryn's eyes were fixed as well. "I see them," the agent said as he reached under his suit jacket for his pistol.

"Henry get back here. There's a pair of minivans in the parking lot outside and I think one of them might be our guys. I've got Doyle and no backup to protect him."

Henry laughed out loud. "Call 911 for some black and whites. We aren't more than a minute or two away. And don't worry about Doyle. You aren't here to protect him. He can handle that on his own. We'll see you soon."

"Hurry," Alanna said before cutting the call.

"I'm gonna bang a U-turn here, and we're gonna get back to the hotel stat. If anything turns to follow us, that'll be our target. Just make sure if we defend ourselves, it's justifiable. Hold on to your skivvies boys," Henry said as he did one last check in the mirrors.

"Justifiable to what authority, Henry?" Ambryn asked, flashing a smile that had a few extra teeth in it.

The will of our dragon is justification enough. Henry spun the wheel after stepping on the brake, and the big SUV turned sharply in the wide road, pulling a full 180. Artur spied every vehicle behind them as Henry pressed the accelerator down, and they sped back towards the hotel. It's tall structure towered in the near distance. "No one has turned," Artur advised.

"Looks clear ahead. Wait, that's a minivan right there

isn't it?" Spoon asked Ambryn, pointing with a finger from his hand on the wheel.

The only one of the three whose brain was able to piece the next moment together was Ambryn, and as he saw the orange flash of a gun's muzzle flare ahead, and then heard, watched and felt the impact of a hundred shotgun pellets simultaneously destroying the windshield, all he could think of was the welfare of his two friends.

Chapter Thirty-Four

Agent Alanna MacTavish

Alanna disconnected from the 911 call and dropped her phone into her suit jacket pocket. It thumped against the stiff Kevlar she wore underneath her agency white shirt. She stood in the ostentatious lobby of the hotel filled with faux gold trim and carvings of exotic animals, all leering down at her, silently threatening her to slide a coin into the myriad slot machines scattered around the giant building. *Cops will be here in less than fifteen minutes. I just need to last that long. Fifteen minutes.* She ignored the artificial beasts and scanned the room for her charge, but Doyle was nowhere to be found.

Dammit! Where did he go? I don't understand how a guy his age can be this damn hard to keep an eye on. Slippery old shit. I bet he kicked ass at hide and seek. She tucked an errant lock of blonde hair that had escaped from the bun on the back of her head behind her ear with her left hand. In her right she held her sidearm, the Tapper standard issue Glock 22. Her firearm, like every other piece issued to the exclusive Tapper agents like herself, had been in the hands of either Mr. Doyle or one of his trusted apprentices for a custom enchantment. The slide of her weapon had a faint tracing of runes and etchings that supposedly gave the weapon enhanced battle capability. She had read the report on the spells active on the weapon, but hadn't seen it in use yet. Neither she nor the handgun had been in a fight since their union. *I think tonight that changes.*

She looked at the counter employees. *They are staring at me and this gun.* "Hey, it would be a good idea if you had all your guests stay away from their windows for the next half hour. And if I were you, I'd get behind a locked door too."

The woman behind the counter, a wilted flower of a young woman who looked like she took community college classes during the day and worked at night at the expense of decent sleep, bit her lip and nodded. She reached for the lobby phone to do what Alanna asked.

On the other side of the wall of glass doors that passed for an entrance to the lobby Alanna saw Mr. Doyle puttering around at the side of the tank. She had parked the bus earlier at the far side of the enormous parking lot, well over fifty yards distant. The old man stood bent over at the waist, doing something to his shoes. Tying them maybe. *There he is.* Alanna took off out of the lobby of the hotel at a trot with all the workers still staring at her in fear. The people of the city stood on a tipping point. Going missing had become a very real possibility for everyone, and the amount of armed police on the prowl city-wide served only to boost paranoia. It felt a lot less like carefree Sin City tonight than it did the Gaza Strip.

Through the doors and into the chilly night she went, focusing on the roads nearby the hotel and keeping the barrel of her pistol pointed at the ground. When she was only twenty yards from the tank, the Brit called out to her.

"Agent MacTavish, your firearm?" he asked, raising his eyebrows and looking at the extended hand with the gun in it.

I'll be damned, but he just reached for something out of his pocket. Is that a stick of wood? He thinks I'm coming to shoot him. Ha. "Mr. Doyle, I just got a call from that Wayne Simmons fellow. He just witnessed a vanload of armed men leave a nearby bar, speaking about hitting a tank." Alanna tilted her head towards the big bus. The misbehaving lock of dirty blonde hair slipped free again, and she restrained it once more.

"Oh dear," he said in reply as his posture eased the tiniest bit.

"I think they are heading this way right now," Alanna said, bringing her attention back to the surrounding area. She could see well. There were few cars in the well-lit lot that night, but that meant the available cover left something lacking. She paid close attention to the entrance of the parking lot.

"Allow me a moment to prepare my battle garb," he said as he slipped up the stairs into the tank. Alanna moved into cover at the corner of the tank and kept watch. In a moment she heard closets opening and closing inside the armored RV and heavy plastic cases being cracked open. As she listened, a strange feeling came over her. *All the hairs on the back of my neck are on-end right now. Static electricity from inside? Battle nerves? Shit, I bet that's magic. Real magic.* Her eyes caught a glimmer of light from below her field of vision and she dared a glance down. The runes on her pistol were no longer dull, lifeless carvings in the flat steel. They were now filigreed light, swimming on the surface of the metal like golden threads swaying, blowing carelessly in a summer breeze. It mesmerized her. A child-like smile crept onto her face. A smile full of wonder. A smile filled with hope. *Well I'll be damned.*

She flinched when she heard the unmistakable

discharge of a shotgun in the near distance. The boom of the weapon seemed an alien noise in the city limits. *Fuck. Fuck. Spoon.*

Alanna found it hard to breathe as she holstered her pistol and bolted up the stairs of the tank. She had but one train of thought—go to her comrade. Go to her friend. Her fumbling hands got the keys out of her pocket and into the ignition faster than she expected. *Practice makes perfect.* The tank rumbled to life, and she threw it into gear.

"Is that gunfire I hear?" Mr. Doyle asked from behind her as the truck jumped forward. He grabbed a cupboard to avoid tumbling to the rear of the big RV. She took a fraction of her focus away from steering the beast of a vehicle and listened over the groan of the big engine. The belching roar of the shotgun had stopped, only to be replaced by the terrorizing ripping sounds of fully automatic gunfire. Ahead she could see diminutive flashes bounce off of cars and buildings near where the guns were being shot.

"Yes," she muttered as the tank turned in the direction of the firefight.

"Do hurry," he said as he moved back to his cases and whatever arcane mysteries were inside them.

"I'm hurrying," Alanna said. The front of the RV had only just straightened on the roadway when they saw the engagement. No attempt at subtlety had been made by the attackers. The dark van the gunmen made their attack from had turned sideways in her lane, and a cluster of men were using it as cover from Spoon's vehicle. They were unleashing a hellacious amount of fire on the black truck in which Spoon, Artur, and Ambryn had left the hotel. It had smashed into a building at the side of the road, both driver's side tires shot out. They'd crashed into an auto parts store, and the SUV sat awkwardly, stuck in the wide glass front, caught on a lip of stone and exposed to the withering gunfire.

I see no return fire. Where's Ambryn? Where's the damn dragon? Don't we have a werewolf here too? God, I hope they aren't dead ... Look at these guys. Changing mags smooth, taking cover, communicating. "Those are professionals. Look at them. Cops, soldiers, something," she said as the bus roared down the street, swerving like a lumbering rhino around cars that had screeched to a halt. *Shit, one of the dudes is huge. Looks like a frigging bear wearing a bandana on his muzzle.*

"Ram them," came Doyle's callous response.

"What? Won't that fuck up the bus?" Alanna asked as the bore down on the van. She forced the pedal down, making the bus pick up speed, and they hadn't turned to her yet. They were caught up in executing their ambush. *Executing my friend.*

"To hell with the bus. It's built to withstand worse, and my spells will hold if they were cast right. If not, to hell with it. Tesser will buy us another. Hit them. Smash them into pulp," Mr. Doyle said.

Fuck, he is angry. "You got it." Alanna floored it harder, and the tank responded as best it could. One of the men looked over his shoulder at them finally and turned to fire.

Watching the muzzle flashes from down the pipe straight at her spiked her adrenaline worse than Alanna had ever experienced. Her fingers were numb and her mouth dry. She couldn't even see in the peripheral; the only world for her in the moment sat right out the windshield in front of her. Not a single bullet spat at her hit her, however. The windshield of the tank cracked and spider webbed, leaving golf ball sized impacts in the ballistic glass. Her brain danced a memory of Humvee windows in Afghanistan firefights for no good reason. "This glass won't hold forever," she said through gritted teeth.

"Then I suggest you duck," Doyle said, right before the moment of impact.

This is what you get for fucking with my people. Alanna held onto the wheel until she felt sure she couldn't miss the van, and then folded over to the side. As her head went behind the dash and the bus' communications gear, she saw the man who'd unloaded on her dive out of the way, avoiding being pulped by no more than a yard. She didn't see what happened to the others. *He gets shot first.*

The tank hit the van, and all she felt came to her as a slight tremor through her seat and a tightening of her seatbelt. The noises though, were terrible. The sounds of screeching metal and tearing rubber penetrated the glass in a way the bullets could not, and it jarred her. Large pieces of plastic and metal erupted into the air like tossed toys or garbage in the wind. The tank demolished the van in whole, all in an instant. Foot on the brake, the tank rumbled to a slow stop in the center of the street, shaking and rumbling with each foot traveled. The broken and hammered van sat wrapped around the front bumper of the tank, no longer recognizable as anything but scrap metal with some wheels somewhat attached.

"I'm out!" Alanna yelled to her passenger before she hit the switch for the exit door on the side of the bus. It flung open smoothly and she drew her pistol again, the golden, glowing runes warming her eyes as they danced more wildly than before, sensing the battle to come as vividly as she herself did. She moved to leave, to engage the enemies outside, and hopefully carry out some kind of rescue.

"Alanna wait!" Doyle yelled, but her mind was set. She didn't even hear him speak. Her people were in harm's way, and she had a job to do. She must help. She could do nothing but help, no matter the cost. Mr. Doyle ran towards the exit to follow her, and he watched what happened next from mere feet away.

Her angry eyes up, searching for the man with the fully automatic weapon who had tried to shoot her, she hit the streets moving quickly. She heard a burst of automatic fire from her right, close enough that she could feel the burn from the barrel's exhaust in her side.

It wasn't the hot gasses she felt hitting her in the side of her torso, impacting and penetrating the body armor she wore beneath her black suit jacket and crisp, starched agency white shirt. She didn't have the time to realize the error in her senses before one of the 7.62mm rounds hit her just above the right ear, and blew the top of her head off, dirty blonde hair and all.

Alanna MacTavish's world went black just shy of nine minutes into the fifteen she wanted to last. By all measures, she could only be called a hero.

Chapter Thirty-Five
Ambryn

Immortality came with an interesting price for those with a soul. It could be argued that vampires had no soul, and certainly Ambryn would staunchly support that stance. The dragon of death had a soul, tarnished and tortured as it might be, and even though his domain was that of the end of life, and despite the eons of time that he had overseen the annihilation of life by his own efforts willingly, when anything died for pointless causes, he felt some sadness, as if he were a child that had accidently dropped their ice cream to the ground while licking it. Something sweet and pure defiled for no reason other than a calamity of bad fortune. He felt less sadness for the simpler forms of Earth's life. He would not fret over the passing of a snail, or an insect, and it would be a rare day indeed that he shed a tear for the death of a mouse or a crocodile. Once in a blue moon when a special human died Ambryn would shed a tear. Tonight, as Spoon laid flat over the center console of the truck they were in and as the windshield disintegrated under a hail of bullets as the car headed towards a collision with a building, Ambryn made a vow.

Not these humans. Not tonight.

"Down down down!" Spoon yelled against the onslaught of projectiles that were eating away his rental. His warnings were cut short as they impacted the windows and entryway of the side of a building. The SUV rode up onto a brick wall and smashed into the interior corner, nearly tossing them all about. Racks of car rims, exhausts, and stereo systems tilted and crashed to and fro, some landing on the SUV, crushing the hood while others fell deeper into the store. In seconds, the entire business was torn asunder. All three occupants in their car were held firm by their seatbelts, which quickly turned from a boon into a bane. Ambryn watched as the van skidded to a stop in the center of the street as their own vehicle's crushed engine died out with a sputter, and they settled, unable to move. The men trying to murder them got out of the van and moved into cover on the hood and behind a light pole, preparing to shoot.

I need to get the humans to safety while they prepare for another round of fire. Ambryn looked at Spoon, who had been knocked half-senseless by the crash. He had a few bumps and bruises, and a few of the shotgun pellets had hit him, but at a quick glance, he seemed like he would survive. His bulletproof vest had proven its worth. In the back seat, Artur had disappeared. Restrained inside the seatbelt instead, covered in the tatters of Artur's torn clothing was a massive wolf, covered in fur as bright white as the highest winter cloud. The wolf whimpered as it attempted to raise its head, and Ambryn saw the blossoming spread of fresh red blood at the werewolf's shoulder. *He has been shot far worse than Spooner.*

Ambryn's left hand slipped down and hit the release on his own seatbelt as a thrown right elbow simultaneously blasted his door right off the vehicle frame. After screeching free from the body of the SUV, it cart wheeled into the dark shop, smashing something glass apart. Perhaps a display case. With his eyes on the men who were about to shoot at he and his friends, the dragon hopped out of the truck and hit Spoon's belt release. It did nothing. It was jammed.

"Help me," Spoon pleaded in a haze, looking in the dark at the dragon. His head was split above his left ear, and a cascade of blood streamed in a sheet down his cheek out of the gash. He spat some of his blood on the dash reflexively when it invaded his mouth. It slid down the fake leather and vinyl like sludge.

"I have you," Ambryn said as he wrapped his hand around the latch and yanked. The anchor of the restraint tore apart in his hand as if it were made of no more than tinfoil and matchsticks. The belt retracted and Ambryn grabbed Spoon roughly, yanking him out of the driver's seat just as automatic gunfire peppered it, ripping the fabric apart. Ambryn watched the invading holes appear in the door like piercing javelins of orange light. He felt some of the slugs impact his chest and face and watched some tear apart the seat fabric, but ignored it all. Their bullets weren't enough to kill or even harm him. He looked to the wolf in the back seat as the bullet holes appearing in the side of the truck walked towards it. *But the bullets can kill him.*

Ambryn dove into the SUV, twisting and contorting between the seats, somehow putting his body between the downpour of bullets and Artur's wolf body. Artur yelped in pain as the dragon shoved the wolf's injured form away from harm. Ambryn winced as round after round tore into him. He feared not for his own safety or pain, but as each bullet bit into his back, it was a strike of doubt and fear for a round that might slide past his body and into the werewolf. Like an umbrella held against the pouring rain, sooner or later drops would defeat him. He pulled, pushed, and wrangled the mewling man-wolf across the back middle row of the SUV towards the passenger side, kicking out as he wrapped up the wolf's body in his arms, creating a draconic cocoon of safety. The door didn't launch away like the first from his foot's impact, though he had caved in the interior molding. As he kicked it again, he risked a glance out the now shattered window of the back seat to see what was happening with the minivan.

He looked up just in time to see the massive black monolith of Doyle's bus hit it at a full clip. The effect looked devastating and entirely entertaining. The men shooting somehow dove out of the way, but the van didn't. All of the van's glass erupted into a shining white froth and broke free of the doors and front in bent sheets of bluish white. The body of the blue minivan bent in half against the heavy front of the bus, practically fusing with it as the brakes engaged, and the bus started to shudder to a stop. The van had been pancaked and ripped apart.

It's like a big bug got smashed on an even bigger windshield, stuck and rather dead. Good, that will buy me a moment. Ambryn used that moment to turn and kick the car door a third time, and with this kick, the metal gave way under his God-like strength. *If I were Garamos or Tesser, the first kick would've been enough. Curse my smaller form. Humans and their engineering too.*

Ambryn slid out of the SUV into the interior of the store with Artur in his arms while the chaos outside was in a lull. The arrival and crash of the bus into the van had sent the four men attacking them astray, and the dragon quickly got the wolf out and behind the engine block of the SUV before they gathered themselves and attacked. Spoon had his back against the front wheel of the vehicle, and he had drawn his big pistol. With closed eyes, he tried to hold it upright and steady. In his daze he still wanted to contribute to their defense. The wobble of the barrel and the unsure look on Spoon's blood streaked face told the dragon he needed time before he was ready to join the fight. A short burst of gunfire told Ambryn the men were coming soon.

"Stay here. Protect Artur. He's hurt worse than you," Ambryn said, crouched.

"All over that. Be safe," Spoon muttered, his words muddled.

"Safe won't tear these men apart," Ambryn said, the thrill of the shape shift coming over him. He winked at Henry, stood to his full height, and vaulted the hood of the truck, landing on two transforming feet.

Not every dragon of Earth could take different forms at will. Garamos and Kiarohn were stuck in dragon-form forever, which wasn't the worst problem an inhabitant of Earth could have. But for most of the dragons who could assume different shapes, there were rules. For instance Fyelrath, dragon of water and ocean, could only assume the forms of things that could swim. Fortunately for her, a human body can swim. Ambryn could assume any form of something he hunted, and in this instance, he had lost interest in being a two-legged, soft skinned, hair covered creature.

He needed to be a bit more natural.

The transformation took mere moments. As he strode into the street his legs extended to their full length, joints reversing painlessly with a fluid series of pops and twists. His torso elongated as his chest widened and thickened, his ribs reaching out to create room for his growing lungs and dragon heart under his darkening and hardening skin. His jaw distended, forming a snout and mouth filled front to back with viciously large and sharp teeth reminiscent of the stone formations in a long forgotten cave. His wings came last. Wide, membranous, and as dark as the night sky above the orange city light they sprouted from his back with a flap, and a loud snap.

There. Much better.

When his arms finished their shift, he dropped to all fours, fifty feet long from nose to tip of tail, and he informed the four men that the dragon of death was ready to finish what they started.

He roared. Glass shattered in a hundred yards in every direction.

The traffic coming in both directions had been stopped or in reverse for some time now, and as he plodded forward towards the center of the street to find the men, the stopped vehicles with their stunned passengers jammed their cars into reverse and fled. A distant gun battle could be a believable reality, horrifying at a minimum to most, but a dragon ... The fear instilled by seeing the world's alpha, entirely dominant life form had a different effect entirely on the human psyche. Ambryn's mouth curled into a satisfied smile as he swung his serpentine neck side to side, looking for the fleeing men. His massive nostril inhaled a cold gust, taking in the sweat, car exhaust, and cordite hanging in the air. He knew two of the men had bolted down an alley beside the auto parts store they had crashed into, and he opted to kill them first.

A single flap of both wings combined with a leap sent him two stories up into the air, allowing him to land on the flat roof of the store they had crashed into minutes before. The brick edge of the building where his rear feet planted gave way, sending bricks tumbling down into the street below, and he had to grab on with a taloned hand to prevent his massive body from falling with them. *That would appear ungraceful. Can't have that.* His long neck, studded down the spine with a row of sharpened bony protrusions, peered over the edge just as one of the men turned. He tripped and fell to his back, grunting in pain, but the man retained enough presence of mind in the narrow gap between buildings to rip off the rest of his magazine ineffectually into Ambryn's face.

He might as well have spat in the dragon's eye for all the damage it did to him. The effect would've been at least insulting.

Speaking of spitting, unlike his larger brothers Tesser and Garamos, and his faster sister Zeud, Ambryn could not conjure forth a stream of immolation from his mouth. He could not breathe fire. There was no reason for him to use the immortal power of the flame in his tasks. He should be able to kill species, not just single enemies or irritants, and the weapon given to him fit such a task masterfully.

Ambryn spat at the man. And woe to that man's life for the dragon of death did not spit mundane saliva, neither acid nor lava or even something so mundane as mud. He spat disease. He spat pestilence. He spat a mixture of cancers and poxes and afflictions custom made by his immortal draconic will to ensure the immediate death of the man below, and only that man. If Ambryn wanted all of humanity to die… he would spit something slightly different.

The small glob of certain doom rifled down between the two buildings as the man struggled to switch out the banana shaped magazine of his rifle. No bigger than a baseball and the consistency of gelatin, it struck him in the chest, knocking the fresh magazine out of his hands and splashing up in a viscous tide against his neck, ripping away the blue bandana he had affixed over his mouth. The brackish, infectious substance slipped over his lips and into his mouth, and the man knew terror. He now owned an inescapable doom, for it had already gotten *inside* him.

Ambryn ignored his screams as his bile and saliva twisted and contorted the man's flesh straight from within, ripping him through too many vicissitudes, too fast for his poor body to survive. Ambryn heard the man's ribcage swell and crack as innumerable growing tumors exploded inside him, spreading pus and blood to places in the alley already most foul. His skin swelled with buboes, festering and sloughing off in sheets. *May your suffering suit the evil you have wrought.*

Ambryn took flight.

The sky. My home away from home. His wings were not as aerially dexterous as Kiarohn's, but his status as one of the smallest dragons meant he was lighter, and coupled with his enormous strength, that meant he was an excellent flyer. With focus and well-timed beats of his massive black wings, he could rise above the flat earth and hover in the air. He looked down upon the square and rectangular buildings of the Las Vegas suburb from a hundred feet above and watched for the flashes of darkness that meant the movement of his prey. It took only seconds to see the leather-jacket wearing goon slip out from an attempted hiding place behind a bright green dumpster. He ran for his life.

So sad. Failure breeds fear.

Ambryn flapped once more with both wings in unison, stabbing his head towards the ground, and his tail to the sky, flipping in midair in a maneuver that defied all manner of science and logic. The dragon grinned like the Devil, and plunged to the ground towards the man that ran away, unaware that in every sense possible, death literally fell from the sky for him.

Ambryn flared his wings just before impact, putting his feet first, his claws splayed wide to smash the man into the ground. The dragon of death tried halfheartedly to keep him alive, but his thousands of pounds hitting the man from above bisected him when his body hit the pavement of the street below. His torso shot away, squirted apart from his hips and legs, arms fishing, gun dropped. His moans were bubbly, blood filled and desperate.

"Oh come now," Ambryn said in a soft dragon voice that rumbled and bellowed. "You can't be surprised that death came for you, playing games as you did. Big boy rules, yes?" The torso's arms stopped moving in response. "Fine. As you wish." *Now to find your friends.*

A single shot from a smaller gun rang out back at the crash scene. *A pistol. I think I'll start looking there.*

Ambryn took flight once more.

Chapter Thirty-Six
Mr. Doyle

Mycroft Rupert Doyle, aged and wise wizard, survivor of two known world wars, master of many arcane arts from around the known world, and the master of a few arts from parts still unknown, watched the top of Agent Alanna MacTavish's head come undone. It broke apart and flipped open with forceful violence that made his stomach turn. He hadn't exited the tank yet, his feet still planted on the recessed steps as it happened. She had hit the ground and panned left, her enchanted handgun up and searching for the men who were trying to kill her friends. But one man had somehow gotten around to her right, behind where she had her attention pointed. She was turning back in the man's direction, but before her gun met the area he stood in, the attacker peeled off a burst of chattering automatic fire into her side at point black range. She could not survive such a blast without more sorcery serving her.

Each flash from the attacker's barrel froze her face in profile in Doyle's mind. Exposures taken through the shutter of his eyes that would be burnt into the film of his memory forever. *Or until I die.*

Each report of the gun walked the barrel an inch

higher, sending the round out a few inches above the last. The final two bullets struck her first in the shoulder, and then in the head. Doyle didn't see exactly where it hit her skull, but the result killed her and ripped his heart apart. Her legs left her. Her arms went limp. She fell to the pavement, irrevocably dead, her loyalty and fearlessness earning her an inglorious death at the hands of an evil person, and a spreading pool of blood.

Her killer surely heard me yell to her to stop. He'll be firing in this doorway next. The young-seeming eyes of the old man fixed on the barrel of the gun. His mind worked fast as the gunman moved on him, his fast-thinking the product of a celeritas spell, and years of being in the wrong place at the wrong time but doing the right things all the same. *Sharp metal ring at the barrel's tip. Short barrel. Gas return above, exposed. It's an AK-47. A custom one. This shooter loves his weapons. I know.*

"Collabefio," Mr. Doyle said with haste, pointing at the tiny edge of the weapon's banana-shaped magazine. He hadn't properly prepared the spell, but he had faith in baby Astrid and everything she brought to the world.

His faith was rewarded. To use a collabefio spell appropriately you would use it during the crafting of an enchanted item. It was intended to be used at a forge, with anvil and flame present, in times of peace and creativity. This application of the smelt spell wouldn't do what it could do under those conditions, but if he instilled enough energy and will into it...

A split second after the last syllable of the word left this lips Doyle felt a flare of power surge in the air between he and his attacker. The steel of the magazine suddenly turned a cherry color, burning red hot within from the incantation. A moment later, as the attacker stepped into view, his identity obscured by a blue bandana and his finger tightening on the trigger of his weapon, the bottom rounds in the magazine cooked off with a series of ear splitting cracks. All hell broke loose in his hand.

In a moment as funny as it was violent, the bottom of the magazine exploded out, warping the steel into a twisted flower petal shape. He pulled the trigger somehow as the gun flew out of his hand, shrapnel penetrated his thigh, and a single 7.62mm round pierced the air a scant half inch from Doyle's left ear.

The gun failed to fire again.

Dirty bitch. In a race to death, the shooter slung his broken AK to his wounded hip smoothly and started to draw a pistol on his belt as Doyle pulled a two hundred year old Pakistani kukri from a sheath he'd moments before the shooting strapped to his leg. Doyle didn't try much more than an underhand toss of the knife at the man, and that's how the race was won. "Exentero!" Doyle shouted fast at the knife just as the pistol's barrel reached the level of his feet. *It would seem the few extra inches of elevation afforded me by the stairs of this bus might save my life.*

The spell ensorcelled the blade, and rather than bouncing off the assailant impotently, it lurched once, spun twice, and soared into the belly of the man just below the bottom of his ribs. He tried to slap the animated, stabbing blade out of the air with his free hand, and lost all his fingers for the trying. They fell to the bloody pavement like a dropped can of Vienna sausages. He screamed as the kukri continued its murderous work. The slicing blade hit something hard below the man's clothing, giving off a 'clacking' sound. *Armor. The bastard is bloody armored.* The blade's magic fought against the science of the Kevlar and the plate as Doyle drew a battle tested Colt 1911 from his hip. The man backpedaled as the blade spun and spun, digging, eating away at the bulletproof material, and backing the desperate man away. With his free hand Doyle tilted the plane of his palm, and then lowered it.

The blade mimicked the motion of his hand, and

Doyle relished it as the blade found a space between the armored plate and the doomed man's belt buckle. "For Alanna," Doyle said under his breath.

The blade devastated. It split him open and dove inside his lower abdomen like a rabid animal, disappearing, chewing, and destroying his intestines, stomach, bladder, and anything else that couldn't get out of the way. The smell of piss, shit and blood sprang into the air as the man fell to the ground on his back, screaming. "Exentero," Doyle whispered, ending the blade's horrible spiral. It remained within the attacker's body

"Oh God. Jesus please, shit," the man said in perfect educated American. Using the hand that still had fingers the man pulled down his bandana and gasped for salvation.

They certainly don't speak the Queen's English here now do they? Doyle lifted his pistol after ensuring the safety was off and the hammer drawn back. He leveled the sights on the man's face, and took a step to him. He whimpered as Doyle kicked the man's dropped pistol away. Nearby, the fully transformed Ambryn made a noise that destroyed every piece of glass for hundred yards around. Doyle reveled in the sound of a deafening dragon's roar. *There he is. My trump card.*

"You brought a machine gun," Doyle said, looking over at the broken AK-47. "I brought a dragon." The man coughed, his eyes wide and dilating fast as he slipped into shock. "Now tell me, do right by the fine young woman you just murdered in the process, and explain to me why this happened."

The man coughed again, and a fleck of blood landed on his lower lip. It was laced with phlegm, and spittle. *The blade managed to find your lung then.* "We just wanted… to live… forever. You wouldn't understand."

"You don't know me that well. You work for the vampire?" He nodded at Doyle. His head lolled to the side and he winced. "Where is Cosmin? He is about to do something stupid young man, and you can help us stop it. He wants to kill thousands. To create a state for the undead here in Nevada. No one else will stop him unless you help me right now. Help me, and I can help you."

"Fuck you," the man said wetly, spitting a thick wad of blood and mucus at Doyle. "I made my bet."

"Have it your way then," Doyle said, and blew the man's head off. This time, the sight of a near decapitation made him feel better instead of worse. As he stood looking down on the man who'd killed his driver, the cold winds whipped up around him, sending dust and trash all about. He turned and looked up. A massive black dragon settled into the middle of the street, looking down intently at the unfolding scene. *Ambryn.*

"Is he dead?" The dragon asked the mage, his voice low and chest rattling.

"Yes. That's a bit of his brain right there. Did we get all four of the shooters?" Doyle asked him, his eyes moving to Alanna's dead body. Sirens could be heard in the distance.

"I killed two," Ambryn said as his long neck descended down to Doyle's level. The dragon's impossibly deep, black eyes looked mournfully at Alanna's body and the enormous pool of blood spreading out around it. "MacTavish?" the dragon asked.

"Yes," Doyle said softly.

"Did she die quickly?" the dragon inquired.

"Aye. She did. No suffering. Henry will not be pleased. They have been friends for a long time." Doyle sighed. "Perhaps more than friends once."

Ambryn's massive head, as large as a bear nodded. "It is good then. She lived as a warrior, and she died as one. Henry will mourn, but he will understand. He too is a warrior. To walk their path you follow in my shadow every step of every day. Death comes to everything, sooner or later."

Doyle pulled his eyes from Alanna's body and looked at the dragon. "But not to your kind."

The same massive head nodded again. "Immortality is not the gift your people think it is. I think this Cosmin Dorinescu misunderstands what he seeks so ardently. What he has fought so long to maintain. Leaving a mark on the world often means you must leave it."

Perhaps you are right. I wonder when I will stop fleeing from the afterlife like Cosmin does. "How are Artur and Henry? Tell me they are alive."

Ambryn puffed up and looked over his massive shoulders and wings. Over the entire bus. "Artur was shot, but I think he will survive. I did not smell death on him. Henry was shot as well, but I think his armor protected him. He was cut on the head and I believe he might have a headache for a month, but he will survive."

At last, something to celebrate. "Good. We will need them both for what is to come before the sun rises. Where is the fourth man?" Doyle asked as the sirens grew louder. They were less than a minute away.

Ambryn lifted his head high, and inhaled deep of the night air. "I cannot get a scent. I'll fly above. Perhaps I can catch sight of him fleeing." The dragon prepared to launch.

"No. Wait."

The dragon stopped his wings just as he was about to thrust them down and take flight. He cocked his giant head, confused. "Why?"

Doyle walked around the front of the bus where the minivan was still attached, destroyed. He looked to the front of the store where the SUV was totaled. "I don't trust the police right now, Ambryn. These men were professionals. I suspect they were police. They might be locals, and if Henry and Artur are hurt, I want you here if the sirens heading our way are coming to finish the job."

Ambryn snarled, turning to face down the street where the cruisers were now visible. "Let the traitors try."

"Have restraint. They are probably innocent. But please, allow me to check in on our two allies."

"See to them," Ambryn said affectionately, full of concern. His angry demeanor had been discarded or well hidden.

Doyle walked around the dragon, stepping over his slender and long tail. His pistol still hung in his hand, forgotten as he walked towards the auto parts store his friend lay hurt in. *May the Lord find and protect this Cosmin Dorinescu. Nothing else will stop us if my friend dies.*

Chapter Thirty-Seven
Henry Spooner

Henry's head buzzed. Static ate away the space where his thoughts were trying to form, and a piercing dagger felt lodged somewhere in a sinus behind his eyes. Maybe two sinuses. His chest felt like he'd been trampled on by a Clydesdale horse, his mouth tasted like the horse had left him a present in it, and he couldn't for the life of him remember quite why he felt like that. His last memory was talking to Alanna on the phone in the SUV.

He felt the familiar grip of his Sig .45 in his hand, and the cold steel made him feel safer. *I have my gun. That's good.* Spoon looked over at the ground beside him—the floor actually, seeing as how he sat inside some kind of shop that had posters of scantily clad women leaning over the hoods of exotic cars—and saw a giant white wolf. It leaned against his right thigh and whimpered. It had an enormous streak of blood that started at its shoulder and ran down to its belly. *Did this wolf bite me? Did I shoot it? No, I don't think so. Where's Ambryn? Where's Artur?*

A gunshot rang out nearby.

Spoon tried to double over behind the cover he was in, but it hurt too much to move. The dagger that felt surely behind his eyes somehow moved into both sides of his torso simultaneously. He felt pinched in a vice. *I'm sitting behind a truck. No, an SUV. Oh, this is my rental. Fuck my head hurts. Shit.* He looked around again. *Okay. I'm behind the engine block, solid cover. Front bumper is snug against the wall of this place, nothing can get me that way.* He looked at the tail of the SUV and saw there was some space there for someone to walk in. *Sirens. BPD, baby. No. I'm in Vegas. LVMPD. Brothers in blue. Shit, we got hit. Rolling ambush when we turned around.* His head started to clear the minutest amount as he heard footsteps at the back of the SUV. His gun came up, but he couldn't hold it steady enough. He realized he had to reach out and protect the wolf, and despite the pain it caused, he knew that was the right thing to do.

"Freeze right there or I'll give you a new hole to shit out of," Spoon said as sternly as he could manage into the dark of the destroyed shop. His voice shook.

"Henry it's me, Doyle. Please don't shoot," a familiar voice said.

"Mr. Doyle?" Spoon said, his memory of the old man flooding in. Visions of absurd goggles, swords crackling with arcs of electricity and the smell of earthy wine. "Come in, what happened?" Spoon asked, lowering his weapon and making it safe. His other hand never left the shaking wolf.

The old wizard stepped over a pile of car rims, tires, jacks and broken brick and glass, making his way to his friend and the wolf that lay beside him. Spoon looked down at the white creature. *That's Artur. That's right, he's a werewolf. Shit, he's really hurt.*

"Henry, we were attacked. Men sent by that bastard vampire we're after. Humans. Cops or soldiers or something. They had machine guns. Professionals. Open your shirt. Get that vest off of you while I take care of the Romanian."

Spoon did as his friend told him to. It felt to him as if

it took forever to get the simple shirt off of him and to undo the Velcro that held his armor on him, but in reality it took only a moment or two. The pain ran from head to toe and nearly sent him back to unconsciousness. He tried to focus on watching Doyle slowly pour some red fluid out of a metal flask into the wolf's mouth. The drink had a strong smell, like wildflowers and spices, but with a musky edge to it. The wolf perked up and ended its whimpering within seconds.

Ha. Healing potion, that's right. Doyle gave one to me. I think it's in the glove box. Maybe center console. Head still hurts.

Doyle came to him then, examining his chest and torso for gunshot wounds. "No holes. No big ones at least. That's a good sign. Plenty of bruising. Cracked ribs possibly." He moved on to Spoon's head, and poked at the cut Spoon didn't know he had up there. It hurt badly.

"Shit, Doyle; that hurts, stop," Spoon said halfheartedly, his protests fueled by waning energy.

"Quit whining. Here, drink this lad," Doyle said, handing him the flask with the red potion inside it.

Spoon took it, ignoring the pain in his head from Doyle's manipulations. "I'm not drinking this. It has werewolf cooties on it."

Doyle stopped and looked at him. "Are you serious? Cooties? How old are you?"

"Old enough to know I don't want werewolf cooties," Spoon said, lifting the bottle to his lips anyway. *Any port in a storm.* Doyle chuckled as the red fluid cascaded over Spoon's tongue. The flavor was spicy and sweet, like cinnamon flavored candy. It had a cool, refreshing character to it, and as soon as he swallowed, he felt his vision tighten, and his headache abate. The harassing knife had disappeared. His chest and side inflated as if the vice squeezing him had been turned. "This is some good shit Doyle. Thank you."

"It’s ogre semen mixed with the blood of a goblin," he

said flatly, pressing a white bandage to Spoon's wound.

What? Spoon coughed hard, and it hurt. "Are you shitting me?" He spat out the taste as fast as he could.

"Yes, I'm 'shitting you.' It's a mending potion. You knew that. I've given you a few before. I brewed them in an alchemical lab and they are no worse for you than one of those energy drinks Abraham loves so. Nothing to worry about, drink up chap," Doyle said as he got to his feet to move back to the wolf. Spoon shook his head in disgust as he heard the cruisers pull up and turn off their sirens. Car doors opened and closed, and after they stopped yelling nonsense at the dragon, things calmed down outside. He took another swig from the metal drink container. *Dragons have a very strange effect on people.*

"What now?" Henry asked the mage as he put the recent few minutes back into order in his head.

"We get this varcolac to good health as fast as we can, and see if we can't get him to take a bite out of the men who just tried to kill you."

"Solid. Where's Agent MacTavish?"

Doyle stopped what he was doing, and turned to face his friend. *I don't like the look on his face.* "Where's Alanna?"

"Henry... When we got here, there was a lot of shooting. I am... I am very sorry, but your friend has been shot."

Complete blankness came over Spoon. His mind stopped working for several seconds before he realized what he'd heard. "Shot, or shot and killed? Tell me."

Doyle moved closer to Spoon, crouching. "One of the men opened up on her at point-blank range with an AK-47. She died quickly. She was brave," Doyle said in a whisper. People were coming closer to them, cops or paramedics. It didn't matter.

Spoon's flesh felt rubbery as pinpricks of grief formed. *Fuck. I got my friend killed. I got... I got Alanna killed. Alanna. What am I going to tell her Mom? Tell her*

Dad? How the hell do I tell her little sister? Emotions swirled up inside him. An entirely different kind of pain.

Doyle put a reassuring hand on Spoon's leg. "Spoon, it wasn't your fault. You must know that. She was doing what she wanted. What she volunteered for, and what she was paid for. She did her job as well as any could, and the fates decided that tonight was the end of her story. Shed no tears. Rejoice. We walked in the company of a hero. I will toast to her when this storm passes. I hope you will toast to her with me."

Hot tears ran down his face as he nodded. All he could do in that moment was mourn.

Chapter Thirty-Eight

Danny Ronan

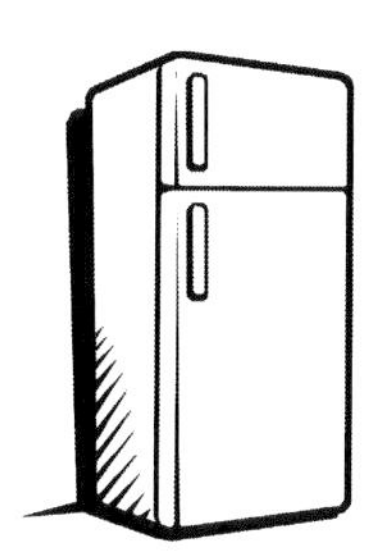

Danny dove out of the way of the maniac black RV, heading to the side he knew the door was opposite of. *I have no idea what the hell the spooks have inside that thing, and I don't aim to be the first to get shot by Gandalf tonight.* He landed on his shoulder and rolled, getting to his feet as the bus annihilated the van. Danny saw in his mind's eye video footage of freight trains creaming cars stuck on the tracks. The van had no chance against the bus. *Guess we won't be returning that van to the long term lot tonight. Hope they had insurance.*

He ran. He stood in the middle of the street and had no cover. Dead man's land against any shooter worth a damn. He looked to the sides and realized the rest of his men were doing the same. *I see Rick, I see Jack; I can't see Cesar. Rick and Jack are taking off. I'm out. We're not prepared for an extended firefight. We'll regroup later after we go to ground.*

Danny's tree trunk legs pumped, and he surged forward at a speed far faster than his giant body would've been thought able to move. Four years of college football breeds a certain kind of athleticism, regardless of your bulk. Danny thanked his coach at

Virginia Tech and a daily workout regimen as he sprinted down the road past several cars that were screeching to a halt, their drivers shocked and amazed by the unfolding debacle ahead of them. He could see how wide their eyes were. He dove in between two buildings and put some brick and mortar between his back and whatever Tapper brought inside that obsidian missile. *Least they won't be able to see me running away.*

A burst of automatic gunfire tore up the quiet behind him back at the wreck. *That' an AK. That'd be Jack.* Screams came next. *That's Jack too. Fuck.* As Danny continued to run, he realized he was running back towards the hotel. *Maybe this is good. Maybe the cops and FBI and whoever else already left, and there's no blue this way. Run to the void. Run Danny. Move.*

So he did. He ran as fast as he could.

Then the noise came. Something he would never forget.

When he heard the roar, memories of watching old Japanese Godzilla flicks as a child flashed into his mind. He saw small toy-scale buildings of Tokyo being toppled and beams of white radiation that set fire to anything they touched. The memories were pleasant. This sound in his presence was not. He imagined a giant bull elephant trumpeting on the African plain, closing on him, then the toothy maw of a polar bear roaring at a meal that desperately tried to escape it. He wanted to run faster, to flee, but couldn't help but slow his sprint to a trot, then to a walk. He had to look. Danny stopped, and built the courage to look around the corner of a building back at the scene of the firefight. To steal a glance at whatever made his courage flee.

Danny regretted it. He caught only a glimpse of the ancient beast and knew without doubt he had made a terrible mistake. A creature as long as the bus—longer if you counted the whole sinewy black tail, tipped with a spike that looked venomous—and had wings even wider.

A row of spikes ran down its spine from skull to tail like some exotic dinosaur, though this was nothing from any history book Danny had ever heard of. It looked demonic, bat-like and alien of the world Danny knew. It couldn't have been less like his south Texas Baptist upbringing if it were Lucifer himself riding in a chariot made of angel corpses, dragged by screaming chained sinners. Danny turned and ran even faster, praying to a God who surely no longer had interest in anything Danny was involved in.

Twenty strides later another shot rang out. A single throaty crack from a big-bore pistol. A .45 or .44 magnum. He couldn't tell. He pulled the bandana off his face and shoved it into the back pocket of his jeans. He glanced around as he ran towards the hotel and saw a gas station. He skirted around it carefully, avoiding any security cameras arrayed to videotape the doors and pumps. He bolted to the back, and slipped into the space between the brown garbage dumpster and the wall of the station. He slung his shotgun and dug out his phone. *I need help. Fast.* He called Rosen.

The beefy Lieutenant answered on the first ring. "Danny, what the fuck is going on. Is the shooting out on the west side you guys? Radio traffic is blowing the hell up here at command. Tell me you killed that European guy and got out."

I didn't think about being out of breath. "Hold on," Danny said as he huffed and puffed enough oxygen into him to steady his speech. After a dry swallow, and a paranoid glance around the gas station parking lot for unfriendly dragons and blue lights heading out to do their job, he returned to the call. "Rosen, we're bent."

"What does that mean? What do I tell Sandy? What do I tell Uncle Cosmo? Explain to me what happened," Rosen asked, angry but hushed.

He must be in the office. "You tell Uncle Cosmo and all of them to get the hell out of Vegas and fast. I don't think we can take what they sent. Man, we unloaded on that car. Two hundred rounds or more. I don't think it did a damn thing."

"What? Are you saying that European dude is vampire? Like, he can't be killed?" Rosen asked.

"I don't know who it was in that car, but a fucking dragon is here in Vegas."

Danny heard Rosen's mouth jawing, drying out from a sudden near-heart attack. "A dragon? Like that big gold dude? The blonde guy? What's his name? Dessert? Desert?"

"Tesser, and no, this was one smaller, and black."

"You don't hear that much," Rosen said impulsively. Neither man laughed.

"I think I remember seeing it on the news when everything happened back in Boston. I want to say this is the dragon that killed the purple one. The one that had been kidnapped by that medical company. It was fucking huge man. Wings wider than a semi. Rosen man, this is the dragon that can kill other dragons."

"Yeah, well, at this point does it matter which dragon is here? That's like being trapped in a burning house and bitching about whether or not the smoke or the fire is gonna kill you. Either way we're dead. What happened to your team? Did they make it out?"

Danny stole another glance into the gas station. A dark red Sonata had pulled in, and a rugged black guy with three day's growth on his face was getting out to get something inside the shop. He looked rough. Danny ignored him. "I don't know. We were ass-ended by that big fucking black bus they have. It creamed the van we stole, and we all had to dive out of the way and into cover. I am almost dead certain Jack got it. I heard a burst of fire from his gun, and then a scream I swear was his, but I got out. I can't imagine that if I was able to run my fat ass out, the others outran the dragon too. Someone had to draw the short straw. Look Aaron, this is a dragon.

They brought a *fucking dragon* to track down Cosmo. Take him out. What the hell are we going to do?"

Danny heard Rosen sigh as his own breathing settled. His lungs were on fire, as were his legs. He hadn't run that far, that fast, in years. *I need more cardio. Less weights.* Rosen finally answered him. "I'm going to call Sandy, let her know someone tried to hit the European. Without our permission. Throw the zebras under the bus, let them take the fall. They're dead or in cuffs anyway from the sounds of it."

"Okay, but then what? The straight cops are going to recognize anyone dead back there, God-for-fucking-bid one of them is arrested and talks, and it won't be long before they figure it out either way. I'm sure the K-9s are already on their way to come find me. And if I do get out of here, they're gonna track us both down. You *and* me. Where do we go? Where do we hide?"

"I don't know. But right now let's focus on getting you away from the site of the shooting, and then we'll deal with the next few hours after. Sit tight. I'll head over in a cruiser and pick you up. Where are you?"

Danny looked around again and got his bearings. "I can't see the street sign, but I'm at that Shell station right at the hotel that conference was at earlier. I'm fucking hiding in the back near the dumpster. Like a goddamn criminal."

"Danny you are a goddamn criminal. Embrace it. I know the spot. Hell, that's less than five minutes from the command here. I'll be right there. Don't move an inch."

"Hey fuck you, buddy. But thanks. I'll see you in a few," Danny said, feeling a small bit of relief, and maybe even hope. He ended the call and hunkered down in the cramped area. He moved his shotgun into the darkness away from anyone's line of sight. "Fuck me," Danny whispered to himself in the dark as he returned to his crouch.

"I won't fuck you, but I'll see to it you're taken care

of," a man's voice said back to him. Danny stood quickly, his lineman knees creaking in protest. He hadn't even seen the man approach. He'd gotten all the way to the edge of the dumpster. He saw the black guy from the red car, and in a steady left hand, he held a pistol aimed at Danny's chest. A revolver. A big one. Danny noticed he had a wedding band on the hand holding the gun. Enough light hit the man's face for Danny to know the guy had planned this. His eyes were furrowed, his lip curled. He didn't come here to rob a guy Danny's size. He came here to get answers, and to right a wrong. *Shit. I just put that Mossberg out of reach. Damn it.*

Danny raised his left hand, the one nearer to the black guy, and kept his draw hand low. *Shit, this guy smells like a bar floor. Maybe that's a good thing.* He started to plan the motion in his head for pulling his new Ruger and sending two shots at the man. But first, he had to distract him. Buy a split second to draw. "Look brother— "

"I ain't your fucking brother!" the black guy said in a shout. "I saw you running. I heard what you just said. Who is Aaron Rosen? He know where my daughter is? Does he know where my wife is? Huh? I saw you earlier too, you big prick. At the bar, with your three boys. I saw you getting in that van. I heard you then too. Live forever? You plotting on the world with some damn *vampires* are you? Twilight looking bastard. You helped them. Whoever has my babies," the black guy was practically foaming he was so angry now. As furious as he was, the plane of his pistol's barrel never wavered. He was in control of the weapon.

Shit, I gotta shoot this guy. He knows too much. "Look, I don't know what you're thinking, but I'm a cop. I work for Las Vegas Metro, and this can all be explained," Danny said as he waved his left hand in a flourish, and simultaneously made a move for his Ruger with his right. He was fast, faster than the black guy, but Danny was betrayed by his brand new pistol and its draw out of an unfamiliar holster. He lifted the plane of the barrel too fast, and the front sight caught on the leather.

The angry man's gun went off like a howitzer in the narrow confines between the dumpster and the stonework designed to hide it from view. The heavy magnum round hit Danny straight between his ribs and punctured his vest easily. Kevlar was bullet resistant, but at that range, without his plate in that night, and with that heavy a slug, the vest was overmatched.

The impact of the round knocked Danny back and into the side of the gas station. Danny remembered being tackled in a televised bowl game. The hollow point round blew into his chest, mushroomed, and lit everything inside him on fire. A second explosion from his killer's hand-cannon gave him mercy from the pain, and ended his life.

Danny died like the criminals he spent a lifetime hunting.

Chapter Thirty-Nine
Wayne Simmons

Wayne's heart pounded. His eyes were wide, his palms sweaty, and everything in the world had jumped out into surreal detail. He could see each letter on the license plate of his car in vivid focus, he could see each hair on his forearms, he could see every drop of blood in the darkness, and perhaps worst of all, he could hear every scream coming from the people nearby who hadn't fled the earlier gunfire. His pair of shots was close to them. The thunderous cracks meant the terror was in their faces, inescapable. The difference between watching someone trip from afar, and it being funny, versus tripping yourself and feeling the burn from your skinned flesh.

Wayne coughed up a wad of thick phlegm and spat it on the chest of the man he just shot. *The cop I just shot.* "Fuck you asshole. Evil motherfucker." Wayne reached into his pocket and dug out his phone. He redialed the number for the Tapper agent from his recent calls, and stood firm, watching the dead cop's body with his gun pointed at it. *Hey. He had a shotgun. Got lucky, didn't I?*

A man answered the phone. He had an accent. It was familiar. "Agent MacTavish's telephone, to whom am I speaking?"

Hey, it's the Irish guy. Wayne's mood lifted off the pavement to ankle height. "Hey, is this that Irish guy? Doyle?"

"I am English young man. To whom do I speak?" he said back.

"Wayne. Wayne Simmons? We met at the bus crash site, and I went and got some DNA of my daughter and my wife for you?" Wayne lowered the gun and watched as several cruisers flew by. Somehow, the sound of the sirens echoed in his ears and in the phone at near the same time.

"Yes, I remember. Melanie and Shauna. What can we help you with tonight, Mr. Simmons? And please be brief, it has not been a good night for us, and there is much for me to attend to."

Wait a second here. I called her, not him. "Why didn't the woman answer?"

"I am not at liberty to discuss Agent MacTavish's whereabouts, Mr. Simmons. Please, what can I do for you?"

Wayne lifted his head and looked down the length of the street to the spot where the cruisers were stopping. Officers were getting out and running further down the street, their weapons drawn. The red and blue flashes were creating a strange ocean of light, and then he knew. It all came together. "I called her. I told her I saw those men. The men in the van." Wayne's voice was somber. Regretful.

"Yes you did. Thank you."

"She got shot didn't she?"

"Mr. Simmons, please."

Damn it all. Another dead girl. "Look I'm real sorry sir. I didn't mean for that to happen. I didn't... I shot someone at the gas station down the street from where you are. Where the big shoot-out was. I saw him running away and recognized him. Big bastard. He was one of the dudes who rolled out on you. I snuck up on his ass when he was hiding and heard him talking on the phone to another cop. They were trying to kill you guys for someone else I think." Wayne looked up to the night sky. He could hear helicopters approaching, dividing the night above with their blue-white search lights.

"Did you hear any names? Locations? Anything of note? Time is of the essence, Mr. Simmons," the Englishman said seriously.

Shit, he's scary. "Yeah. Aaron Rosen, and Uncle Cosmo."

"Bollocks," Doyle said through gritted teeth. "Rosen. Where are you?"

"Gas station down the way between your position and the hotel. I dropped the dude near the trash in the back. What should I do?"

"Stay still, Mr. Simmons. You've done a good thing this day. Brilliant in fact. I must warn you, however, your life is about to take an abrupt turn into the strange, and you must prepare yourself for it. You have crossed the line into the weird, and there's no unseeing what you are about to see."

"If it means I find my daughter and wife, or it means I'll put whoever hurt them to justice, I'll carry an ice cream cone through Hell wearing a winter coat."

"Perhaps then we should start looking for ice cream. I will be to you in a moment, post haste. Let no one near that body; if anyone asks you who you are or approaches you, identify yourself as a Tapper asset, and tell them you work for me directly," the Englishman said. "Mr. Doyle."

"You got it."

"And if they press you, you shoot them. Trust no one. Expect treachery."

Chapter Forty
Artur Cojocaru

When you hunted evil, getting injured had to be expected, and for the werewolf this was far from being the first time he'd been shot or wounded. His ample and impressive collection of injuries spanned two decades of hunting some of the worst things the world had to offer, and he had a story for every scar. Shot in Frankfurt by a police man's submachine gun. Stabbed in the back by a rogue priest in Barcelona. Gutted by a possessed fisherman's hook on a pier in Greece. Impaled with a pitchfork by a fear struck farmer. His legs had long ragged scars running from waist to knee from a feral werewolf Artur had to put down in a Ukrainian village as a teenager, and the burns on his left arm were from a night Artur did everything he could to forget. Those particular scars were penance, and he bore them.

Getting shot twice in the side by a handful of Americans with assault rifles should be expected on a trip to Las Vegas really. '*Murica.*

Artur sat in a pile of glass on the floor of some small business, his body curled into a canine ball of blood soaked white. They had been heading to the morgue. They'd turned when a threat had been reported on the phone by MacTavish. The threat had found them. He had remained beside his companion Henry Spooner after the dark figure of Ambryn pulled him from the car in which he'd been shot. Artur knew he was safe—safe enough at least—and let the fear leave him as the old wizard he knew to be Mr. Doyle knelt beside him and poured a sticky-sweet drink into his long wolf-mouth. The warmth across his tongue and down his throat told him it was magical and good. Artur's tongue lapped at it, and he drank deep. He quickly drifted into the sleep of the varcolac, and let his werewolf body mend.

*****

"Hey," a man's voice said to him quietly over the din beyond the darkness of the SUV's body.

Artur opened his wolf eyes slowly, and looked at the speaker. It was Henry. *Best I should change now. He can't understand me in this form.* Artur shifted to his man-form. It hurt, the change. It always hurt some. Bones softening, bending, disappearing sometimes, appearing the others. Muscles stretching, swelling, tearing and shaping. Skin shedding hair or growing it, tearing and healing right before his eyes. On the best days, the moments of the change were painful. Tonight, the agony ate him alive, and he fought against a chorus of screams inside his body. His four legs warped and reformed into two legs and two arms, and his trunk stretched out into his tall human body's version as his face shortened, flattened, and his teeth retracted and reshaped into what passed for normal human. When the shift over, he sat naked on the broken glass beside Henry, and the two gunshots that had been under his fur near his armpit were bare to the open and cold night. They stood out as bright red circles the size of American dimes. The bleeding had halted, but the pain ran deep.

"Holy hell," Spoon said. "Cool."

"Yes. I am cold. Is there a blanket?" Artur asked him, folding his arms across his chest carefully so as not to pinch or move his wounds too much.

"You're just gonna leave your dick hanging out?" Henry asked him as he got to his feet. He pointed at Artur's groin with his free hand as he holstered his pistol.

"This bothers you?" Artur said, looking down at his exposed manhood.

"Well I mean no, but generally when your dick is hanging out in front of another dude you put at least minimal effort into covering it up. Maybe that's an American thing. Hey! Blanket!" Spoon yelled out to the mass of people Artur could hear nearby. *Police. Emergency people.* Out of modesty Artur lowered one hand to his genitals with a wince while they waited, and a moment later a dull gray blanket landed in his lap. He unfolded it carefully and placed it across his midsection.

"I feel better already. Doyle's drink and my sleep in the wolf-body has helped. I need food and more rest, or time in the man-wolf form," Artur said as Spoon handed him an opened bottle of water. He sipped at it.

"Wolf-body, man-wolf, what do you mean? It all sounds the same to me," Henry asked as he kept watch on the group outside the shop. Artur noticed his eyes lifting high, as if he was periodically looking at the nearby rooftops.

"We have words for it, but the wolf-body is all wolf. Then we have a dire wolf form, which is a very big wolf, and then we have the man-wolf body, which is upright, like a human, but also part wolf. Claws, teeth, fur." Artur sipped again. *Cold. Clean. Good water.* "That is the body we most often go to war in."

"So four different shapes all together in one person? Crazy."

"Yes. How is Ambryn?"

Spoon laughed. "Huge. He's fine. It'll take more than automatic gunfire to put his game on pause. He dragged both of us out of the truck as it was getting shot up. Saved us."

Interesting. "The dragon of death saves lives. What next, yes? I know I saw Doyle. Where is the other one? The lady MacTavish?"

Spoon's eyes stayed high for a moment too long and Artur knew before he said anything. "She took a few rounds point blank. She didn't make it. I'm told it was quick." Henry looked... old.

"I am sorry Spoon. She seemed a good person. I will kill our enemies in her name. She deserves that."

"You and me both. Are you okay to stand?" Henry finally looked down at Artur.

Artur shifted his torso, testing his range of motion. The left side of his chest felt like he had a kitchen knife stuck in it, but if he was careful... He extended his right arm to Spoon, and the American took it. Together they got him slowly to his feet. The blanket fell. Spoon unfolded it and wrapped it around Artur, looking away the whole time. Suddenly the space above the truck went dark, as if the entire city had lost power. Artur looked up, and learned it hadn't.

Blocking the entire space above the bullet punctured hood was Ambryn's gargantuan dragon head. His eyes were at least the size of car headlamps, but impossibly dark, and deep, like a well with no bottom. Artur immediately smiled in innocent wonder. A child's dream fulfilled. "You are... in the dragon. Majestic. Beautiful beyond words."

Ambryn somehow tilted his head in thanks. "A man's body for man's work. A dragon's body for a dragon's work. Are you feeling better? I noticed you were hurt."

"More of the juice Doyle gave me earlier, and some food and rest, and I will be right soon. Thank you for saving my life. Our lives," Artur said, pointing to Henry as he led him out of the shop.

Ambryn's head pulled back and up like a massive

studio camera boom, reaching ten, twenty feet up. His body came into view as Artur walked into the open, so big it obscured and made irrelevant the hundred police and firefighters all around. A fire truck behind him looked like a well-lit couch for the dragon. His body was thick, but elegant, his legs long. His tail was snakelike, but had a talon at the end that reminded the werewolf of a scorpion's stinger. His claws looked like an eagle's, but twenty times the size. The dragon spoke, "It is good. I do not wish for you to die, not like this. There is much left for us to do."

"Speaking of which," Mr. Doyle said as he approached them, walking fast. "We must move. An opportunity has arisen literally down the way that we must move to. Ambryn, realizing fully I will regret this question, could you fly us a half mile or so down the street to the gas station?" *He shows regret on his face. He is scared to fly.*

The dragon grinned, showing a dozen teeth each big enough to impale a pig. "Pick you three up and fly you? Of course. Two of you in one hand, one the other."

Mr. Doyle nodded, affirming his insanity. "Then, if Henry and The Romanian don't object, I would like to go now, before our opportunity passes."

I will fly? Yes. I will fly. "Take me. I wish to see how a dragon soars," Artur said with another wide smile. All his pain had faded.

"I'll fucking walk," Henry said with a wave, starting down the street on foot.

"Your loss Henry," Ambryn said as he gingerly scooped the werewolf and the wizard up, one in each enormous clawed hand. *So big. Claws…*

And the ground fell away.

Ambryn's enormous downward wing buffet, timed with his legs propelling them upward, put them fifty feet above the street in a split second. The g-force on his body made his gunshot wounds belch a cry of pain, and Artur saw red. He fought it. Across the dragon's shoulders, he watched Mr. Doyle fight against a joyous smile. *I wonder if this is his first dragon flight.*

They weren't in the air long, or high, but the memory made of it would live with him until his death. Looking down on the all cars with their flashing lights and over the tops of all the buildings around; seeing the shallow glitz of The Strip in the distance, and hearing the heavy beat of the helicopters above. Everything seemed small. All of the world temporary and fleeting. Time stood still for him as he looked at the city and the dragon holding him, and he felt a purity he had never felt before. A oneness with the world that had eluded him his whole life.

They landed incredibly soft in the street beside the large petrol station, and the feeling faded. A black man came out of the rear of the station, a huge pistol in hand. He had a look of awe on his face. Artur fought against the pain again as the dragon set him and Doyle down.

"Mr. Doyle, wow," the dark skinned man said to the sorcerer, his eyes on the dragon.

Before replying he straightened out his clothes and looked to the dragon. "Yes, well. As I said, you cannot un-see what you are about to see. Wayne Simmons, I present to you Ambryn. The other man with the blanket is a consultant for Tapper."

Artur bowed, his good arm holding the modesty bestowing blanket cinched. "Artur. You may know me as The Romanian." He said it with pride.

The man named Wayne never took his eyes off the giant dragon. "That's cool man. So a dragon, huh? I never thought I'd be in the same place as one of you."

Ambryn lowered his body to the ground, tucking his legs in and wrapping his tail around his form. He looked so much like a big black cat Artur actually laughed. Ambryn gave Artur a mock angry sneer, and then smiled. "Mr. Simmons, strange times are upon the city of Las Vegas. We dragons flock to these kinds of things. That or we stirred them up in the first place. It can be hard to tell if we've got the donkey in front of the cart at times."

"That's crazy. So hey, Doyle. That guy is in the back near the dumpster. You want me to show him to you? He's dead. But he doesn't look that bad. I hit him center mass twice. There's some blood, that's all." Wayne threw a thumb over his shoulder, indicating where the dead, bloody man lay.

"That's quite alright. The expert on bodies here is The Romanian. Artur, I thought if you were to perhaps, you know... Do your thing?"

Fresh flesh of a traitor? What secrets do you hold for me? "I would be delighted. Thank you," Artur said to Wayne as he strode past him, ignoring the pain in his side and chest. He walked around the edge of the concrete wall as police threw up tape in a wide radius around, blocking off the street and intersection. He saw the dead man's foot, and felt a thrill. Against rationality, his mouth began to water.

True to Wayne's word for a dead body, the man's corpse seemed clean. He wasn't dismembered, or disemboweled. His head and face remained intact, and save for the blank expression of death he wore and the enormous red stain on his shirt, he might've been a drunk staring into space. *But he is not. He has the smell of death on him. Rot and ruin.*

Artur held the blanket tight and went to a knee beside the body. He ripped the shirt open with one hand, and after fumbling angrily with the bulletproof vest, he found the Velcro straps, and got the front of it up over the large man's head exposing the two finger-sized entry wounds. *Such small holes for such a large gun. A pomegranate seed. I wonder what the holes on the other side look like. A seed going in, a whole pomegranate coming out I think.*

Artur looked behind him, and when he saw no one, he sat his blanket aside and fell back into the form of the white wolf. The shift gave him less pain than the last transformation, and walking on all four paws somehow spread the pain out so it was less intense. *I am healing faster than usual. Doyle's drink.* The smells of the world jumped out at him. The rank garbage, the piss of the homeless. He smelled the chemical odor of the petrol nearby, and the intense … absence of a scent coming from the dragon. Ambryn smelled of oblivion. He carried the odor of the inescapable end, and that realization shook Artur.

The wolf nose hovered over the gunshot wounds in the body. *I will save his face. Spare his family further tragedy.* Artur revealed his fangs and sank them into the meat at the wound, digging deep and freeing up a mouthful of human flesh. He tore at it, twisting until it came free of the bone. He swallowed. The cooling skin, fat and muscle slid down his throat, salty, coppery, taboo, and delicious.

The visions it gave him were a delicacy as well.

Chapter Forty-One
Aaron Rosen

Aaron closed the clam shell on the burner and leaned back in his office chair. It felt chilly to him in the office, and the hair on his arms stood up straight. The upright posts holding the armrests up on his chair dug into the side of his thighs. It hurt. The situation of his entire life was summed up for him by the chair and the vice sensation it put on his lower body. If he stayed where he sat, he would be squeezed, and there would be pain to endure. Possibly… more pain than he could stand if he sat still. Agony most likely would come in the cards. But if he got up and moved… There would less pain. At least the burn in the meat of his legs helped him to focus and make a decision on just how to proceed next.

He weighed his options as the command office emptied. He could hear the chairs pulling out from the desks, and the drawers being yanked open so the pistols could be put on belts. He could hear the doors open and close and all the hustle and bustle of a crisis unfolding. He knew each officer walking out the door headed to where Danny and his crew were. Where they had tried to kill the European, and where the dragon held court. The cops were hungry for justice. The missing people from the buses had weighed heavily on all of the good cops for too long. Every cop takes every crime at least a little personally.

Aaron laughed, thinking about it all, and his mind was made. *I am not going anywhere near a fire breathing monster. I saw Reign of Fire. Dragonheart too. No way I'm getting set on fire. Sorry brother, but Danny, you're on your own. And as far as everyone else goes…Oh well. Uncle Cosmo is badass, but he's peanuts stacked against a dragon. I'm out. I'll find a different vampire somewhere else.*

Aaron got to his feet and the pain in his legs disappeared immediately.

*****

He already had a bug-out-bag in his locker at the station. With every officer in the city running towards the gun battle, Aaron made it to his bank in five minutes. He withdrew several hundred dollars from the drive through ATM, and went to the used car lot that he knew to be open late. Gamblers who won after business hours often needed an opportunity to blow their winnings, and this one dealer had placed his lot in a clever location towards the highway and kept hours that meant he got that late night business. Rosen hedged his bets, abandoned dedication in favor of self-preservation, and traded in his family's Durango and picked up a fuel efficient black Honda Civic. He had a lot of driving planned, and fuel economy mattered.

Danny headed towards Interstate 40 down the 95 and into California no more than two hours after leaving his office and the iron maiden chair. He drove with his service Sig 229 tucked under his right leg, a spare magazine slid under his left, and his personal cell phone ringing incessantly from the cup holder.

His wife undoubtedly, wanting to know when he was coming home to the kids and dinner.

Maybe she'll turn on the news and think I'm at the shooting. A few hours of obliviousness won't kill her. Aaron hit ignore on her call and picked up the shitty burner phone he'd gotten from Sandy at The Arabian Nights. Uncle Cosmo's Chief Bitch and one of the few women on the planet that gave Aaron the chills. She reminded him of the white witch from Narnia.

"Lieutenant? We are busy here. Make your business quick, and make it useful," she said, cold as ever.

"Miss Brown, have you watched the local news the last hour or so?" Rosen asked her. The Nevada Public Radio had been set to live feed on Danny's shit storm the entire time he'd been in the Honda, and he knew the television coverage would be worse. He also knew his brothers on the force had located all four of the bodies from Danny's crew, and that meant Danny had eaten a bullet after the phone call, and it meant the only story that would reach Sandy's ears would be his. *A gift if I ever saw one.*

"No, I work for a living. Why?"

"The unit of men I assigned to track your European friend decided to hit him in west Vegas a few hours ago. Call it an attack of opportunity. Their attempt on him was spectacularly unsuccessful."

Rosen could hear her scathing exhalation. "Goddamn it, Lieutenant. I told you. *Low profile.* We have political irons in the fire that you can't possibly understand. Aggression, *open* aggression on our part is just about the worst damned thing for us right now. It will endanger everything."

"I think that's the least of your worries. Tapper brought a dragon to Vegas. I think he's here to kill Cosmo."

"Are you fooling around Lieutenant? Because now is not the time for bad jokes," Sandy said entirely as a threat.

"Turn on the television. See for yourself. Big black

one. Not the gold one, or that huge red and brown one, but the black one."

Aaron listened as she clicked her mouse several times and typed something into her keyboard. *She's looking at the news website. Shat pants in three... two... one...* "Oh boy. Okay. Stay low. Find a place to hide. Do not come to the casino unless I tell you to. If the dragon really is here for Cosmo, he's going to want to change plans and we need to be ready. Can they track your errant minions back to you?"

"If they are dead, then not to my knowledge. The worst thing they could do is get his burner and then find mine. I'm gonna trash my SIM card after this call so even if they do, they won't find me. If I need you, I'll call the club direct with a new burner and leave you a message so there's no electronic trail."

"Good. Smart. You've handled this well it would seem. I'll make sure Uncle Cosmo hears about your fuckup, and how you've kept us out of the loop. Maybe he'll promote you to vampire status. No promises, but keep hope alive."

Yeah, fuck you. I'm gone. Minneapolis, here I come. Maybe Calgary. Maybe I'll buy a boat and be a fisherman. We'll see where the wind blows. "Thanks, I know this went south on us, but I'm trying to protect Uncle Cosmo and the business. You know what my endgame is. Where my loyalties are."

"Good. And Lieutenant, don't try running. Uncle Cosmo has family in places you think might be safe, but they aren't. Be smart and lay low. Call me when you have a new phone," she said, and hung up.

Fuck that bitch. I am never talking to her again. Rosen threw the burner phone out the driver's side window and into the south Nevada night. It hit the pavement and smashed into a thousand tiny and sharp plastic pieces. *Hope none of them are big enough for a print.*

He set the cruise control on the steering wheel for five

miles an hour over the limit, and tried to think of a way for him to stomach leaving his wife and kids behind. He had crossed into Arizona and saw the signs of dawn ahead before he thought of a way to move on.

Chapter Forty-Two
Sandy Brown

Sandy shut the piece of shit convenience store disposable phone and started to hurl it at the concrete wall of her office. She snarled and at the last moment pulled the power from her arm. Her calculating, logical manner wouldn't allow her to destroy the phone no matter how angry she had become at the message she'd received through it. *I still need this phone. I need to get to Cosmo.*

Sandy got to her feet, slipped the phone into her pocket, and looked over at her locked electrical closet where she kept her food. She had an itch. One that fresh blood could scratch. *No time for a taste right now, no matter how bad I want it. I should turn her before Uncle Cosmo realizes I've left her alive for feeding. Make more vampires, Sandy. Maybe if her blood wasn't so damn delicious. I must move on. Always a damn calamity to deal with.* She left her office, letting the heavy steel door to her office shut with a clang.

She knew Uncle Cosmo had been at wit's edge since he'd sent one of his 'family members' from Europe out to drop off the USB stick with the video on it. The young eastern European kid had gone to the hotel where the authorities were meeting about what to do. He'd gotten in and out, slick as a whistle.

Everything Uncle Cosmo and all his sired vampires had worked so hard for was either going to come to fruition imminently, or it would all crumble to dust. The see saw had to settle one way or the other. Either way, Uncle Cosmo had been moving about the lower levels of the casino for hours now, awake far before the safety of sunset, issuing a hundred and one commands to seemingly everyone who could achieve even the most basic of things. Expectations were high. Sandy had been spared from the tasks only because she worked diligently in her office spiriting away casino funds in a hundred different off-shore rainy day accounts he had set up months ago.

Uncle Cosmo apparently expected storms. Hundreds of them.

"Where is Uncle Cosmo?" Sandy asked one of the dhampyr security guys standing at a hallway intersection.

The suit wearing, big Slav grunted back at her in shitty English, "Meeting room. Wiss Yimmy."

"Jimmy?"

"Ya," he said, adjusting the assault rifle slung across his chest.

What the hell is he meeting with Jimmy for? Why am I not involved? Orders go through me to Jimmy, not direct. Little upstart prick. Sandy smoothed out the wrinkles in her attitude and went to the double doors of the conference room. She knocked hard with bony knuckles.

"Enter," she heard Uncle Cosmo say sternly.

She pulled the double doors open and walked in, shutting them deliberately slow. She turned and smiled for the two men. Cosmo looked pissed, and Jimmy was shuffling through a massive stack of manila folders, arranging the order they were in. On the huge wall-mounted television she saw the local newscasters talking excitedly. Over their shoulders she could see footage taken from a helicopter. The screen showed a large black bus with a smashed apart van at the front of it. Several blood-stained white sheets covered bodies lying in the open, and most disturbing of all, she could see the enormous black reptile sitting in the middle of what should've been a busy street. It sat prim and proper near a gas station, big as the Tapper bus, a crowd of cops around it. "Sorry to bother you gentlemen. I've some news. Though it looks like you are aware of most of it already." She pointed at the screen.

"Yes," Uncle Cosmo said. "Certainly changes the stakes. Jimmy, go. And make sure not a one of them makes a mistake. Each of them gets a folder with what they need to know. We've only hours before it is too late. Less."

Jimmy Romita stood and tucked the folders under his arm. "On it Uncle Cosmo. And for the record, thanks. I appreciate your trust."

"Do your job Jimmy. Don't fail us," Uncle Cosmo said.

Jimmy was solemn. "I won't." He left the room after giving Sandy a weird expression. He shut the doors behind him, leaving Cosmo and Sandy in the room with the muted television.

Bastard. What the hell is he doing for Uncle Cosmo? "I don't want to sound unappreciative, but what's so important that Jimmy needed to be summoned and sent away without my knowledge? I really need to know what assets the casino has to deal with issues that come up, and Jimmy is an asset I need to keep track of."

"You sound very unappreciative Sandra. It is not becoming of a woman so intelligent and confident. Is it the hour we sit at that ruffles your feathers? The battleship coming over the horizon that sends your fleet into chaos? I can understand that. Rest assured your place on the totem pole has not been challenged. Every tool for its job, yes? Right now Jimmy is working on what you could call my plan B, which is far more important than anything else that could come up that would trouble you. I have complete faith in your ability to solve problems, Sandra. You have your job for that reason, amongst others. Now, you mentioned news for me."

Whatever. Okay. "Yes. We have a dragon in the city. Lieutenant Rosen informed me that several of his men made an attempt on the European's life. The man you referred to as 'The Romanian' I believe escaped alive, and further as the television shows, he was with a dragon. It's only a matter of time before the police figure out they have rotten apples in the barrel, and someone starts talking. It might already be too late."

For a brief moment, a fraction of a second really, Sandy saw Uncle Cosmo's composure fail him and she understood true, honest fear. He snarled, baring fangs and hatred for a flash, then smiled like the cat with a feather poking out of its mouth. "The timing of this could not be worse."

"I understand," Sandy said sympathetically.

It was the wrong thing to say. Cosmo launched out of his high back leather seat as fast a viper's strike and had his hand around her throat before she could do anything to stop him. Not that any effort she could muster would've changed what he wanted to do to her. He had her up and off the floor, her heels coming free and dangling at her toes. "You understand?" He stared at her, his eyes all manner of bloodshot and fierce. "You understand *nothing*, Sandra Brown. You have been the tiniest part of my life's plan for the 59th second of the 59th minute of the 12th hour. What could you possibly understand about all I've wrought? Gears within gears. Misdirection on so many levels. All of what's at stake here?"

She tried to answer him, but he was choking her. Oddly, it did not make her panic. Air was something she no longer needed. Her response was to hang limp in his iron-strong hand until he sat her down. Which he did. He put his fangs away as she adjusted her feet in her heels. "I'm sorry."

"There is no need for your being sorry. I lost my temper. You are one of my children, and a loyal one at that. You deserve a better father than what you just experienced. I apologize." Sandy was mum while he sat. "We must accelerate matters. Take the city by force before dawn. We do not have much time left. Our army could be set forth within the hour, and we could spread like a carpet of fire ants, taking everything before us. The dragon could not kill us all. Not fast enough at least. Vegas will be ours. The necropolis at long last."

"What if… what if the dragon can kill us all? What if he breathes fire like the one in Boston?"

"Well let's be honest Sandra, we're already dead. And the gold dragon is in Norway according to CNN. And should the dragon we have on our hands here succeed against us, I've already long since had a plan in motion. Vegas was never the only objective we were working towards."

"Jimmy?"

Cosmo nodded, all-knowing. "Jimmy, and a few other little things here and there, two decades in the making. Now, phone the Lieutenant—no, phone the Captain—and tell him that the assault on the city is tonight and to have all his loyal men fight alongside my children. They shall be rewarded with eternal life, as they expect to be. They will know when it begins."

"Yes sir," Sandy said, feeling important again.

"And see to it our children are set free in their proper playgrounds. As soon as possible. The most amount of wreckage we can cause the better. We rule in the chaos my dear. Our kingdom becomes real tonight. Celebrate with me on the morrow. Now go, issue the orders as we've discussed, and when you're done…" Cosmo looked at her with a pleasant look of hunger on his face, "go out and play with the humans. You've earned a few hours of barbarism."

Sandy felt that itch come back stronger than ever.

Chapter Forty-Three
Ambryn

Ambryn sat in the middle of the road beside the human gas station, still in his dragon form. Above several mechanical contraptions with whirling blades of steel and plastic on their tops buzzed about in the air, shining beams of light down to illuminate the different areas of violence in the street and surrounding neighborhoods. The humans themselves swarmed about like ants, marking evidence, measuring distances, gawking at his massive size and presence, and being wasteful of the precious little time they had. *Your tape measure will not lead us to Cosmo, officer. Put it down; leave and track the leads we have given you.*

Ambryn looked over to the ambulance that contained his human companions, and the werewolf. Artur had eaten the flesh of one of their attackers to seek visions, and he had fallen into a deep sleep. You might call it a coma, though when his wolfen lids were parted, his eyes flickered about in a dream. He had been like this for almost two hours. In an attempt to make him more comfortable, Doyle had him moved to the back of the emergency vehicle where an EMT with veterinary experience put an IV in and nourishing oxygen was given to him. Henry and Doyle were in the ambulance with him, sitting nervously at his side. Wayne, the man who had killed the traitor cop, and the father and husband to two missing to the vampires, sat on the curb nearby. Doyle had taken his gun but asked him to stay close.

Artur's little wolf legs kicked. "He's rousing some. I didn't imagine this would take that long. Do you think there's something wrong with him? Bad trip?" Henry asked Doyle.

"I can't say. Perhaps he can seek out more memory and detail by sleeping like this? Varcolacs are exceedingly rare and what we know about them is minimal. Secretive bunch. I've learned more about them in just the past few days from Artur than I've properly known up until now. Fascinating creatures."

Ambryn leaned his long neck down and put his head at the rear of the open ambulance. With his dragon's ears he heard the wolf's small heart flutter faster and faster, coming out of the stupor it had sunken into. It sounded much like the helicopters in the air above. Thup-thup-thup. "I can hear his breathing becoming more rapid. His heart too when it quiets for a moment out here."

Doyle looked from the dragon to the wolf. "Good. Time is wasting away. I don't know what Cosmin and his minions are up to, but this attack against us on the heels of that video seems ill-timed."

"I agree," Ambryn said. "He seemed to be making a serious attempt at resolving this peacefully through poorly designed political means."

Henry scratched the top of his head, confused. "I've been thinking. That video is strange. If Cosmin was serious about making a political attempt at settling this now, why would he go all Al-Qaeda in the video? Why wouldn't he just make a serious attempt via viral media, in a suit, with money. Dude has to have a ton of cash on hand, being immortal and all that. It seems like an ill-designed play to kill a young guy and issue out threats with one corner of your mouth while you beg for peace out of the other."

Doyle looked thoughtful to the dragon. "You have an excellent point. Why release the video then? To what end?"

"Perhaps he felt the noose tightening? Or his agents made him aware of Artur's arrival? It is clear the police here cannot be trusted," Ambryn offered in his rumbling dragon voice. Several local cops looked over after hearing his accusations. They had grounds to be offended, but the truth of what he said couldn't be argued. They returned to their work, feelings left unsaid.

"Well, what has the video actually achieved since its delivery?" Spoon asked the group.

"It has spurred discourse at the highest levels," Doyle responded. "He has gotten the president's attention."

"It has distracted us for several hours. It took us off the hunt to plan a response," Ambryn said.

"Hm," spoon muttered, looking at the wolf. "Maybe that was it all along. Maybe he knew his time was short, and he released the video to buy time to escape? And then he sets up a hit on us to further trip us up."

"No," Doyle said shaking his head, "If he wanted us dead or truly disrupted, he could've hit the entire upper echelon at the hotel during our meeting. He knew we were there in a large gathering. He must have access to some kind of explosives, and a single bomb would've been a smarter choice than this drive-by shooting. This smacks of a second decision. Separate from the larger logic at play."

"I agree," Ambryn said. It makes sense. "Perhaps an ambitious underling? Police on the take trying to impress him?"

Spoon spoke, "That might be it, but it still doesn’t answer the video question. The message in that video is relevant. It has to be. Must be important to him and whatever cause he's actually working for. He wants the world or at least the U.S. to think about a vampire nation—or laws at the barest minimum—but something's off. I can't put my finger on it, but we're missing something. Whatever it is, it's big."

The wolf's head lifted off the pillow on the stretcher. Fog filled the human sized clear plastic oxygen mask and Henry took it off. Artur shifted to human form, quicker than Spoon imagined possible. Plain as day the wounds he suffered earlier were healed. Only a pair of puckered red craters in the skin remained. He looked refreshed as he sat up. "I listened to your talk now. And Ambryn is right. I saw visions of another police man. Big, with slick black hair. They spoke of moving up. Trying to be promoted."

"Rosen," Doyle said gruffly with an upturned lip.

"Yes," Artur said enthusiastically, hearing a name he recognized. "They know of me here. Pictures taken at the airport of us when I landed. They came tonight to kill me."

"Well, fuck them," Henry said. "Alanna really saved your ass, didn't she?"

Artur reached out and took an offered blanket from Spoon. He covered his midsection with it. "She did, but at great cost to her and our cause. I will name my next child after her."

"What else did the flesh tell you?" Ambryn asked him.

The werewolf looked out the end of the ambulance at the massive dragon and simply smiled. Such joy sat on his face. "The flesh told me the vampire owns a casino. And a woman they called the 'Ice Queen' is involved. Someone who works at the casino. I also saw a vision of something Middle Eastern. Domes of a mosque, and heat. A winding bright blue river. Perhaps there is an Islamic connection."

Wait. The muscle-bound guards at the nightclub. "When I killed those guards at the nightclub, they spoke of working the floor, or the money room. I would bet for certain that they had escorted their vampire from whatever casino you speak of."

Spoon hopped out of the ambulance and stormed off, looking with purpose for someone or something. As he ran by the disconsolate Wayne he motioned for the man to follow, and he got off the curb and did so. The two went off together.

"Did I anger him? Did Ambryn anger him?" Artur asked the dragon and Doyle.

"I suspect he is going to ask someone if they know about an Ice Queen at a casino. That or directions to find the closest Mosque that encourages gambling. Continue please, what else did your visions tell you?" Doyle prodded him.

Artur gave a wide smile. "He is planning a massive attack on the city. Soon. The man, Danny, only knows this because of the Rosen man, who learned it all from another police man. Someone more senior. Perhaps the boss of Rosen. A familiar face to me. Someone I have met."

"That could be Captain Reilly. We'll need the FBI agents here to remand him into custody. We have questions for him. Continue."

"Yes. The rude man from the meeting. With the gray hair. It was him. He serves the vampire."

Ambryn lifted his massive head and looked around. He recognized a badge on a chain swinging on an older woman's chest. In the dark at thirty paces he could read the three letters on it; FBI. "Ma'am," Ambryn called out to her, stopping every human in a thirty foot radius in their tracks.

The pretty and strong woman looked in every direction, sure the dragon was speaking to some other ma'am. After a moment of searching eyes looking around, she realized he spoke to her. "Yes?" she asked him, walking closer in trepidation.

"You're an FBI agent?" Ambryn asked her cordially.

She looks about to wet herself. "Special Agent Brand. Is there something I can help Tapper with?" she asked, walking slowly as spoke.

"Indeed. We need to speak with a Captain Reilly and a Lieutenant Rosen. They are both Vegas cops."

She gave him a sour face. "Why?"

"We have strong reason to believe both have colluded with Cosmin Dorinescu. We must question them immediately. See to it. Do not involve the local officials if possible."

"I don't think I can take orders from a dragon," she said with a hint of an apology.

"You can take orders from me. Do as the dragon wishes. His will is mine," Doyle said authoritatively.

She looked befuddled, but snapped to. "You got it. Where should we bring them? Federal building?"

Doyle leaned out the back of ambulance now. "Hold them and get in touch with me immediately. You have my number?"

"I can get it fast if I don't," Agent Brand replied.

"That's the spirit. Now go. Please," Doyle pleaded to her. She obliged, and disappeared, running.

The dragon and the man turned back to the werewolf. Artur continued. "The Danny knew there were hundreds of vampires here. I feel that there are more than we know of. Locked away and hidden. For years this has been growing, like a tumor beneath the skin. We only now can see it at the surface, but it is fat and rotten deep below. A cancer hidden by flashing lights, parlor tricks, and money. Soon there will be terror here. Death beyond our greatest fears."

"Are we too late?" Doyle asked, fear of the worst in his voice.

Artur shrugged. "If we can find the homes of the dead and kill them before they are set loose, perhaps not."

It is not too late. If I must kill every human, insect, and animal for ten miles in every direction to stop this, it is not too late. "Are they separate? Or is there a single place where we can find many?" Ambryn asked as Henry trotted up, Wayne hot on his heels. *He seems... angry.*

Before Artur could reply, Henry spoke. "Good news and bad news."

"Not that game, Henry," Doyle said, disappointed.

"There's a casino, fairly new on the outskirts of the city. It's called 'The Arabian Nights,' and has a big dome, and all that imagery you described. It's owned by some Sheikh and managed independently by a woman named Sandy Brown. One of my ATF guys said she's a huge bitch. I think that's our place."

Artur's eyes glazed over. His brain assembled someone else's memories. "Yes. That is what I see. Less memory of being there, and more memory of thinking of the place. It is hard to decipher another's mind."

Spoon looked at him, waiting patiently for him to finish. "So yeah, that. That's the good news. Bad news is," the sound of a dozen sirens kicking up down the street and leaving the area paused him. "The bad news is, there are vampires on The Strip. A lot of them, and they are ripping people apart."

Something crawled up Ambryn's throat. Rage. "I will destroy them all," Ambryn growled. Raising up off the blacktop and spreading his wings.

"Wait," Doyle cautioned the massive dragon. "Henry, did they come from the Casino?"

He shook his head. "Sounds like they came from a bus. One of our missing buses I'd bet. Maybe both. No idea where the bus came from yet."

Doyle looked at the dragon that itched to fly away. "Ambryn, what makes more sense? For you to head to the strip to kill a handful of baby vampires, or for you to go to the casino and find Cosmin? Either way you can move over the city faster than we can if you find nothing."

"You want us to split up?" Henry asked his British friend. "Don't you watch horror movies?"

"Always being funny when serious is needed Henry. Ambryn, what say you?"

He raises a good point. "Cosmin is ancient I reckon. One of the oldest perhaps. He will be superhuman. Time is generous to the vampire blood. His baby vampires will be strong as well, but nowhere near his level. I should go to Cosmin if he is at the casino."

"I agree. The rest of us shall go to the city and deal with the bulk," Doyle said. "He also cannot distract us from something happening at the casino if you head there as well. I must prepare my spells and gear. I need five minutes."

"Me too," Spoon said.

"I am naked," Artur threw out, lifting the edge of the orange blanket on his lap revealing a bare thigh.

The men laughed, dragon included. Doyle offered him a hand to get off the stretcher. "I have pants in the bus. Though I suppose you won't be fighting vampires wearing pants." They all laughed again as Ambryn prepared to launch into the night's fray, wherever he found it.

"Where should I go? What should I do?" Wayne asked. *He doesn't want to be left out. He has a horse in this race as the humans would say.*

"You have military experience?" Doyle asked him.

"I do. I'm a Marine. I can shoot, you already know that," Wayne said.

"Come to the bus. Consider yourself hired as a trial agent in Tapper. Tonight is your interview. It's settled, let's do what we need to do," the old man said as he exited the ambulance.

"Anyone want to say something stoic and quotable before we rush off to our certain doom?" Henry asked the group, grinning.

"Do not fail," Ambryn said. And then he took off into the night.

Chapter Forty-Four

Carnage at The Strip

The bus emptied, and the undead feasted. They were hungry.

So very hungry. Starving really.

Tall and short, old and young alike, they bared fangs and grew claws, and ran and jumped, moving from one unsuspecting victim to the next.

Biting, tearing, ripping, drinking.

At first, the tens of thousands of tourists and local workers just ending their long shifts working at the clubs, casinos, and hotels thought it was a stunt for a new movie or a comic book. Maybe a new video game. The screams of the dead and dying were quickly too real however, and after the first ten innocents met their demise outside of the Bellagio and Planet Hollywood, bled dry and consumed, the reality became apparent.

The living ran.

The vampires ran faster, and the spilled blood of their food ran faster yet.

Chapter Forty-Five
Spoon

"Hook the damn chain on the frame," Henry said to a scrawny mechanic. The grease covered tool had been working on detaching the van from the front of the tank for nearly twenty minutes, and now that Spoon, Doyle, and a shirtless Artur were ready to head downtown to confront the rampaging vampires, the man needed to finish what he was doing immediately or hundreds could die.

The mechanic hooked a chain on to an exposed piece of the frame of the van and activated his winch, glaring at Spoon.

"Fuck you," Spoon said to him. *Look at me like that. You don't fucking know me. You're not my mom.* "People are dying man. Hooking the damn chain up to a fucking piece of the fender. Where'd you learn to tow shit? Back of a Cracker Jack box?"

The mechanic stepped from the groaning winch as the chain went taut, ready to fight the agent. "Fuck off buddy. This isn't easy," he said angrily.

"Boys. Enough," Doyle said with finality as the creaking steel of the destroyed van began to wrench free. Spoon took a few steps back, half because he didn't want to be hit by the falling wreck, and half because he didn't want an assault charge for punching the mechanic's teeth down his neck.

With a crash, the van pulled away and rolled, leaving the tank's front end exposed. Spoon ran inside the giant armored RV past the massive blood stain that his friend and former lover Alanna had left as her last mark on the world. He tried to ignore it and turned the key as he sat in the driver's chair.

The tank rumbled to life. "Let's go!" Spoon yelled out the open side door. Artur scrambled up the steps and in, showing no sign of the grievous injuries he had suffered earlier in the night. *Hell, even I can't feel any pain now. That red stuff is good shit.* Doyle moved a bit slower, but boarded and sat down fast, adjusting the chain mail armor he wore, as well as his scabbard and pistol. He looked ready for war once more.

Wayne got in last, and as he put his foot on the first step of the tank's entrance, he stopped. His hand trembled on the grip of a loaned M-4 rifle. "Mr. Doyle?"

"Yes, Mr. Simmons?"

"I think I should go to that casino. I think you guys will be okay, and I got this feeling the dragon is going to need some help."

Doyle looked at him peculiarly, then stood and grabbed a small black bag out of a large plastic case on the floor. He tossed the heavy bag to the father and nodded in approval after the other man caught it. "Do be safe Mr. Simmons, and I hope before this night ends we find out the fate of your family, for better or for worse."

"Thank you. Kick some ass," Wayne said, and then he took off running.

"What's that all about?" Spoon asked Doyle.

The old man sighed. "Call it intuition. The man has been in multiple places where he was needed or helpful, and we've nothing else to credit except for good fortune or fate. I feel it is a small risk to take this night to trust the man's gut. With any luck, he will miss all the fighting and go home to be a father to his son. Drive us Henry."

Spoon put the tank in drive and let the engine's idle move the beast until the side door was parallel to the mechanic who was already unchaining the van and preparing it to be loaded onto his flatbed. *Damn it. Be the bigger man.* He braked as the door met the grease monkey. "Hey uh," Spoon said apologetically, but loud enough for the man to hear.

The tow truck operator stopped and looked inside the tank at Spoon. "Yeah?" he asked the ex-cop, half angry.

"Sorry I yelled at you. I lost a good friend tonight," Spoon said.

The skinny man with bad teeth looked down at the massive red stain on the pavement. He looked up, humbled. "It's cool man. I'm not angry. Sorry I couldn't get this shit done faster. Nervous. Go get some for us. For your friend."

Spoon's eyes moistened. "Yeah. Yeah I'll do that. Find someplace safe. It's going to be a bad night for Las Vegas."

"Nice jacket," the kid said, looking at Spoon's enchanted pilot's leather jacket, a gift from the sorcerer Doyle.

"Thanks. It's seen some stuff. Be safe tonight."

The driver of the flatbed tipped the brim of his Lakers ball cap in an old-fashioned gesture of thanks, and Spoon shut the door and gave the tank some gas. The engine picked up, and within seconds they were sliding through the night like a black missile filled with a hundred tons of dynamite, ready to blow.

*****

Navigating the streets to the downtown cluster of casinos and hotels turned out to be easy. The massive tank divided the insane amounts of fleeing traffic like a boulder dropped into a stream. If he drove straight, peering carefully out of the shot-up windshield, the oncoming cars went around him, gunning their engines and racing to get away from the madness the trio drove towards. Artur breathed heavily, the smell of fresh blood and vampires on the air.

"Artur," Spoon asked him, "what do we need to know about fighting with you?"

Artur's mind drifted in another word for a second as he stared through the busted windshield, but he snapped to. "I am in control. Do not fear my rage."

"What of your past excesses? I know you have gone too far. Recently, even as my good friend Belyakov can attest. Should we worry about that tonight?" Doyle asked.

Artur looked offended. "No. I only did these things when I was drinking, and I am not drinking. Tonight, I do this for my daughters. For Alanna, and to regain the honor of the Cojocaru family. I have been a stain. Now, I change this."

"What else?" Spoon asked as he made a turn that would take them onto Las Vegas Boulevard. The heart of Vegas, and the site of the massacre they were heading to try and stop.

"I rip and tear and shred. When in the war form, I heal from injuries as fast as they occur, sans fire, or silver. Some vampires and monsters have magic enough to harm me, but tonight… I care not about pain."

"Do I need to worry about shooting you?" Spoon asked.

Artur shook his head. "So long as you do not shoot my head off, or damage my brain so badly I cannot heal properly, you may shoot me if need be."

A loud crack hit the front of the bus. Spoon looked over to the passenger side of the windshield and saw a pockmark where one hadn't been a moment before. A bullet had struck them. "Pistol round, see why I asked?

There's going to be some serious gunplay. Look," Spoon said lifting his chin towards the melee ahead.

It could've been a Roman orgy, if the streets, light posts, parked cars, and sidewalks weren't all covered in blood. Fresh blood, still red and wet, running from torn and tattered bodies that were cast aside like garbage.

"Holy shit," Spoon said. A horde of maniacs ran about up and down the street, inflicting pain and misery. As they closed the distance to the center of the madness, Spoon could see that they were not feeding to survive, they were murdering for pleasure. No blood was drank from ripped open necks, and no flesh was eaten when a stomach was torn into like tissue paper, the victim fighting frantically to push *everything back in* as it spilled out. They leapt over cars in bounds, scampered up stairs, and blasted into hotel lobbies as if they were pantries filled with forbidden sweets. The undead made indiscriminate wreckage of everything living they got to.

"Drive us into the middle of it," Doyle said as he got to his feet.

"My M-4 won't touch these guys," Spoon said as a teenaged vampire ran and dove onto the front of the bus. The impact of the vehicle against his body was bone breaking, and he lost hold of the grill, tumbling under. The bus shook as the fat tires rolled over his body. *I hope that puts him down for a bit.*

"The bandolier of ammunition I gave to you is enchanted. Same sort of bullets I supplied Abraham with the night Kaula died. The bullets are blessed thrice or more, and have a solid silver chip inside. Ballistically they will perform almost as well as a normal round, though they tumble and break apart at great distance. Shoot at things less than fifty yards away and you will be fine."

"What about my pistol?" Spoon asked the mage as he applied the brakes. Vampires, long in the tooth and drooling rivulets of human vitae were everywhere, chasing the few survivors left. Some started to turn towards the bus, murder in their eyes.

"Your pistol has been heavily enchanted by me. You could shoot a hippopotamus and kill it with one shot," Doyle said proudly, drawing his own handgun. His sword remained in its jewel-laden scabbard.

"You choose a hippo as an example? Why not a lion?" Spoon said, putting the tank in park.

"Take a trip to Africa with me soon. We can watch the hippos eat the lions together," Mr. Doyle said with a wink.

Artur went to the door as Spoon grabbed the magazines of special ammo off the floor. Spoon dropped the mundane magazine out of the weapon and slid a special one home. He charged the weapon as Artur reached for the door handle.

"Stop," Doyle said. Artur did as he was told, but he looked like a dog straining at the end of his chain. Lips quivering, hackles raised. "We need some space. They are already crowding us in."

He's right. Two dozen of the vampires had rushed the tank and were beating on the door, the sides, and the windows. Were it not for the thick bulletproof armor and glass, the three would have claws at their necks already. "Do it up, Doyle."

Mr. Doyle turned to Spoon and had a somber expression. "For Alanna," he offered.

"Yes. For Alanna MacTavish. Warrior woman," Artur said resolutely.

"For Alanna," Spoon whispered. *I'm so sorry.*

Doyle reached into one of the myriad pouches at his belt and produced a tiny jar filled with dark colored earth. The jar and the material inside it looked rich and old. He smiled, and spoke a short phrase of power as he threw it to the hard floor of the tank. "Et movebitur terra!"

Nothing happened. "Dud?" Spoon asked him as he

adjusted his custom made vest. It was light body armor, but over it straight to his chin was a fine mesh of silver alloy. His gloves matched it, Nomex under studs made of silver.

"No," Doyle said with relish. "This one just takes a moment... to…" the bus shook. "Build."

With a violent upheaval, Las Vegas Boulevard had an intense and focused earthquake, and the vampires were thrown off the bus, and tossed to the ground. Car alarms bleated in every direction.

"Now, for me," Artur said, and he flung the door open.

Chapter Forty-Six

Ambryn

Ambryn moved like a shark in the sky, swimming through the air, his entire length undulating, when his nostrils caught the scent of the blood. He looked towards the glitz and glamour of The Strip, miles away. *From so far off? There must be piles of the dead. Such fools Kaula and I were to tamper with the way of things in Tesser's absence. Arrogance and impatience reaps such sweet rewards. Tonight, oh tonight I bring more of my mistakes to reckoning. Cosmin Dorinescu, may you stand and fight me. I pray you do not flee like the cockroach you are.*

The flight to the outskirts of the city where the massive domed casino sat was a short one for the dragon. His black wings spread wide, flushing the air to his aft to pick up speed, he rode atop a buoyant warm air thermal, lubricated by it, sliding along it with minimal effort at maximum speed. He felt... perfect.

The casino from high above spread large, though it did no not reach the scope of the city's biggest. Golden domes dotted the roof, spires in between. Swaying arches were in every conceivable place, lending an air of fluidity and grace. On the roof a giant yellow H stood out against a gray backdrop where a helicopter could land. Beyond the ornate architecture, the casino and hotel's chief attraction had to be the massive series of steel loops forming a roller coaster that dove into and out of the interior of the sand colored building and above its parking lot. Ambryn could see a pair of cars blitzing along on the tubular tracks, the passengers screaming for joy, and he knew the coaster would be his ticket into the casino's guts.

He twisted and dove through the sky, plummeting five hundred feet in a single breath. He spread his wings like a parachute, and buffeted them down, coming to a hover at a low spot on the rail of the coaster, outside the casino, above the parking lot. People below—idiots who had no idea what was happening elsewhere in the city—looked up to the dragon and screamed in fear. Here came a monster, they thought.

They weren't completely wrong in their fear.

As the cars rifled down the tracks he could see they slowed. Someone somewhere sees me. Good. Let them have their moment of dismay. He put his feet down on the track, and gripped hard, holding on. The cars slid to a stop within his arm's reach, the passengers held still behind padded steel restraints. They fought to escape.

Ambryn shushed them with a massive clawed hand. "Shhhh. Quiet. It's alright. I am not here to eat you. You are safe," he said in as soft a tone as he could imagine.

They screamed. Ambryn sighed.

"I'm going to get you out of the cars now, and put you on the ground where it's safe. Please hold on." Ambryn chose a large man in the front row as the first. He tried his best to smile at the wide-eyed human, forgetting that a dragon's smile looked terrifying. The man's hair stood on end as Ambryn's teeth were revealed from behind lips that looked to be snarling. "Sorry," he said as he reached forward and gently ripped the restraint off the man. The metal gave way with a crack and a shriek, and the young passenger screamed in fear again. Ambryn put a dexterous hand around his midsection, and lifted him gently into the night, twenty feet above the ground below. The man leaned his head down and bit his finger in defense, but the chomp did nothing to the dense scales on his flesh.

"Aaahhhhh!" he yelled as Ambryn put him down on the blacktop below with all his fingers and toes, sans even a bruise. The man went quiet abruptly, looked up at the dragon, and ran away into the sea of parked cars huffing and puffing as he went.

"You are welcome," Ambryn said as he lifted his body back up to remove another stranded passenger from the coaster car. One by one their screams became sedated, and eventually they sat patiently waiting for their turn on the 'dragon ride.' The children squealed in delight when he helped them down and that made the adults that much more calm.

He got to the last older lady, a woman who had at length told him to be careful because she had two children in college and they couldn't afford tuition without her and her husband, before the security in the casino opened fire on him. *They're going to kill someone, and it won't be me.*

He shielded the now insane woman from the reckless gunfire with his own body, dropping to the ground below. He let the woman run free and turned to seek out the small orange-white flashes of the loud weapons. To his rear he saw a handful of men leaning over the hoods of cars, and peering around pillars of stone alongside the building, all shooting at him. He felt their bullet hit his skin and fall off, pinpricks of sensation like falling raindrops. He looked over his shoulder to ensure Gina had reached safety, and then he launched into the sky, gliding the hundred yards between him and them, and spitting twice into the areas from where the men were attacking him.

His saliva—pestilent, thick, and aggressive—splashed

two of the men, and their interest in shooting at him came to an immediate halt. All that they could do was scratch at the gray-green ooze, and the hundreds of hives that had sprouted in their mouths, and on their faces, even on the whites of their eyes. They fell to the ground, tearing their own skin off to save their lives. *That won't work sillies.* As their fellows died, the other two men shot at him continuously with automatic weapons, but the bullets did no more to harm him than the man's bite had done earlier. *You need bigger guns. Much bigger guns.*

Ambryn pounced, leaping over a series of parked pickups as if they were no more than stepping stones in a riverbed. The trucks didn't hold up to his weight as well as a stone their size would've. *I should hope these gamblers invested in automobile insurance.* He landed straddling one of the last two guards, and simply punched his foe's body once into a crater in the asphalt. He wasn't dead, but a few pints of blood leaked later, he would be. *I give him sixty seconds.* The lone remaining guard had some sense and ran back to the entrance of the casino, but Ambryn running on all fours was an opponent in the sprint the man could not defeat.

You could run away from death, but to escape from it? In all things, death would be inevitable.

Ambryn snatched out, his jaws turned sideways, and severed the man into thirds. He swallowed the center of the man, his trunk, and turned back towards the rails of the coaster as the man's head tumbled away. With a hop he flew up and grabbed the iron tubes, and began to shimmy along them, entering the casino and hotel through the gap they created in the wall.

He didn't notice Wayne speeding up in his Sonata to the casino entrance behind him.

*****

The lobby of The Arabian Nights exceeded the exterior's opulence by leaps and bounds. Everything not intricately carved was covered in a hundred shades of gold and platinum, much of it fake, but some of it real. All of it dazzled. Full size palm trees and cacti grew under the watchful eyes of caretakers and the ultraviolet lights embedded in the ceiling. A small stream of crystal clear water flowed through a blue tiled river of amethyst and lapis lazuli, glittering under the lights, creating an otherworldly feeling, transporting the visitors to the hotel to another time, and place. *Heh. A river of blue.*

Right now the time was 1945, and the place was Berlin. *A bit of a botch, but I suppose the feeling of all-out war wasn't the impression they were trying to convey when they built the place.*

The lobby erupted into a tornado of bullets the moment Ambryn poked his head in. A score and more of heavily armed men and women had taken strategic positions around the multiple tiers of the giant room, taking cover behind stone railings, rock outcroppings designed to look natural, and more stone and plaster pillars. Ambryn felt each and every bullet tick off of his hard scales and fall to the floor with a hundred inaudible clicks. Piles of spent rounds would be everywhere in a few short minutes. Rounds that somehow missed him chewed into the drywall and mortar of the walls around, sending up clouds of white, dry powder and debris, making it progressively harder to see and breathe with every passing moment. They shooters seemed human in the din of the assault, but it was hard for the dragon to decipher their natures without a taste of their flesh or more evidence of their true nature.

Now. In what order do they die? I know. Top to bottom. The leech likely lives below anyhow.

Ambryn in full form could move about the cavernous lobby so long as he didn't hit the tubes of the coaster as they spiraled through and out the other side. He used the steel as a child would climb a jungle gym, and headed up.

A leap, a scramble, and a launch later, bullets pinging off of his side harmlessly, Ambryn grabbed onto the thick stone edging that doubled as a railing on the third floor of the hotel. The highest level from where he was being shot. His claws wrapped over the top of the smooth stone and embedded in the other side, nearly splitting the man behind it in two. The dragon pulled his body up and rocketed his head over the top, biting the man nearly in half. With a toss of his head he threw the remains out into the lobby, where it fell to the hard floor and broke apart completely. The body parts twitched below as Ambryn dropped a level to where two more shooters poured lead at him. He spat at one and swiped a claw at the other, sending him and freshly severed parts over the ledge and careening off the side of the coaster rails.

That looks to be about half of them. He saw two of them move into the open another level below to find better cover and he spat a wad of death at them. He missed the second target—a much faster woman, and he'd led her too far—but she slipped in the slime he'd sent her way, and when she landed in it, the spontaneous mutations it caused nearly ripped her apart. *I can hear her bone breaking over all the gunfire. Poor thing. Serving vampires doesn't pay.*

Out of the corner of his eyes he saw a pair of unarmed guards moving into the huge lobby. Their skin was thinly colored, ashen. As they walked with confidence, they shook off their suit coats and looked up at him. Bullets tore the room apart everywhere around them, but they paid the chaos no attention. They were fixated on his black eyes. *They have fear in their faces, but they also have fangs there. I would bet Tesser's virility their boss told them to come kill me.* The men snapped their hands down, and the tips of their fingers burst open, revealing cat-like claws. *Ah. Clawed vampires. They hurt.*

The vampires took off at a sprint, heading for the stairs that ringed the open lobby.

Might as well go and say hi.

Chapter Forty-Seven

Artur Cojocaru

The werewolf wearing the skin of a human transformed as his bare feet left the steps of the armored Tapper bus. He landed on the smooth concrete sidewalk already well into the shift into his *forma război,* the war-form.

To cry havoc, and let slip me.

Artur howled laughter as his lungs and throat changed savagely from human to werewolf, his cartilage and muscle ripping and reforming, causing his body to put out a guttural, soul screeching bellow that touched on secret fears from the midnight hours in all who heard it. Here came a sound that told you in no uncertain terms: death has come for you.

The *forma război* existed only to destroy, and over time the werewolf war-form had evolved into a body exceedingly suitable for the destruction of anything put in front of it. Artur's height drew out and up to nearly eight feet from the toe to the top of the skull, his legs reversed at the knee joint, and his feet lengthened to rise up almost twelve inches, becoming a giant bipedal bastardization of a normal wolf's leg. Such legs would make him faster than nearly everything on land.

His center mass, his torso, drew out as well, with the ribcage thickening, rising, and narrowing simultaneously. His arms fell long, bones cracking over and over until each arm was four feet long, and tipped with paws that were almost as dextrous as a human's and just as lethal as a bear's. Perhaps worst of all for those who stood in the way of the varcolac was the head. A vicious skull faced with a snout and with a jaw that sported forty-two teeth, each able to sever muscle and skin. Artur's yellowed upper canines were two inches long each and dripped with his saliva. From head to toe he wore a white coat of fur, thick and rough.

I hunger. Give me the flesh of the dead. Show me their nightmares. Show my face in their last moments.

Artur dropped to all fours and used his hind legs to spring forward into the chest of a female vampire who tried to get to her feet from Doyle's small quake. His hands hit her at the collar bones, breaking them in half and bending the shards of bone downward and into her chest. Her shrieks of pain ended with a frothy gasp as Artur sank his fangs into her throat around her trachea and ripped backwards. He nearly tore her head off. He roared another howl—another laugh—and spit her neck out. The wound would be enough to kill the immortal, so he jumped off of her and went to the next man coming at him, a brawny teenager, apparently one of the football players from the missing bus. He still wore his jersey, #81, though now it had been stained nearly black from old and new blood.

They leapt at each other and collided in midair at the front of the bus.

Artur's mass won the battle against the vampiric blood, and the young bloodsucker was tackled to the pavement and put on his back snarling like a feral dog. As the werewolf used his ample claws to rake a series of inch wide slashes down his chest, the vampire tried the same on his sides. The baby vampire's claws were small, less than half an inch. *It hurts, but he cannot cut me deep enough, fast enough.* Artur did something decidedly human; he headbutted the vampire in the face with the flat of his broad wolfen skull.

The young vampire—only a boy, despite his status as being undead—had his nose and brow crushed by the blow and the back of his head smashed into the pavement. Artur watched as his eyes rolled up momentarily, and the werewolf used that second of weakness to plunge his claws into the vampire's stomach just above the navel. He shoved his hand up into the undead's chest, under the ribcage, until everything beyond his elbow was under the skin and bones, and then he grabbed the heart and lungs, and yanked.

He nearly turned the boy inside out.

Artur backhanded the interior of the vampire into the street and stood. He watched as a circle of undead formed around him ... six, then seven. Ten then twelve. The wounds on his side from the boy's small claws stung, but he could feel the supernatural itch of his flesh mending already. *They will have to do more than scratch me to kill me.*

One of them—an old lady, so old her agile movements looked inappropriate and alien for her advanced age—leapt out at him, slashing him across the upper chest, just missing the vital artery at his neck. The cut went deep, scratching bone and tendon, sending immeasurable pain into his skull. He growled at her and slashed back with his own claws, slapping the cheek right off her face, exposing her skull, half her teeth, and one of her vampiric fangs. She screamed in rage, and Artur slashed across the woman's neck again as she reared up for another blow. He hit her so strongly she spun wildly in a circle and fell down, near dead and defeated. *Yes. Act your age.* Artur stepped forward and stomped mightily on her skull, and it cracked open. Ten more vampires had filled in her spot in the semi circle around him. Artur's blazing confidence began to form cracks.

A deafening sound tore the tense moment apart. A buzzing noise, powerful enough to shake the lungs inside Artur's chest. It sounded to him like a thousand tiny explosions all happening at nearly the very same time, sustained for several endless seconds. Artur's eyes barely registered three of the vampires evaporating into a dark red mist in the air right in front of where he stood. Chunks of the bodies fell to the street like meat dropped from the sky above. The noise stopped, leaving only a mechanical whirring noise in its wake. *What in all the world could do that?*

He looked quickly over his shoulder to the Tapper bus, and saw Doyle's head poking out from behind a massive multi-barrelled machine gun. The six barrels in rotation came to a slow stop, pouring small strings of smoke into the air. *A gatling gun?* Doyle lined up the sights, and Artur watched as he thumbed some kind of trigger, letting loose another eardrum-shattering burst of gunfire. Artur turned to see what Doyle shot at, but when his eyes caught up to the laser streams of bullets, the target had disintegrated, just like the first. Doyle stopped firing.

"The M-134 Minigun!" Doyle shouted with glee. His accent was thicker than usual. *Perhaps it is the excitement?* "Enchanted and blessed rounds dispatched at three thousand per minute! Let's measure their mettle against this, shall we? You're going to want to duck, Artur!"

Artur did as the gun toting mage told him to, and the old British man on top of the bus in a turret with the Gatling gun showed the vampires the power of ancient magic and modern military technology brought together as one.

Artur danced in the rain of vampire blood.

Chapter Forty-Eight

Mycroft Rupert Doyle

Doyle thumbed the minigun's trigger and the weapon came to life in his hand. It buzzed, vibrated, roared, and spit out round after round of 7.62mm death at the semi-circle of vampires that had approached the bus and threatened to murder Artur. Not that the werewolf had experienced any difficulty dispatching the undead or needed help. Doyle had fought ardently to have the M134's installed in each of the Tapper buses at great expense to the agency, and this seemed like a perfectly good time to put the weaponry to the test against something paranormal.

I believe they call this a validating moment. Or is it proof-of-concept?

The blessed ammunition flecked with rare magical metals coupled with the enchantment on the weapon erased the vampires from the street as fully as an eraser would remove pencil from paper. Where Doyle walked the stream of tracer fire, anything living or dead ceased to exist. He watched as the heavy fire of bullets ate away at the pavement, leaving pockmarks and furrows behind. He followed a sprinting vampire down the street and let loose a two second burst, the rough equivalent of a hundred rounds. Half the shells split the vampire in half, and the other half destroyed the hood and engine of a parked police cruiser. *Oops. The department can invoice us for that.*

After the initial rush of the undead met destruction at his hands from a hail of ensorcelled bullets, he became choosy with what he shot at. *Ammunition of this type doesn't grow on trees and I must be judicious in its use.* The upside of Doyle slowing down his punishing rate of fire meant Artur had been freed to roam. The werewolf moved to the rear of the tank, out of the field of fire Doyle had chosen. Watching the werewolf destroy the undead had chilled and thrilled the old wizard.

I've only seen a werewolf kill like that once before, and the memories haunt me. A murderous shape shifter in northern Europe. Belgium. I'm glad we took her down before she killed too many. How I wish we had a gun like this back in that day. Bravery is easy when you shoot so many bullets so fast. But it is a thing to see something I once called monster do good like this. It changes how I feel. And as an old dog…that is no easy feat.

Doyle scoured the street for fewer and fewer targets. Anything with fangs and claws, or anyone who had their mouths and necks covered in blood received a burst from his Gatling gun. To his rear, he could hear Artur's soul-curdling howls as he dismembered and tore apart vampire after vampire. When he paused his own onslaught, Doyle could also hear the disciplined crack-crack of Henry's rifle alongside the sounds of Artur's terror. *If I know Henry, he'll be keeping the vampires off of Artur's back. A good team, if I ever saw one. Not quite the equal of Belyakov and me in our heyday, but you can't have everything. Back in our day, we had to kill werewolves, and vampires, and wendigo in the snow, uphill both …*

Doyle's eyes moved upward during a lull in the shooting. They'd only been in the street fighting for fifteen, maybe twenty minutes, but his hands, ears and whole body made it feel like it had been hours. He scanned the smooth side of the towering casino hotels and saw window after window of gawking onlooker. Smart hotel patrons that hid behind their locked doors and shatter-resistant glass. Smart patrons who watched professionals kill nightmares right in front of their eyes on the street below. *What a sight we must be to them. Not the holiday they expected, I imagine.*

Wait, what was that?

Something changed in one of the rooms his eyes had just passed over. He looked back, searching for the change. Where there had been open curtains and the light of several lamps before, there emitted now a dim red glow, and the curtains had been half drawn and left askew. He watched as the curtains moved suddenly, as if they were jerked aside by a struggle. Suddenly, a face appeared pressed hard against the glass. Bloody and in panic, the tiny face, so distant it might as well have been on the moon, mouthed two words that broke Doyle's heart: *help me.*

Doyle turned the small turret to face the hotel and raised the axis of the weapon but he couldn't get the angle. If he shot and missed, he'd destroy more than a handful of rooms, all potentially filled with innocents. None of his spells would work either. Not fast enough. "Henry!" Doyle shouted.

The crack-crack of Henry's rifle stopped, and a few seconds later Doyle heard the man below the edge of the bus. "Mr. Doyle? You okay?" Crack-crack.

Doyle pulled his body up out of the turret and onto the roof of the tank. He drew his 1911 from his hip and blasted a vampire that had reached a full running sprint towards Henry's back. It stumbled and face-planted in the middle of the road, and he blasted it once more in the back. "Thank me later. Look." He pointed with his pistol at the room where the people were being killed. "They're in the hotels. Can you get up there fast? Help those people?"

Doyle watched as Henry counted the floors. "Yeah, that looks like the tenth floor. Can you and Artur hold down the street?"

Doyle looked around. The piles of vampire bodies were now starting to outnumber the piles of dead innocents. That spoke less to their ability in killing vampires and more to the sea of the undead that they had waded through to accumulate such success. *Thankfully the creation of a vampire is a long and arduous process. This battle would've been lost before we arrived if not so.* "As long as my ammunition supplies hold. I've a spell or two as well I can cast. It appears the police are at the ends of the boulevard. They are moving in our direction. Reinforcements will be clutch."

"Alright, I'm out. Be safe Doyle," Henry said, and he took off running towards the casino entrance.

"You as well, Henry," Doyle said to the man's back. *Run fast Henry Spooner. Every second wasted is another dead body, I fear.* Doyle dropped back down into the turret and started looking for vampires. When he found one, he destroyed it with a burst of blessed silver gunfire.

Chapter Forty-Nine

Wayne Simmons

Wayne got out of the car as Ambryn, in full-sized Dragon form, comically slinked along the top of the casino's roller coaster and into the side of the building. *Funny as hell watching a thing that big try to be small. Now what'd Doyle put in this bag for me?*

Wayne looked around to ensure he wasn't about to be shot and dragged the bag to the driver's seat of the car. He took a knee, and unzipped it. *What the hell is this stuff?*

Wayne picked up another series of magazines, each marked like the special ones in the magazine pouches he'd gotten from Spooner earlier. *Magic bullets. Or something like that.* Beside those Wayne saw a heavy ballistic-resistant helmet, similar to the ones SWAT officers wore. The insignia for Tapper had been stenciled on the front and back of the helmet, but on the sides there were strange symbols that seemed to be lit from within the helmet. Wayne looked inside, but there he found no light source. *Hell. That must be magic too.* He popped the helmet on his head and snapped the chin strap together, fastening it. He saw a brief flare of yellow light inside his car, and knew it emanated from the symbols on the helmet. Once he had the thing on, he realized that there was a recessed piece of black glass or plastic just above the brow. With prying fingers he pulled down on it, and a smoky piece of glass slid down over his eyes.

Immediately a faint yellow line appeared inside his car wherever an opening might have been. The outline of the glove box became immediately apparent, as well as the ash tray and several small storage compartments secreted away. *Ha. It tells me what can be opened. Neat.*

Wayne pushed the black glass back up inside the helmet and returned to the bag.

A belt with two canister pouches on it held small steel flasks marked with more strange runes. Stenciled in English below the odd writing was the words; Drink immediately in the event of injury. Attached to the same belt he saw a pair of familiar M-67 fragmentation grenades, and a single AN-M14 incendiary grenade. *Ah, the good stuff.*

In the bottom of the bag below some mundane bandages, a first aid kit, and a fairly generic change of clothes that may or may not fit him, Wayne found a polished steel knight's gauntlet. *What the hell is this thing doing here?* Wayne lifted it and examined it. *Damn thing is heavy man. Battle worn too, look at the scratches and shit. Super-fine writing on it. German?* It was for the left hand. Wayne looked up as gunfire broke out inside the hotel lobby. Punishing, wretched amounts of it from the wall of noise that tried to escape the inside of the hotel. He watched as the glass doors of the building rattled and pulsed from the cacophony within. *Man. Hella gunfight in there.* Wayne looked back down to the gauntlet, and slipped it on his left hand. It fit as if it were made for him. A tingle followed by pleasant warmth fell over his hand and cascaded up his arm. He flexed the heavy steel fingers—bright as silver—and laughed, astounded by how well the armor moved. He'd lost no motion, and it felt as if it weighed no more than a thin fabric glove. As a test, he dropped the magazine out of his rifle and slid it back in. Easy as normal.

Wayne stood and made sure all of his new goodies were attached properly around his waist and below his Kevlar vest. He felt immeasurably better with the helmet and single gauntlet on, and laughed at the thought. *One metal glove and a pot on the head won't make me bullet proof, and I doubt it'll stop a vampire from biting the crap out of me. Now, let's go see if I can find my daughter and wife. In Jesus' name, I do your work, Lord.*

Wayne ran to the doors that stood between him and a gun battle bigger than any he had ever experienced as a Marine.

*****

Watching the dragon soar and leap around the massive indoor lobby filled with trees and a sparkling blue gem encrusted river was something Wayne simply couldn't wrap his mind around. Bigger and better than anything Hollywood had ever done. He took cover behind a series of ATMs just inside the hotel's entrance, and watched as the dragon bit and tore people apart with a savage grace that reminded Wayne of a lion on the savannah. *A pissed-off lion chasing squirrels maybe.*

The game changed when two card-carrying bad asses walked into the lobby, threw off their suit coats, and grew fangs and claws. Wayne's mind—the very same one that had refused to believe the dragon right in front of his eyes was real and actually killing people—twisted from disbelief to anger as the vampires took off at a sprint up the wide and spiraling stairs to get higher at the dragon. The gunfire in the room died out as they leapt from the stone stair railing, soaring through the air to latch on to the dragon that held on to the side of the upper exposed floors. *He looks like a cross between King Kong, Mothra, and Godzilla.*

Ambryn timed a part of his defense perfectly, and

with a single backward swipe of his claw, he sent the first vampire screaming through the air, hitting him hard enough to tear most of his clothes off. Rags fell like snow to the floor below. *Looked like a tennis pro's backhand.* The vampire flew the hundred feet across the lobby without losing an inch of elevation before it crashed into the opposing stone wall. Wayne heard the crunch and waited to see him fall to the floor. Wayne celebrated as the body of the vampire hit the hard tiled floor twenty feet ahead a second later. The body stayed still as Wayne watched the other vampire rip and claw at Ambryn's chest. The vampire looked like an angry tick, digging for the red meal below. *Hell. That looks like blood. That dude is hurting him.*

The vampire on the floor near Wayne twitched. The man's broken legs began to straighten, and Wayne could hear the dead fellow grunt in pain as his body began to repair itself.

"Oh hell, no," Wayne said out loud. The vampire spun its head and hissed at him. Without a beat missed, the Marine put the M-4 to his shoulder and thumbed the fire selector to SEMI. He squeezed the trigger twice after the pretty red dot lined up on his target's center mass. The two rounds cooked through the vampire like normal rounds would, but the effect they had on the undead's body seemed far from normal.

A typical 5.56 millimeter round travels so fast that when you shoot someone with it, they often get a step or two in before they even realize they've been shot. A second or two after that, the bleeding starts, then the pain, and about then they fall down, or take cover as best they can considering they've just been shot. These bullets... the magical, blessed, supernatural bullets Mr. Doyle had given Wayne, were in no way a typical 5.56 round. The impact site on the vampire's now bare chest blossomed out with a gray stain laced with cracks in the skin, like when an anvil fell on a sidewalk in a cartoon.

But the cracks didn't stop, they spread, and so did the harsh gray mottling until it had spread to the size of a dinner plate. Wayne watched as the vampire's mouth fell open, his fangs revealed but now somehow impotent. The man's eyes turned black, and he fell face down on the floor, a spent husk, rotted out from within.

"These are some good bullets," Wayne said under his breath as he watched the dragon pluck the vampire off his chest, and squeeze him until he burst. A red stream fell from his massive black hand to the floor like he'd squeezed a blood orange the size of a couch.

The gunfire returned, and as it did, more fanged adversaries spilled out of the far hotel hallway, issuing forth like a river of the damned. Some ran at the dragon, but worse yet, some ran at him. Drooling, slavering, hungry and angry, they ran impossibly fast. Wayne shouldered his rifle, and started to put the red dot on new people. He pulled the trigger over and over until he couldn't hear himself scream anymore.

Then he reloaded, and did it again.

Chapter Fifty

Cosmin Dorinescu

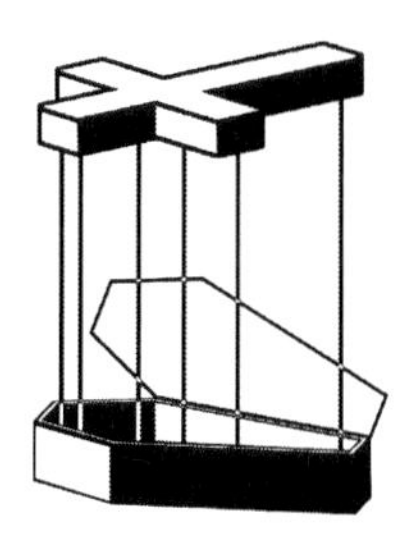

The walls were thick. The floors were thick. The doors barring the way were strong and held shut by locks equally strong. There were a hundred men and women, half of them vampires, many dhampyr, and all armed literally to the teeth with the best weapons money could buy. Still, the distant hammer of heavy gunfire, and the rumbling of the building's destruction at the claws and teeth of the dragon could be felt and heard.

Thunder over the mountain. And here I sit, listening to the battle rage above in greater fear than I have ever experienced. My children die by the dozen as I sit here and do nothing.

Cosmin leaned back in the rich leather chair he had imported from Italy, and watched the ungodly carnage unfold on the security monitors in his office. From five different angles he watched the black dragon rip and tear every poor soul apart that ran into the lobby. Bodies were thrown like garbage, smashed like ants, torn apart like old mail, and occasionally eaten like an hors d'oeuvre. His strongest vampire, his eldest from Europe even, stood no more a chance at hurting the dragon than he did, and Cosmin had killed and murdered the most powerful of men and monster alike for well over five centuries...

I have done the right thing. I have made the right choices. I have walked away from the path of torment and embraced the path of enlightenment. The path of life. He stood, sure more than ever he had put the right events into motion. He walked to the door of his office, and the three dhampyr guards standing against the wall moved to follow.

"No, boys. My children," Cosmin said sorrowfully. "You must go. Take all the dhampyr below, and all the baby vampires, and use the tunnel to the garage. If you are quick, you can all escape in cars. Live full lives. Make your papa proud of you."

The guards—children of his from a union between he and a living woman decades ago—looked at one another, confounded. One asked the question they all thought, "You are going to face the dragon? We will go, we will fight with you. Die with you if we must." The others agreed immediately.

Cosmin walked to the young man and brushed his cheek, "Your loyalty to your father is a beautiful thing. And now, after all these years, the weight of time has shown me that the death and destruction I have wrought has been... ill advised. But that is my concern, not yours. Do your father proud, and live full lives. Protect the vampires, your cousins. Give my people a chance at the happiness I was not afforded in my time." Cosmin laughed. "The happiness I failed to seek."

They cried, and Cosmin kissed their foreheads as if he were the Pope. As Cosmin left the third son and went to the door, he gasped a final question to his undead father, "Papa, what will you do?"

Cosmin turned. "I have done something tonight I should have done a long time ago. Now, I will engage my tormentor one last time to ensure that my wishes are carried out. Be well my sons."

Cosmin left the room and headed to the stairs to greet the dragon that dug and clawed to meet and kill him.

The eldest of all vampires felt a peace that he had never experienced, and he let it coalesce over him and embrace his cold heart. His fear had left him, and in its void he realized what that fear had driven him to do since he'd been turned into a vampire so long ago.

As he reached out to push the final heavy door open that would allow him to ascend the stairs to the surface levels, he looked over and saw a phone mounted on the wall. *I should speak to the dragon. End his destruction.* Cosmin stepped away from the door and walked to the phone. He read the small card with extension instructions on it and picked up the handset. He dialed the number that would call on the entire hotel and casino speaker system, and he spoke. "My vampires, my employees, my servants I implore you; stop fighting the dragon and allow me to speak to him."

The gunfire above tapered off within seconds, and the booming sounds of the dragon ripping his way through the building stopped with it. Cosmin imagined what the scene looked like. His scared and bloody vampires facing down a dragon that they had no chance at stopping and no ability to escape from. *Poor things. Goldfish thrown to the barracuda in a tank.* "Black dragon, I seek council. Kill no more of my children and I will come to you this moment and face you with honor."

Cosmin waited, and after many seconds filled with dread, he heard a deep voice so powerful he could feel its bass in his chest, two stories below ground. "Come to me, cheater of death."

Cosmin sighed in victory, hung up the phone, and walked slowly and with a clear mind to his doom.

Chapter Fifty-One
Spoon

The elevator had been the only place Henry hadn't shot a vampire since he'd stepped out of the tank on Las Vegas Boulevard. He had to kill three in the hotel lobby after he'd pushed the button to hail the elevator. He used the precious few seconds of elevator Muzak induced calm to refresh the magazine in his rifle, take a few deep breaths, and wipe the sweat from his brow. He felt the tender flesh where his skin had been ruptured in the earlier car crash. It healed quickly.

This is worse than the daemons. Or is it? The daemons were pretty bad. At least none of these things have arms and legs made out of baby parts. The elevator dinged for the tenth floor arrival, and Spoon snapped to and shouldered his rifle. *Hope I guess right on the floor.* The twin metallic doors covered in thin trails of blood and viscera parted, revealing a taupe colored wall and a coral colored rug. The flooring had been spattered with blood, and in spots it tracked up the wall like flung paint. He saw faint footprints outlined in blood heading down the way as well. *Well right or wrong, I suspect I'll be able to do some damage on this floor.* Spoon took a deep breath and stepped into the hallway facing where the footprints headed.

Ten paces distant he saw a scarecrow of a man with raven black hair hunched down on his knees, gnawing at the inside thigh of a young girl, no more than ten. She was still and surrounded by a halo of dark blood on the rug. Mercifully, she had already died. *Son of a bitch.*

"Hey fuck face!" Spoon yelled to the vampire. It stopped feeding and popped a little too fast to its feet for Spoon's comfort. The ex-paratrooper put two rounds through the vampire's chest and neck, and watched as the silver-impregnated rounds infected and ruined him. The rotting vampire dropped first to his knees, and then collapsed backwards. It shook and convulsed in a series of violent death throes before going still. *At least he didn't fall on the kid.* Spoon's ears were ringing from the rifle's reports in the narrow hall. He wore an earpiece which helped one eardrum, but the other felt swollen and lethargic from the last thirty minute's noise. *Going deaf is a real concern in this line of work.*

He couldn't hear anything at the closed hotel room doors as he started to walk slowly, one half pace at a time, moving only from the knees down, keeping his shoulders level and the rifle's barrel at waist height. He stopped at every opposing set of doors and listened for the sounds of murder within. The sounds of feeding and death.

Four sets of doors and who knows how many passed corpses in rooms later, Spoon heard the sound he dreaded. A thick, gurgling slurp noise followed by a breathless laugh. He faced the door and swung his rifle to his hip. He drew his Sig .45 and aimed it at the door jamb where the lock was. Poom-poom went the heavy handgun and Spoon's foot followed a heartbeat later, smashing the door open with authority. As the door's hydraulics fought to slow the opening, Spoon's mind took a snapshot of the layout and situation in the room. He saw a mother and son standing, shaking, at the back of the room against the windows with the tinted glass and the curtains, the mother holding the son under her wing as a teenage girl literally ate the face of the dead-or-dying father on the floor at the foot of the bed. The mother covered her boy's eyes to save him from the horror. He could see the parent and young boy were in his line of fire, and the narrow room entrance gave him no space to slide to the side for a clear shot.

"Move!" he screamed as he drew a bead on the high school vampire with the bad dye job and the stained Abercrombie shirt. The mother moved too slow, and Spoon held his trigger discipline. It cost him. Fortunately, his armor plate was made real strong. The girl must've played football or dated a lineman at some point, because she got up and under his arms from a crouch faster than Spoon thought was possible. She slammed her palms into his chest right at the base of the ribs, and were it not for the ceramic plate under his Kevlar and the dubiously indestructible leather jacket he wore over it, she'd have broken every bone where she struck him. Even with the armor the force of her blow hit hard enough to throw him out of the room and across the hall, where he hit the opposite hotel room door with a thud hard enough to evict all the air from his lungs. He dropped his pistol right before his ass hit the coral carpet. It was tucked under his right butt cheek. *Oh fuck me.*

"Silly police man. Is your leather jacket made out of pigskin?" the teenaged girl taunted, licking the dead man's blood from her teeth. She looked down at the palms of her hand. They sizzled, wafting smoke. Spoon could see a fine meshwork of burns etched into her flesh. Spoon remembered the thin vest of silver Doyle insisted he wear under his leather jacket. *The silver alloy. Ha. That'll teach you.* She spat a piece of skin on the rug. "Pig," she said, reveling in the power of the word in the face of the man she was about to kill. "You should try dying, it's not nearly as scary as all the old people say it is," she said with a wicked lick of her lips.

Enough air got back into his lungs with a gasp that he could reply to her. His words bought the wife and boy time to get out of the hotel room and scamper to the stairs, the mother still covering her son's eyes. Even if he died, they now had a shot at living. "You know we have a werewolf here."

She stopped her approach a few feet short, her bravado tested. "Well I guess we'll drink that thing's blood too."

"What about the dragon? You going to try and drink his blood too?" Spoon asked her with his own wicked smile. "You got a plan for that?"

She looked at him, her bloodshot and yellow streaked eyes narrowing between blood soaked cheeks and brows. "You're lying. Filthy pig."

Spoon had used the distraction to get his offhand under his ass, and onto the grip of his Sig. All he had to do was lean to the left... "I may be filthy, but I tell you no lies."

"Whatever. And dragon or not, it won't matter. Half the cops in this town are on Uncle Cosmo's payroll anyway. Soon enough, everyone in this whole city will either be a vampire or working for one. We're unstoppable. Just me and Darren were able to kill all these people on this floor by ourselves. Think of what a hundred of us could do with the cops helping." She ran a poorly painted fingernail down her neck and between her no longer budding breasts. Spoon couldn't decide if she wanted to seduce him or kill him. *Fucking teenagers. Shit or get off the pot already.*

Spoon thought of Doyle's last comment before he left. *'Reinforcements will be clutch.' Fuck. Fuck-fuck.* "Hey guess what?" Spoon blurted, feeling an urgency he felt wasn't nearly powerful enough.

"What?" she asked as if the situation wasn't what it was.

"Cops or not, you're not faster than a bullet." Spoon tilted to the left and got the pistol up and at her chest just as she dove towards him, teeth bared, and poorly painted fingernails spread out to slash at his eyes. The girl had been ungodly fast, and with his offhand he grabbed her throat with his silver-studded Nomex gloves. Her strength wilted as he twisted his wrist, dragging the sharp studs across her chin and neck, leaving behind smoking streaks of ashen destruction. Twice the gun bucked in his hand, and when her body landed atop his, she had lost her strength and will to kill. Her previously brazen eyes went soft, staring into his with a sudden lament. A second later, they went black, and she stiffened. Spoon pushed her off and thumbed the microphone that linked him and Doyle. "Mr. Doyle," Spoon said into the mic as he got to his feet. *Shit my back hurts. Tailbone too. I will not be known as the guy who broke his ass fighting a vampire.*

"Yes, Henry, are you alright? Is the hotel dealt with?"

"This floor appears to be. Hey I took out a vampire up here that reminded me of something. She said that half the cops in the city are on the vampire payroll. Those clutch reinforcements heading your way… they might not be our reinforcements, but theirs." Henry holstered his handgun and got his M-4 back into firing position as he walked slowly back towards the elevator. Doyle didn't answer him. "Mr. Doyle, you hear me?" He waited a few second, but the old man didn't answer. Spoon sprinted back to the door he shot and kicked in and burst back in, jumping over the dead father and rushing to the window. He looked out and quickly saw Mr. Doyle's problem.

A blue armored personnel carrier marked with police markings was approaching the big black tank where Doyle was located. He sat in the turret, still firing at full tilt at the APC as a large, remote controlled water gun on the vehicle's roof began to spray at him, knocking the heavy weapon from its aimed state. A blast of white water hit the old man hard in the face, and Henry watched as he slid down into the bottom of the turret, dead or unconscious from the cannon's direct hit on his skull.

"Motherfucker!" Spoon yelled, and he took off running again, this time to get to the street to save his friend's life and to put down the worst kind of villains.

Men who promised to do good ... but instead did evil.

Chapter Fifty-Two
Ambryn

Ambryn had destroyed a hundred feet of hallway and two descending stairwells when the centuries-old vampire made his plea over the hotel's paging system. Ambryn's hunt hadn't been about the baby vampires since he learned of Cosmin's presence, and when the old cheater of death offered him a chance at a face to face meeting, the eternal dragon played the game. He had forever to try again after all, and he'd already killed so many cheaters that night that his own brand of bloodlust had been sated. The big black creature of death meandered back through piles of the dead, staring down the vampires that he hadn't yet killed, who thirsted for their chance at a tiny sip of his rare blood.

Let them have their taste. Ambryn had been wounded a hundred and one times in the hotel and casino battle. The vampiric claws and fangs were inherently magical and special enough when coupled with their incredible strength to pierce his bulletproof hide now and then. His body was laced with fine cuts that at a distance looked to be tiny, but were in fact yards long in places, and as deep as stabbed pencils. They stung, and reminded the dragon that though he could not die, he could be made to suffer.

Ambryn got down into his resting position, arms and legs folded under his body, wings swept back, and began the wait for his prize. He knew he looked catlike and found humor in the association. As he watched the hundred vampires circle him, he heard a familiar voice.

"Hey you alright? You're cut up pretty good," the man called out.

Ambryn turned his massive head and saw Wayne, the black man, the good man, the devoted father, and the one who had made the call to Alanna that allowed them to barely survive the earlier ambush. He had just stood from a crouched shooting position behind several slot machines that had been themselves shot to hell. Ambryn saw he wore a strange silver gauntlet on his left hand. He looked frightened at the encroaching vampires, but made himself visible nonetheless. *I like this man. He looks death in the face and thinks only of trying to do the right thing again and again. A rare breed.* "I will heal. The opportunity to destroy the undead tonight has made any blood I lose well worth it."

He nodded repeatedly, as if the words the dragon spoke needed to be reaffirmed in his own brain by consistent nodding. "Cool. I got hit once in the head, but this helmet saved me. Can you believe Doyle put it in the bag he handed to me? It's like he knew."

Ambryn chuckled, and the vampires nearby withdrew, thinking it was an attack. "I don't think giving a man going to battle a helmet is that much of a stretch Wayne. It has the scent of sorcery on it. It must be a special helmet indeed."

Wayne nodded again as his wary eyes surveyed the stalking vampires surrounding them. "Hey ... um. I wanted to go look for my daughter Melanie and my wife Shauna. I think they're here. Will you go with me?"

The dragon cocked his head, and thought. "I must meet with Cosmin. We are at a standstill until that moment. I cannot protect you, as I gave my word to harm no more of these cheaters."

Another voice joined the conversation. A thinly disguised foreigner's voice. Someone for whom English had been learned as a second or third language. A familiar voice. "Go with my blessing, father and husband."

Wayne and Ambryn turned to look at the speaker, and Ambryn knew the speaker's identity at once. The stink of him alone told the dragon everything he needed to know. "Cosmin Dorinescu," Ambryn grunted in a hiss.

The vampire looked in awe of the dragon, openly showing deference. He spoke to Wayne though. "Sir, please. All those here with me know now that this man is under my protection. He shall be allowed to pass. And those who act against him shall suffer the curse of treachery."

"Curse of treachery?" Wayne asked him, taking a few hopeful steps forward.

Cosmin, skin as white as bleached ivory inclined his head. "Yes. My blood is rare, enchanted and cursed even amongst the vampires. It suffers no action against m, and acts on my behalf even as it flows inside the veins of my children."

"You cannot be betrayed?" Ambryn asked him, his head lowering down.

"No," Cosmin said softly as he looked with affection at the vampires everywhere around. They returned the very same look to him. "The dhampyrs and vampires that come from my line can say nothing against me, nor take action against me. To do so… would result in the blood turning against them."

"They would die, then?" Ambryn asked.

Cosmin nodded. "The vampire, Simon? The one you hunted at the club? It was you at the club, wasn't it?"

Ambryn grinned, the same dragon smile that frightened those on the roller coaster earlier. The vampires recoiled from it the same. "Yes, it was me."

"It could've only been you. I should've thought of it. Too late now. But Simon tried to betray me and my family, did he not? Was he?" Cosmin asked, already knowing the answer. He had a satisfied smile on his thin, pursed lips.

"Aye, he was about to lead me to you," Ambryn said before he chuckled. "Then he blew up."

"Yes. The curse is... explosive. Sir." Cosmin turned back to Wayne. "Please go tend to your search. May you find your daughter and your wife. I know down below there are still surviving humans and some vampires as well. I wish you luck, and I sincerely apologize for the pain my family has visited on you."

Wayne took a few more steps forward. "So if any of your people fuck with me, they'll blow up?"

Cosmin nodded. *He looks happy to be able to help Wayne. How strange.*

"I'm out. For what it's worth, I hope you rot in hell," Wayne said to the vampire.

Cosmin smiled sadly. More sadly than Ambryn thought any vampire could. "For my past I am sure if there is a hell, I will be headed there."

Wayne and Ambryn exchanged glances, and the Marine and father took off running down the hallway on his quest.

Silence blanketed the room as the onlookers watched the ancient vampire and the dragon of death. Cosmin tried several times to start talking, to say something, but nothing materialized.

He doesn't know where to start. "Speak. Confess what it is you need to say. I have already made my decision about how this ends. Nothing you can say will change that," Ambryn said.

The vampire found his voice and spoke. "You are the black dragon, I see. The dragon of death? The one who decides what lives and what dies? Ambryn is what the internet calls you."

"Yes. I am Ambryn. And tonight there has been too much death of the living, and too little death of the undying."

Cosmin looked again to his children all about, and the sadness came back. "I am the eldest vampire alive," he said to the room, not so much the dragon. "I think. My brethren have been starved out and hunted for as long as we have walked the earth. We have been hated by everything that has known of us since our kind came to be, and I have spent nearly all my years trying to survive, to avoid this persecution, and to eke out some kind of existence; to better my lot."

"You have done horrible things, Dorinescu. I have heard tales of your crimes against humanity. You have been wretched beyond what you are in half-death."

"Oh yes. In my worst years, yes. I have killed tens of thousands to keep myself alive. I have enslaved, tortured, and worse. I ask for no forgiveness, dragon. I ask for answers. Maybe you know them. Why has my kind been hunted so thoroughly? Why are we so cursed?"

"Because you are an aberration. The original vampires were a mistake so epic that I have spent centuries hunting them down. The past decade has been particularly fruitful in that endeavor. So few vampire have been made that your kind have died out at the hands of the humans."

"Are you saying we are a mistake? Whose mistake? Our creation was an error to that person? That we are even… not natural?" Cosmin asked the dragon as if he were praying at an altar to a god that finally turned an ear his way.

Fine. Let the truth come. "You are a creation. Born of Kaula's magic and my blood and essence. No better than a machine. You were meant to cull the human herd, but instead you nearly eradicated them. It has taken effort, even with your age it would be hard for you to comprehend to make your infection go away."

"We came from your blood?" Cosmin asked in joyous disbelief.

"Yes," the dragon answered, disgusted by the reminder.

Cosmin lit up further. "Then we are all your children. You are the first of our line. We have descended from you, in your image. Eternal in life, dealers of death. We are in your image black dragon. Can you not see that? See that we are not a mistake, but that we instead simply... *lack proper guidance.*"

Ambryn felt a strange, beyond bizarre sensation in his chest. Anxiety.

"Have we ever been brought under your wing and taught how to do what you intended for us to do?" Cosmin asked.

"No."

"Have we tried so hard, blindly doing what we were created to do, but unwise and unwell to the ways of your wishes? I swear a thousand times over Ambryn, dragon of death, that were you to simply guide us, you would have the tool you had sought for so long," Cosmin pleaded, near fanatical. "We do not have be the monsters we have become. We can be more than that." The crowd of fellow vampires had begun to catch their father's fever. They were blurting out evangelical praise for the dragon and the vampire alike now. They created a stranger scene out of the already strange one they started with.

"No, you are undeath, you violate the cycle. I cannot abide it," the dragon said tersely without giving what the vampire said any thought.

"Can you not see? We are not an accident. We are an evolution. We are *life,* Ambryn. Not machines. Simply a form of life you have disdain for. Ask your brother Tesser how many times his meddling in the affairs of living things led to a creation that was unexpected. I think he would tell you many times."

Ambryn roared, and Cosmin stumbled back until he

tripped and fell into the rubble of his casino. "You do not think of what my brother feels! You know nothing of his wishes and plans for Earth, nor mine! Do not be so arrogant!"

The vampire rose up off his back, resting on his elbows. He looked up, and for the first time perhaps ever, the dragon saw a rare emotion aimed in his direction. Disappointment.

"I am sorry, father."

"Do not call me that," Ambryn said by way of a threat.

"But that is what you are. We are all your children, bastards that we are," Cosmin waved a hand around, still on his back. "Teach us now. Show us the way to be what you need. Give us purpose. Do not destroy us. Redeem us."

Ambryn grunted in anger. "I came here to destroy you, Cosmin, and nothing you say will change that. You are beyond redemption."

Cosmin accepted the statement. "So be it. I have done more than enough to earn a thousand deaths. To die at your hands is the most appropriate way to die, I imagine. An honor I have not earned. All I ask is that you spare my children, and give what I said thought before you destroy us all. We do not have to hunt like monsters if we are given purpose Ambryn, and you can give us that purpose. When I said I wanted to create a nation where we could exist, I meant it. It does not have to be here, now; but my kind, *your* kind, we deserve a chance at a peaceful life, free of the fears that have driven us to centuries of murder and other unspeakable acts. I beg this of you. Take my life, but give my children—your grandchildren—a chance."

Doubt. Uncertainty. I ... have never thought something like this could happen. "I will take it under advisement," Ambryn said, and in front of all his offspring, he ate Cosmin Dorinescu.

Chapter Fifty-Three

Wayne Simmons

After taking a security guard's electronic key card off of his dead body, Wayne had been in the bowels of the hotel and casino for the better part of twenty minutes. He hadn't seen a soul since he'd swiped the card on an electronic lock and descended down the wide white walled stairs to the area marked "Executive Areas—No admittance."

Might as well have said vampire lair this way.

Moving down the stairs felt to Wayne like leaving an air conditioned room and heading into the outdoor heat of summer. The temperatures grew, and so too did a pungent scent in the air. Wayne had smelled it before. Copper and iron, rot and ruin. Blood. Spilled blood, and the further he walked the denser and more invasive the smell grew. It clung to the inside of his nose like a growing cancer. He followed the stench like a divining rod, leading him towards the worst of what he might discover, while hoping for the best of all scenarios.

Unlike the floors above, the basement seemed pristine, and despite the smell of blood everywhere, none could be seen. It was a ghost town. Every employee and vampire had disappeared. The stink of death seemingly had sunk into the wall. Wayne used his acquired card to open door after door, gun in hand, and when the card didn't work he used his size eleven boot as a key, and he'd yet to find a dead body, or a drop of blood. All he discovered was a maze of pipe filled hallways, bland offices, cubicles clustered together against the doldrums of business life, and a bedroom.

A bedroom?

Wayne's M-4 was equipped with a tiny but powerful rail mounted flashlight below the barrel, and he'd used it to illuminate the dark rooms he encountered before he found the light switches. When he opened one heavy door with the card, the two inch long flashlight showed him an empty bedroom. A wide king sized bed sat to the left of center, covered in unmade satin sheets. Dressers, bureaus, and a comfy looking slate gray couch were arranged fashionably all about. Each wall had been covered in plasma screens, creating a strange feeling of overwhelming technology. Wayne scanned side to side with the gun mounted light, and stepped inside. He found the switch on the wall, and he flicked it.

Rather than lights in the ceiling turning on or a lamp on a bed stand flaring to life, the walls of screens powered up in unison. *What in the world?* Wayne stepped back, and within a second a panoramic series of images loaded onto the screens, creating a false vista of the city of Las Vegas. If you forgot you were thirty feet below the desert, you would've thought you were in a penthouse suite. *Ha. Fake windows complete with fake sunshine for a vampire. Nice.*

Wayne examined the room. Small spatters of blood could be seen on the navy blue sheets and that sparked his curiosity. Using his rifle mounted light he followed the trail of drops to the side of the bed where they moved to a wall. *How?* High quality wooden paneling covered the wall, and the trail of drops terminated no more than two inches from it. *It's like the wall was bleeding. Or maybe someone was cut here and then taken to the bed? I don't get it. And the smell. It's worse over here.* He felt the wall and floor for several minutes, but found nothing. The trail cold, and his curiosity still peaked, Wayne turned and headed towards the door to retrace his steps. *There's gotta be something I'm missing.*

Wait. Wayne stopped short of the door and turned back around. The wall and the blood drops at its base taunted him with its secret. He skirted the bed and reached up with his gauntleted hand and pulled down the tinted black glass from inside his helmet until it covered his eyes.

There we go. I knew it. His enchanted helm drew out a yellow line on the wall, telling him it was, in fact, some form of door. He approached the wall and felt with his bare hand up and down, searching for some kind of switch or lever. He searched the dresser drawers, the bureau, the small bathroom, and the rails under the bed. He found nothing. Frustrated, he went to the bed stand where the remote controls were. He hit button after button trying to find a special combination that would open the false door but all he managed to do was scroll the panoramic screens through a series of world scenes. At the end, he was surrounded by the vista of the French Alps.

"Shit!" Wayne yelled as he gunned the remote across the room. It broke apart when it hit a dresser. He stormed back and forth in front of the wall, trying to think of a solution, but nothing came. I've searched everywhere. I pushed every button. "Shit!" he yelled again, and he punched the wall with his gauntleted hand.

The fist went through the layered wood and drywall as if it were less than paper. He yanked his fist out and punched again. Debris fell to the floor. Wayne took a step back and brought his M-4 up, and triggered the flashlight. Using its beam of illumination, he looked through the holes he'd made and saw what lay hidden beyond. Before he saw anything, he caught wind of the source of the stench inside. Sweat, shit, dried blood and suffering were in the air thicker than flies over a mass grave.

The concealed room couldn't have been more than ten feet deep, and half that wide. On the left and right Wayne saw two females tied to wooden frames that held their arms and legs spread. They were stark naked, utterly vulnerable, and had crusted blood and scabs at their necks, and on their inner thighs. On the floor between their legs Wayne could see meager piles of thin, sickly feces. It might've been mixed with thin foodless vomit. At the rear of the room from floor to ceiling were a dozen shelves stacked atop one another, each shelf filled from wall to wall with small jars, all labeled with writing Wayne couldn't read and filled with liquid darkness. But worst of all, strapped immobile and in pain directly between he and the shelves at the back of the room he saw a familiar dark skinned woman.

Shauna. Baby.

At the sight of his shackled, emaciated and drained wife, Wayne went berserk. He rained blows down on the wall with the silver gauntlet as fast and as hard as his body could manage them. Pieces of wood broke off and flew in the air, bouncing off his face and chest. He ignored the tiny bites of their pain and kept hitting. Inch by inch he smashed a hole larger and larger in the wall until he could fit his body through, and as soon as he could, he crawled through, screaming her name every moment of every step. "Shauna! Shauna baby I am here! Shauna!"

As Wayne stepped into the blackened room and found the switch on the wall, his wife meekly opened her eyes, and said his name. "Wayne David, where you been? Where's Trevor?"

"I've been looking for you. Trevor's with Marsha. Far away and safe," Wayne said as he sat his rifle down, and went to the bindings on her legs.

"Your hat lights up. It's cute," she said, sounding tired.

Wayne hadn't noticed, but the yellow symbols on the side of the helmet had flared up since he sat his rifle down. They were lighting his way. The restraints holding his wife's ankles were made of two semi-circular pieces of hardened steel, fastened shut with hiking carabineers. As he undid them, he talked to her. "I've been working with the cops, Shauna. That's where I got the helmet. It's magical. I've been helping them, trying to find you and Melanie. They have a werewolf helping, and one of the dragons. A dragon, Shauna. Thing is huge. Once I get you undone, we'll go looking for Mel. How long have you been locked up like this?"

Her words took supreme effort. They were precious. "Since we were taken. He… He's been bleeding me slow. But then he got bored. He killed Charice there, and then Elaine. But he saved me. For something else."

Both leg locks released, Wayne stood and started on her arm. "Well I'm glad he saved you. I don't know what I'd do without you. Have you seen Mel? Where's my baby girl?"

"Wayne, stop. Don't. Please. Listen," she pleaded to him.

I hate the way she's talking to me. Like she's already given up. Wayne looked her in the eyes. The whites were stained a gray that looked unhealthy, like ashes stirred in milk, and her chocolate skin around her eyes was bruised and purple. She'd been hit more than once. Wayne felt his anger rise in his throat. It burnt. "Shauna, let me get you undone and let's get out of here. Find our girl."

"Wayne, I can't go. He saved me. The man. Jimmy was his name. Jimmy saved me to turn me. I'm becoming a vampire, Wayne. I can't be a mother no more. Not like this. Feel my pulse, Wayne. Put your finger on my neck. Feel me."

Wayne's hand shook, but he did as his wife told him.

Her soft skin was cold, unlike her. She always ran hot. He pushed his fingers around where the thump of her heart's beat should've been, but found nothing. He counted to twenty but still no beat. He counted to twenty again. He noticed she hadn't taken a breath since he touched her. He withdrew his hand. "You're dead."

Her head tipped up and down, and her lips quivered. "It's painful. Everything inside me is dying. Shriveling up, falling out. Such pain Wayne. I prayed. I begged for salvation but none came for me. It must be God's will I thought, so here I am. A freak. Dracula. Don't touch me anymore. I know I need to drink. And you... You smell good." She began to weep, but had no tears. Her body shook with grief, and all Wayne could do was put a hand on her shoulder.

"What should I do?" Wayne asked, his own grief boiling over. His eyes made tears, and he wiped them away. Watching her sob with no breathing or tears felt discordant for the husband and father of two. It seemed fake. Forced somehow. The act cast a strange light on his feelings and threw all his emotions into even more turbulent conflict.

"You should kill me," Shauna said in between quakes of sadness. "And don't tell Trevor or Melanie. Tell them I died early. You found my body. Something." Shauna looked at the floor, unwilling to meet Wayne's gaze.

Wayne felt something go still inside him. He lifted her chin with a soft hand and looked her in the eye. "No. I can't kill you. No more than I could kill our daughter. They'll fix this. There has to be a way. They have this guy, his name is Mr. Doyle, he gave me this helmet, and this metal glove. He can fix you," Wayne said as he dropped to his knee. He quickly closed his wife's leg back in the clasp, and slipped the carabineer back through the lock.

"Wayne, no."

Wayne looked up at her after locking her other squirming leg in place. *She feels weak.* "Do you know where Melanie is? Tell me if you do."

Shauna lolled her head side to side in great dismay. "Jimmy said Sandy had her. I don't know who Sandy is."

"Sandy Brown, must be. I heard she runs the casino."

Shauna forced a weak laugh. "Yeah. That's her."

Wayne felt a thrill. "I bet that bitch's office or bedroom is down here. I bet Melanie is in a room just like this. I'm gonna go find our baby girl, and then we're going to sort you out." Ignoring the danger, Wayne leaned in and kissed his wife on the cool forehead. Out of a brand new instinct, she weakly opened her mouth and bit at him. She was slow though, and depleted. *She has little fangs now. Sweet Jesus.*

"Okay, Wayne."

Wayne caressed her cheek. "I don't care if you're dead. I don't care if you need to drink blood. I said for better or for worse, in sickness and in health, and I meant it when I said it. I can't think of what might be worse, or sicker, and I'm still here. Shauna Simmons, I love you, and nothing will change that. I won't go back on my word."

Her lips trembled, and Wayne kissed her on the forehead once more. This time, she didn't try to bite him.

*****

Wayne had left the dungeon inside the underground bedroom with the televised vista of the Alps with savage, singular purpose. From door to door down hallway after hallway, he looked for one thing: Sandy Brown's name. He discarded every other thought.

His search didn't take long. At the end of the hallway past an unmarked, heavily fortified door with a nameplate that read 'Uncle Cosmo' he found a matching bronze wall placard that read her name. Wayne didn't even try to swipe the security card. Instinctively he flicked the M-4 to three-round burst, and unloaded several bursts into the door where the lock met the jam.

Nine rounds later he kicked the door and it rocked free of the lock, swinging in wildly. Inside he saw a Spartan concrete office, devoid of personality and charm. A remarkably pretty woman stood behind a simple desk; hands that were loading a small briefcase with stacks of papers paused. The woman had a look of terror on her face. She flashed her teeth at Wayne, and sat the bag down. She was ready to fight.

Wayne stabbed the barrel of the rifle in her direction, and barked at her. "Where is my daughter? Where is Melanie?"

Sandy's threatening visage melted away, and she took on a demeanor more appropriate to dealing with a petulant child. "Are you Daddy?"

Bitch. "Your Uncle Cosmo sent me down here to find my wife and daughter. I found my wife, and you are between me and my daughter. Now if you don't want me to treat you like I just handled that door, then take me to my daughter right now."

The woman licked her lips in a gesture of frustration. "Uncle Cosmo sent you? Try telling me something remotely believable."

Condescending bitch. Wayne took a step forward. "He made a truce with the dragon. Sent me down here. I want my daughter back. I will let you go if you show me where she is. No jokes. No lies. Tell me where Melanie is, and you can take your briefcase to wherever it is you want to go. Act fast, the dragon is still upstairs, and he's on a tear. I won't ask again." Sandy looked down at the bag filled with hastily stuffed paperwork, and Wayne suddenly understood what it held—her getaway fund.

Sandy looked at him with evil eyes. Abandoning her hard stance she walked over in heels that clicked on the hard floor to a yellow mechanical closet marked with a sign that read: 'Danger: High Voltage.' Never taking her narrowed, angry gaze off of Wayne and his rifle, she reached to her tiny leather belt and pulled a ring of keys from a spring loaded holder. She found the key by shape with her finger, and inserted it into the door. With a feline grace, she stepped back, pulling the door open. "Your delicious little girl is in here. Now if you are a man of your word, I'll be leaving now."

"Get out, bitch," Wayne said, moving forward aggressively, forcing her away from the door and back towards her desk. I like that she looks afraid. The light of the office lit the interior of the closet, but it didn't hold back the smell. Just like the chamber where he'd found his wife, this cramped space smelled of waste and blood. His heart dropped when he saw his tiny girl curled up on the floor, still. Wayne forgot what he was doing, and went to the door jamb of the closet, and he dropped to his knee, turning his back on the woman who had imprisoned his daughter. "If you know what's good for you," he said to Sandy as he reached out to his daughter, "then you'll leave right now."

"After transferring half a million dollars into 53 accounts, I guess I'll decide what's good for me. Now that I've set aside a few million of Uncle Cosmo's money for myself to start over, I think it would be smart of me to leave no witnesses," he heard her say just before her feet clattered hard on the floor, and she launched herself at his back.

Protect me Lord.

It may not have been the Lord that prevented Sandy Brown from killing Wayne Simmons, and surely afterward, his daughter, but a force she could not best intervened. Wayne heard a noise that reminded him of a grenade going off in close confines—a muffled whoomph—just a few steps away as she lunged, and though parts of her touched him, there wasn't enough of her left to do any harm.

Cosmin Dorinescu's tale of his curse of the blood held true. Sandy Brown's act against his will resulted in her imploding into a pile of sludge. Bits of her ran down

Wayne's back, but he didn't care. Not at all. No, he didn't.

My baby girl has a pulse.

Chapter Fifty-Four

Spoon

The glitz and glamour of all the neon on the Las Vegas Strip made the terrible slaughter on the street below that much more alien. The blinking signs denoting each hotel and casino operated independently of reality, unaware of the horrors just yards beneath their lofty homes above, almost remarking to the world that the death and destruction below could not be remarked on, would pass, and that they couldn't be bothered to stop their incessant promotion for a moment because of it. The only thing the lights could care about was their own mechanical pulsing. The announcement of wealth. The heartbeat of greed.

Henry had the drop on two of the dirty cops. They had exited the SWAT vehicle with the water cannon on the roof to get at Doyle inside the tank, but the heavily armored bus had thus far repelled their attempts to get into it. As they pried at the steel and carbon fiber door, their backs were turned to Spoon, and with no hesitation he made them pay for their turncoat ways. The experienced shooter put the sights of his rifle on the back of their heads, and two focused squeezes of his trigger finger later, they were in a heap on the ground beside the tank, and the unconscious Doyle inside had a short reprieve.

Wake the fuck up, limey; I need you.

Henry watched something amazing happen as he leapfrogged from cover to cover, getting closer to the APC that held more of the traitor cops.

Multiple policemen were standing in the street near the APC and the bus, some in cover, some not. Whether because they were dirty, or simply scared of what they faced, all had drawn a bead on Artur in his werewolf form. *They're dirty. Gotta be. They all sat there while that SWAT truck hit Doyle.* Each was unloading their heavy rifles, carbines, and shotguns at Artur as fast as they could pull the trigger, and against all logic and reason, the werewolf still advanced. If the world was silent, it looked like he advanced against a gale force wind, leaning, fighting against resistance. Yes, he was knocked down over and over again from the heavy shotgun blasts, and yes, at times he had to crawl and not walk, but no matter how many rounds they put into him, none was the killing bullet. They had no silver, and none of the shooters had managed to strike his head from his shoulders or destroy his brain.

Artur howled in pain and anger, and he pushed forward. Relentless, angry at their foolish betrayal. *He'll never reach them before one of them gets lucky and kills him.* As he had that thought a cop with a bolt action rifle took aim on Artur, using the side of the SWAT APC as a firing position. Spoon eyed the distance from where he'd ducked behind a steel garbage barrel housing to the SWAT vehicle. *It's far, but they're at the curb. That dude's gonna blow Artur's head clean off. Fuck it, I'll do it.*

Spoon slung his M-4 to his left hip and went to his tactical belt. He got his incendiary grenade free from the pouch that held it and quickly pulled the pin. A glance over the top of the barrel housing told him where the APC was positioned, and he popped up like a meerkat, and hurled the grenade at the armored vehicle. He ducked down before they saw him.

The canister landed well short of the armored vehicle, but as the smoke began to billow out of it, and the sparks began to shoot from the end of it, it rolled. It skittered and spun, eventually hitting the hard stone curb and bouncing back several feet until it stopped, streaming smoke and sparks angrily directly underneath the hull of the APC. Intense, roaring flames appeared. The man with the bolt action rifle stepped away, unsure of what transpired at his feet.

Bird shoots, he scores. And the Celtics take the lead. Spoon got his M-4 up and betrayed his position by plugging the man with the sniper rifle as he backpedaled away from the scalding heat of the grenade. He then emptied the remaining 24 rounds in his magazine into the front tire of the vehicle. The tough rubber wheel exploded with a deafening thump that drowned out the volume of gunfire and the hiss of the grenade. The armored personnel carrier listed to the side like a sinking boat. Several of the rogue police officers shooting at Artur realized they were now being flanked, and they turned to shoot at Spoon.

The smoke obscuring their vision coupled with the thousands of degrees of heat spitting off under the tank meant that they couldn't focus well enough to hit him. It also meant the gunfire that had kept Artur from making forward progress slowed. Almost as if physical bonds had been broken, The Romanian sprang forward, vaulting over a trash barrel identical to the one Spoon hid behind, and landing on one of his assailants. He ended the man's life with a lightning fast rip and tear.

Spoon stayed low and slapped in a new magazine as the thermite grenade cooked the interior of the APC. The driver seemed to realize the alarming brevity of their situation too late, and Spoon guessed that the APC's errant spurt forward and coasting crash into the Tapper bus ahead meant he had succumbed to the heat of the steel of his own APC melting under him. Using the new cover of the personnel carrier, Spoon displaced to a stone fountain edge several yards away and waited for the men to get out of the armored vehicle.

When they came out of the hatch, he cut them down one by one with short bursts from his rifle. Three dead traitors fell in a pile, half cooked and shot dead. *Suck on that. Got a head start on burning in hell, didn't ya?*

Spoon saw an opening in the battle and ran. The street had cleared of the undead and rogue police. He couldn't see any blood soaked undead running wild murdering, and there were no police or civilians anywhere near their position. No police that weren't shot or being torn apart by Artur, that is. With no threats in sight, Spoon got his phone free and called the number for the local police command. He'd dialed that number enough lately to know it by heart.

An operator answered. Spoon cut him off. "This is Special Agent Henry Spooner with The International Agency for Paranormal Response. I'm engaged heavily on The Strip with vampire as well as hostile forces dressed as Las Vegas Metro police officers. I am asking you to call off all additional local officers. Keep all police away from The Strip or they will be fired on. Do you understand?" Spoon was practically screaming at the poor guy on the other side of the line.

He stammered, steamrolled by Spoon's commands. "I … uh. I don't have the … "

"Shut the fuck up and get the call out. I will shoot anyone with a police uniform on, do you understand? ATF, FBI, CIA only. Got it. Federal forces only, and they better have three letters in their acronym or I'll shoot at them too. Send the fucking IRS before you have another local cop come here."

"I … uh, okay, what's your badge number?"

"I'll look it up later. Keep your people at a distance

and tell them to watch each other. You've got a few foxes in your henhouse," Spoon said, and he hung up the phone. I hope that idiot gets that call out. When Spoon hung up the phone he stood at the back of the Tapper bus, skirting the still intense heat coming off the thermite-torched APC. The molten steel could take hours to cool, and he didn't want to catch a tan.

Artur stood only ten paces away, looming over the corpse of a cop that made a few poor life choices. The werewolf truly seemed a machine made for war. His enormous jaw was filled front to back with teeth designed for tearing enemies apart, and his claws were no different. As Spoon watched his heaving chest he could see the individual bullet holes tightening and healing shut one by one, as if they were the eyes of someone falling asleep. Only the dreams of prior pain would remain.

"You are genuinely fucking scary, Artur," Spoon called out to the monster that he called a friend.

In a particularly human gesture the gargantuan beast bent at the waist, thanking the agent. Spoon laughed. "If you see any cops, rip them a new asshole."

Artur nodded, dropped to all fours, and loped off into the center of the street, looking for more vampires to kill.

As he left, Spoon laughed again and looked at the tank. He had reached the bus' door, and with the keys he fished out of his pocket, he unlocked it and prepared for the worst.

Water fell out of the door in an even cascade, and it had streams of thin blood in it. Spoon felt the writhing of tension in his belly before the door opened fully, but he fought it and pushed his way inside.

The secret turret that Mr. Doyle had fought so hard to have installed was cleverly hidden in the bathroom. When the water cannon hit the sorcerer-turned heavy machine gunner, he fell through the opening in the roof and plummeted nearly seven feet to the floor, smashing into the footrests that he had stood on. The old man's body lay sideways in the narrow hall, having knocked the bathroom door open, and his head lay cocked at an unhealthy angle against a cupboard. Trickles of blood streamed from the side and back of his head where he'd been cut. Everything was soaked.

Spoon dropped to his knees and got his rifle out of the way. "Doyle. Doyle can you hear me?" Spoon asked softly, checking the old man's pulse and respiration. He didn't dare to move his neck. It was bent too far to not be injured somehow. Within a few seconds of feeling Doyle's neck, and hovering a hand over his mouth, he knew the old man still lived. Would he heal though?

"Henry?" Doyle said, detached and oddly still.

"Hey buddy," Spoon said softly, checking the rest of the old man's body for wounds. The enchanted chain mail he wore made the task particularly difficult.

"What happened?"

"You got hit in the face from a water cannon blast. Right in the chops. Fell down into the bus. Hit your head a few times I think. You're leaking gravy and warm beer everywhere."

Doyle looked around with his eyes only, searching for memories. "I can't see. My glasses are gone." Doyle's eyes moved to Spoon's face. "Henry, I can't feel my feet."

"I think your neck might be broken, Doyle. You've got a few lacerations on your head too."

"Belyakov will have a field day when he hears I'll be in a wheelchair," Doyle said with surprising humor.

"Yeah well, I think Abe is going to fart a potato out when he hears you got hurt. Tesser's going to have my hide too," Spoon joked grimly.

"Tesser knows the game. He understands the stakes. Abraham might be cross; that I can agree with. What has happened? Have we carried the day?"

"Well," Spoon started, fishing a bandage out of his blow-out kit, "Artur is a fucking beast. He kept them from killing you for far longer than he had any business doing, and he wrecked some ass."

"Profanity Henry, please," Doyle said politely.

"Sorry. I bet you anything there are still fifty vampires here. More. In the hotels, casinos, hiding or killing. We'll get them. You remember the bad cops coming?"

"I remember you calling me about it. Beyond that, I assume my memory lapse is to be attributed to them?"

"Roger that. We've got some rats to find, but we'll do it. I'm gonna get the Feds rolling in here. They're cleaner than the locals, at least a little, and with Artur, we'll find them all. I haven't heard anything from Ambryn wherever that Arabian casino is."

"Have you heard any massive explosions?" Doyle asked weakly.

Spoon shook his head and gently tied a bandage around the Brit's head. "No, nothing."

"Well that's well and good. That bandage hurts a fair bit you know. Give me one of my healing potions when you're finished torturing me. Fish out Alanna's telephone from my bag on the couch. Call Wayne and see if he answers. Perhaps that will tell you what we need to know. If Cosmin is dead, we may be situated well."

"I don't want to speak too soon, but I think we have this contained, Mr. Doyle. If Ambryn got to Cosmin … I think we're going to be okay." Spoon poured a dollop of the red elixir into Doyle's oddly angled mouth and laughed at the world. *Man. I have the weirdest job.*

Chapter Fifty-Five

Ambryn

Ambryn hadn't moved since swallowing the vampire that had started the nightmare in Las Vegas. Frozen in his image were the hundred odd servants of Cosmin arrayed around him, standing in wait as the dragon debated what to do next. *I swear I can feel that monster trying to claw his way out of me. Impossible ... but still.*

The vampires had been still for more than twenty minutes, anxiously awaiting their fate. Anxiously awaiting the judgment of their maker.

A conundrum. Cosmin spoke truths, and I cannot walk away from some of his wisdom easily, desperate as it might have been – though I hate to admit it. He looked about at the faces of the undead. *They have hopes and dreams in their eyes, not murder and destruction. I've never seen them acting… human before. Perhaps there is some hope in teaching them.*

From beyond the destroyed hotel lobby atrium, Wayne returned with two women, one under each arm. Ambryn could see one was younger and had a similar nose. She bore a deep, ugly scar on her temple. Ambryn thought of Alanna. The other had to be his wife. *She stinks of death. She has been turned. And in her eyes I see despair...*

And love.

Ambryn's inner conflict grew. "Wayne. You survived the search. I'm very happy for you. Introduce me to your wife and daughter, please," Ambryn said. The vampires in the room fanned away from Wayne, openly fearful of the man and his small family. He had left the room with Cosmin's blessing, and returned almost as if he were a prophet of the dragon Ambryn.

Wayne's face showed some elation, but clearly also trepidation. "Ambryn, this is my daughter Melanie. This is my wife Shauna. She's..." Wayne started.

Ambryn interrupted, saving the man the awkward moment. The dreaded confession. "She's very beautiful. So is your daughter. Tell me Wayne, do you love your family?" Ambryn asked innocently and genuinely.

Wayne seemed surprised at the question. He looked to the arrayed undead, almost reaching out for their support. "Yeah. That's a stupid question man. I will always love my family. Why do you ask?"

"Your wife. She has become what I would call a monster. You love her even now that she has become a vampire? Knowing that she will need to drink blood to survive, and could visit violence on you or strangers at any moment?" Ambryn posed.

"You think death or sickness changes anything, Ambryn? She didn't ask to be changed into a vampire. I bet most of these people didn't ask for it. They're scared, the same as anyone who is sick. My wife is a good person. Gentle and kind. A wonderful mother. And I know life won't be the same, and it'll take work, but I won't abandon her. Some... some things about her may have changed, but I know in my heart her soul is still here."

"Sick," Ambryn said aloud, considering what that single word meant. *The sick can be healed, cured, taught to live with illness. Taught to adapt.*

"What are you thinking about?" Melanie, the tired and wounded daughter asked the dragon.

Ambryn looked to her and saw her worry. *She thinks of her mother. She expects me to kill her. To kill all the undead here.* Ambryn sighed through his enormous dragon nostrils, blowing dust and detritus around. "I am debating a change little Melanie."

"A change?" she asked.

"Yes. I wonder how I could change the course of vampiric existence if I were to become a guiding force in their lives. I wonder if I should give them a chance. Some of them a chance. I know some have forfeited their rights to survival due to inexcusable behavior, but still, I wonder."

"My mom deserves a chance," Melanie said.

And with that, Ambryn changed. "So be it. Let us begin a grand experiment. Vampires gathered here, children of Cosmin Dorinescu, here are the terms I set forth. Should you want to survive beyond this night and the coming dawn, remain in wait here. I will see to it you are protected, and tomorrow we will work together to try and build a new way."

The dead rejoiced. Salvation had arrived and a chance at redemption had become reality.

Chapter Fifty-Six
Spoon

Spoon had been on the phone for an hour. A luxury that hadn't made itself available to him since the catastrophe on The Strip a week prior. The calendar said the month had almost reached Christmas, and the whole city of Las Vegas would probably skip celebrating the holiday this year. There remained a lot of rebuilding left. Both of the people, and of the city.

Rebuilding of trust as well.

"Tell me more," the woman on the other end of the line asked him. "How was Alanna's funeral?" *I love her voice. Sultry.*

Spoon lay in his hotel room bed, his shoes off, his shirt unbuttoned. His horsehide leather jacket hung on a permanent hangar in the closet, and his trusted Sig sat on the bed stand next to a glass of whiskey on ice. "It was pretty. She had full military honors. She was buried in her hometown outside of Sacramento. Four hundred and thirteen police officers came in uniform for her. You had to see it. She would've been so pissed such a big deal was made over her."

"I'm so sorry for your loss, Henry. I know you two had been very close. She was a hero."

"Thank you. I don't know if she'd see it that way. She was doing what she wanted to do, even if it was dangerous. She knew it had to be done," Spoon said, and then sipped his whiskey.

"How is that not the definition of a hero?"

"Fair. Nevada Highway Patrol assumed command of the Vegas precincts today officially. They're getting oversight from the Justice Department. They're all working with the FBI on tracking down all of the turncoats that haven't run off and hidden under a rock somewhere. It's going to get real ugly when they start flipping over rocks. Tapper agents are working with Artur around the clock right now on The Strip, trying to find any of the vampires that we might've missed."

"Do you think there are any left?" she asked.

Spoon shrugged, even though no one could see the gesture. "Hard to say. I think we either killed or have all of the bloodsuckers from The Strip in custody. I can't think they might still be hiding there. It's been days, and I don't know how they could've fed. I think the two we found in a restaurant closet yesterday are going to wind up being the last."

"Where are they being taken?"

Spoon sat up and sipped his whisky. He'd spoiled himself and picked up a fifty dollar bottle of Larue Bourbon. The sizzle and the smoke in it satisfied him. "Ambryn has all of them at the Arabian Nights. The basement over there is set up to house a few hundred people, and the police have set up a perimeter around it to keep it safe. Get this: they have had to arrest almost forty people the past few days who have tried to attack the casino to kill the vampires inside. Ha. To think we spent how long trying to kill these fuckers only to turn around and try to keep them alive in the end. Ambryn. I tell ya."

"Dragons are able to change their mind, you know," she teased.

"You would say that," Spoon said after another sip of the bourbon. "Of course, there's the dilemma that the goons at McCarran didn't shut the airport down until well into the night, and a whole shitload of vampires got on planes. A few of the vampires were on delayed eastbound flights and wound up going up in smoke when they landed. Imagine that shock. Welcome to your new life, and poof, you're a ball of flame. We found some half shredded documents about dozens of off-shore accounts set up to bankroll the vamps that traveled. Fifty plus accounts, one for each of the squirters. We're trying to track them down, but international laws, and red tape, and all that shit has probably cost us our chance. Who knows how many slipped the noose and are now roaming the country."

"What of Doyle? What do the doctors say?"

"The old man is like that jacket he gave me. Unbreakable. He fractured two vertebrae in his neck. He's currently going crazy in Philly waiting for surgery. Doctors claimed that his little moonshine health potions staved off the worst of the damage, and with a fusing or two—or whatever—he'll be okay eventually. He'll need therapy, and I'm sure he'll drive a substantial amount of medical professionals quite batty, but he'll walk again. He might limp or need a cane, but he'll walk again. I think his field days might be numbered."

"That would be a loss for you, but he's had a good run. He's been around a long time and the world is the better for it."

"Longer than he has any business being around. I'm hoping this will push him into being more hands-on at the Tapper academy. He's a good teacher, and we need more magically educated agents. Abe will be one of the first graduates once he exits Quantico."

"How is Abe?"

Spoon smiled. "He's great. Texted me last night, said he and Alexis are doing well, and he's almost done in

Virginia. He's excited to be out in the field. Again, I guess."

"Good. They're a good fit, as strange as they are," she said.

"You would say that."

"I would. What's next then?"

"For me and Tapper? I think we're here in Vegas until early next year. Tesser's on his way back from Norway now, and he's going to come here to establish some order. I heard the President is on his way too. Some kind of joint announcement about the video Cosmin sent out, and how he wasn't representative of the vampire race, and how the government will be working to clarify laws to shore up the rights around... Weird shit. There's talk of three to five new constitutional amendments. I hope they all realize that this house of cards they're building is going to come crashing down the moment some fuck face vampire gets caught eating another cheerleader in the heart of the Bible belt."

"The world is changing very fast, Henry. Tesser's return and Astrid's birth have thrown everything into chaos. I, for one, think it's great."

"You would say that," Spoon said, baiting her.

"I would. When will I see you again?"

Spoon sighed. "When this simmers down. I have a few days off lined up, and Tesser will be available should anything happen. Where are you going to be in the middle of January? Any chance I can talk you into coming to Boston again?"

"Eh. It's a little chilly for me that time of year in Beantown. How about you fly to Tahiti? I'll cover the cost of your ticket. Relatively speaking, I'm buried in human money right now."

"Talk dirty to me. Tell me more about your money," Spoon said in a husky voice.

She laughed. *I love that sound.* "Henry. Henry. Henry. Call me in a couple days. We'll sort out getting you to the

South Pacific and back into a bed with me."

"Deal, Zeud."

"And tell my brothers I said hello," she said.

"I will, talk to you soon." They ended the call at the same time, and Henry sat there smiling, warmed by the expensive drink and the thoughts of a profoundly beautiful and smart woman in his life. It had been a long time since that'd happened and he'd been okay with it. His eyes drifted over to the foot of the bed and his mind drifted back to the last person who'd sat there.

Alanna. Alanna and her loneliness. Alanna and her memories of what was and what might be again. *Maybe she and I were more alike than I care to think about.*

Spoon picked up his glass of bourbon and toasted to the memory of his friend.

Epilogue

The City of Angels got a bit of tarnish on its halo when Jimmy got out of his cab just shy of the crack of dawn. He looked to the edge of the eastern horizon and felt the twangs of oncoming panic. In twenty minutes the sun would begin to crest, and he would die shortly after in a smoking heap of flame if he didn't get inside. He paid the fare and watched as his assistant vampire Andy got out of the other side. The driver popped the trunk on the beaten up Crown Victoria and like a good Igor should, Andy fetched their two bags. Andy grabbed his UNLV athletic bag, and Jimmy's too. Jimmy's stood far apart; it was a Victorinox with built in hangers to keep his Armani suits clean and wrinkle free. He'd packed four suits.

"Jimmy, here's your bag," Andy said as the cab pulled away.

"I don't know that name anymore, Adam," Jimmy said with a wink. "I'm Jesus Chavez. Hay-soos Shah-vezz. Say it with me. Hay-soos Shah-vezz."

Andy-Adam looked embarrassed as he pushed the expensive luggage towards his new boss. "Sorry, Jesus. It's just, you know."

"Yeah I feel ya. Let's get inside this damn hotel and black out the windows of the penthouse suite. And let's hope all the other vampires landed with no delays, right? Hard to spread the vampire population across the world when the sun cooks us up, right? How smart was Cosmo. eh? Distract the feds while we put all the smart vampires on planes; money and safe houses set up all over the country for them already. Pure genius. What'd I tell you, Adam? I told you I would take care of you, right?" Jimmy-Jesus put an arm around his lackey's shoulders as they walked towards the entrance to the Ritz-Carlton. Jesus already knew they had the suite reserved.

"You did, Jesus. Thanks for looking out," the new Adam said with appreciation. "What do we do now?"

"We start over. Uncle Cosmo has a dream, you know? Independent vampires, free from persecution. I think the City of Angels is a nice place to try to build that dream."

Adam looked around at the posh hotel's exterior and the unreal glamour of the city they'd just arrived in. "It is. We could do well here. So long as we don't need to start any fires in the desert again."

Jesus looked at a harem of beautiful women strutting down the street dressed in trampy club clothes and with immaculately pruned hair and nails. They exuded sex and youth. They were exotic.

They look delicious. "Ha, right. No more gasoline and piles of wood for us. We'll do real well here, Adam. Now vamonos. Let's get that room for the day, and tonight we tackle the future. Don't forget, we got thirty baby Marine vampires to take care of. They'll be our new shock troops brother, once we take off their training wheels," Jimmy said with a triumphant smile.

Adam and Jesus walked into the lobby of the hotel, and fell off the map.

For now.

About The Author

CHRIS PHILBROOK is the creator and author of the *Reemergence* novels, as well as the popular webfiction series *Adrian's Undead Diary* and *Elmoryn: The Kinless Trilogy*.

Chris calls the wonderful state of New Hampshire his home. He is an avid reader, writer, role player, miniatures game player, video game player, and part time athlete, as well as a member of the Horror Writers Association. If you weren't impressed enough, he also works full time while writing for Reemergence as well as the worlds of Adrian's Undead Diary and Elmoryn.

Find More Online

Check out Chris Philbrook's official website **thechrisphilbrook.com** to contact the author and keep tabs on his many exciting projects, or follow Chris on Facebook at **www.facebook.com/ChrisPhilbrookAuthor** for special announcements.

Visit **adragonamongus.com** to access additional content and learn more about Ambryn and the world of the Reemergence Novels.

Don't miss Chris Philbrook's smash hit: *Adrian's Undead Diary*. Follow the exploits of Adrian Ring in this epic eight-book series as he searches for meaning, survival, and hope in a world ravaged by the dead. Visit **adriansundeaddiary.com** to learn more about Adrian's world. Available in print, Kindle, and online.

Read more by author Chris Philbrook in *The Kinless Trilogy*. Explore Elmoryn, a world of dark fantasy where death is not the end. The story begins in *Book One: The Wrath of the Orphans*, available in print, Kindle, and online. Visit **elmoryn.com** to learn more about Elmoryn, view concept art, and much more.

Can't Wait for More?

Look for Chris Philbrook's **FREE** short fiction eBook, *At Least He's Not on Fire*.

Find it on Amazon, Goodreads, or Smashwords today!

Amazon: http://www.amazon.com/dp/B00JSGEKIK
Goodreads: https://www.goodreads.com/book/show/21948978-at-least-he-s-not-on-fire
Smashwords: https://www.smashwords.com/books/view/430970

Made in United States
North Haven, CT
15 February 2022